AGELESS

AGELESS

RENÉE SCHAEFFER

CamCat
Books

CamCat Publishing, LLC
Fort Collins, Colorado 80524
camcatpublishing.com

Paperback ISBN 9780744310023
eBook ISBN 9780744310047

Library of Congress Control Number: 2024933804

Book and cover design by Maryann Appel
Interior artwork by Dencake, Ganna Bozhko, George Peters, Lyubov Ovsyannikova

5   3   1   2   4

For my grandmother, Gertrude Jenny Gorman, who loved me best.
And for David Levine, my husband and best friend.

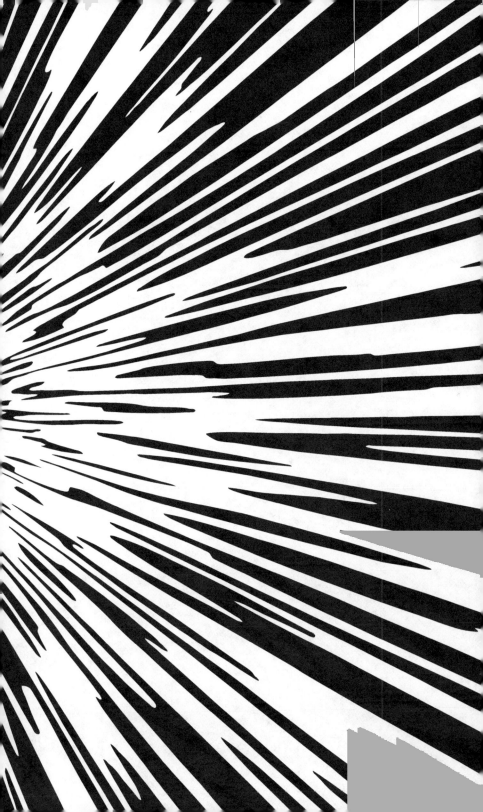

Our greatest glory is not in never falling,
but in rising every time we fall.
—Confucius

PROLOGUE

TIME. FOR MOST of my life, others thought of it as the ticking of a clock carrying change relentlessly forward. There was never enough time. It could fly away. Time was for memories, and for dreams of the future. It was the precious, tenuous, present moment. Some had plenty on their hands, others wasted it.

Many years later, people would look at time differently. Time became as bountiful as the universe. It became the air. Time was irrelevant. It was ignored.

But for me, time is beyond those things. Time is—and has always been—my immortal enemy, the cause of my grief. Battling the monster gives me strength to fight life's brutal blows. It gives me the power to find equanimity when it all goes off the rails.

CHAPTER ONE

1850–1866

Naissa

❦

T HE CRYSTAL PALACE *at Hyde Park, London, was the site of the first world's fair, the Great Exhibition of the Works of Industry of All Nations of 1851. Produced by Sir Charles Cole and Prince Albert, Queen Victoria's husband, the Exhibition showcased cutting-edge industrial technologies from the Western world.*

Among these were the world's first modern pay toilets, which cost one penny to lock. Charles Darwin, who attended the Great Exhibition, published On the Origin of Species by Means of Natural Selection *in 1859, generating international debate, acclaim, and calls of heresy.*

In the United States, railroads began to replace canals, and rumblings of secession by Southern states burgeoned. Harriet Beecher Stowe's Uncle Tom's Cabin *vilified slavery and was all but banned in the South. John Brown attempted a slave revolt in Harpers Ferry in the Shenandoah Valley and failed, becoming a martyr for the abolitionist cause.*

By 1861, Confederate secessionists defeated Federal forces at Fort Sumter, initiating four years of the bloodiest war on American soil, leaving up to a million dead.

In 1850, the year I was born, most American babies enjoyed names derived from British royalty or the Bible. My first name, Naissa, which means rebirth, was a little out of the ordinary. Perhaps my parents were giving homage to the Renaissance or displaying some sort of inexplicable presentiment. Sadly, I never thought to ask why they chose Naissa.

My father, John Nolan, was descended from a long line of Irish silver and goldsmiths who had settled in Philadelphia early in the eighteenth century. My father's contribution to the family jewelry business was exquisite design. Finely wrought Nolan jewelry and tableware were in demand by the haut monde across the country.

Father often invited me to his workshop to watch him turn metals into his jewelry designs. My job was buffing finished jewelry with a soft cloth. I loved the workshop's smells of oil and solder and the sound of his hammer tapping against the small anvil. In the summer, however, I did not like to visit on days when the hot forge was running.

My paternal grandfather, Patrick Nolan, my only grandparent still alive when I was born, had bucked family tradition and been an attorney of some renown before he retired and lived with us.

He tended the grape arbor adjacent to our large garden, as well as several beehives from which he harvested the most delicious honey. While I couldn't speak for Grandfather's wines, his grape juice was fit for a queen and the best part of autumn.

My mother, whom Father called Maggie but whose name was Margaret, adored numbers. Keeping the household and business books was a chore for most people, but not for Mother. She could find numbers in just about everything: a honeycomb, the shell of a chambered nautilus, or peppermints in a crystal candy bowl. No one was her match at the billiards table, much to the chagrin of any visiting gentleman foolish enough to accept an invitation to play. There was always a book by Mother's side or in her skirt pocket.

I remember one sunny afternoon when I was walking in the park with Mother and Father and a young woman in a lavender frock stopped us, thanking my mother for donating funds to send her to school. The woman said she was employed as a secretary and would never forget Mother's generosity. Throughout my childhood, such scenes were not uncommon.

When we camped outside at our country house, which we did often in the summer, the best times were at the campfire after dinner. We would sing songs and toast nuts and popcorn. I would watch Mother and Father exchanging little smiles that made them both glow. Sometimes Father would sneakily reach out to hold Mother's hand when he thought no one was looking. It was as if their love were a warm, invisible blanket wrapped around me, making me feel secure and happy.

My sixth birthday was a morning to remember. I awoke with the sun, and my little sister, Trudy, who was three years old, was still sleeping. I could not wait for my celebration day to begin. I quietly opened the shutters and marveled at the golds and pinks painted across the sky, the sun a fireball peeking from behind Jessup's Hill. The awakening world was new and fresh. I stretched out my arms and twirled until I fell down laughing. Trudy woke and rubbed her eyes with tiny fists and climbed down from our canopied bed to kiss me.

"Happy birthday, Naissa!"

Kissing Trudy back on her soft face, I said, "Thank you. I am sorry I awakened you."

Just then, Father and Mother came into our room.

"Happy birthday, Naissa!" they said together. I gave each of them a hug.

"Now that you are six, I would like you to have something of mine," Mother said, handing me a small parcel.

Lying in tissue paper was a sky-blue porcelain egg standing on three golden legs and decorated with ivory angels. Lifting the egg's lid, I found a ring of lace spun from silver. It had a diamond in the center and a sapphire heart on either side. The ring fit perfectly.

Mother touched the ring tenderly. "My mother, who died before you were born, gave me this ring for my sixth birthday. I pray it brings you as much happiness as it did me and that someday you will pass it on to your own daughter."

"Oh, thank you, Mother!" When Mother wrapped me in her arms, her love filled me with joy.

Trudy and I skipped and danced together around the room. At three and six years old, we had become inseparable. Everyone said that except for my brunette hair and Trudy's red, we looked like twins.

On bad weather days, our bed became the Enchanted Bed taking Trudy and me on adventures in which we became anyone we chose and experienced whatever we wanted. The Enchanted Bed took us to ancient Greece and into the mysterious future.

At times, the bed was a cloud upon which we ascended to heaven. The angels played their harps for us and lent us their wings so we could fly down over our house and around the world.

After saying goodnight and sharing hugs and kisses with Grandfather, Mother, and Father, we nestled under the covers for our last adventure of the day. Trudy and I whispered to each other until our eyes could stay open no longer, and the Enchanted Bed transported us through the starry night and into our dreams.

When I was ten, Father and I worked together on a brooch for Mother's birthday. The design was a silver framework shaped like a lilac spray, where each tiny blossom was a cut amethyst.

After I'd watched him create the framework and solder on its hammered leaves, Father said, with a smile, "Now, Naissa, are you ready to begin mounting the blossoms?"

With excitement, I watched as Father opened the safe and removed his sparkle box, a small chest of polished walnut inlaid with mother-of-pearl. Setting the box on the workbench, he unlatched and lifted the lid. Nestled in lush, purple velvet were a rainbow of gems, all to be used in the jewelry he made. Father handed me a satin pouch from the box, and I poured its contents onto one of the black velvet-lined trays on the workbench. A hundred tiny gems glinted in shades from light to darkest purple.

"The crystal from which these stones were cut came from a one-meter-tall Russian geode." Father handed me his brass loupe. "The color is brilliant. If you look closely, you can see there are virtually no imperfections in the crystal. They are the highest quality."

I held the small device to my eye and bent forward until a few gems were in focus. The stones were like the finest glass, transparent and without a single striation.

"We will mount each one and then solder them to the framework," Father said. "Are you ready to begin?"

"Yes!" I said eagerly. And we got to work.

My first efforts at mounting the gems were clumsy, but Father was a patient teacher. We worked two days, and by the afternoon of Mother's birthday, we were finished. We put the brooch in a velvet Nolan Jewelers box, which I gave to Mother at dinner.

Mother opened the box and gasped. "Oh, this is exquisite! My favorite, lilacs. I thank you with all my heart. I shall wear this with pride."

I beamed as Father pinned the brooch on Mother's dress. She scooped me into a tight embrace.

"Darling Naissa, I shall treasure your gift always. I love you so much, my sweet one."

<hr />

Exactly one year later, I was eleven years old and in a foreign land when a black curtain dropped, ravaging my childhood. My entire family was torn from me.

Every one of them, gone: Mother. Father. Grandfather. Even Trudy, my best friend and playmate, only eight years old.

We had steamed to France for an autumn holiday to celebrate Mother's birthday away from the troubles between the states. The days were brisk and sunny as we explored the streets of Paris amid the sharp, earthy smell of fallen leaves mingled with the delicious aromas from patisseries and cafés. Our lodging was at Brodeur Inn on Rue de la Paix, near the heart of the city and overlooking the breathtaking Tuileries Garden. The innkeeper, Madame Brodeur, took a liking to Trudy and me. While Mother's and Father's attention was elsewhere, she snuck us hard butterscotch candies, which she retrieved from her skirt pockets as her silver and agate bracelets softly clinked.

For Mother's birthday, my family went to a luxurious restaurant known for its fresh seafood and views of the Seine and Notre-Dame Cathedral. Dinner was magnificent. Everyone agreed our favorites were the buttery escargots and mussels mariniere. Mother's birthday cake was almost too pretty to eat: a tree of pastry balls and wispy threads of spun caramel nestled in a wreath of silvered leaves and wheeled to our table on a shiny brass trolley.

After dinner we went across the river to tour the cathedral, and I was disappointed that scaffolding hid much of the facade's gargoyles and other carvings I had seen in books. Once inside the cathedral, the explosion of color was entrancing: the late afternoon sun shone through multihued windows and painted the floors in rainbow brilliance.

When Mother tucked me in that night, holding me close and giving me my goodnight kiss, she smelled odd. There was a strange, sour odor underneath Mother's usual lilac fragrance as she whispered, "Sweet dreams, my darling Naissa." I told Mother I loved her.

Awakened by a nightmare of sound rising out of my dreams, I became aware that Mother was screaming in the bed next to me as she held Trudy, who hung limp as a sock doll from her arms. Trudy's face was oddly blue in the lamplight, her lips dark. A thick string of spittle hung from the corner of her mouth. Mother just screamed and screamed. I jumped up to get Father, but when I saw the door to Grandfather's adjoining room ajar, I changed course. Entering the room, I froze when I saw Father weeping by Grandfather's bed. The old man lay hanging half off the bed, bedclothes askew, his nightshirt immodestly high. Grandfather's open lips were the color of indigo ink in his ashen face, and his eyes stared at nothing.

I ran back to Mother, only to find her whimpering and trying to speak. Trudy slowly sank out of her arms and back onto the bed. Mother, voicing unintelligible words and looking around wildly, did not seem to know I was there.

"Mother! Mother, I am here," I sobbed, grabbing her arm. Mother brought a trembling hand to my cheek, but quickly moved it to her eyes. She poked her eyeball and blinked hard, as if surprised she had done such a thing. Moaning and reaching out again to me, Mother groped, but looked over my head. A cold grip of panic tightened around me—Mother could not see. She kept trying to say something, but the words came out as if in another language. Then she vomited and began gasping for breath from bluing lips, her mouth moving as I had seen fish do when too long out of water.

"Mon Dieu! Mon Dieu!" Suddenly, Madame Brodeur was in front of me, pushing me aside and helping Mother sit on the bed. This was a futile effort because Mother kept sliding over and down, as if she had turned into one of the marionettes we had seen at the street theater. Tears dripped from Mother's bulging eyes.

Then Father was beside us, his face overcome with horror. "Maggie!" He knelt by the bed and held Mother's hand. There was nothing we could do but watch as Mother drifted away, her gasping breaths coming farther and farther apart until at last they were no more. "Oh, Maggie," Father murmured.

Mother! How will I survive without your kisses?

It was impossible to believe she would never hold me again, never whisper how she loved me more than rainbows and stars. And never again would I play with my sister, never hug her when she trembled in the dark. And Grandfather, how I would miss his smell of tobacco and peppermint and the rough prickle of his whiskers.

"Father, what is happening?" I wished with all my heart for Father to tell me this was only a bad dream.

Father staggered to his feet, wavering as if he had played too many games of ring-around-the-rosy. He tried to speak, but his words were nonsense. Father clutched Madame's hand and looked at her beseechingly, and then looked at me.

She said, "Oui, yes, I shall take care of her; do not worry."

He staggered to his room. Mme Brodeur told me to stay in her rooms while she summoned a doctor, but I wanted to be with Father. She put her hands on my face and said, "Pauvre enfant," but I knew I was not a poor child; Father had always said we were Philly big bugs. I believed he would tell her so himself when he was better.

But Father did not get better. My once strong and indomitable father lay dying. "Father," I begged, "please do not leave me. Father, please!"

Father's mouth formed words with no sound. Grabbing Father, I held him tight, as though I could keep his life from flowing away. But my embrace was no match for death's. In a stillness so deep I was lost in it, I watched with weeping, aching eyes as Father's features softened into blankness. I put my ear to his lips, but there was no breath at all. Father had left his body and had left me with nothing but emptiness. I cried and cried and could not stop.

The next day after a brief chapel service, I found myself walking down the streets of Paris behind a pair of black, ornate carriages, their horses' hooves clattering upon the cobblestones. At the cemetery, the clergyman's nauseating cologne overpowered his words. I watched as a huge hole swallowed four ebony coffins, three large and one small.

Leaning over the maw, I whispered, "Trudy, dear sister, do not be afraid of the dark." Now, Trudy had to sleep alone.

I was emptied bit by bit as three workers threw shovelful after shovelful of French dirt onto my beautiful family. Then, sweat-drenched and dripping, the men levered a massive, granite slab over the grave.

Madame lay a small bouquet on the stone. She said gently, her voice far away, "By God's grace, enfant, you have been spared. Viens, Naissa, let us go." She tried to take my hand, but my fists were buried in the pockets of my cloak. An enormity of dirt and granite were piled upon my chest, so how could I move?

Somehow, I turned my back and walked away from my family.

On the way out of the cemetery, I paused in front of a stone woman sitting on a pedestal with her face in her hands, grieving. My own grief reached out to hers and joined in recognition.

That night, at Madame's, I lay sleepless, envisioning my family in the blackness of their earth-covered coffins. When breathing became difficult, I moved my visions out of the dark: Mother, her smile showering me in endless love, and wearing the brooch I had given her and that she now wore in her grave; Father, whose whiskers smelled of orange blossom and bergamot and whose eyes twinkled more than gems, waltzing with me in the parlor; Grandfather, deep in his grape arbor, clipping lush bunches from the vines, smiling at me as the sun dappled his face.

I remembered Trudy at night in our big bed, our arms wrapped around each other as we whispered stories and secrets. I remembered how joyfully she had played at various roles, especially that of mother to her doll babies. But now, Trudy would never have the chance to grow up, to live her life.

Where were they? In heaven with the angels, as Trudy and I had imagined? Could they see me?

I wished with all my heart to be with them so we could go on adventures together once more. Trudy and I would run and play and watch people like tiny ants in the world below.

But no. They were all under the ground. Trudy was sleeping alone in her box, without me. In my mind, I climbed into Trudy's dark and cold, lonely casket and lay with her. Although my heart still beat, I was dead, too.

<hr />

My Uncle James Leighton and his wife, Aunt Josephine, came to fetch me back to Philadelphia. Because Aunt Josephine bore an unsettling resemblance to her sister, my beautiful, red-haired mother, I could hardly look into her hazel eyes without my raw wounds bleeding anew. I was told that the gangling and humorless Uncle James had been appointed my guardian. This deepened my melancholy because he and Aunt Josephine had always been overly formal and cold toward my family.

One luncheon at the captain's table soon after we embarked, the steward offered potted mussels to Aunt Josephine. She recoiled. "Oh dear, no! Are you trying to poison me? Take those monstrosities away at once!" She turned to Uncle James and sniffed, "The nerve! Everyone knows what happened to my dear father and sister. One should think the chef would be more considerate." She glowered at me from under her feathered hat.

Unsure why, I felt as if I had done something wrong. Then, her words struck home. *The mussels.* My stomach roiled.

"Please excuse me, Uncle, I feel ill," I begged of Uncle James, and ran from the table the instant he nodded assent. In my cabin, I cried myself to sleep.

I returned to America across an ocean of sorrow. Every day, I stood at the ship's stern and gazed at the dark expanse. As the distance widened between me and those I loved and had left behind in a French cemetery, a numbing emptiness spread and I knew that a large part of me, the part I recognized, was vanishing into the past along with my family.

The Leighton house felt barren, despite being elegantly appointed and full of bustling servants. My aunt and uncle had a daughter my age, Claudia, whom I had met a few times before. Claudia attended a posh boarding school in Vienna but had stayed home that fall because of illness. Now recovered, Cousin Claudia disregarded me, and complained bitterly to her mother about any attention I was given. Claudia became visibly annoyed when people remarked that we looked like sisters. It bothered me, too. *Trudy* was my sister.

I pined for my real family as time ticked on. Food tasted like cardboard, and even my corset began to hang loose. Most days, I was left to fend for myself.

No one ever went into the Leightons' library, so I spent hours there reading from the collection of books whose crisp pages seemed untouched by human hands. It was difficult to focus on the words. Gazing out over the library garden where leaves rustled in the crackling aftermath of the season's growth, I found it painful to focus on my future.

One afternoon, the stern housekeeper discovered my library hideaway and admonished me to take good care of the valuable books. After that, the housemaid would sneak me tea and small cakes or warm biscuits with honey, saying she had been sent by the housekeeper. Otherwise, I was left alone and empty in the depths of my despair.

A few things from home had been brought to my room at the Leightons', including Father's sparkle box. With shaking hands, I unlocked the box with its silver key. It was empty, save for a gold, heart-shaped locket with intertwined hearts etched on front, Trudy's initials on the back, and two photographs on the inside. One was of Mother and Father, smiling, and the other of Trudy and me. Father must have made the locket for Trudy's next birthday. Donning the necklace and pressing the locket against my skin, I received some of the comfort I so badly needed. I would wear the locket most of my life.

At Christmas Eve dinner with the extended family, Aunt Josephine announced that after the holidays, I was to join Claudia at school in Vienna. The table murmured with approval. My Uncle William, Mother's elder brother, was the only one who spoke up.

"Surely," he said firmly, looking from my aunt to Uncle James, "the poor child ought to stay home with family until her grief abates. Look at her, she looks like a wisp of vapor. And with the War Between the States, traveling has risks."

I loved Uncle William from that moment on.

Aunt Josephine disregarded her brother and Uncle James booked Claudia's and my passage on a stately ocean liner. On our carriage ride to the ship's mooring, I contemplated an unfamiliar life outside the country. I did not know whether I was more heartened to be getting away from the

Leighton house or frightened of living alone in another strange place. What would it be like going to school in Vienna? Claudia, who hated me, was the only person I would know. I did not allow myself to cry.

Aunt and Uncle had invited their coterie to an ostentatious bon voyage party on board so all might see how well I was treated. Their guests murmured approvingly as they toured the ship and were impressed by our large stateroom and its fine furnishings.

A long, linen-covered table, adorned with golden candelabra and centered with a glistening dolphin sculpted from ice, was laden with oysters on the half shell, roasted beef, poached fish in aspic, sweetmeats, and sundry exotic morsels. Multitudes of yellow and white orchids graced the room. The wartime ostentation was startling.

An elegantly dressed woman—I think she was one of Uncle James's sisters, judging by her excessive height and thin frame—approached me carrying a small plate with a sampling of the delicacies.

"Naissa, dear child, why don't you have some of this lovely food?" Her eyes were kind as she proffered the plate.

"Thank you," I murmured, accepting the offering even though I was far from hungry. The few bites I managed to eat became a lump in my stomach, and I fought both nausea and tears. Easing into a corner chair, I lost myself in happier times.

We were camping at our country summer house. Grandfather and I had foraged for wild leeks and fiddleheads while Trudy and Father fished.

Grandfather was stooped over, motionless, cradling something in his hand.

"Naissa, come here—slowly," he said quietly.

I approached, and his treasure was revealed: a dragonfly perched on his first finger, ashine in iridescent blues and greens. Its wings flashed the rainbow as they flickered in sunlight. The matchstick-long creature ran a foreleg over its head from back to front, back to front, grooming itself.

"Class and order?" Grandfather whispered.

"Insecta," I answered promptly, but paused to consider the order. Neither hymenoptera nor lepidoptera, but . . . "Odonata!" I exclaimed, triumphant. The

dragonfly, startled by my voice, darted away, settling in the middle of an amethyst cluster of wild bergamot.

"Dragonflies are marvelous creatures," Grandfather said as we walked on to a large oak at the edge of the field. "They are pure predator. They can snatch a mosquito out of the air quick as lightening. And fast! They say the darners, family Aeshnidae, are faster than a racehorse." He stopped by the oak. "Let's wait here, in the shade. They should be along any minute."

After we sat down in the cool beneath the tree's canopy and Grandfather dabbed his forehead with his kerchief, he asked, "Do you know what sort of oak this is?"

I looked up. The sun sparkled through the rustling leaves, and squirrels scampered and chittered among the thick branches. Each leathery leaf had six or so deep lobes.

"A white oak?" I ventured.

"Excellent guess. This is a tricky one, because white oaks are similar. This old beauty is a pin oak. You can tell because the lobes are sharply pointed, like pins."

Just then, we heard laughter from across the field by the stream. Father and Trudy were walking up the hill toward us. Trudy started running and I jumped up to meet her.

We collided like puppies and rolled laughing in the grass. My knee burned from where it grazed a rock. I stopped to pull up my trouser leg, which now had grass stains and a small tear. I was glad Mother allowed Trudy and me to dress in boys' trousers for these adventures so we would not muss our good dresses. I watched as the crimson scrapes quickly faded, and pulled the trouser leg back down as Father approached.

"Watch out, my rough-and-tumble sons!" Father feigned shock at our behavior and then laughed, tousling Trudy's thick, red mane. "Come on, girls, let us fetch Grandfather and head back to the campsite. We shall cook these fish for dinner." He held up a string of glistening trout.

After we returned to the campsite, Grandfather stoked the fire with wood Trudy and I had collected earlier. Father and Grandfather were cleaning fish *when Mother arrived carrying a hamper. She and Cook must have finished canning tomatoes. I ran up to her.*

"Mother, Mother! Guess what? This morning Trudy and I pretended we were explorers and look what I found!" I dug into my pocket to produce my treasure: several flint arrowheads and a long, fluted spearpoint made from obsidian.

"Oh my, these are beautiful, Naissa! I would guess the spearpoint is Lenape, and very old. Very rare."

"That is what Grandfather said. He said they used it to fish and hunt."

"You are a good hunter yourself, my darling." Mother bent down to hug me in a snug embrace. I breathed in her scent of fresh soap and lilacs, and my heart sang with joy.

The minute the guests departed, Aunt Josephine whispered something to Sylvia, Claudia's maidservant and our chaperone.

Josephine's voice jolted me from my memories. She faced us. "Claudia, Naissa, I expect you to attend your studies to the utmost of your abilities."

Before either of us could do more than utter a feeble, "Yes, ma'am," she turned on her heel and was gone, a waft of verbena and the swish of silk skirts lingering for a moment in the space she left behind.

I went out to the rail. People around me held onto streamers and tossed the other ends to the crowd on the pier. Everyone held their ends until the ship pulled away and the streamers broke. I, too, was breaking—from sorrow, loneliness, and apprehension.

The air itself trembled. I lingered on deck even while the sky began to writhe, and huge, bruised thunderheads grew ripe to disgorge their innards. The sea breezes became winds blowing straight through my clothing until my insides were gust-whipped and brined. Evaporating. The salt I tasted was more than sea mist.

I wiped my eyes and made my way back to the stateroom. While changing for supper, Claudia and I stood in front of the looking glass and silently arranged our hair. We did appear to be sisters, with our brunette hair and hazel eyes. But that was where the similarities ended. Claudia was two months younger than me but looked mature and statuesque for her age. Her navy ensemble was well pressed and sophisticated. Shorter, less developed, and thin, I was a little girl next to her. I felt awkward and self-conscious in my smocked, yellow dress.

That night, I threw myself onto my bed and thought about a terrifying nightmare I had when I was five years old. No matter how I strained, I could only remember it was about being a grown-up with an unhappy life. My life was already unhappy. My tears wouldn't stop.

Among the throng meeting the ship in Trieste, Italy, was one of our schoolteachers sent to accompany Claudia and me on the train to Vienna. She was middle-aged with a genial face, her graying hair pulled back in a thick bun.

"Herzlich willkommen, I am pleased to see you again, Miss Leighton," she exclaimed as she shook Claudia's hand before turning to me. "And this must be Miss Nolan. Willkommen. I am Frau Klein. I teach the German language at Miss Sinclair's English School for Girls. I wish you a fruitful and pleasant stay at our school. My, my, you and Claudia could be sisters."

"How do you do, Frau Klein? What a lovely thing for you to say." I curtsied while thinking that looking like Claudia was not lovely at all, especially with that sour look on her face.

Too agitated to sleep the previous night, I dozed for most of the long train ride. When we arrived in Vienna, Frau Klein ushered us to a waiting carriage. The driver, a freckle-faced boy, helped the three of us in and then loaded the trunks and travel bags.

The view on our bumpy ride to Miss Sinclair's School consisted of farms and vineyards occasionally interrupted by patches of old forest. After about an hour, the carriage slowed.

My breath caught at a Baroque building fifty feet ahead. It stood monsterlike in the gloom, its many eyes glowering. As we drew closer, I saw the eyes were numerous small windows with faces pressed against them. I released my breath.

Most of the girls, having been at school since autumn, ran out to greet us. Claudia jumped out of the carriage to meet them, but I hung back, watching the reunions. Frau Klein introduced me to the group and ushered me inside.

A smothering, claustrophobic sensation pervaded the building. The tiny dark rooms contained too much heavy furniture and smelled of mustiness and decayed possibilities. At night, the window was a mirror in which I tried to fathom my future but saw only my own sad, glittering eyes. My room had one pleasing feature, discovered only when spring arrived: the window looked out on a shapely maple tree. Its leaves, like green butterfly wings, reflected the sun's rays as fluttery glints of my happier past.

As I readied for breakfast the next morning, there was a soft rapping on my door. When I swung it open, a girl about my age was standing there.

"Good morning! I am Anna Winchester, from across the hall." She gestured to her room's door. "You are Miss Nolan, are you not? You may call me Anna. Do you know where the dining hall is? I could show you. May I accompany you to breakfast?"

I did not know where the dining hall was but was not keen on company at the moment.

"I am not quite ready. Perhaps I could—"

"Oh wonderful!" She brushed past me and sat herself on my reading chair. "I will wait. Say, I heard you are from Philadelphia. I hail from New York City. Do you have Parisian fashions in Philadelphia as we do in my city? We have the most wonderful fashions. I must show you the most divine bonnet I acquired over the holiday. May I help you with your hair?"

I looked at the hairbrush in my hand. It was all too much for me.

"Anna, I am sorry. It seems the long journey has suddenly caught up with me. I feel an urgent need to rest. Perhaps we will meet at dinner."

In the early days of school, Anna and others tried to connect with me, but I felt like an outsider who had nothing in common with them or their happy lives. Discussions of hair ribbons or so-and-so's inheritance meant nothing in the face of my grief. If I were to be honest, I also feared losing anyone I might come to care for. As a result of my standoffishness, the others began to ignore me.

For some reason, I made George, the boy who had been our carriage driver, an exception. Twelve days after my arrival, we met again on a Sunday afternoon when he saw me reading behind the stables, under a pair of ancient fir trees. Hearing the gravel crunch, I looked up and saw him walking toward me, his hair bleached almost white by the sun. His lack of a coat and cap made me shiver beneath my cloak.

George's smile lit his face and eyes, melting away my melancholy. His breath came in clouds as he said with a faint German accent, "I beg pardon, miss. Perhaps you remember me? I was your driver to the school. My name is George Johnson, eldest son of the Reverend George Johnson." He gave a slight bow. "I work for Miss Sinclair after school and on weekends, to help provide for my family. May I—may I speak with you?"

"I am pleased to meet you, Mr. Johnson. My name is Miss Nolan. It would be my pleasure to speak with you."

"Why do you sit here by yourself, miss?" Although surprised at his forwardness, I appreciated his earnest manner. Well, if he could be forward, then so could I.

"I am uncomfortable with the other girls." Yet I was not uncomfortable with him, and we appeared to be of similar age.

Surprise flashed across George's face before he gave me a quick, lopsided smile that begot a deep dimple in his left cheek.

He nodded toward my book. "When I am able to find solitude and time, I also enjoy reading. If I may ask, miss, what other pursuits do you fancy?"

"I like exploring the outdoors. And you?"

"It seems we have similar interests, miss. I have found some wonderful places not far from here. Would you care to see them? I could show you."

It was against the rules to be in the company of a young man without an escort. I looked around and saw no other students or teachers. The possibility of an outdoor adventure rekindled a spot in my heart that had been dark for long months.

"Yes, thank you, Mr. Johnson. I should like that very much. But only if you call me Naissa from here on."

With that same half-smile, George answered, "Of course, Miss Naissa. And please call me George."

"Very well, George. I must don my boots and gymnastics costume. I shall be right back." Once in my room and breathless from running, I cursed the slowness of my fingers as I untied my crinolette. Trudy and I used to be so free in our trousers whenever we played outside. Feeling gratitude for Mother allowing us that freedom, I laced and buttoned my gymnastic pantaloons and shift, and, last, pulled on my new Aigle Wellingtons. Redone, I stepped out the door and tried not to run.

When I returned to the fir trees, George had a lantern. He led me to a secret cave he had discovered two miles from Miss Sinclair's. As we crawled through the cave's small opening, the light receded and darkness assailed me. It was not a shadowy or hazy darkness one's eyes could adjust to, but a world of deep and utter black. A darkness that contained who-knows-what kind of horrible monsters that reached out to touch me with icy fingers, whispering of their hunger.

All at once, I heard fluttering from above, and something brushed my cheek. I screamed and grabbed for George, but then laughed at my foolishness when I realized it was only a bat.

George lit the lantern. Wondrous, otherworldly glory! All around us shone marble-like walls, ceilings, and floors with lustrous rock icicles—stalactites—growing from them. There were many limestone formations, some shaped like castles, flowers, and mythical creatures. It was a fairyland, and well worth the tongue-lashing I later received from Miss Sinclair for my unchaperoned adventure.

The following Sunday, not caring about the consequences, I went on another trek with George. He led us deeper into the cave to a lake. Its startling, cobalt-blue water put the sky to shame, even by lantern light. We waded in barefoot with clothes hiked up, but George and I became drenched anyway. It was fun but freezing.

When the lantern oil waned, we reluctantly backtracked to the cave's entrance, with George as guide. I was grateful for his knowledge of the cave because I would have been completely lost in the maze of passages.

Once out of the cave, George and I relaxed for a time in the sun while he whittled a small block of wood he carried in his pocket. On our way back down the hill, I pointed out edibles such as bilberries, meadow salsify, and lawyer's wig mushrooms. George and I hungrily ate some, and then gathered all we could carry to George's mother for supper.

Mrs. Johnson was free with her smiles, hugs, and delicious meals. She invited me to spend Sundays after church with George and the rest of the family while the reverend made Sunday visits to his congregation.

Miss Sinclair agreed because Mrs. Johnson was an acquaintance, so she knew the family was a wholesome and pious one. Nonetheless, she lambasted me regularly about proper behavior with George and his family. Her admonitions did not matter to me, because George was a comfort in my otherwise solitary life.

Over the next few years, while war raged between America's Northern and Southern states, I excelled academically. Toiling on schoolwork kept emptiness from the loss of my family at bay. Interested in foreign languages, I took all those available, even though just two were required: Latin, Greek, French, and German.

I was intrigued by unlocking secrets hidden within books written in diverse languages, and the way words in other tongues corresponded to English. Most of my other classes were trivial "gentlewomanly" pursuits, such as needlework, deportment, and elocution.

I enjoyed drawing class but was miserable at it. My father's words, however, kept encouraging me: "Nothing worthwhile is gained without hard work." Needing more instruction than was offered by the school's curriculum, I successfully petitioned Uncle James for private drawing lessons with a local artist. At times, I nearly gave up because my progress was so slow, but I didn't want to let Father down.

George and I spent many Sunday afternoons on hikes together. The two of us combed every nook and cranny within a six-mile radius of the school during our Sunday roaming. Curious about what could be seen, we climbed the tallest trees upon the highest hills.

We walked through shallow streams to find out where they led and used some medieval ruins we found as the background for impromptu melodramas. George and I observed the ways of the animals, and after a time recognized and named individuals.

In the beginning, George was a playmate and protector. As the years progressed, our relationship matured.

One autumn day in my third year, George and I sat next to each other in a copse of birch trees overlooking the valley. The gray of the sky matched my melancholy, for I was reminded of autumn in Paris. Sensing my gloom, George reached over and put his arm around me.

I froze. Then I relaxed into the warmth of him. I leaned my head against his shoulder, and we sat like that for a long while. George leaned down, and I felt a soft kiss atop my head. My heart was soothed, as if kindness flowed from his lips to my very core.

After that, we would lie under the shelter of trees, holding each other and talking while sunlight sparkled through the leaves and danced over us with tremulous, golden fingers. Occasionally, we shared a brief kiss. The warm softness of his lips on mine became the best moments of my days.

Throughout my time at school, anguish from the loss of my family lingered. I often anticipated a glimpse of someone, a shadow, a motion at the door— something of my family filling the void. This expectation of their presence caused me to take second looks when shadows teased the periphery of my vision.

One March afternoon warmer and more humid than it should have been, George and I took a walk in the woods before returning to loll behind the stables under the firs. George stirred a small pile of fallen needles into patterns with his fingers, while I braided a chain of buttercups collected on our walk. In that moment with George, I felt sufficiently at ease to confide my struggle with grief.

"Do you think the loss of loved ones triggers the loss of oneself?" I asked.

George's gray eyes darted to mine before he looked back at the pile of dry needles, which he studied for a bit. Then he replied, "I think it is clear the people we love each occupy a part of our heart, and when they die, that part in us might be lost, too, no? I think also, perhaps we fill the holes a little bit with memories of them."

I considered George's answer. "But what if the memories fade and disappear? Then a person would be left with nothing but the holes."

"It seems to me," he said, "in such a situation it would be important to preserve the memories as best we can, while we still have them. Perhaps that could be done by transcribing the memories or finding or making other mementos."

"Is that what you would do?"

My friend gazed out over the mountains. After a moment, he nodded. "I have my carving."

He always carried a small piece of wood in his pocket for whittling. Sometimes he showed me the finished products: animals and figurines of happy families at play.

I pondered how I might best preserve memories of my family, which grew fainter every day. Trudy's locket with its pictures was a piece of them I could always hold on to. I had a few more photographs of Trudy, Mother and Father, and one of Grandfather with his beehives. But these were paltry means to fill my emptiness.

During my drawing lesson the following week, I suddenly thought of a way to keep memories of my family from fading. The grave in Paris where they lay was unadorned, with only the words *Famille de Nolan* carved upon its granite cover.

What if there were an ornamented monument honoring my family at Père Lachaise necropolis? Memories of them would become ageless in marble, gracing the world with beauty for eons to come.

I had neglected my drawing lessons for a few weeks, but began again, redoubling my efforts with the goal of sketching the monument design forming in my mind. Whenever I thought to give up—which happened many times—the memory of my father, his skill, and his words pushed me to keep trying.

Late April of 1865 held a shocking week of tidings from America. Its zenith: the South had surrendered; the war was over. The nadir: our president, Abraham Lincoln, was assassinated just days afterward. I wondered about the America I would return to the following year. Would the peace hold? What would be the situation of the former slaves? I wished I could have discussed these questions with my parents.

I was still puzzling such questions a few days later when I was invited to Sunday dinner with the Johnsons. My fifteenth birthday had been the day before, and Mrs. Johnson prepared a celebratory meal crowned with my favorite dessert, her apfelstrudel.

Mrs. Johnson gave me a delicate lace collar she had tatted, which I treasured and wore often. My gift from George was a tiny, kicking Lipizzaner horse he had carved from a piece of ash and polished until it shone like one of the stallions themselves.

Later that evening in the woods, with the sky still light and crickets chirping in a chaotic symphony, George and I fell asleep in a hemlock grove. We did not awaken until dawn.

Miss Sinclair was by nature an angry woman, but that morning she was angrier than I had ever seen her. It was clear from her flushed countenance that she was steaming in her dark silks. She paced back and forth in front of the leaded windows of her office, a silhouette of iron intensity in the morning light, her heels a staccato on the mosaic tile floor.

Every now and then, a muffled crack or shout came through the windows from the gymnastics class, where a game of ground billiards waged on the front lawn.

Once she began, Miss Sinclair spat words at me, her voice an octave higher than usual.

"Miss Nolan, I should not have allowed you to spend Sundays with that . . . that . . . boy. I consider your behavior last evening to be a failure of the utmost severity. You have shamed me, our school, your schoolmates, and your esteemed family."

What family?

"Have you not learned a single lesson in deportment since you have been with us? Where is your propriety? This is utterly shameful. What you and that boy have done is an abomination. An abomination."

Perhaps she has been rehearsing this speech for decades. I am so fortunate to be its witness. Joy unbounded.

"You have dragged the reputation of this fine school into the ditches. For all we know . . . How many times have you lain with that boy? What have you to say for yourself?"

Her fury of words and striding came to a sudden halt as she turned to fix me with raging eyes. Girls' laughter drifted into the room from the game outside. A woodlark in the rhododendron below the window sang its cheery *toolooeat, toolooeat, toolooeat*.

Instinctively, I reached for Trudy's locket, rubbing its golden warmth into my fingers. I knew humble pie would be the best offering, but one must defend oneself when no one else would. "Miss Sinclair, I adamantly disagree, as your conclusion is false. I did not surrender my virtue, not once. I have always done as you asked and been a model student. Your lessons have not gone unheeded."

The headmistress's ears flamed red, her rage rising even further. "We shall see, we shall see, Miss Nolan. You shall submit to an examination by our physician and the truth of the matter shall be exposed. You may go." She turned her back to stare stonily out the window at the girls and their game.

I suffered through a humiliating examination by Herr von Graben, the school physician, who pronounced me still *intact*. Nevertheless, a cloud of hissing whispers followed me, and Claudia, instead of ignoring me as was customary, glared. Miss Sinclair never apologized for her false accusations or even mentioned the doctor's findings. Far worse, one of George's sisters told me their father had beaten him severely, and we were to be kept apart permanently.

I considered defying the injunction, but truth be told, I was afraid of Reverend Johnson. More than once, I had seen his eyes spark with anger and his children flinch.

Without George in my life, I was broken. Nevertheless, I determined to take George's advice about keeping the memory of my family alive, and wrote to Uncle William, asking him to persuade Uncle James to allow construction of a monument at the Paris gravesite.

After Uncle James agreed to the monument, my drawing tutor gave me the names of two Parisian sculptors who could be hired to do quality work. To meet the sculptors and commission one of them to create the monument, I obtained Miss Sinclair's permission to travel to Paris that summer with Frau Klein.

I speculated that Miss Sinclair's approval, given with dramatized reluctance, was to keep me from complaining to my aunt and uncle about her treatment of me.

The day of our departure for Paris dawned warm and humid, thus I was glad to be wearing my cage crinoline, which allowed me to forego layers of heavy petticoats. Frau Klein and I rode the Kaiserin Elisabeth-Bahn to Salzburg, where we overnighted at a small inn near the station. The next morning, we headed for Stuttgart and the Rhône valley.

During our journey west, Frau Klein was often engrossed in reading her book. She had tried to keep the title covered, but I knew it to be *Incidents in the Life of a Slave Girl, Written by Herself*. I had heard of this book, which was said to be a description of the horrors of slavery but was rather scandalous owing to some indelicate content.

AGELESS

I wanted to understand Frau Klein's interest. "Frau Klein, please forgive me for interrupting your reading. I should like to ask your thoughts on a topic related to the book you are reading."

Frau Klein closed her book, removed her spectacles, and mopped her brow. She looked at me expectantly.

"Frau Klein, what do you think shall happen to the former slaves in America, now that the war is over?"

"That is a good question. It may be some years before all Americans accept the end of slavery, and so the dangers to the former slaves may not be insignificant."

"I hope not. It couldn't be worse than slavery was. My parents used to attend antislavery meetings, and they made sure my sister and I treated all with respect. Perhaps they were more involved, I will never know. Once, I overheard a family friend tell Father about his visit to a Louisiana plantation. The plantation owner tried to have, um, relations with a nine-year-old slave girl. When her mother begged and tried to save her girl, both mother and daughter were tied up and their backs whipped until the skin shredded. Father was furious to hear of such a thing."

"How horrible, Naissa. Thank goodness slavery is at an end. I pray when you return to America, you will find your country's people coming back together." We talked more about current events before the conversation moved to what I would do upon returning to my guardians that summer.

"Frau Klein, living in my aunt and uncle's house is difficult for me, thus I hope to find a position that allows me to live on my own, or with another family."

"I do not wish to pry, but what is the nature of this difficulty?"

I was unsure how much to say but felt comfortable with Frau Klein. "To be honest, the Leightons and Nolans have never been close. I suppose Aunt Josephine disliked my beautiful, outgoing mother. My Uncle James is of dour disposition and barely acknowledges me, and Claudia resents my presence."

Frau Klein's eyes glistened as she took my hands in hers.

"You deserve a loving homelife, my child. Every child should have unconditional love. I am sorry."

I was warmed by my teacher's empathy and concern. "Thank you, Frau Klein."

"Naissa, dear, please call me Marta." She paused and gave me a slight smile. "When we are not at school, of course."

It was the first time since my parents had died that I conversed openly with an adult. As we talked, Marta confided that she had once been married and there was to have been a baby, but none of it had worked out. Marta told me the rest of her story, and I told her mine. Time passed quickly.

<hr/>

It was bittersweet to be back in Paris and see some of the places I had enjoyed with my family. When I asked our hotel's concierge about the restaurant where my family shared our last meal together, he said it was shut down five years before because a number of diners had consumed tainted seafood, which had proved fatal.

The first sculptor Marta and I visited, Monsieur Auguste Clésinger, had been described by my drawing tutor as a sculptor of somewhat scandalous reputation but breathtaking skill. He had created the acclaimed tomb of Frédéric Chopin, in which the muse Euterpe wept over a broken lyre. When we met Clésinger in his studio, he was polite and, although his eyebrows quirked at my design sketch for the monument, he seemed pleased with my ideas. Clésinger, full-bearded and rather unkempt in a baggy suit grayed with stone dust, had the strong, aquiline nose common to many of the French. Wisps of white in his dark beard and hair softened his angles, but his eyes were so black and sharp, I would not have been surprised if he used their gaze to bore straight through marble.

As we discussed his fee, my attention was caught by a low figure in the corner of the studio. I excused myself and approached it. My limbs suddenly froze and I gasped at the sight of a nude, reclining woman of white marble. Her nakedness was carved in such exquisite detail, my cheeks burned. She had the generous curves of a real woman, the stunning result of intricate chisel work. I could almost smell the morning glories, roses, and lilies upon which she lay, their rendering was so lifelike. Most striking, even beyond the exquisiteness of the work, was her pose. The woman's head arched back at an extreme angle, while her spine twisted and was locked in an eternal convulsion. Her torso was in the throes of death. She reminded me of my mother in her last, agonizing moments.

And yet, this woman held peace in her countenance. Her feet and hands were in languorous repose, as if the final relaxation was having its way with her. The dichotomy was unsettling and intriguing.

"Elle est *Femme Piquée par un Serpent—Woman Bitten by a Serpent,*" said Monsieur Clésinger at the very moment I spied the tiny snake curled around her wrist like a bracelet. One could easily forget this was a piece of marble. I turned away from her and walked toward him.

"When would you start on the monument? And how long might it take?" I offered silent thanks to Mother, Father, and Grandfather for the funds with which I was able to pay Monsieur Clésinger's exorbitant commission. I told Frau Klein there was no need to visit the other sculptor.

After returning to Vienna, I suffered through my remaining months at school without George. My only consolation was a second trip to Paris with Frau Klein, this one at the close of my final exams, to oversee installation of my family's monument. Frau Klein and I found lodging on Rue de la Roquette, near the Père Lachaise main entrance, and took pleasure in daily jaunts to the necropolis.

The walk up to Section Ten where my family was interred was not long, yet it was a journey to a universe separate from the living chaos just outside the gates. As we strolled deeper into the stone garden, up its narrow cobblestone and flagstone alleys, the voices of wrens and nuthatches gradually overtook the din of the city. The many residents of the narrow and ornate stone houses packed among spreading maples and chestnuts infused us with their quiet repose, coaxing worries to fall away.

Monsieur Clésinger and his apprentices had worked exclusively on my commission over the past year. The final installation took several weeks' effort, with Clésinger, his two apprentices, and a number of laborers working dawn to dusk.

I enjoyed the worksite with its marble dust, clanging and banging, and laborers stripped to their trousers, their iron muscles glistening as they wielded hammers and hefted hunks of marble. Clésinger, barking orders and working with singular focus, somehow never failed to pause and provide a colorful update on the progress, pointing out what was newly accomplished, what was yet to be done, and the infuriating details, which, if not rectified, would mar his artistic excellence.

One morning, Clésinger called on Frau Klein and me at the inn. As we sat in the parlor, he beamed.

"Madame et mademoiselle, I have excellent news for you this morning. The work is accomplished. C'est fini."

Frau Klein and I both exclaimed in excitement.

"How wonderful!" Frau Klein said, "When may we see it?"

Clésinger turned his beret in his hands. "I would be honored if you would accompany me at present, maintenant."

I hesitated. "Thank you, monsieur, I am happy to hear your news. Please excuse me a moment, and I will get the balance of your fee."

I needed a minute to think. Going to my room, I retrieved the note I'd previously written with the balance of the agreed-upon price. While I was anxious to see the finished monument, I wanted to be alone for my first viewing of my family's tribute.

Back in the parlor, Clésinger accepted the note with thanks.

"Monsieur, in order to fully appreciate your work, I would like to view it in private, if you do not mind. I will go to the cemetery later in the day, by myself. Would that be acceptable to you?"

Clésinger seemed to deflate. "Mais oui, of course, mademoiselle. As you wish."

"Perhaps Frau Klein would like to view the monument with you now? She is anxious to see it."

After they left, I went to a nearby café and had a small dinner while watching colorful Paris flow by on the busy street. Afterward, I walked to the library to return a book I had borrowed earlier in our stay and then browsed a few of the shops. Finally, as the sun began slanting and shadows grew longer, I turned toward the necropolis.

The monument was exquisitely beautiful in the late afternoon light, its sparkling, colorful marble mimicking nature with perfect pitch. It was exactly what I had envisioned. Clésinger had brilliantly executed the ornamented, eight-foot-tall arch over the sepulcher, and a marble bench where one could sit and look upon, and through, the archway. Everything was hewn not from the austere marbles of muted white and gray so common in the necropolis, but from a rainbow of richly hued marbles: crimson Griotte from France, the palest pink Rosetta Vene from Egypt, yellow and orange Numidian from Tunisia, green Cipollino Versilia from Italy, Blue Sky from Brazil, purple-veined Pavonazzo from Italy, ebony Noir Belge from Belgium, ivory Proconnesian from Turkey, and Artesian White from Greece.

Carved in high relief on the arch were two smiling goddesses whose benevolent gaze, I was sure, comforted the spirits of my family as they passed through the archway. Gaea, Mother Earth, was on the left column of the arch and honored Mother and Father's love and respect for the natural world. The shaft of the tall spear Gaea held was encircled with tea roses and represented Trudy, whose name meant *spear*. Rays hewn from Numidian marble radiated from the spear's tip, up and across the span of the arch, where they met and intermingled with vines of ivy. The ivy grew from Physis, the goddess of nature, who was on the right-hand column. She honored my parents' study of the world around them. The scales she carried represented Grandfather's profession as a barrister. His beehives and honey, grapes and wine balanced the scales. The goddesses were adorned with brightly colored tiaras, necklaces, bracelets, and rings, representing the Nolan jewelry business. Masses of carved dahlia and lilac, Mother's favorite, grew from the base of the arch, and flowers of all sorts rose up and around the arch in bas-relief, all reaching out toward the apex, the sun.

Too many of the figures in the cemetery were sorrowful. I wanted my family to instead spend their eternity in beauty. Each stroke of Clésinger's chisel sang of Mother, Father, Trudy, and Grandfather—forever beautiful, forever joyful.

I sat upon the marble bench in front of the archway and allowed the world to settle around me. The scent of freshly turned earth drifted by on puffs of air while wrens' clear voices warbled. A pair of lovers whispered and laughed softly as they ambled past with arms interlocked. I stayed until the light started to dim and the marbles burned with the lowering sun's fiery reds and golds. The lovely surroundings and the splendor of the monument brought memories of my family into sharper focus. As the songbirds quieted and the nighthawks began their raspy calls, I had the satisfaction of knowing I had honored my family in a manner they would have been proud of.

On the way down to the exit from Père Lachaise, I paused at the grieving woman sitting upon her pedestal, whom I now knew was *La Douleur*, or *Grief*, sculpted by François Dominique Milhomme in 1815. She was more beautiful than I remembered, more human. I empathized with her.

◦─◦~◦─◦~◦─◦

Before returning to Philadelphia, I sent Monsieur Clésinger a letter apologizing for excluding him from my first viewing of the completed monument, describing what it was like for me to experience the monument, and how perfectly he had carried out my intention. My thanks for bringing my family closer to my heart, exactly as I had wished, were sincere.

Because my sketch had accurately communicated my wishes for the monument to Clésinger, I was encouraged to keep drawing. I carried a small sketchbook with me and developed the habit of drawing whenever I could.

Regarding Frau Klein, I corresponded with her until her death over thirty years later. She became my Aunt Marta for whom I cared deeply, and who genuinely cared about me and my success. When I received a letter from Aunt Marta's sister informing me of her death, I felt the last remnant of family ripped from my grasp.

All I ever learned of George was that he left home a few months after my departure and joined the clergy. I hoped he found happiness—as I did upon my return to Philadelphia.

CHAPTER TWO

1866–1893

Naissa

B Y THE END *of the Civil War, states were rebuilding, and former slaves were beginning to build their free lives in America. May 10, 1869, saw the last spike driven into the country's first transcontinental railway, opening the West to settlement. In the autumn of 1871, a fire in Chicago decimated over seventeen thousand structures, leaving an estimated three hundred dead. Two years later, an economic depression in Europe spread to America. Since the country had been so prosperous, most were completely unprepared for financial hardship when banks and railroads failed, and the New York Stock Exchange shut down. The breathtaking Brooklyn Bridge, designed by John Roebling, opened in 1883; a scandalous rumor circulated that his wife, Emily Warren Roebling, had served as construction supervisor. In the spring of 1876, Philadelphia commemorated the one hundredth anniversary of the signing of the Declaration of Independence with a massive International Exposition. Among the marvels were a railway refrigerator car, a giant steam engine, and a machine called a* typewriter *that printed words upon a page. Most astonishing was the exhibit showcasing Alexander Bell's talking instrument, which seemingly used magic to transport voices over long distances.*

In 1890, the US military waged a campaign against the Lakota Sioux, cul-minating in the Seventh Cavalry, armed with four rapid-fire Hotchkiss M1875 1.65-inch mountain guns, surrounding and massacring almost 300 men, women, and children at Wounded Knee, South Dakota, nearly extinguishing the Lakota.

⁓⁓⁓⁓⁓

Upon completing school and returning to Philadelphia, my sixteen-year-old cousin and I were introduced into society at an elegant Dancing Assembly Ball. In the grandiose Music Hall's second floor ballroom, the Grand Foyer, I was introduced to Peter Jones, a handsome young man in crisp linen, whose manner reminded me of my sweet and gentle father.

After Peter escorted me to the dance floor and we began twirling in a waltz, he glanced up at the arched ceiling.

"Were you aware, Miss Nolan, this poor, plain ceiling was intended to be lavishly frescoed in the Italian style? The funds, however, have yet to be allocated for the job."

"Is that so? And what do you know of the Italian style, Mr. Jones?"

The chandeliers could not compete with his smile. "Ah, Miss Nolan, I applied to the building commission to decorate this ceiling, as I have previously created works in the Italian style."

"You have? Were you not introduced to me as a student of the law?"

"Well, yes, that is my current state of affairs. But I am, in my heart, an artist. And for an aspiring artist such as myself, such a commission would be the thrill of a lifetime."

"Indeed, it would. You must have admirable skill to contemplate such a work."

He laughed, and his eyes locked on mine. "I have many talents, Miss Nolan."

"Indeed."

I had promised dances to other eligible young men, but risking my aunt's displeasure, I danced exclusively with Peter in the glow of sparkling glass chandeliers, mesmerized by his sapphire eyes and feeling as if the orchestra played only for us.

During the musicians' break for refreshment, Peter and I went through the tall folding doors and onto the narrow balcony where we could talk. We found we enjoyed many of the same artists, authors, and playwrights. We even shared a dislike for foods in aspic, such as some of those being served that evening.

When I learned Peter was in his final year of reading law at Oxford University, we exchanged our experiences of school abroad. Josephine, vigilant as a hawk, intermittently paraded past us on the balcony, making her presence known by clearing her throat and casting sidelong glances at me. I feigned I did not see her, but Peter gave her a gentlemanly nod and a charming smile each time she passed. Before we knew it, the ball was over, and we were saying goodnight.

"Miss Nolan. This has been a most enchanting evening. May I . . . may I write your uncle for permission to call upon you?"

I consented wholeheartedly.

Because the Jones family was of considerable station, Uncle James gave his approval to the courtship after he received Peter's note the next day. Aunt Josephine chaperoned us for only three short visits in her parlor before, sadly, Peter voyaged back to Oxford to complete his studies.

Our relationship unfolded through frequent, lengthy letters. It pleased me greatly to find Peter and I held the same views on current affairs. We were thrilled that the slaves had been freed but horrified at the war's death and destruction.

Our letters enabled Peter and me to understand each other more thoroughly than through mere conversation. The letters gradually became more intimate. What had started out as *Dear Mr.* or *Miss* and *Sincerely* evolved into *My darling* and *With all tenderness*. I had fallen in love with Peter, but propriety forbade my writing it to him. I hoped his feelings toward me were as strong as those surging through my heart. I consoled myself by writing love poems to Peter that I never sent.

The summer after the ball, the prestigious Central High School for boys reorganized its entire curriculum, and all new staff were hired to implement it. The school's male teachers hired only unmarried female assistants, and so, with a good word from Uncle James and the foreign language skills I acquired in school, I was employed as the language teachers' assistant. My duties mainly included tutoring the students in Latin, German, and French. Once the teachers saw my capability, I sometimes taught their classes when they were unable.

The first time I led one of the classes, I was nearly brought to tears. As I stood in front of the French class and tried to begin a lesson on the pluperfect tense, the boys became restless and noisy. One boy, Theodore Ellsworth, started throwing wadded-up pieces of paper at another student.

"Mr. Ellsworth, please stop that," I begged.

Theodore laughed. "You cannot make me! You're just a girl."

My face burned. He was right, of course. I was barely older than the students.

Wads of paper and raucous laughter flew around the room. When one of the wads hit me, the boys nearly fell off their seats.

Suddenly, the door opened and Mr. Shippen, the principal, thundered in. "Gentlemen!"

The room fell into an immediate hush. "What in the blazes goes on here?" He glared at the class before turning to me.

"I—I was trying to begin the lesson . . ."

Mr. Shippen had a way of looking over his glasses and down his nose that made me feel an inch tall.

He said sternly to the class, "You shall quietly continue your work. Miss Nolan is my representative, and you are to treat her accordingly."

With a slam of the door, he was gone.

That night, reliving the nightmare of my first class, I knew there must be a better way to take charge.

The next time I was tasked with teaching a class, I stood as tall as I could and spoke in the firmer, louder voice I had practiced.

"If we complete the lesson quickly and accurately, we shall have extra time to enjoy this beautiful day during recess."

The boys were model students from then on. Before long, I held hours at the beginning and end of the school day, meeting with my charges and helping with their studies. When I listened carefully to what they said and guided them in finding solutions, it was exhilarating to see their eyes light up. I became a privileged advisor when the boys confided to me their difficulties at home, their infatuations, and other secrets. This job made me realize I adored teaching.

⟡⟡⟡

After twelve interminable months, Peter was coming home to Philadelphia for good. In a white heat for weeks prior to his return, I was too worked up the day before to be of much use to the students. At last, the final bell rang. That night, sleep evaded me.

Dressed by dawn, wishing it were already late afternoon, I tried calming my agitated insides. After pacing the floor, fussing with my hair, and changing outfits three times, I decided to go to the port hours early. Mary, one of the Leightons' maidservants around my age, was only too happy to leave off polishing silver when I beckoned. Having no desire to involve Aunt Josephine in my reunion with Peter, I trusted Mary to be a discreet chaperone.

Tingling with anticipation as we stepped into a cloudless summer Saturday, I felt attractive in my slate and black damask frock with its matching parasol and bonnet. Even though I felt like running, I walked decorously toward the cabbie stand to hail a hansom. As we rumbled toward the river, Mary talked animatedly about the return of my "handsome young man." She said from the times she saw us together in the parlor, she knew he was the perfect man for me. The cab provided us the cover to be more familiar, and it helped settle my nerves to have someone with whom I could share my excitement. At the waterfront, instead of jumping from the carriage after Mary, I waited genteelly for the portly hackman to help me down.

"Girlie," he said with a gap-toothed smile, "You looks as like Cupid did shoot ye."

Embarrassed, I paid him and stammered, "G-good day, sir." He tittered as he drove off.

"See?" Mary giggled, "Everyone can tell true love."

When we arrived at the wharf, others were already waiting to greet the transatlantic vessel. Giggling girls fidgeting with their dresses chatted with their chaperones. Sweethearts twisted handkerchiefs and sighed, as I found myself doing. A few boys chased hoops the same way my heartbeats chased after one another. Would Peter still be attracted to me? Would he love me as I loved him?

The air of excitement multiplied as those waiting became a sizable crowd. After what seemed like forever, a man's shout of "I see the ship, I see her!" rose above the sounds of shouting dockworkers, crying infants, barking dogs, and laughing, hollering boys. Mary squealed and grabbed hold of my arm before realizing she had overstepped. She quickly withdrew her hand.

"I am sorry, miss. That was not proper of me, miss."

I smiled and patted her hand.

"I am glad you are here with me, Mary, for I think I am going to burst!" I strained and narrowed my eyes but could not tell one ship from the many others in the river. "Which ship is it?"

Then one ship turned slowly toward the pier and we were surrounded by cries of, "Here she is!" and "The ship has arrived!" We waited impatiently while the ship gradually sidled up to the pier and was secured. At last, the gangplank was lowered amid a cacophony of shouts and calls of recognition.

I scrutinized the people on deck for a sign of Peter. And then I saw him, scanning the crowd. I waved and called to him, and before I knew it, Peter lifted me in his arms. When he put me down, I beheld joy on his face. We embraced, oblivious to propriety and those around us. The world consisted only of our embrace.

I had lost the love of my sister, parents, and grandfather, but now I was enfolded in an incandescent, overpowering kind of love. Peter took my hand and squeezed it fleetingly. I shivered with the lingering thrill of his touch as we strolled away from the crowd, Mary following a few paces behind.

Peter tilted his head toward me and smiled in a way that made me blush. "I am so very happy to see you again. You are more beautiful than I remembered."

He took my arm as he flagged a cab and directed his trunks to be loaded. As the cab pulled into the city traffic, Peter's smile faded. "We must stop at my parents' house. I did not notify them of my imminent return."

I was still pondering that bit of information when we reached the Joneses' mansion a few blocks away on Washington Square, not far from where Grandfather's office used to be. The house was stately and intimidating. As were Peter's parents.

As Peter and I stood in the parlor, they inquired about his health.

Peter replied, "I should like you to meet Miss Nolan. As you know from my letters, she is a fine schoolteacher from an upstanding family and a treasured acquaintance of mine."

Peter's mother nodded to me and glanced over my shoulder, doubtless looking for my chaperone. Her eyes passed right through Mary, who stood a short distance behind us, but apparently Mrs. Jones was satisfied. Peter's parents neither acknowledged my curtsey nor invited us for tea. After strained pleasantries, Peter and I said goodbye and returned to the cab.

Once we were out of sight of the house, Peter signaled the driver to stop, helped me down, and gestured for Mary to stay where she was. After apologizing for his parents, he said, "One cannot choose one's parents, but one *can* choose with whom one spends his life." He took both my hands in his. "Miss Nolan, will you please do me the honor of becoming my wife?"

Mary gasped.

Dazzled, thrilled by his proposal, I searched my sweetheart's face. It radiated sincerity. "Yes! Oh, Peter, yes! I would love to be your wife."

Peter kissed me deeply and after a momentary panic at the shattered taboo, I opened to him, my heart racing in surprise at stirrings that began in an unmentionable place and spread heat throughout my body. I was dying for our bodies to melt together as our lips were doing. Reluctantly, Peter let me go and kissed my forehead.

"You have made me the happiest man of all time." He squeezed my hands. "Now, my beloved Naissa, shall we meet your guardians?" he asked, opening the cab door for me with a flourish.

At the Leighton house, I was proud of the earnest formality with which Peter asked Uncle James for my hand. Uncle James and Aunt Josephine seemed pleased by our news. No doubt they were relieved to be rid of the burden I represented.

I was overjoyed at the prospect of leaving behind the cold loneliness of the Leighton house to live with Peter. *My* Peter.

⁂

I was seventeen years old and Peter twenty-three when we married at Christ Church, which was redolent of joy and roses. I sailed down the aisle in Mother's champagne satin wedding dress, her linen handkerchief in my waistband, and her elder brother, Uncle William, at my side. Uncle William had forged my heavenly gold wedding band in an interlaced Celtic design with a small, brilliant diamond at the knot's center. As Peter and I had requested, there were no bridesmaids or groomsmen. I had reserved the honor of bridesmaid for my adored, departed sister.

In addition to the Leightons' guests and Peter's friends, my pupils and their parents filled the pews. The wedding breakfast Aunt Josephine hosted was ostentatious, and Peter's stone-faced parents left before the cheese course. Nothing, however, could dampen my euphoria: I was to be mistress of a home of my own and Peter's lifelong companion.

In place of a nuptial journey, Peter and I honeymooned at the charming cottage we had bought in Haddington Woods. Set on the outskirts of town, it was secluded from the closest neighbor and encircled by a profusion of flowers and fruit trees, courtesy of its green-thumbed previous inhabitant.

Before the wedding, my aunt had told me, without elaborating, to be brave on our first marital night and to do what Peter asked. Consequently, I trembled as I modestly pulled my nightgown over my dress and attempted to disrobe.

Peter stripped and started getting into his nightshirt. My eyes strayed to the difference in Peter's anatomy and I felt heat rise in my face.

Noticing my embarrassment, Peter asked, "May I touch you?"

My breath caught, and I nodded.

Later, as I lingered in Peter's arms, our plain room, furnished with a simple bed, chest, and chair, became a glorious royal chamber, for it was Peter's and mine. I slept in Peter's embrace until dawn. When I woke to his kisses, I no longer felt shame at being naked in front of him. I was never so joyful and free.

We filled the days making love on a blanket under the whispering awning of trees behind the house, our nights loving one another until sleep overpowered us. We took so little time out to eat, it was a miracle we did not starve.

Peter's real interest and talent lay in painting, yet he had studied law in deference to his parents' expectations. To their vexation, he decided to devote himself to his art, instead of practicing as a lawyer. Fortunately, my large inheritance enabled us to live comfortably after I was compelled to vacate my position at Central High School because of my marriage. While it was difficult to leave a job I loved, my compensation was living blissfully with Peter in our little cocoon.

I spent my time keeping house, reading, drawing, and dabbling in writing poetry. Sometimes I modeled for Peter, but only after he swore on his life he would not show my nakedness to anyone else. Because Peter and I were perfectly happy alone together, we rarely socialized beyond obligatory family events. Peter's parents continued to be cool and distant, so we mostly avoided their company.

Peter and I both yearned for a loving family; we longed for children. Despite our repeated attempts to conceive, our dream remained unfulfilled. I quietly grieved as time passed and our family never grew. My only consolation was having Peter in the center of my universe. At first, Peter supplemented our livelihood with sporadic portrait commissions. This frustrated him because he was forced to limit his creativity in order to make the commissions as flattering as possible. Yet, Peter forged ahead in his more exploratory art, and found an occasional buyer for these innovative works.

When the economy collapsed and Peter's commissions dried up, we lived thoughtfully and frugally. Peter painted steadily, but when he became morose at the lack of sales, we supported each other and found strength in simply being together, realizing a little more happiness every passing day. Although Peter returned to his old self before the economy did the same, we had depleted half of my inheritance. Peter redoubled his efforts to gain patrons and was sometimes obliged to journey many miles to fulfill a commission.

⚜

Of all Peter's work, his dreamlike landscapes were my favorite. We searched for suitable scenes on walks together. Peter painted directly from nature, as opposed to doing sketches and later painting at home. He used wet canvas to intermingle colors, and short strokes of bold pigments to seize the essence of the subject instead of its details.

One day as Peter worked quickly to capture the qualities of movement and light, I asked, "How did you decide to paint in this fashion, rather than in the classical style you use for portraits?"

"While on holiday in Paris, I saw the Impressionist technique and became enmeshed in its possibilities. I am glad you appreciate my style of painting. Some people mock my work and call it absurd. Naturally, people have different tastes, but I have to say, the criticism brings back my childhood. My parents often criticized and seldom praised."

"I am sorry your parents treated you so unfairly, my darling. It seems to me your confidence and skill have more than overcome your childhood disadvantage. Your work is imbued with a place's soul and aura and all the passions it elicits. It compels me to perceive nature in a larger, more resplendent beauty I had not known existed. I am sure many others will feel the same."

Peter and I intrinsically understood the ideas and emotions in each other's art. Peter said reading my poems in which I had captured the perceptions he tried to convey in his paintings made him feel even more as one with me. Together with our physical selves, our minds had married: mind shaping mind, tracing back and forth along the ties between us. Our union helped me regain the serenity and wonder of my childhood.

Peter was invited to show his work at the Philadelphia World's Fair at an exhibit of up-and-coming artists. As a result of Peter's triumph at the exhibition, his paintings were in great demand. Peter had always hoped his art would live on, and now he was becoming famous.

I sorely missed a child in our life. Sometimes, Peter came home drunk after going out with his artist friends, and when Peter asked me to join them for a night out in the city, I often begged off, claiming a headache. Despite any disagreements, Peter and I got along well and almost never went to bed angry.

Seventeen years into our marriage, on a late summer afternoon of unnatural calm and stagnant air, Peter went riding on our horse, Toby, while I shelled beans and shucked corn for supper. When he did not return in a timely manner, a premonition of calamity began gnawing at me. When I could wait no longer, I burst outside, dashed to the back meadow, and ran faster and faster through the woods, Peter's name on my lips as a prayer for his safety. My calls were answered only by the fluting of a solitary wood thrush.

Finally, I spied Toby grazing in a clearing by the stream. Peter lay motionless close by. Attempting to revive him, I splashed water on his face. But when I lifted his head, sticky ooze seeping from his broken skull told me Peter would never awaken again.

I mounted Toby and galloped him to the nearest house, and choking on stifled screams, told the neighbors where to find Peter. Then I folded in on myself like a broken fan. I could barely move the air in and out of my lungs.

The neighbors, Theodore and Malvina Holmes, took me back to our house in their buckboard wagon. While Theodore went to collect Peter and lay him on the kitchen table, Malvina made us chamomile tea and tried to comfort me. For Peter, there was nothing but an infinite eternity: odorless, soundless, sightless. Mindless.

Kindhearted locals brought me food and words of consolation. The women offered to sit with me and help prepare Peter's body for burial. But I would do this last thing for Peter, myself. After their departure, my tears fell on Peter as I washed him and dressed him in his best suit. I slipped off my wedding ring, pushed it as far as it would go onto Peter's left little finger, and crossed his hands over his heart. Then I kissed Peter for the last time.

Most of those who were at our wedding and many of Peter's customers and admirers came to pay their respects. There were few dry eyes during the service. Peter's parents looked through me as though I were invisible.

My mind could not make sense of any of it. Why had my own breath not stopped? On the way home from the cemetery, the minister was kind enough to offer me a couple of sips from his whisky flask, but even they could not take the edge off my despair.

Declining all offers of companionship and help, I secluded myself in our cottage. Peter's absence was so new, I would catch myself about to share a thought with him, only to have my heart plunge at his nonexistence. Our idyllic marriage was annihilated. Never again would I gaze into Peter's loving eyes or hold him close. Gone were his voice, his fragrance, his touch. The only reason I did not unite with Peter in death was an immobilizing numbness that prevented me even from changing clothes. I hardly left our bed for weeks. I knew Peter would not have wanted this for me. He had attained his goals and was gratified. He would have wanted me to pursue goals for myself. This thought gave me the strength to make myself presentable and leave our little nest.

Hitching Toby to the buggy, I went to town to shop. Aimlessly, I perused Mr. Samuel's shelves. I peered into a jar of pickled beetroot trying to see how it was spiced but could not focus on the contents through my muddied eyes. I quickly returned the jar to its place on the shelf. Picking through a crate of summer squash, I vainly tried to find one not washed in gray. Peter had taken all his artist's colors when he left the world, and none remained for me.

I was stepping toward the door with my empty basket when a tiny sound caught my ear. It was a lilting version of "Baa, Baa, Black Sheep." I found Mr. Samuel's young daughter, Lily, sitting on the floor behind the counter, singing quietly to herself and playing with a wooden pull-along sheep. What a sweet sight. She was so like Trudy, I could not help the smile that began stiffly on my lips and then widened fully.

On the drive home, I wondered whether the nearby Reed Orphan Asylum was in need of assistance.

In the morning, I set off for the orphanage, a two-mile drive from Haddington Woods. It was an unimposing brick building, but thanks to the efforts of local church ladies and their wood-chopping husbands, both comfortable and warm inside. I wanted to help the children, and at the same time distract myself from grief, from the pain of living a life devoid of loved ones.

As I tied up Toby, exuberant children in all sizes scampered outdoors to meet their visitor. Two of the littlest tugged at my skirts while I introduced myself to Patience and Gerald Reed, the sister and brother who ran the orphanage, and offered my assistance. They thanked me profusely for my offer, asking about my skills and when I might start.

Patience, a plump, good-natured woman of indeterminate age, had an apt name. She never scolded or was cross and used logic and kindness to persuade the children to act in harmony with the Golden Rule. Her brother, Gerald, was affable and quick with a joke or a laugh. The two were fruit from the same tree, and their charges were fortunate to have them as guardians.

Every morning I awakened at dawn to ride to Reed's and assist the youngest children in getting ready for the day. Although the eldest children also pitched in, everyone appreciated an extra pair of hands. I told the little ones stories, taught them, listened to their cares, bathed them, and sang them to sleep.

Dr. Bartley Westerbrooke, who lived near the University of Pennsylvania, saw to the orphans' medical needs. Dr. Westerbrooke always sported elegant attire. Everything about him shone: his shiny brown eyes and dark hair, his shiny silver sideburns and mustache, his shiny boots and silk top hat, and his gold pocket watch etched with an ornate fleur-de-lis. Dr. Westerbrooke was broad-shouldered and not very tall, although he was taller than I.

One day, Mrs. Reed asked me to assist Dr. Westerbrooke in examining young Sadie Rose, who had developed a cough. As he worked, I handed him the items he requested.

"So, Mrs. Jones, when did you begin working here?"

"It has only been a fortnight, Dr. Westerbrooke. I very much enjoy working with the children, and the Reeds are delightful."

"And your husband, he does not mind you working outside the home?"

"I am recently widowed, sir."

"My condolences, madam. I am also widowed, nearly two years."

"Then, my condolences, as well. Have you any children?"

"Alas, no, my wife and I were never so blessed. And you?"

I shook my head and stroked Sadie Rose's hair.

Whenever Dr. Westerbrooke came to the orphanage, we paused in our work to converse about the orphans and the weather. One day, he invited me to dinner.

Our discourse centered around our mutual experience in marriage and coping with the loss of a spouse. From there, our conversation moved to the orphanage.

"The one I most pity," I said, "is little Tommy. Poor boy, he is alone all the time. I give him small tasks to assist me, just for the company. He is the only child I have seen who never has visitors or prospects."

The corner of Dr. Westerbrooke's mouth turned down. "I have known Tommy since he arrived at the Reeds' two years ago, when the lad was a toddler. I understand his parents succumbed to pneumonia shortly after they moved here. They were from somewhere in the Midwest. Maybe Kansas City."

"Are there no other relatives nearby?"

"Not to anyone's knowledge."

I thought for a moment. "Perhaps I might write to Kansas City to inquire."

"I admire your initiative, Miss Nolan," he said, smiling. "City Hall has records; you might try there. If you write the inquiry, I shall be pleased to take it to the telegraph office on my way home tonight."

I looked into his shiny eyes and saw compassion and friendliness. "Then, we are a team on a mission," I said resolutely.

By dinner's end, Bart and I were on a first-name basis. Thereafter, we saw each other often and soothed one another in our bereavement, bonded by our shared pain. Loneliness dimmed when we were together.

One month later, Mrs. Reed excitedly informed me that she had a telegraph from Tommy's previously unknown aunt and uncle in Lenexa, Kansas. They had sent fare for a ticket so Tommy might travel there and reside with the extended family. Bart's and my mission was a success.

We married on my thirty-fifth birthday. As this was the second marriage for each of us, we had a civil ceremony performed by a judge in his chambers. We skipped the wedding holiday because Bart's many patients needed him.

I sold my little house with its treasured memories and moved into Bart's well-appointed, three-story brick home in the city. Marriage forced me to leave work at the orphanage, but my regret was eased when Bart asked me to be the receptionist for his practice in the house's medical wing.

I wrote Uncle William a note explaining my situation and asking him to tell Uncle James and Aunt Josephine I was fine, and nothing more. I had no desire for any further connection with the uppity Leightons. Surely our distaste was mutual, because, as far as I knew, they never tried to contact me. However, I loved Uncle William dearly, and he joined Bart and me for dinner on many a Sunday. My uncle and Bart developed a friendship, and after-dinner parlor sessions were lively, with loud debates on politics and current events, or games of rather aggressive chess.

Work in Bart's medical office was both tedious and fascinating. The hours dragged when performing administrative and clerical work but flew when interacting with patients. In the few quiet times between patients, I perused Bart's medical journals. Early in our marriage, after Bart and I had our fill of commiserating about our deceased spouses and discovering we were both Darwinists, we had little else to talk about. I hoped learning more about his practice might improve our discourse.

One day, an article in the local *Journal of the Medical and Physical Sciences* sparked my interest. A surgeon at the nearby School of Anatomy, William Williams Keen Jr., had given the author a tour of his surgery, which highlighted several methods of germ theory Dr. Keen used for infection control.

At lunch with Bart that day, I said, "Bart, darling, I just read a fascinating article about Dr. Keen at the School of Anatomy in town."

Bart's eyebrows twitched up. "You did?"

"Yes. I often browse your journals. I have also read a few books from your medical library. I find the body's systems, operations, and malfunctions intriguing."

He rubbed his chin and regarded me. "You do?"

"Of course. Anyway, Dr. Keen uses several methods to prevent infections, to positive result. First, the surgery is wiped down with carbolic acid, and he assures his own cleanliness by wearing a clean, white coat and washing his hands for a long time. Then, he boils instruments and dressings before using them."

Bart's gaze became more intense. "He does?"

"Yes. Apparently, heat is more effective than carbolic acid. Also, he uses a diluted solution of carbolic acid for cleaning and dressing wounds which is less noxious than pure carbolic acid—although, I am not sure of his recipe for dilution. At any rate, his methods appear to be rather successful."

"Intriguing," Bart mused, "and so simple."

"Yes, I thought so, too. It would be simple to adopt his boiling method. I have a kettle in the kitchen perfect for your instruments and bandages. And, I could inquire at the school about their recipe for carbolic solution."

"Yes, quite. Let us try Dr. Keen's method. Please proceed as soon as possible." Bart looked at me with a twinkle in his eyes. "And Naissa, dear. Please keep reading those journals."

My life with Bart was generally satisfying, with a few exceptions. I still missed Peter and the children at the orphanage. Worse, I took no pleasure in relations with Bart. I cringed when he insisted I carry out, as he put it, my "wifely duties."

He was a clumsy lover who paid no mind to my needs and fell asleep immediately after his gratification. Trying to imagine Bart was Peter did not help. My escape in those moments was to think about the minutiae of keeping house and managing Bart's office.

A year and a half into our marriage, I discovered I was with child. I could hardly believe it—at long last, I would be a mother! My soul soared. Bart was thrilled. Although my relationship with Bart was more business partner than beloved spouse, I felt he had the makings of a good father.

Throughout my pregnancy, I dreamed of giving birth to a daughter who looked like Trudy. Bart and I eagerly awaited this longed-for child and counted the days till its arrival. My short, uneventful labor brought, to my wonder and delight, the fulfillment of my dreams when Bart delivered our beautiful, red-haired daughter. Erupting with happiness as I held her for the first time, I wanted to shout my jubilation from the rooftops.

"Let us call her Cecile."

Bart was busy assisting in delivery of the afterbirth. He mused, "That's . . . odd."

"What is odd, Bart?" A tingle of worry drew my attention from the babe.

"I thought you had torn, but I see no wound. Peculiar."

"I have always healed quickly. Perhaps it was not what you thought."

"Perhaps." Bart turned to our daughter. "She is beautiful. Yes, Cecile fits her."

I was so delighted by Cecile's little life, I spent hours feeding her in my rocking chair by the nursery window, the golden sunlight filtering through the maples onto her silky hair. I sang the songs I had learned from my mother, such as "So Early in the Morning" and "Buffalo Gals." She would sleep contentedly in my arms as I breathed the sweet, sweet smell of her.

As she grew to a toddler, Cecile flourished and proved to have Trudy's angelic disposition. Some of my favorite moments were at bedtime, when Cecile snuggled close and was entranced as we read or I told stories about the animals in the forest and fanciful tales about little girls in faraway lands. She would ask questions and giggle in amusement, and then, exhausted from her day, sigh and droop and rest her long lashes upon her rosy cheeks. Because I read to her frequently, Cecile spoke sentences at fourteen months. I began sketching again, with Cecile as my muse.

Bart adored his new daughter and was entirely dedicated to her, giving in to whatever Cecile wanted. After long calls at patients' homes, he often brought back treats or small presents for her. She would reach for him to pick her up, and giggle as she played with his shiny mustache and side whiskers.

Cecile was a child of joy, even under trying circumstances. The month following her second birthday, the Great White Hurricane, a sudden and powerful blizzard, howled through Philadelphia. We had wood and food aplenty, and Cecile and I played games and nestled together by the cozy warmth of the fire while the rest of the world fretted over ruined houses, stalled street cars and trains, abandoned wagons, and downed trees. When the storm finally cleared and mounds of snow sparkled in the sun, I made a slide for Cecile down the front steps. Laughter erupted from her belly and rang out over the muffled streets, bringing smiles to passersby.

In warmer weather, Cecile toddled after me in the garden and took great interest in the vegetables and flowers. She loved watching leaves dance in the sun. She was particularly fond of insects—overly fond. One afternoon, I turned from my sketchbook, just in time. Cecile, sitting cross-legged in the grass, held up a garden spider, ogled it with gleaming eyes, and slowly lowered it toward her mouth. Fortunately, my sharp cry halted her snacking midact.

By the time our daughter was four, I relived my happy childhood teaching her about the world around us, just as my parents and grandfather had done for me. Cecile absorbed the knowledge like a scholar. Her fascination with every new discovery and her sunny personality filled my heart. I couldn't even be upset with her when she cried and refused to leave the park when we had to return home because I, too, would have loved to spend more time out of doors. She was just like me, with a fascination for the natural world around her. She played in the grassy yard and presented me with gifts of dandelions, acorns, and pinecones. She skipped and bounced along when we walked to the park, laughing and exclaiming, scattering squirrels and pigeons. Cecile charmed everyone she met and made friends easily.

It was an unusually warm day for February. We were walking home from Sunday meeting at Fletcher Methodist Episcopal as rivulets ran from underneath the mounds of dirty, icy snow. Little Cecile and I struggled to keep up with Bart as he strode down Franklin Street. The weight of my skirts and coat, already sopping from the melting snow, dragged at my steps. The grip of my corset was a tourniquet around my lungs.

"For goodness' sake, Bart, what is your rush? Could you please slow down?" I panted.

Just then, Bart turned the corner onto our street and nearly collided with an elegantly dressed couple.

"Good day to you, Dr. Westerbrooke," said the gentleman, tipping his hat.

Bart was momentarily nonplussed but recovered quickly. "How do you do, Mr. Simpson? It is a pleasure, madam." He gave a wave in my direction as I caught up to them. "May I introduce Naissa? And this is my daughter, Cecile."

Bart was so flustered, he had introduced me with my given name instead of as Mrs. Westerbrooke, as was proper.

Mr. Simpson's smile was genuine. "Well, old fellow, you never mentioned how lovely your daughters are. I am delighted." He bowed to Cecile and me.

My cheeks burned as if they had been slapped.

Bart's eyes narrowed. With an air of nonchalance, he responded, "I beg pardon, but Mrs. Westerbrooke is my wife and Cecile our daughter."

This seemed to delight Mr. Simpson even further. He clapped Bart on the shoulder enthusiastically. "Well done, sir. What a fine family you have."

Mrs. Simpson was not so admiring. Her eyes darted back and forth between Bart and me, her expression as if she had just eaten a cherry that was not quite ripe.

Before we bade our adieus, promises were made for an evening at the theater at some unspecified date. Bart marched double-time the rest of the way home, leaving Cecile and me behind to sing nursery songs and laugh as we meandered down the street. For some reason, Bart would not speak to me, persisting with his stony silence throughout dinner and the rest of the day, intermittently piercing me with cold looks when he thought I was attending elsewhere. That night as we prepared for bed, I could stand his coldness no longer.

"Bart, please tell me, *what* is troubling you?"

He paused for a moment, his mustache twitching and the vein in his forehead protruding. Then he spat out, "People think you are my daughter! And this was not the first time. It is simply shameful." Before I could respond, Bart left the room.

My face in the mirror was the same as always: no worry lines, no gray hairs, just me. Had I known Mother and Father when they were older, I might have learned which one I took after in maintaining a girlish appearance at nearly forty-one years old.

In the days following our meeting with the Simpsons, Bart rarely came to the family wing of our house. He said there were several diseases at large, and he would take his meals at the practice and sleep there, so as not to risk exposing us. Before this, he had always joined us when his work was done.

Cecile and I went about our merry business of abandoning ourselves to whatever joy a four-year-old mind could conjure. Cecile especially loved making snowballs. She insisted upon taking a bite of each one before tossing it ahead of her, a miniature chef sampling her creations before hurling them out into the world.

One day, Cecile put down the rag doll she had been playing with and came over to me. She pushed aside my knitting. "Mama, my tummy hurts."

Putting my hand on Cecile's forehead, I noted that she did feel a little warm. "Come on," I said. "Let's make some ginger tea, and we will have your stomach better in no time."

If only it had been true.

Cecile became increasingly feverish. She expelled anything she tried to eat or drink. When I told Bart of the pink spots on her chest and abdomen, he looked stricken and rushed to Cecile's bedside, taking the stairs two at a time. He flung aside the covers, pulled up her nightdress, and peered at the ivory skin stretched tight over her round belly, so like a porcelain pot hand-painted with tiny rosettes. He tenderly pulled her nightdress back down and patted it into place, and then drew the covers up to our daughter's chin. When Bart looked at me, he was ashen. The shine in his eyes had gone flat. Then, his stare turned to ice, as if the temperature had instantly cooled in direct proportion to Cecile's fever.

Bart stood and whispered fiercely in my ear, "Give her fluids, as much as she will take, and wipe her skin with damp cloths as often as is practical."

He looked through me as he left the room. Moments later, the front door slammed and I fell to my knees.

It was beyond horrible watching my daughter slip from me, from existence. All the light withdrew from my life when, a fortnight after becoming ill, Cecile died.

She was buried with the sapphire and diamond ring Mother and Father had given me on my sixth birthday. I had planned to give it to Cecile on her sixth, so she could pass it down to her own daughter as hope for the future in each succeeding generation.

Having suffered so many visions of Mother, Father, Trudy, and Grandfather in their black forever, I could not allow my darling Cecile to be alone in the cold and pitch black. The only thing to do was follow Cecile into her grave.

I flung myself toward the hole where she lay, a moth to a dark flame. Bart grabbed me hard by the arms and yanked me back. I screamed and fought him until I could fight no more.

Cecile and Trudy were so alike, the loss of both little angels melded together. Their sweetness, their potential—gone.

Typhoid fever took many that spring. *Ashes to ashes, dust to dust. Everything goes to ashes and dust.*

Lost in a maze of foreign streets, I'm looking for something important and cannot remember what it is. Beyond panicked, I finally see two police officers and ask for their help. One hands me a cup of coffee. Taking calming sips, I begin describing my problem, when suddenly I am back home in Philadelphia, and I am overjoyed. The next instant, the ground drops out from under me when I realize what I've forgotten.

As I fall, my screams are so loud they rattle my eardrums and scorch my throat. My head cracks open on the floor below.

⁂

My cheek pressed against the cold floor into something sticky and metallic smelling. Then, I recognized my screams as words, repeated loud and long.

"Ceciiile! Cecile!"

I was on the bedroom floor, wailing and sobbing. Blood was on my temple, which I must have cracked on the nightstand when I fell out of bed. Although there was no physical pain, a wrenching, full-body agony overwhelmed me.

My darling, my beautiful, my perfect, my girl, was gone. My stomach roiled and heaved.

Oh, my darling, my Cecile. Why did you leave me?

Everything faded to blackness.

⁂

The soft light of dawn began to glow. I straightened out my leg, peeling it from the cold wood. I placed my hand on the floor in front of me, thinking to push myself up, but the fibers of my muscles were only water.

⁂

"Naissa! Get up. Get *up*!"

Someone was tugging at me, trying to pull me up. Bart.

"Leave me alone," I croaked.

Bart pulled me up to the bed and roughly set me down, my legs hanging over the side. Then he took my feet and pulled them around and onto the bed. He panted from the effort.

"Get up, Naissa. It has been days. You must come out of this."

I rolled over, turning my back to him.

A small spider scurried back and forth across the ceiling. How did it get here? How long could a spider live? Not longer than its children. I lay on my back, watching. I shuddered and hoped it wouldn't drop onto the bed. I turned to Bart's side of the bed. Empty.

I closed my eyes, leaving the spider to its busyness.

The sound of children playing a game came from outside. Their shouts and laughter sliced in like daggers to where I lay. The light was hard. It was probably afternoon and school had let out. I pulled the blanket over my head.

It was nighttime and all was quiet.

My child was gone.

I thought back to playing in the front yard, pulling Cecile, who giggled and squealed with happiness in her red wagon. She was so tiny and sweet, with a musical laugh.

If I had just . . .

I became lost in endings to that thought.

My little Cecile, my dear one, died before she had truly lived. I wished there was something I could have done to save her. My sorrow and remorse would never subside. I did not know if I could tear off the woeful shroud, cast it aside, and go on. Pulled relentlessly into a dark hole inside myself, I screamed until I had no voice left to scream.

Cecile had not been part of my life. She *was* my life. I had believed I already knew what it was to lose someone beloved. But Cecile's death ripped out my core, leaving an everlasting, open wound. Dazed, moving through life like a puppet, I made only the motions. *I want Cecile* was my only thought. I took the curl of Cecile's baby hair from my vanity and tucked it into my gold locket to keep her close to my heart.

"You're nothing but a freak!" Bart yelled as he bolted the doors between the house's family and medical wings, leaving me completely alone. Freak? I shuddered. Perhaps no one else suffered such loss as mine.

Did that mean there was something wrong with me? *Was* there something wrong with me? Would I be cast out and held apart for the rest of my life because I could not keep my daughter alive? Because I could not save my family?

Bart had the housemaid pack up and send my things to Uncle William's. He divorced me. For the rest of his life, Bart refused to communicate with or see me. It was distressing to be thrown away, to be unable to share my grief over our daughter. Maybe I should have hated Bart for this, but I could not. He had loved Cecile deeply and I knew the heartache causing his bitterness.

Uncle William was caring, but not a compassionate soul. Even so, it helped to be in his household as I grieved. I was, however, not much company for him, spending my days cloistered in his guest room, doodling, reading, and sleeping.

I swore I would never again have another relationship or be a parent. The pain was too much to bear.

Cecile's death forced me to ask *Why?* in an agonizing cycle in which there was no hope. Yet, I finally withstood every urge to curl in a fetal position and succumb by telling myself there might be hope. My numbness at Cecile's death turned into simmering anger, which I had no place to direct.

I chose to make time my enemy. It had sneered as those I held most dear were taken from me. It laughed every time I looked in the mirror.

I spat on time. And faced forward.

The evening was still light and warm enough to sit on the back porch with my sewing. Uncle William was at Josephine's for the evening. Earlier in the day, I had attended Easter service at church. The pastor's sermon was an uplifting eulogy for Reverend Carson, a much-loved pastor at the church down the street who died on Good Friday. Our pastor's sermon focused on the significance of the reverend's final journey coinciding with Christ's and the celebration of rebirth. Among the quotes the pastor shared was one from the Psalms about the Lord healing the brokenhearted and binding up their wounds.

I sewed as those words rolled over and over in my mind. I didn't know how to mend my broken heart, or to bind up its gashes. I thought of how wounds from the deaths of those I loved never disappeared. They eventually softened around the edges, but their centers stayed raw. It had been years since my family and Peter had died, but the trauma from their loss was still as fresh as Cecile's. Some injuries never healed, while others . . .

Why do my cuts and burns always heal so quickly? What is the mechanism? There must be a scientific explanation. Then, as if it were an echo bouncing back across an enormous canyon, I heard Bart's final word as he left me. Freak. *Freak!*

My forty-second birthday was in a few days, and I was frequently hearing pointed comments about what a fresh, young face I had. I must have inherited some ancestor's excellent traits. But *freak*?

The thread in my needle ran out, so I tied off the ends and trimmed them with my scissors. I pulled a long piece from the spool, cut it, carefully threaded it through the needle's eye, and twisted the two ends into a quick knot. Instead of pushing the needle back through the cloth where the other thread had left off, I held the needle up and studied it. Then I tightened my grip and jammed the needle into my palm at the base of my thumb. A tiny ruby of blood appeared. When I wiped it away, the pain was just about gone, no mark was visible. No more blood. A deep sigh escaped me.

Setting down the sewing, I picked up my scissors. I hesitated. Then I snipped at the same place on my palm. I gasped at the fiery pain. Hot liquid smelling of iron flowed from the throbbing, half-inch gash. Panic rose and I cursed my stupidity. Such a wound would be serious if it were to fester.

I grabbed a scrap of cloth from the sewing basket, pressed it tightly to my hand, and ran to the kitchen sink. Pulling the cloth from my hand, I ran cool water over my palm. The sides of the slice were already knitting together.

A dark cloud filled my mind. *No one heals that fast. Am I a freak?*

Yes, I healed quickly. I had a strong constitution; I always had. But it was a far cry from being a freak.

I am not sure how long I stood at the sink and stared at my hand. All I knew was that I was over forty years old and did not look like someone who had seen nearly half a century. Perhaps I would, someday.

<hr />

Returning to teaching might have allowed me to distract myself with work once more, but I had not realized the extent of unease my youthful appearance caused. Small-town gossip and stares followed me, and I was rejected for positions at every turn. I needed to flee to a place where I was unknown.

Before marrying Bart, I had hired a Philadelphia attorney whom Uncle William had employed and trusted. Gerard Semler, the immaculately dressed proprietor of Semler and Associates, was a middle-aged, no-nonsense lawyer whom I liked straight away. He was willing to discreetly do anything necessary to meet my goals. Mr. Semler agreed to securely store journals and other items important to me. Taking advantage of laws allowing married women to own property, I safeguarded my inheritance and property through a trust managed by the firm, which enabled me to keep my own assets separate upon my marriage to Bart. When Bart cast me aside, this served me well.

That summer, I met with Mr. Semler to discuss my financial arrangements.

When we concluded the discussion of property, Mr. Semler asked, "Is there anything else I may help you with today?"

"Yes, in fact, there is a somewhat delicate matter, for which I would ask your confidence."

"I pride myself in my discretion, Mrs. Westerbrooke."

"Of late, I have found acquaintances react to me rather unkindly."

"They do? How so?" he asked with surprise.

"I receive comments regarding my, um, youthful aspect. Negative remarks."

"Yes, go on."

"I am unable to socialize or find employment. People are unsettled because my appearance conflicts with my age. Might you be able to help me? Is there— Is there a way I could pass as someone younger, legally?"

"Of course, Mrs. Westerbrooke. We will submit records with a new birthdate, say, 1870. Would that do?"

"Yes, thank you. And could you please change my name back to Nolan, so I will not have to explain my lack of a husband?"

"Yes, of course, Miss Nolan. I will prepare the documents myself. You have my complete discretion."

"Oh, Mr. Semler," I said with relief, "Thank you so much."

INTERLUDE

Notebook 49.300451-p91, Genome Project P_0.
Dr. V.N. Singh, Project Leader.

Results Summary, Ex. 55-300

As anticipated, tests have confirmed the P_0 phenomenon is a complex but discrete set of MNLPs ranging across all autosomes.

However, specific factors contributing to the anomalies remain indeterminate. Attempts to isolate viable genetic material from the French P_{-1} samples are ongoing. Once the P_0 genome is derived, testing may reveal a basis for the phenomenon.

To meet the GP project objective of isolating the origin and action responsible for the P_0 phenomenon(a), genomic abnormalities must be identified utilizing Cas13-X2 sequencing and Morris-Ashton analyses. Next focus after sequencing will be experiments on P_0 cultured nucleotides regarding their impact on normal cells and tissues.

That said, I have developed serious reservations about the pace and scope of this project. The implications from such significant manipulations of the human genome must be first studied, reported, and standard operating procedures proposed. To continue this work feels unethical. Furthermore, such manipulations may be, in many countries, outside current legal boundaries.

I have detailed my concerns under separate cover, with supporting data, which I have forwarded to management.

Signed: _____

V.N. Singh, PhD, P-REG Lead Researcher

CHAPTER THREE

Rys

W HAT WAS IT like? I hated the doctor most of all. His gloved hands were like icicles, as were his eyes behind the safety glasses. His lab coat was blindingly white and hard, like it was starched stiff. He didn't care if it scratched me. He acted as if I were invisible, never looked me in the eye. As if I were a dumb monster or something. Or maybe he was ashamed. Who knows?

Medical testing days were the worst. As soon as the aides came in, I ran, trying to get anything I could between us—chairs, meal trays, clothes, whatever was at hand. Inevitably, they cornered me and picked me up like a sack of flour. I screamed as loud as I could. I scratched, spit, and bit. Some of the aides were nice, but they had to follow orders. As you can imagine, there was a lot of turnover among them.

Once the aides wrestled me into the medical office, I was strapped down so I couldn't even turn my head. I was punctured with needles everywhere.

When the doctor took samples, he never used enough anesthetic. Sometimes he just knocked me out, and I woke later in my bed, alone.

No, no, don't cry! I know, it sounds awful. It was. But it was also all I knew, so I had nothing to compare it to. It just was.

Except for testing in the medical room, I remember being always alone. I slept a lot. There really wasn't anything to do. After a while, they left paper and crayons in my room. I didn't know what to do with them, so I crumpled up the paper and threw it at the aides. The crayons, too.

I must have been around three at the time.

CHAPTER FOUR

1893–1950

Naissa

⸺

T HE EARLY HALF *of the twentieth century soared with humanity's first flights in heavier-than-air vehicles. Roads grew busy with automobiles, and the rails moved countless people and goods. Wondrous electric lights opened nighttime to the world, and new machines appeared at a dizzying pace, including those for performing tedious tasks like laundering clothing. The largest and only "unsinkable" ship, the* Titanic, *sank on its maiden voyage in 1912, briefly shaking people's confidence in modern technology. Two years later, massive war began in Europe and waged for four years on land, sea, and sky, turning marvelous new machines into tools of annihilation.*

Meanwhile, the US waged relentless war on the remaining Indigenous people by breaking treaties and trying to erase all remnants of native culture. The government forced children into "schools" designed to culturally assimilate them to the United States. The government also waged war on unarmed women by refusing them suffrage. Women were attacked and imprisoned for picketing peacefully near the White House, and force-fed with tubes down their throats when hunger strikes were the last option for protest. Their suffering and determination drew enough attention to the cause that, one hundred and forty-four

years after the United States' founding, the Nineteenth Amendment to the Con-
stitution passed, enabling women to vote. Women across the country celebrated
upon hearing the news on wireless radios—a piece of technology that helped
people feel connected to the larger world. Then telephones made the distances
smaller still.

The 1929 stock market crash and ensuing Great Depression challenged the
roaring innovation. President Roosevelt's New Deal programs helped ease the
Depression's hardships, but it took a war to turn things around. After the shock
of Japan's attack on Pearl Harbor, the United States entered the fight the follow-
ing day. The Second World War was ended by a technological invention like no
other: atomic weapons deployed by the US on Japan. With two bombs, the world
entered the atomic age.

⁘⸱⸱⸱⸱⸱⸱⸱⸱⸱⸱

During my few months at Uncle William's, I cast about for my next steps. It
was time to get away from nosy questions about my youthful appearance.
The gossip was beginning to cause Uncle William discomfort, which dis-
tressed me.

One day, the sermon at church centered on the unremitting plight of
dispossessed Native Americans and the horrors they endured every day.
Because of military actions, forced migrations, and children's removal from
their families, I seethed at the Native Americans' suffering at the hands of
their fellow men. Rather than despairing over the situation, it was time to acknowledge my advantages and do something to help. Bidding a sad farewell
to Uncle William, with whom I often corresponded over his few remaining
years, I left Philadelphia for a position teaching Navajo and Hopi children
in Arizona. I was elated at the prospect of helping them—and starting anew
as a presumed twenty-year-old.

I had thought Phoenix would be a dusty desert plain. To be sure, there
was ample dust and desert, and the late-summer air was hot and dry, but
breathtaking mountains surrounded the young city, igniting in a rusty glow

when touched by the sun. Shade-giving trees—not just cacti—grew throughout the desert town: ironwood, majestic Emory oaks, and spicy-smelling cypress.

The Phoenix Indian School, rather than the rustic, primitive institution I had imagined, consisted of two dozen buildings on a 160-acre campus on the outskirts of town. I was pleasantly surprised by the school's electric lighting and steam heat. However, I had grown used to Philadelphia's new flush toilets, and the Indian School still relied upon outhouses. These were suffocatingly odorous in the Arizona heat, and the first thing to dim the rosy view of my new home.

I was dismayed to find the students by and large sickly and their medical care haphazard. The children, some of them quite young, were grouped in military-style regiments, and marched to and fro in sharp lines.

The worst was learning that my job was not so much to educate as it was to train the children to renounce their culture. The federal Indian Boarding School Policy's goal was to "destroy the Indian within the Indian." The Indian School was in fact a prison for children torn from their families in order to teach them English, Christianity, and Anglo culture. The poor children were even forced to bear English names, abandoning those of their ancestors. I knew I had hard work ahead of me.

The first time I tried to intercede on a student's behalf—a boy's meals were being withheld because he said a Native word in class—I was reprimanded by Mr. Whitworth, the superintendent. "Our mandate is to follow federal policy," he lectured. "Our institution complies with policy, as shall you. There are, Miss Nolan, severe consequences for disobeying federal policy."

"Is it federal policy to starve children?" I demanded.

Whitworth frowned. "Miss Nolan, do you wish to continue employment here? Yes? Then consider this a warning of the most severe sort."

From then on, I did my best to provide comfort to the children and honor their independence, while playing at dutiful employee with the staff and administration.

Once, I came upon the grammar teacher using his riding crop to flog a young girl, Lizzy, in the dormitory hall.

"Mr. Little, what are you doing? Please stop!"

He looked up with rage in his rheumatic eyes. "Mind your business!" he hissed.

Lizzy whimpered painfully with each blow. Bleeding welts showed through her torn smock. What happened next was not in my control.

I found myself between Mr. Little and his victim, facing the man with fury in my heart. "*No!*" I roared. "You shall have to come through me before you lay another hand on her."

The man sneered. "If that is what you want." He lunged at me with the crop raised and hit me on my arm. I flinched but remained still. He paused for a moment, and then furiously hit me again and again with the crop, on my chest, my head, my face. I stood like a statue through the pain, knowing my wounds were healing as soon as they were inflicted.

At last, the man stopped, his chest heaving with the effort. He looked at me with wide, horrified eyes.

"What devil are you?"

"Never again, Mr. Little, will you lay a hand on any of the students, or on me. Now, *go!*"

As he scurried away, I turned to Lizzy and took her hand. "Come on, dear, let us take care of you."

A short while later, the superintendent summoned me to his office. Mr. Little stood beside Mr. Whitworth's desk, arms crossed and a mocking smile on his face.

"Mr. Little accuses you of an unprovoked attack. This charge will result in your dismissal, as well as arrest." I was already judged guilty. "Explain yourself," Whitworth said sternly.

When I described the situation and showed the damage to my dress from the crop, and described Lizzy's injuries, Whitworth sent his assistant to verify Lizzy's injuries and story. I was returned to work with a lengthy admonition. The reason I was not dismissed was because the school had difficulty recruiting and retaining teachers. Mr. Little, unpunished, gave me a wide berth the rest of my time in Phoenix.

Over my years at the Phoenix school, it was a constant struggle to protect the children while trying to help them become strong, independent human beings. How could I do otherwise? The students' situation was outrageous. Once, I asked Lizzy her true name, but she was taken so young from her family, she could not remember. After the hallway incident, Lizzy became my shadow, a special friend and assistant. In some ways, she reminded me of Cecile, whom I missed every day with a bone-deep ache. Being around Lizzy softened the pain.

Thanks to Little, the staff ostracized me, which aligned with my wish to keep distance from others; relationships other than those required for work and town life were too risky. Looking young appealed to my vanity, but I was anxious about the consequences if people learned my true age.

When I had been at the school long enough for questioning stares and gossip to begin, it was Lizzy who was the most difficult to leave. As I bade her a tearful goodbye, she pressed a small parcel into my hand. Inside was an exquisite headband, tender deerskin beaded and quilled with expert care. I had no idea how she kept her work hidden or acquired her materials.

"Lizzy, dear, this is extraordinarily beautiful. I thank you with my whole heart. I shall treasure it always. Please, dear one, be careful these next few months until you graduate." Our embrace was long and close.

❦

As the train rolled away from Phoenix, my heart was heavy for the children I left behind. My throat closed up tight as I remembered Lizzy's beautiful face. Praying her beadwork remained undetected at the school, I pulled the headband from my pocket and looped it through my belt.

The deeper the train descended into the Mississippi Delta, the more drenched I became. The humidity was increasingly oppressive. Thank goodness corsets were falling out of fashion, or I would have succumbed to the heat and humidity well before reaching my destination. As it was, throwing modesty aside, I removed my travel jacket and stood in my shirtsleeves on the observation platform at the rear of the train. Even that proved too sheltered for a reliable breeze, and before long it seemed every particle of soot from the locomotive was clinging to my perspiring skin. I wished I could ride atop the train, full into the wind.

I had found a position teaching classical history and languages at Mrs. Camellia Courtney's Academy for Young Ladies, a New Orleans finishing and college preparatory school for daughters of the elite Garden District. I had read that the Crescent City was a melting pot where Creoles, Africans, Americans, and Europeans lived in relative harmony. The vision of a diverse society had drawn me toward New Orleans even more than the proffered employment.

The city of New Orleans was a flood upon the senses after the aridity of Phoenix. When I first disembarked at Union Station, the humidity and the variety of faces and clothing styles reassured me that I was no longer in Arizona. The myriad smells of the river and city were amplified by the water in the air. A group of musicians, busking on cornet, trombone, clarinet, banjo, string bass, and drum filled the station with wonderful and strange music in lively, complex rhythms.

Suzanne Durand, Mrs. Courtney's tall, tawny-haired assistant language instructor, welcomed me at the station. Her lilting accent was not quite French. On the carriage ride to the Academy, Suzanne told me about her Cajun background and, obviously charmed by her city, pointed out some of its unique architectural styles. Because Suzanne seemed genuine and kind, I was instantly at ease with her.

The Academy's founder and namesake, Camellia Courtney, had purchased the school's sprawling Greek Revival mansion and outbuildings in the Garden District. She remodeled the interior to mimic classrooms and dormitories she had toured in England, and then proclaimed her Academy open for the daughters of the New Orleans gentry. Now in its nineteenth year, Courtney Academy was the center of New Orleans debutante society.

"Welcome, *wel*-come, Miss Nolan!" Mrs. Courtney sang out when Suzanne and I arrived at the school. She was a short, round woman with rouged cheeks and a silver topknot, and wore a black silk mourning dress that was brightened by her lavish personality.

Surprising me with a firm embrace, Mrs. Courtney clasped my hands and studied my face. "We are thr-*illed* you have chosen to join us, Naissa. May I call you Naissa? Oh, just *look* at you, such a beauty! To match the brains, no doubt. Your résumé and essay were exquisite, simply *ex*-quisite. What a fine addition you shall make to our staff!"

I felt my color rise. Mrs. Courtney turned and called, "Yvette!" A young woman entered and curtsied. "Please bring blackberry cordials for our sw-*eet* Miss Nolan and Miss Durand."

Mrs. Courtney invited Suzanne and me to sit in the parlor with her. The refreshing drink was welcome after the hot train. We discussed the school and its upcoming curricula. Finally, sensing my exhaustion from the lengthy journey, Mrs. Courtney said, "Well then! You simply *must* freshen up, my girl, those trains can be devastating to one's comfort. Suzanne, dear, will you please show Naissa to her quarters?"

Suzanne led me up a flight of stairs and through a long hallway to my room in the staff wing. She explained when and where meals would be served and said she would come back at suppertime to escort me to the dining room. My room was well-appointed with an oak bed, next to which my luggage was neatly arranged. There was an armoire, a set of antique chestnut bookshelves, and a night table and writing desk, each graced with an electric lamp. The space was filled with light, its window taking up a good portion of the outside wall. There were lace curtains on the window and a vase of pink lilies upon the night table. Best of all, one of the new electric fans hung from the ceiling and cooled the room.

In the bathroom down the hall, I could not get my well-soaked traveling clothes off fast enough. I decided I must visit a seamstress at the earliest opportunity and order a few of the summery linen and cotton blouses and short skirts I had seen on the city's ladies. Drawing a bath of cool water, I washed away the layers of dried sweat and cinders. How marvelous to have a plumbed bathtub with hot and cold water, a tub drain, and an odorless, flushing toilet.

⁂

"You are acclimated, no?" Suzanne asked as she lifted a stack of books from the crate we were unpacking. It was two days before the new school year and we were readying my classroom with textbooks, boxes of pungent cedar pencils, composition books, slates, chalk, erasers, pens, and ink—all the trappings of scholastic life. I had requested a good-sized world map and chalkboard, which had arrived the day before and were already installed on the classroom's front wall.

The room itself was bright, airy, and tiered, with desks arranged on five ascending levels in the European style. My desk was nearly as tall as a lectern, with an equally tall chair so every student could have an uninterrupted view of me, and I of them. The size of the room was a little intimidating, as it could seat fifty students. I had never taught so large a class.

I quickly appreciated that Suzanne was often direct to the point of bluntness, but not in a malicious way. She was a fresh breeze, crisp and concise. I enjoyed her company and her forthrightness.

"Acclimated?" I asked. "I suppose so, as much as possible. It was quite warm in Arizona, but far drier than here. I do not know if I shall ever become acclimated to this dampness." I wiped the hair from my sweat-covered forehead.

Suzanne laughed softly. Her dark eyes shimmered and her twin dimples deepened. "No, no, Naissa. Please forgive me. Here in New Orleans, there is special meaning to the word *acclimated*. When we say someone is acclimated it is because they have survived the yellow fever and thus are immune to the disease. For years now, if one is not acclimated in our Crescent City, many doors are closed. You were asked this question before you took the position, yes?"

I shook my head. Suzanne mused, "It has been four summers since the last yellow fever outbreak, so perhaps the school board did not wish to frighten you away.

"The fever is a dreadful disease that tortures its victims. The sick endure terrible headaches, nausea, and pain. In the worst cases, the skin turns yellow and one bleeds from the eyes and other places. The poor souls go crazy and vomit black blood. Several thousand were stricken during the last epidemic alone. We lost eight of our girls and two instructors. It was heartbreaking. So many have succumbed, sometimes we call our city *Necropolis*."

My thoughts jumped to the Père Lachaise necropolis. Indeed, there were similarities between the two crowded, ornate dwelling places—aside from the obvious difference in the residents' animation. After the plain-faced adobe of Arizona, New Orleans was an intricate and exotic wonderland, as teeming and mysterious as Père Lachaise.

Suzanne continued, "Thank heaven the city has enforced Dr. Matas's antimosquito program. We now have compulsory window screening and a ban on standing water. Mosquitos are the reason outbreaks occur in summer. Thus far, the mosquito program appears to be working. There has not been another outbreak of the fever and I will attest to fewer mosquitos. Oh, the clouds of them in summer were awful." Suzanne waved away invisible mosquito hoards and rolled her eyes theatrically.

I smiled and told her I was generally healthy, so she and the inhabitants of Courtney Academy had nothing to fear.

"How do you find the students?" I asked. "Are they hard workers?"

"*Oh, the girls are so courtly at Madame Courtney's, there are none so fair, to be sure*—so goes our school song." Suzanne surprised me with her lilting, clear-voiced alto. "I think you shall find our students to be the typical daughters of wealthy families. Some are brilliant, some slow, and most in between. Some are kind, some petty, but most are in between. We provide them the best education their fortunes can buy."

"And French, do they speak it at home?" I asked, hoping to dust off my conversational skills in the language.

"Our girls? Oh, heavens, no." Suzanne chuckled. "French in this town belongs to the Creoles. Although every debutante is expected to perfect her *vouses* and *êtres* in case she goes to Paris, she knows which side of Canal Street she is on. I shall soon take you to Canal Street, which is the neutral ground between the English-speaking and Creole neighborhoods. It is quite lively there, mon amie."

Suzanne made good on her promise to introduce me to the many colors of New Orleans, and I could not have asked for a more insightful tour guide and companion. Because Suzanne was at ease in all parts of the city, explorations with her were always fascinating. New Orleans was a city of water: myriad fountains, the river, the lakes, canals, ocean, bayous, water even in the air itself. The city's architecture swung wildly between Creole cottages, Italian villas, double-galleries, tiny shotgun houses, and neo-classical plantation homes. I never tired of touring the neighborhoods and fell in love with the French Quarter's epicureanism and vibrancy.

My years at Courtney Academy passed pleasantly. I adored almost everything about the city set in the crescent of the slow-flowing Mississippi: its people, music, culture, cuisine, architecture, and liveliness. I came to feel that breathing the night-blooming jasmine was as vital to life as oxygen, and I learned to take the humidity in stride.

Twice a month, I took the Saint Charles streetcar downtown to volunteer at Charity Hospital. Sometimes Suzanne and I volunteered at the Poydras Orphan Asylum, in both the classrooms and kitchen. Once, I attended a meeting at the local arm of the National American Woman Suffrage Association. I was shocked to realize its members believed votes for women should include only votes for *white* women. I never returned to their meetings.

Every year, I eagerly awaited the raucous madness and colors of Mardi Gras: its floats, the tribes' magnificent costumes, the dancing, and the joyous music unlike any I had heard elsewhere. I savored crawfish season every spring, when the messy, crimson feasts were as much social affairs as meals. During the two weeks of spring recess, Suzanne, Ida Collins—who taught the primary grades—and I would rent a cottage on the beach at Grand Isle and go to the community crawfish boils on Friday nights. We spent happy hours walking the shoreline of the long white-sand beach. Dolphins, rays, schools of silvery fish, and even sharks frolicked in the waves, and pelicans, gulls, and albatross flew back and forth looking for a meal. Raised stands of sea oaks in the salt marshes were enchanting to explore in the spring, when thousands of migrating hummingbirds, iridescent buntings, and elegant swallow-tailed kites swooped in and rested after their five-hundred-mile nonstop flights across the gulf. Some afternoons, thousands of those exhausted travelers literally fell into the trees and onto the ground.

Most of my students were good learners. I enjoyed opening the doors to ancient worlds and showing the girls what remarkable cultures and languages could be found therein. Occasionally, a student would be genuinely inspired by and excel in the classics, which made my countless classroom hours worthwhile.

As in Phoenix, teaching was my defense against unwanted advances. It was easy to say I loved my job and did not want to risk it with an amorous relationship. I instead found satisfaction in my students, my friends, and my work.

⚜

In late September of 1915, a devastating hurricane struck the city. Several days before, the National Weather Service informed our city that a dangerous storm was approaching. New Orleans burst into a flurry of activity as people secured their homes and businesses. Many residents from the barrier islands descended upon the city, seeking shelter wherever it could be found. At the Academy, students were returned to their families. The staff prepared the school buildings as best we could, and then boarded an uptown train to Mississippi. Rooms were taken at the Terrace Inn in Mc-Comb, and I billeted with Suzanne, Ida, and Clara, the home arts instructor.

Although the hurricane's center was a hundred miles away when it struck, it had power far beyond anything I had ever experienced. The storm screamed as if banshees were tearing around outside and crashing into each other as they cavorted in the roaring thunder.

Newspaper reports following the storm were far from encouraging, thus our confinement in McComb was prolonged. We learned that levees had overtopped and failed, and waters from Lake Pontchartrain had backed up into the canals, leaving thousands of homes flooded.

At the river, hundreds of boats and ships had been submerged and the docks destroyed. Buildings and churches had collapsed, roofs and steeples were ripped away, electric and telegraph lines had been severed and the stalwart *Times-Picayune* building was so damaged it could not print our local news.

Upon our eventual return to New Orleans, the damage to the city was horrifying. Between flooding and powerful winds, the city was almost unrecognizable. Everywhere one looked, what were once structures were now piles of debris. Nearly every building in the city had suffered damage, and the cloying stench of death was inescapable. Our Academy was fortunate in that most of it was still standing. Two of the outbuildings had been obliterated, as had the main building's cupola and west wing roof.

All told, at least 275 lost their lives and thousands more their livelihoods in the Great Storm. Countless were injured. I wondered how this place would ever be the same. An outside observer might have concluded that, this time, New Orleans was surely defeated. But I believed our city's intrepid people would emerge from the rubble and rebuild.

⁂

Shortly after our return to Courtney Academy, I received a letter from Gerard Semler, my Philadelphia attorney. As he was about to retire, Mr.

Semler sought my approval to transfer my account to his son under a new company name, Semler Family Law, and promised continued confidentiality of the kind to which I had become accustomed.

Among papers summarizing my assets was a clipping from the *Philadelphia Inquirer* entitled, "Socialite Mourned," which was an obituary featuring a photograph of a severe-looking older woman with a corona of white hair. There was something about the stern expression of the eyes and the way the woman held her chin high. Curious, I read that friends and associates of the esteemed Reginald Coxe were invited to view the remains of his wife of forty-one years. Claudia, the fifty-nine-year-old mother of six, grandmother many times over and a great-grandmother, daughter of the late James and Josephine Leighton.

The thin paper fluttered to the floor beside my writing table. Claudia! My cousin, my age. A mother, a great-grandmother. For a few moments, I was unable to inhale and my chest burned. Anger rose to the back of my throat, up into my sinuses, and poured out of my eyes as hot tears. How could *she* have had such a life? Claudia, who was as shallow as a piece of parchment, as cold as a tin cup in winter. A vision of Claudia surrounded by a horde of babies, three generations of children, with a loving husband standing by her side, bombarded my mind. How dare Claudia invade my consciousness here in New Orleans, after I had worked so hard to make a life after losing my family, my Peter, and my precious Cecile? How could this be, how could this possibly be? The overwhelming injustice of it was too much to bear.

It is not injustice. It is time's will, part of a normal life. Why am I so outraged? Am I simply jealous of Claudia? Life changes are the natural progression. It is basic biology. Claudia lived a normal life. She procreated successfully and grew old. While I—

I rushed outside, turned uptown, and ran blindly, a loud buzzing in my ears. My reality was ripped asunder, just as the city all around me had been torn by the Great Storm's fury. I ran and ran, and only slowed when I realized I was well inside Lafayette Cemetery.

Music stopped me. It was a funeral parade, with brass and woodwinds and drums, one of too many such parades since the storm. The uniformed band played an alluring dirge in the local style, which in the future would be known as *jazz*. A large group of mourners walked behind the band, stepping and swaying with the music. Their parasols seemed to float in the air, twirling here and there to the slow beat. I watched until the bereaved made their solemn way to an open, above-ground grave. In New Orleans, all graves were above ground; otherwise, the omnipresent water would inevitably push what was buried back up into the light.

On my walk back to Courtney Academy, the sounds of rebuilding, of hammering and sawing, energized my steps.

<hr />

On September 16, 1917, three cases of influenza were found on an oil tanker in New Orleans port, and less than one month later, thousands of cases were reported in the city every day. On October ninth, all schools, churches, and other nonessential public places were ordered closed, excepting eateries and drinkeries.

All our girls were sent home. I hoped we would see them again. Suzanne, alarmed for herself and her family, made the difficult decision to leave New Orleans for her family's rice farm outside of Marksville, Louisiana. She begged me to join her, but I didn't want to risk becoming too involved with another family. Besides, I wanted to stay in New Orleans to help with the pandemic. I was heartbroken to see Suzanne go. She had been a constant, beloved companion since I arrived in New Orleans.

I offered my services to the Red Cross at Charity Hospital, where the Sisters of Charity had given over three entire floors to influenza patients. Never had I seen the hospital so overcrowded. Influenza patients packed the wards and hallways as well as tents, which had been set up outside for additional beds and triage. The din alone was enough to make one wonder whether the hospital environs were helping or hurting the sick. Physicians, nursing staff, sisters, and clergy shouted orders, trying in vain to tend the endless rows of patients.

Are you acclimated? Suzanne's question about my health during my first days at the Academy echoed in my head.

I was told to report to Sister Evangeline, an austere woman with whom I had occasionally worked as a volunteer. Her blue eyes were haggard and bloodshot above her white mask.

"Thank you for being here. I need you to string sheets between the beds in B and C wards to help isolate patients. Sheets and rope are in linen supply," she said crisply, gesturing toward the closet down the hall. "You know where to find a frock and cap. Take a few face masks." She turned and walked brusquely in the direction of the east wing, a full board-and-clip in hand. The sister shouted at me over her shoulder, "And be sure to wear them!"

"Do not worry about her," a nurse said as she passed by. "She is all business with everyone."

Before I could reply, the nurse had rushed around the corner and was gone. I felt a stranger at this Charity Hospital where everyone dashed about, held conversations in motion, and were disguised in white frocks and face masks. If I did not already know my way around, I would have been at quite a loss. I made my way to the floor's supply closet, donned frock and cap, tied a cotton mask over my mouth and nose, and then put several spares in my frock pocket. I found an idle cart in the hallway and filled it with sheets, rope, and a pair of shears. Wheeling around fast-moving medics, patient cots, and other mayhem, I made my way to ward C.

Standing in the doorway, it took a moment to grasp the situation. Ward C was a large, long room that normally held a score of indigent patients. Now, however, the ward was overfull times three. This was going to take a while.

Are you acclimated?

As I worked between the tightly packed beds, stringing lines over which I draped sheets, I observed the influenza patients. What surprised me was their age: most of the patients seemed to be young adults, in the prime of their lives. A few slept, others tossed in pain, and all were feverish and coughed frequently and violently. Many an emesis basin and bedpan were filled with noxious liquid. Some patients bled from the mouth, nose, and ears. The most severe cases coughed incessantly, blue spots on their cheeks, their lips and ears indigo as the fluid filling their lungs leisurely drowned them.

The only comfort we could grant the patients was aspirin to dull the pain and quinine for the fever. Windows were mercifully left open to provide fresh air.

In time, my jobs were as varied as the people giving orders. I bathed patients, changed hospital gowns and linens, cleaned pans and basins, and provided water, blankets, and emotional comfort.

Am I acclimated?

Every day it was more difficult to close the eyes of the dead and pull sheets over their heads. Just getting to and from the hospital was an arduous and overlong task because strict limits had been imposed on the number of persons allowed per streetcar. In the wards, the coughing and cries for help were constant—a harsh, clamoring drone from which there was no respite. The stench of waste and death never left me. Every day, hospital staff themselves became patients.

The sisters had to beg for help from outside the city. The worst were the children, their tiny frames wracked with coughing, their skin so transparent one could clearly see the networks of purple and blue veins. How they cried. It wore me down further with each ensuing day.

When I looked into those blue faces, I saw what I had tried so hard, for so long, to make invisible. The blue death turned every woman into my mother, the men into my father, the elderly into my grandfather, and the children into my sister and my daughter. With each death, the brightness I had sought in life dimmed.

Oh, my sweet Cecile. After these many years, the ache in my womb and in my heart had begun to ease, but I retained enough agony to weaken my knees. I would have given anything and everything to be with Cecile, wherever she was.

I stopped wearing a mask at the hospital. What difference would it make? None. Everyone I cared about would still be gone—and I would still be here. Every time a concerned doctor or sister admonished me to put on a face mask, I went through the motions of compliance, but never wore it for long. One afternoon, trudging with a cartload of quinine and aspirin from patient to patient, I worked off a board on which Sister Evangeline had clipped a many-paged list. I went sluggishly up and down the rows of beds, offering little pills and cups of water, checking off patients on the medication list and noting any patients who required a physician's, orderly's, or clergy's attention.

Perhaps it was because I was one of the only workers without a mask, showing a human face, or perhaps it was the air of professionalism the board with its clipped-on papers gave me. For whatever reason, the patient in row three, bed twelve, thought I was someone who could do what she needed. After swallowing her quinine, the young woman grabbed me by the wrist. I tried to pull away, but she clutched me fiercely.

"Help!" she gasped through bluing lips. "You must help me, please! My daughter . . . four years old . . ." She broke into a storm of coughing, while never loosening her hold on me. Fighting down the attack, she continued, "She is only four . . . all alone, my husband, dead . . . family, dead."

I met her hazel eyes so like mine and a chill started in my scalp and crept along my spine. "Please. If I die . . ." She stopped for breath, tears pooling in her eyes. "When I die . . . please . . . take her . . . make sure . . . good home. Clarice, she is . . . only four."

I was stunned at the request, too stunned to answer. The woman continued, wheezing, "She is here . . . somewhere . . . Please, find her . . . I beg you." A convulsion of coughing hit her so severely, it finally broke her hold on my arm.

When the coughing eased, she whispered, "Please. Promise. I beg you."

With that, she slumped into the bed and did not breathe again.

My hand covered my mouth in horror as the room receded, and blackness crept in from the corners until all I could see was an immense hole in the ground. I saw the woman and her daughter tumble into that blackness. Then I saw four coffins, then five, then six, then too many to count.

I ran from the ward, pills and papers scattering in the hallway, ran down spiraling flights of stairs, slammed open a side door. Once outside, I doubled over and vomited.

The blackness washed in again from the edges, until this time it overwhelmed everything with an inky nothingness in which I floated, weightless. Everyone else was gone. Everyone I had ever loved. Everyone I had ever known. Everyone who had ever been—was gone. Even Earth itself and the other planets, and all the myriad stars. Gone.

At the end of the universe, there was nothing left but time's empty blackness.

Nothing—but me.

Alone.

⸻

"Ma'am? Ma'am! You okay? Ma'am, is you okay?"

A deep voice pulled me back from the darkness. With feeling returning to my shaking limbs, I gradually focused on a masked orderly, a worried look on his brow, a handkerchief proffered.

"Ma'am? Can I help you? Git you some water?"

Somehow, I found my voice and the ability to lie. "No, thank you, I am fine. I just needed a little air."

He persisted, handing me his handkerchief. "Well, would you please let me escort you to wherever you goin'?"

"You are very kind, sir, but I am fine, really. I shall go back inside now. I thank you for your concern."

He appeared unconvinced but gave a slight bow. "Ain't no trouble, ma'am. These times is mighty hard on all of us."

As I opened the door and stepped inside, I felt his eyes following me and I was grateful. I started up the stairs. Somewhere in the hospital was a little girl who needed to be found.

❦❦❦

I located little Clarice hiding in a corner of B ward. She was placed in an orphanage and, once the influenza abated, a loving home was found for her. I now recognized that I would never—ever—find the same. What use would an endless life be to me? It brought nothing but heartache, no lasting connections. I would move on from New Orleans two years after the pandemic, before my ageless face came under suspicion. I was unsure how to proceed: an infinite life apparently lay ahead, but I was leery of taking the first step. What if I took the wrong direction? The safest path forward, for now, seemed to be the one I was already on.

Mrs. Courtney and I cried when I gave her my notice and the falsehood that my mother in Pennsylvania had passed away and my invalid father needed care. On the summer morning I left the academy, Mrs. Courtney pressed a fat envelope into my hand "to help Mr. Nolan." I tried to refuse it, but, as I should have known by then, even the collapse of heaven or hell would not change Camellia Courtney's mind once she had made it up. Heavy with guilt, I accepted the generous severance and left Louisiana.

Aboard a Gulf and Western steamship somewhere between New Orleans and Tampa, the captain reported over the ship's intercom that the Nineteenth Amendment to the United States Constitution had passed. Female cries of joy soared ship-wide upon the realization that our voices would at long last be heard in the running of our country. The ship's lounge became the scene of an impromptu and raucous victory celebration. I was buoyed by the energy from the room and thrilled by the prospect of voting for the first time.

Florida's Southern College offered programs in education that resulted in a teaching certification, which schools were starting to require. References and transcripts for applying in accord with my apparent age were not very difficult to obtain, thanks to my trusted and discreet Philadelphia law firm. Southern's campus near Orlando, in Sutherland, had been damaged by fire, but buildings were being constructed on a new site in Lakeland, halfway between Orlando and Tampa. In the meantime, the campus was housed temporarily in nearby Clearwater Beach, a strip of bright white sand and emerald waters just outside Tampa.

In addition to immersing myself in my education studies, I took painting and sculpting classes, joined the women's basketball team, and learned to swim, which I loved. Sometimes I joined my teammates at local dance halls. The new dance styles were fun and energetic, but at first I was uncomfortable with the physical closeness and touching. I drew the line at the Shimmy.

Within four years, I earned a college degree and teaching certification. I hoped they would help me find a use for my long life. On graduation day, I felt the absence of my family keenly.

In Tampa's booming economy, I had no trouble obtaining a job teaching geography and mathematics at Gorrie Elementary School. Gorrie was an excellent school with a new, progressive curriculum, and I enjoyed the coastal lifestyle. Deciding to stay a few more years before moving on, I joined the new American Federation of Teachers.

Then the stock market crashed. Our school was in a wealthier district and remained open, but with reduced classes and staff. My salary was cut drastically. Fortunately, Tampa was an inexpensive place to live, so I did not need to draw from my savings or investments to get by. I was even able to help my landlords pay their electricity bills when they had problems making ends meet.

⧫⧫⧫

In 1935, my endless youth made it time to move on once more. I could go about fifteen years before my youthful appearance attracted negative attention and drove me to relocate and start anew. I kept asking myself, *Why don't I age? What is the root cause? Are there others somewhere with my condition?*

I tried the local library's limited selection of science journals and found nothing. For all I knew, I could be an anomaly of nature.

Freak. I am nothing but a freak. Bart was right.

No, wait! I am not a freak. There must be some force, some physiological property causing my condition. How frustrating to find no explanation!

Yet . . . discoveries happen every day—just look at the new polio vaccines and sulfa to fight infection. If science cannot help me—yet—someone will find the answer. Someday, I will learn who I am. I will keep searching. I must. I need a better library.

The Social Security program required everyone to register with the government. My attorneys had a new birth certificate fabricated for me, and I became Naissa Nolan, aged eighteen. I chose the city of Atlanta, Georgia, as my new home. Georgia's capital appealed to me because of its cultural offerings, such as its recently opened regional ballet company and its renown as one of the country's more beautiful cities. Most importantly, Atlanta boasted the well-respected and extensive Carnegie Public Library and Emory University Library School, where I planned to conduct a couple of research projects. The Carnegie seemed ideal for my needs, as it included a large medical section tied to the Emory University School of Medicine. Could an explanation for my condition be buried somewhere in the library's many stacks? My second project would make use of the library's considerable periodicals section to try to discover what had become of people I cared about in my previous incarnations.

Despite the Depression and the overall scarcity of jobs, my Florida certification opened the door to a part-time position teaching composition at the Emory University Library School, where I also took courses leading to a degree in library science. After I graduated, I was hired to teach future librarians at the library school.

Armed with research skills and in-depth knowledge of the Carnegie Library, my private research proceeded with as much speed as my busy schedule allowed. Seeking out maladies even slightly resembling mine, I scoured medical volumes. Ancient texts from Greece, the Middle East, and Far East were particularly fascinating.

I studied the four humors, miasma theory, Pasteur's germ theory, smallpox inoculation, and vaccination. I combed medical journal articles on immunity and fungi published by researchers such as Duchesne, Paine, Gratia and Dath, and Twight. A Scotsman, Alexander Fleming, was making a splash with his penicillin. Its future applications seemed promising, if a few hurdles could be cleared. It was all interesting, but I was unable to work out a connection to my situation.

Eventually, I returned to Darwin's writings. When I was a child, my parents and their friends held many drawing-room discussions, sometimes heated, about Darwin's then-scandalous *Origin of Species*. How was it that my physical attributes were similar to everyone else's on the planet, while the traits of immunity, healing, and aging could be so strikingly different? What were they, exactly, and where did they come from? Were there others like me? If so, where were they? Realistically, the chance of finding any others was nearly zero.

Who in their right mind would announce such news, only to end up prodded and cut and queried, spending the rest of their days as a circus oddity? No. Any sane person would no doubt keep his or her head low, as I did. Someday, there would be a way to flush out my sisters and brothers in unending youth. If they existed.

I carried on with my after-hours research at the library and in private. Keeping detailed notebooks as I had learned from Bart, I experimented with my immunity to injury. I drew up a list of questions and hypotheses, and tested them one by one. Using a Bunsen burner, I tried to burn the tip of my index finger, and then held my palm over the flame. The excruciating pain dissipated almost immediately. I liberated a piece of dry ice from the science lab, clutching it for one second, five seconds, ten seconds, sixty seconds. I sliced open my thigh with a butcher knife. I cut a small slit in the radial artery of my left wrist. I hit my nose with a dictionary, hard enough to hear a sharp crack. I hit my left hand with a hammer, my right foot with a sledgehammer. In the dead of night, I jumped from a one-story building. Then a five-story building.

Each test had the same result: within seconds of injury, the offended flesh would simply close and whatever was broken would mend—as if the damage had never occurred. It wasn't that I didn't feel pain. Some of the experiments were more excruciating than others, forcing me to stifle cries of agony. The pain, however, like the injuries themselves, always dissipated immediately; I felt nothing more than flashes of varying intensity.

After years of always achieving the same results, I decided against further experiments.

My ability to remain healthy and unharmed was a frightening power to have. Some might call it a challenge to the Almighty. I saw a new comic at the newsstand about a man from another planet who could not be injured. He was strong, and could fly, too. *Superman.* Was *I* a superwoman? Could my ability to be unharmed somehow help people?

Who am I fooling? Women aren't supposed to be powerful. I would be run out of town by a mob. I'd be Freakwoman. That's no life for me. Better to just keep trying to find the science.

For my second project, I spent many hours in the library's archives, searching for familiar names in the *Philadelphia Inquirer,* the *Arizona Republic,* the *Times-Picayune,* and the *Saint Petersburg Times.* I sat at a corner table in the large room scented with the spicy smell of old newspapers, glints of dust swirling under the lamp as old memories rose from the pages I turned with ink-smudged fingers. I marveled at how different life had become: from the musky odor of leather and horse sweat to exhaust fumes, from fireplaces to radiators, from oil lamps to electric, from walking on the ground to flying above it.

Rarely did I find what I had been searching for, but there were a few. One of my most promising students from Philadelphia, Nathanial Stern, became the editor of a well-regarded national magazine before he died. I cried when learning my husband, Bart, had perished in a housefire with his third wife and their four children. The obituary did not mention Bart's second wife.

That was the day I stopped searching the old newspapers. They were too distressing.

<hr/>

After the Pearl Harbor attack, our home front sprang into action: men and boys enlisting, factories firing up, women rolling up their sleeves to work outside the home. A constant river of recruits flowed through Atlanta to Fort McPherson on their way to the war's various fronts. Atlanta swelled with an influx of laborers from the countryside—mostly women—ready to earn a decent factory wage instead of scraping a bare living from the red clay. Georgia and the other states became cogs in the great machine of war.

When victory was at last declared, celebrations were deafening. The unabashedly ornate Fox Theatre was the go-to place for newsreels about the war. The stark evidence projected on screens around the world of Nazi mass exterminations in Germany and the US annihilation of two hundred thousand people in Hiroshima and Nagasaki by atomic bombs horrified audiences. I was gutted.

And what of the effects of those bombs? They obliterated *all* life at their targets, leaving only poison behind. What madmen conceived of such weapons, with utter disregard for life? It seemed ridiculous for people to motivate themselves and strive, when the promises of life in an abundant world were in fact one, always kept: the promise of extinction after a brief consciousness—a momentary flicker in an endless nothing. And now, humans threatened the Earth itself.

<hr/>

When it was time to move on, I relocated to the farming community of Webster, New York, near Rochester and Lake Ontario, where I took employment as a high school English and French teacher. It was time to get back to a simpler way of life after my distress at the war and the failure to reach my goals in Atlanta.

Webster was a small town set amid fragrant orchards. There was no cinema, but the village boasted a fair library, a large basket factory, and numerous farm markets. When I first arrived in September of 1945, my fingers and toes were always chilled. It was as if the hellish newsreels from which I was running, and which continued to invade my thoughts and dreams, had sapped my inner heat. I still could not comprehend a world where such horrors could happen.

When I first unlocked the front door of my small house in the village of Webster, things started looking up. What a pleasure to find someone had stocked the shelves in my cupboards and refrigerator! There was a vase of fresh-cut flowers on the dining room table, and a basket with fruit, cheese and crackers, and chocolates, and a bottle of wine on the sideboard.

My second night in Webster, I was invited by my new boss, the Webster High School principal, to a performance at the high school. The show was to celebrate the end of the war, and most of the community was expected. I was tired from a long day of unpacking and settling in, but Mr. Miller insisted with a dazzling smile.

"Oh, come on, Miss Nolan, all you need do is relax and enjoy the show. I'll even give you a quick tour of the building before the show starts, okay? The kids have been working on this for weeks. Besides, what else are you going to do on a Wednesday night in our charming village?"

"All right, Mr. Miller, it would be a pleasure to join you."

"Call me *Mr. Miller* again, and I am going to give it to you! You must call me Frank. Got it?"

"I've got it . . . Frank." I laughed. "And it's Naissa."

When Frank Miller had interviewed me on the telephone, his brio was one of the things that attracted me to the Webster job. It was rare to find such enthusiasm in administrators. Maybe it was because he was surprisingly young for a principal—around thirty, I guessed. He was tall and lean, with hair the color of ravens and emerald eyes that twinkled as if he knew a secret you would soon be in on. As tired as I was, I was curious about my new principal, his school, and the community.

I tried to keep up with Frank's long legs as he moved and talked a mile a minute and guided my whirlwind tour of the three-story school while he greeted people in the halls. "We became Webster Central School District two years ago, and we're expanding fast. We brought in not only Webster students, but those from the neighboring communities of Ontario, Penfield, and Walworth—Oh hello, darling Betty! How are you this evening, cooking with gas?—We have a large gymnasium, and the auditorium can hold nine hundred folks. And here we are!"

We stepped into the hall, which was buzzing with preperformance jitters. Frank sat me next to him near the end of the front row. The curtain rose and the performance began. After the Pledge of Allegiance, everyone sang patriotic songs, the mayor and superintendent gave speeches, and students of all ages performed a play about a family rescued from the Nazis. At the end, the stage lights were lowered and the children's sweet, clear voices filled the hall as they sang "Amazing Grace." Students held candles, lit one from the other, representing the people of all the allied nations involved in the war. When the curtain fell, I wasn't the only one blotting tears.

Shooting to his feet, Frank hooted and clapped exuberantly, as did the rest of the audience. He then jumped up to the podium at the side of the stage.

Still clapping, he exclaimed, "Let's hear it for our fabulously talented students! Mrs. Flynn, what a swell production!"

The audience cheered and whistled. The children and their director bowed again and again.

When the ovation quieted, Frank said to audience and performers alike, "Let us all be thankful for our brave soldiers who brought us to victory. And let us, by living our lives well, honor those who suffered and died and lost everything. May President Truman bring peace and prosperity to our great country. Bless you all! Good night."

As the applause again thundered then faded to quiet, I started to feel that Webster might be less an escape than a place of healing.

I had heard it said that rural folk, even though polite and generous, were slow to welcome new people into their community. Even fifty-year residents could be considered "newcomers." The heartfelt welcome I received from everyone I met—teachers, staff, parents, and other Webster residents—put that theory to rest. The farming community accepted me readily and warmly, a testament to the high value the hardworking people placed on education. The first time I went to the village market, the grocer put a whole chicken in my shopping basket, "Because of your good work with the kids." After that, an extra orange or container of coffee was in my grocery bag whenever I unpacked.

Before long, Frank was my best friend. What could have been an awkward boss-and-employee association never materialized. When I first realized we were becoming close, I dreaded the uncomfortable discussion we were bound to have about my needing to concentrate on my work and not be distracted by romance. But the necessity for the conversation never arose, and for that I was grateful. Instead, we were completely satisfied with friendship.

Frank and I had a compatibility which, I think, surprised us both. We shared a similar sense of humor, "Dry, like a good brut," as Frank would say. We both appreciated fine art. He grew up in Cleveland and had earned his master's in education at Harvard. Frank never spoke of his family, demurring when I asked, saying he no longer had a family. I was curious as to why, but it was clear Frank did not want to discuss it. Lucky for me, he also respected the boundaries around my own background. We kept our friendship removed from work as much as possible, focusing on Webster High School when in Webster High School, and saving the fun for weekends and breaks.

Frank's other best buddy, the physical education teacher, Bill Kuhn, was frequently a third Musketeer in Frank's and my leisure adventures. Muscular and somewhat short, Bill had bottle-blond hair in tight curls, light-brown eyes, and a ready laugh. His warped sense of humor kept us highly entertained, plus he was a virtuoso with impressions.

The three of us had a good time playing many a cutthroat game of Monopoly in Frank's front room while washing down local cheeses and crackers with olive-garnished martinis. We also enjoyed going to Rochester's dance halls, movie theaters, and other attractions. I loved the Museum of Arts and Sciences, with its archeological, historical, and scientific artifacts, even though it was strange to see familiar items from my youth resting in the display cases. My favorite destination was the Memorial Art Gallery's permanent collection of paintings because it included three of Peter's works.

A few years after I moved to Webster, a drive-in theater opened on Empire Boulevard. Many summer nights, Frank, Bill, and I would hop into Bill's 1947 gold Chevy Fleetmaster, and with the top down and a basketful of sandwiches, popcorn, and beer, we would spend the evening dining alfresco under the huge screen. A sad portent of the long winter-to-come was the Empire's marquee at the end of summer:

CLOSED FOR THE SEASON
REASON? FREEZIN'!
SEE YOU IN MARCH

Once, the three of us drove south to Letchworth State Park, also known as the Grand Canyon of the East, to hike and admire its breathtaking gorge and waterfalls. Frank and Bill wanted to trek across the railroad bridge hundreds of feet above the gorge, but I refused. What if one of my friends fell? I let them think it was because I was afraid of heights. Frank's and Bill's well-being was worth the endless ribbing.

One unseasonably warm Saturday evening in late April 1950, when I had been in Webster nearly five years, Frank dropped by my house with his customary, "What's buzzin', cousin?" and demanded I accompany him on a night out. "It's a gorgeous Saturday night and the lilacs are opening, so let's go paint the town. Dinner and a movie in Irondequoit, how 'bout it?"

When I gestured toward my attire, secretary trousers and an old blouse, Frank lit up and offered, "No need to deck out, just throw on your yellow swing and some slides, and you're good to go."

It was no use arguing with Frank, as his stubborn streak was as strong as he was tall. Besides, I had spent the afternoon preparing for the intro to drawing class I was teaching, so I jumped at the prospect of time out in the crisp, spring air. Quickly changing into my swing dress, I ran a comb through my hair, dabbed on some lipstick, grabbed my white angora cardigan, and out we went. We sailed west toward the bay in Frank's peacock-green Starlight Champ, windows down and Frankie Laine on high volume.

When we arrived at Bay View Restaurant, the maître d' escorted us to the rear banquet room because, he said, the front tables had all been reserved, as was normally the case on a Saturday night, and since we had no reservation, we could not possibly sit in the main dining room. Frank and I looked at each other with raised eyebrows. I thought it peculiar that the banquet room's lights had not been turned on. Then, the maître d' flicked the switch with a flourish.

Surprise! Happy Birthday, Naissa!

Enthusiastic shouts filled the room at the same instant its darkness flew away. Blinking in the sudden brilliance, it took a moment to realize there were many people in the room and they were all grinning at me, excitedly awaiting some type of response. One by one, faces came into focus and I first recognized Bill, then the others. Was the entire staff of Webster High School in the room? Oh gosh. My colleagues had conspired to throw me a surprise party. I fought the impulse to turn and bound away into the night.

All I could think, after the initial jolt, was that my colleagues couldn't possibly have known it was my birthday. What on Earth were they all doing there, looking at me as if I were a shiny toy in a toy shop? Had I won a prize? An award? And yet they had shouted "Happy birthday."

Frank! It must have been Frank's doing. As principal, he had my personnel file. I silently groaned. My file listed my real birthdate but a fictitious year. Everyone in the banquet room thought it was my twenty-fifth birthday. They didn't know the staggering truth. This birthday was my one hundredth.

I turned to Frank and whispered menacingly, "I will get you for this." Frank laughed brightly while steering me into the room.

As parties go, it was a good one. When I recovered from the shock, I relaxed and took in the goodwill that had brought us all together. Usually, I wasn't comfortable in big groups, but this was easier because I knew everyone. There was an excellent meal of savory roasted trout with tart cherry sauce, plenty of libations, and dancing. The shy young man who taught algebra asked me to dance more times than I would have liked.

I grabbed Frank's wrist and hissed in his ear, "Please, please dance with me! If I have to dance once more with his smelly pomade, I'll lose my dinner!"

Frank chuckled and cut in minutes later. "What else are friends for?" he said.

After the next song, however, he handed me off to Bill, instructing him, "Here, keep her out of trouble for a few minutes. There's something I need to do." And off he went.

Bill was a good dancer, so we cut the rug for a couple of songs and gossiped about who in the room was secretly dating whom. The minute we took a break and started toward the bar for a drink, a new song began: a loud, mostly unmusical rendition of the "Happy Birthday" song. Turning around, I saw a crowd standing around a skirted cart upon which sat a very large, three-tiered cake adorned with spring lilacs, both white and lavender. I didn't have to count to know there were only twenty-five candles on the top layer.

Laughing, I shouted over the din, "I hope you're not auditioning for Community Chorus!"

When the spirited song ended, it was supplanted with calls of "Make a wish! Make a wish!"

I sensed time lurking among the smiling faces.

One hundred birthdays. A century of birthdays. How did I get here? It seemed I was home in Philadelphia just yesterday.

What was my wish? I thought of a much smaller cake, many years ago in Philadelphia. Mother had put fresh lilac sprigs around the base of that layered sweet. There were eight candles that year. The memory shifted and visions of other candled cakes came, one after the other.

I saw Father and Grandfather, beaming, singing "Happy Birthday" harmonies in their rich baritones. Then there was my eleventh birthday—the last with my family. Trudy had sewn a dress for one of my dolls. Next was the Vienna birthday dinner George's mother had made for my fifteenth, topped off with her apfelstrudel and the Lipizzaner stallion George had painstakingly carved for me.

A picnic and cake by the creek with Peter. And then a birthday with little Cecile, her chubby toddler hands reaching for the cake and candles, her cherubic face glowing in the lamplight. There were Suzanne and Ida on the beach, singing "Joyeux Anniversaire" and pinning dollars to my blouse as we laughed so hard, we cried.

The montage evolved one scene after another, picking up speed, until I was seeing only the candles, more and more and more candles, and finally thousands, millions, billions of candles. As many as the stars. And then I was at the end of it all, in time's nothingness.

What could I possibly wish for? To never again lose someone I loved? To have a family, without watching them grow old and fade away? To be unaware that all the knowledge and the parts of me I poured into my students eventually decayed and crumbled?

To not have another friend's flesh melt into the earth? To not leave Frank and Bill in a few years? To not witness the end of the universe? To defeat time?

What had I done in all this time? Had I accomplished anything? I still didn't understand why I was the way I was. I needed to do something more with my life, but what? I wish I knew.

I looked around at the familiar faces, their expressions just beginning to hover between gaiety and concern because it was taking me so long to blow out the candles. There was no escaping the warmth these people were sending toward me, no escaping the warmth of all those candles.

I smiled at my friends. Then I took a deep breath, and blew.

CHAPTER FIVE

1950-2019

Naissa

⌐∽⌐∽⌐⌐∽⌐

T HE WORLD BOOMED *after World War II, growing ever smaller through rapid transportation, communications, and mass media. Broadcast television brought living images into homes, and before long the black-and-white format evolved to full color. The land was prickly with columns of telephone poles marching down every street and antennas sprouting from rooftops like artificial trees. There was record growth in manufacturing, farms became industrialized, and the abundant sea was harvested. Commercial air travel became commonplace.*

In 1962, the Soviets and Americans brought humanity to the brink of nuclear war in Cuba. For nearly two weeks, humankind held its breath because it realized there might not be a future. In the end, there was no war, but the blow to the illusion of security was difficult to repair following this most dangerous episode in human history.

In the United States, times were turbulent, rocked by a spiral of shocking events: the murder of three civil rights workers in Mississippi, a mounting involvement in the Vietnamese civil war, and Martin Luther King's and the Kennedys' assassinations. Laws still supported unequal treatment of the races, and a civil rights movement fought for equality for all citizens. A woman's right to control her body's procreation became legal. The Vietnam War dragged on and divided the country as the body count rose. Soldiers who made it home, broken in spirit if not body, were sometimes greeted with hostility and indifference rather than compassion.

Nationwide anti-war protests were large and frequent. US involvement in the war ended after President Richard Nixon resigned instead of facing impeachment for non-prosecuted criminal acts, and President Lyndon Johnson began troop drawdown.

By the late twentieth century, fast-changing communications and computing technologies emerged as the Digital Revolution, with devices becoming smaller and more powerful every year. A massive communications network, the Internet, developed and grew like an infinitely tentacled beast, becoming indispensable to daily life.

As the twenty-first century neared, panicked information technology personnel sweated the lack of programming to process third-millennium dates, but apocalyptic predictions of huge systems failures didn't materialize.

Globally, extreme conservative moments spawned hate crimes and groups. Some ruled with repressive, oppressive, and terrorist tactics in the name of religion. In the US, White nationalists and supremacists, as well as groups organized around misogynistic hatred, were emboldened by government leaders with similar goals.

Advances in medicine included more effective antibiotics and vaccines. Scanning technologies enabled looks inside the body in ways previously unimagined. Electron microscopes captured images under two-million power magnification. Four researchers untangled the building blocks of all life: the DNA double helix. Dolly the sheep was announced as the first mammal cloned from an adult cell.

Automobiles were made larger and faster, and as an afterthought, more fossil fuel efficient. Toxic waste, burning fossil fuels, waste accumulation, and proliferation of new chemicals defiled the planet's land, water, and air, while humans made their first, dramatic steps off Earth toward the stars.

I never stopped missing and mourning the people important to me. I came to understand that the fabric of my being—the emotional fiber and stitches fastening me to the present day—had snagged on the Enchanted Bed of my childhood. I was dragged forward while held back, pulling the past with me in pieces and rolling across the years of my life, inch by day, foot by week, yard by years, slowly coming undone. My perpetual life forced me to move on from Webster two years after my one hundredth birthday. Giving notice to the school, I told everyone I had to return to Atlanta to help my family. It was hardest saying goodbye to Frank and Bill.

I became a third-grade teacher at a community school in Papillion, Nebraska. My time in the New York farming community had raised my appreciation for the hardworking people who cultivated the land. I settled easily into my new home and made friends with a few of my coworkers. After work hours, aside from the movie theater and a new bowling alley, there were few options for leisure activity in Papillion, so we made occasional trips to Omaha. I regularly carried a sketchbook or easel with me in and around town, creating a sizable record of local flora and fauna. I found ink and watercolors to be the perfect media to portray the delicate and bold hues of nature, especially with subjects like Nebraska's expanse of dawn sky over the fields and abundant wildflowers.

I began reading books to my class every day after recess, initially as a transition from play to serious studies, and eventually for the joy of it. The children and I looked forward to our reading time more than any other part of our day. We were transported into children's classics and tales by exciting new authors, such as E. B. White and Mary Norton. I became adept at voicing different characters, which helped hold even the most restless listeners' attention and often garnered giggles and guffaws. Sometimes the principal and other teachers would sit in on their lunch breaks.

One evening in the spring of my third year in Papillion, the school's principal was at my front door. He looked stricken.

"Miss Nolan, may I come in? I'm afraid I have sad news."

"Come in, Mr. Myers. Please sit. May I offer you anything?"

"No, thank you. It's just terrible. You know Hap Schlauderaff, the crop duster? Well, he'd been halfway through spraying the Hansen's soybean field this afternoon when his duster developed engine trouble. Hap couldn't restart the motor and needed to make an emergency landing. Hap didn't want to risk an explosion, of course, so he did what seemed like the best course of action. He dumped his fuel and chemical tanks. Then he pointed the plane's nose down the middle of West Lincoln Street. Lucky for Hap, the road was clear and he made a solid landing. A little rough, though."

"He is lucky." It could have been a disaster.

"Well, here's the hard part. Johanna Swenson, little Gertie's mother, was concerned when the girl hadn't come home from school."

Gertie? My student!

"She went looking and found Gertie on the side of the street. Apparently, she'd been walking home when Hap passed over, emptying his tanks. The poor girl was drenched in pesticide and aviation fuel from Hap's tanks. I'm told she was gasping for breath. By the time the doctor got to Gertie, her airway had closed."

"Oh my god! That poor girl! How is she?"

"Well, she's in a coma. The doctors think it may be irreversible—probably a blessing because she's got chemical burns all over. Johanna and Herb are destroyed. Anyways, I thought you should know why Gertie won't be in class."

Every day for the rest of the year, Gertie's empty seat shook me with the horror of her fate and her parents' grief. Gertie never awakened from her coma.

⚜⚜⚜

After the missile crisis in Cuba, which caused our world to stop in Papillion, people went back to living their lives, urgently embracing the everyday things that had to be done—bulwarks to avoid facing eventual nothing-ness. Around that time, I purchased a copy of *Silent Spring*, Rachel Carson's deeply moving exploration of the dangers of indiscriminate use of chemical pesticides. As news of the book spread throughout Papillion, a community dependent on what Carson called *poison*, I was disturbed by the outright rejection of Carson's premise. Had everyone already forgotten the horror of Gertie Swenson, whose parents moved about town like ghosts?

It was incredible that those whose lives depended on the land would choose to patronize the same corporations whose products were poisoning the earth. My unique perspective aggravated my alarm, because there was no way I could spend an interminable life in a poisoned world. For my own and the world's well-being, I had no choice but to fight for preservation of a healthy ecosystem.

I studied on my own time to learn all I could. I became outspoken around town about the issues, to the point where people changed sides of the street to avoid me. My principal summoned me to his office and warned me about complaints he was receiving from parents. It seemed people were so entrenched in their ways and their belief in the government and corpo-rations, they would not be moved. And then I realized: young people were the agents of change.

I finally knew my direction. I would use the changes I'd experienced over the years to help the environment by training young people to be its stewards. I could have broad reach by teaching science at a junior high or high school, while emphasizing environmental principles. But first, a new teaching certification would be necessary. So, in 1963, I left the Midwest and enrolled in Columbia University's Teachers College in Manhattan and specialized in the sciences.

I rented a flat overlooking Morningside Park. I loved walking through neighborhoods in the vibrant melting pot, taking in its people, their actions and interactions. Cosmopolitan, cultured Manhattan was the perfect place to absorb the mid-twentieth century.

I straddled a divide between the current world and a slower time of grace. Belonging to neither world, I was drawn in by both. Today breathed yesterday's air. A block of skyscrapers was a field where sheep grazed. Cars exhaling clouds of exhaust became horse-drawn carriages, clip-clopping down cobblestone streets.

Parking lots were ponds with splashing, laughing children. Cemeteries full of cancer victims became graveyards full of children who died from polio, typhus, pertussis, and tetanus. My view from the divide fortified my dedication to the goal of safeguarding our environment.

I was drunk with the polarities of emotion people experience before jumping off into the unknown—exhilaration and uneasiness, giddy expectation punctuated with pangs of dread—and my life beat with the frantic wings of a desperate, caged bird. Ready to soar.

I felt like a girl again and loved being a student. To fit in with my hip peers, I wore the current fashions and listened to popular music, especially to my new favorite, rock 'n' roll. I joined a circle of classmates with whom, in the hours between classes and studying, I crammed in as much fun as possible. We took the train to beach parties in Rockaway, played at Coney Island, and went to the city's many museums. We saw many excellent movies. I enjoyed the dramas, excluding historical re-creations in which history was fiction and fiction, history.

My friends and I often rented bicycles and rode around the parks. One day, however, the brakes failed on my bike on its way down a small bridge, and it sped faster and faster until the front wheel caught, and I flew over the handlebars. I had the wind knocked out of me. My companions were concerned but amazed that my scrapes seemed mere illusions only moments later. I joked that I had a tough hide, hopped on my bike, and took off, yelling, "Race you!"

During the summer, I volunteered as a counselor at Green World Day Camp. Supporting and encouraging children brought life meaning.

⚜⚜⚜

After graduation in the spring of 1966, my lawyers acquired a Social Security card for me with a new number. They informed Social Security that Naissa Nolan had "died" at the age of forty-nine. I became twenty-year-old Kerri Gordon, a young, certified science teacher with a honey-blond pixie and wire-rimmed glasses—nonprescription, naturally.

I couldn't help but think, *I killed Naissa to became Kerri. What a waste.*

It was true—Naissa Nolan no longer existed, officially.

But I'm still here. It's just documentation.

⚜⚜⚜

I took a position teaching high school science at a private school, the Du Bois Academy, in Ossining, New York, an economically and racially diverse river town famous for its penitentiary, Sing Sing. I moved to a lovely condo in Tarrytown, a thirty-five-minute train ride to Manhattan and a short ride to Ossining. The condominium development had twenty two-story buildings, each with four units. Its great variety of plantings made me feel like I was living in a botanical garden.

I became a high-energy young teacher who loved my students and helped them in class and out. Besides hosting environmental outings for my classes, I organized students to write our government representatives and newspapers about environmental issues, ran the art club, and was faculty advisor for student government. I tried to pave my students' way to become the best they could be, which sometimes drew in the rest of their families. Parents freely discussed their children, confident nothing they said would be repeated or written in their children's records. My circle of influence grew.

Because I had lived from the preindustrial to the postindustrial eras, I was able to speak meaningfully to my students about environmental changes over the years. When I was a child, we rode in horse-drawn carriages, and products were made from natural materials and renewable resources. Now, we had a "new and improved" lifestyle in which goods were manufactured from synthetics. We breathed toxic emissions from their processing, from the exhaust of vehicles transporting the goods, and from the incineration of the junk when we were through with it. The dirty air, tainted water, and food laced with chemicals correlated with an epidemic of untimely deaths from cancer.

In my science classroom, I did my best to open my students' eyes to their part in the environment around them.

"What do we take away from how the Native Americans used the animals they hunted?"

Silence.

"Joey?" I prodded one of my star young scientists. "Any ideas?"

He shrugged.

Susan raised her hand.

"Miss Gordon, was it so nothing was wasted? And the animals were respected?"

"Yes! Very good. The important thing to remember is, if we don't treasure our world, as did the Native Americans, we might push our planet to its demise. Let me read the words of Chief Seattle:

"'The Earth does not belong to man, man belongs to the Earth. All things are connected, like the blood that unites us all. Man did not weave the web of life; he is but a strand in it. Whatever he does to the web, he does to himself.'"

I made friends with a few colleagues and started going to Greenwich Village with them on weekends. I wore bell-bottom jeans and the Navajo headband given to me by my student in Arizona. We listened to poetry readings and original music that became the narrative of change. We danced, smoked pot, and protested in Washington Square Park—at least until the police chased us off. We joined growing numbers of young people looking for a different future.

The sixties counterculture's optimistic visions for a world of peace and cooperation were instead a reality of snarled hopes. I wished there were forces strong enough to comb them out. My very long life had provided a unique perspective in which noteworthy events and people became insignificant as I watched them fade first into obscurity, then oblivion.

There were always pointless games of war waging somewhere in the name of nationalism, religion, power, revenge, or greed. The players changed places every few years, former enemies becoming allies, and vice versa.

Fighting for the environment was a war I'd wage as long as I could.

The image on the television screen in shades of gray, black, and white was coarse and blurry. It was alien, but unmistakable: the top half of a sphere marbled with wispy, white swirls, suspended above an ashen, pockmarked plain. My neighbor Robin and I gasped at the same instant. Earth, viewed from the moon.

Robin exclaimed, "Would ya look at that! Cool!" With her accent and Italian roots, Robin was as much a product of Queens as Mr. Met and Shea Stadium.

The immense majesty of our Earth had compressed to less than the size of a TV screen. The astronauts' voices were only slightly distorted, as if they and their beeping equipment were broadcast from a New York TV studio with a cheap microphone and not from a quarter million miles away. Then I recognized the words I was hearing. The *Apollo 8* astronauts were reading verses from the book of Genesis.

It was Christmas Eve, 1968, and Robin had invited me over to watch the broadcast of the first manned lunar orbit and drink hot Frangelico toddies. Robin Roselli Ames was a year older than I was supposed to be, and our birthdays were only a day apart. She had moved into the condo next door over the summer with her husband, Lon, and their two- and three-year-old toddlers. Their condo always smelled heavenly of tomato, oregano, and parmesan cheese.

Robin was born into an Italian-immigrant family. She'd grown up in Queens, had married Lon Ames when she was nineteen, and dropped out of college when she became pregnant at twenty. Robin had a big heart, big hair, a big voice, and big opinions, and was always dressed in eye-popping, bright prints.

And, oh, that laugh from deep in her belly—it was hard to believe it came from that perky little woman. Robin made me smile.

When Robin invited me over to watch the broadcast, she had rolled her eyes while saying Lon was last-minute Christmas shopping. I often wondered about Robin's eyesight, considering how frequently she rolled her eyes when mentioning Lon. He, on account of work at his insurance agency, was rarely home and always did things last minute. Robin plainly resented it.

"This is like a sci-fi novel!" Robin exclaimed. Then her excitement visibly fizzled, and her belly laugh became tinged with bitter tones. She pulled at her dark curls.

"I think I'm through with novels, ya know? I told you, I've wanted to be a writer since forever. Just today, I carved out some time to work, sat down with the Selectric in the den, a blank page rolled in and ready to go. And just as an idea hits me, Brian screams."

"Oh, no!"

"Yeah, he caught his little finger in the wheel of that darn Batmobile toy. The noise of course woke up baby Lee, and now *he's* crying." Robin shook her head. "With all the stops and starts, my writing is *so* disjointed. And that's how the Great American Novel falls. Fuhgeddaboudit." Robin laughed again, but a tear brimmed the corner of her eye.

Then she said, "All I do is clean and cook and break up the kids' fights. It's like, I've lost myself in a prison of meaningless detail. Years from now, I'll probably be in the same boat, filling my emptiness with cooking and TV. Having achieved nothing."

I tried to give Robin's hand a squeeze, but she waved me off. "Would you like something? I picked up some sfogliatell' at Longhitano's today.

They make the best, so flakey and the cream's to die for. Who knows when Lon's getting back, so we may as well enjoy 'em."

Before we brought the desserts into the living room, Robin said, "It's definitely time for some toddy refills, don't you think?"

"Absolutely."

Several toddies later and the mission broadcast over, we stared at the TV, not caring what we were watching.

After a while, Robin said, "You know, besides being a writer, I wish even more I could've been a child actress. That would've been so cool."

"Really?" I was surprised, but somehow it made sense. "You would've been great."

"Yeah. Thanks. You know what I'd like? If I could wake up as a kid again and do things differently."

Robin's voice became soft. "Do you dream? I don't dream anymore. Maybe I'm just too tired."

I held the warm toddy in both hands, inhaled its hazelnut aroma and said, "Sometimes."

After a minute, Robin continued. "When I was five, I had my first nightmare. It was about being a grownup caught in some sort of awful reality. It was terrible. I woke up in a cold sweat but couldn't remember any details. Still, I knew it was about my adult life—a foreshadowing?—and it scared the bejeezus out of me."

As Robin spoke, all the warmth of the toddies left me. I gaped at her.

"What?" she asked, frowning.

I set down the toddy and laced my fingers together, hoping to steady my hands.

"You won't believe this." Robin looked at me impatiently while I tried to believe my own words. "I had the same dream. When I was five."

Robin's eyes widened.

"Holy shit!" we said in unison. And laughed until we nearly peed ourselves.

For many years, Robin was a good friend. I loved her pluck. She told me that right before they moved to Tarrytown, Brian got a terrible cough from the incinerators in their apartment complex. When Lon refused to move, she took the boys to Honolulu by herself and stayed there on Lon's dime until he agreed to move to a place with cleaner air.

Robin and I spent a lot of time with each other; she had a way of making me feel better when I was down, even though I could never confide in her entirely. After we'd shared our strange nightmare, we became especially close and often spent weekend mornings together in the park while her children played. Robin was a deep and sensitive thinker, and I valued her opinion.

One weekend, I was hanging out at Robin's place when the phone rang. Robin listened for a minute and said, "See ya then," and hung up.

She said dryly, "That was Lon. He promised he'd be home by seven, but now he says he won't be home 'til ten. What a chooch. Want to stay for dinner?"

We fed the kids TV dinners and put them to bed, but not before the kids and I sang goodnight songs, and I told *Auntie Kerri* stories. At eleven years old, Brian was losing interest in my sometimes-fictional adventures, but I could still command Lee and little Dawn's attention. It gave Robin a break.

Robin cooked the chicken and bacon for our cobb salad while I stood at the pass-through countertop peeling hard-boiled eggs and slicing tomatoes and avocado. The news show *60 Minutes* was on in the background.

"Lon was late last night, too," Robin said, frowning. "We had a big fight. When we went to bed, Lon said he was sorry and bumped his hard little cazzo against my backside, like it was asking, 'Pretty please?'"

We both cackled.

"Dare I ask what happened next?"

"I shut him down with the early-morning-teacher's-conference excuse."

As I set up dinner trays in front of the TV, *60 Minutes* launched into a segment on a rare disease called *progeria*. Mike Wallace, the newscaster, said the name was derived from the Greek and meant *prematurely old*. Progeria victims—all children—had organs which aged at an astonishing rate, so the little ones had the appearance and all the physical symptoms and diseases of the very elderly.

"Robin, look at these poor kids! They're like tiny old people. It's heartbreaking!"

Robin turned from the stove toward the TV. Her mouth formed a neat *O*.

"Oh, Maronna mia! Those poor babies! Imagine having a child like that. It would tear my heart apart."

Progeria, as Mr. Wallace explained, resulted from a gene mutation that sped up the life clocks of afflicted children, causing them to age and die by their midtwenties at the latest.

I nearly sliced through my finger instead of the tomato as my heart pounded with a rush of adrenaline. What if my condition was related to progeria, causing my life clock, instead of running too fast, to stand stock still? And what about others? Wallace said it was estimated one child in twenty million was born with progeria. If my condition were related, there could be more people like me.

Given the world population, that would mean there could be fifty others. If any ever made themselves known, there might be someone I could be together with in an unending span of time. And, oh my god, the children of such a union might be immortal!

I had to laugh at myself for jumping so quickly into an immortal family fantasy. But with the puzzle of my predicament possibly unscrambled, I was more hopeful than I'd been in ages.

"What's so funny?" Robin asked.

"Oh, that Mike Wallace. He's full of surprises."

Robin turned to look at me, her eyes narrowed and one brow elevated. "Uh-huh," she said before shaking her head and returning to the stove.

The next day, I borrowed a colleague's card for the New York Medical School's Health Sciences Library in Valhalla, after assuring him I knew my way around stacks and medical journals. In the library's sparse literature on progeria, I learned the disease, also called Hutchinson-Gilford progeria syndrome (HGPS), had been first described nearly a hundred years earlier. Very little was understood about progeria, other than it was probably a genetic mutation of some kind. I read that it wasn't known if the disease was inherited, a de novo (new) disease, or acquired.

I sensed there was something in the literature I was missing, some connection that might explain my case. Most progeria articles sought relationships between the disease and the natural aging process in order to discover more about normal aging.

For me to have stopped aging around my twenties, and to have the self-repair abilities I had demonstrated over the years, something must have been working differently on the cellular level. The answer felt nearer than ever before.

Was my agelessness the result of a rare, recessive gene? If that were the cause, there could be others like me out there somewhere. I might not end up alone. And, if such a gene had caused my condition, would it be inheritable? Would any children I might bear be ageless like me? Or, if it were a random mutation, then chances were I was the only one. If I could find others, at least that question might be answered. But how to find them?

Because Robin and I had a friendship I valued and appreciated, I wanted to bounce ideas off her. What if I told Robin the truth? Would she think I was a freak? My aberration would become a wall between us. I couldn't lose Robin's friendship; it had been so long since I had a close friend. I cringed when I realized I hadn't seen Frank in over twenty years. Fortunately, we still kept in touch by mail and an occasional phone call. I couldn't lose Robin, too.

Instead, I ran an ad in major newspapers around the world, inquiring about families or individuals with longevity and excellent health for an academic study, and listing a post office box. After two months, the box yielded fewer than a dozen responses, none of which described anything remotely like my condition.

⚜⚜⚜

On a Saturday night in early April, I met Julian Lange at the Katonah House, a new place that was becoming known for its good food and live music. Robin and Lon had hired a sitter, and we were having a rare evening out together.

We had just ordered dinner when the show began. The man who took the stage was at least six feet tall with an athletic body, Scandinavian features, and long blond hair pulled back in a ponytail. Robin and I exchanged a glance.

"Who is *that*?" Robin whispered. I spied a chalkboard near the stage and pointed, "Julian Lange, singer-songwriter."

This Nordic god played acoustic guitar and sang folk-pop music, entrancing his audience with a clear, soothing voice for almost two hours. His most poignant song, "Their Light Forever," was about remembering loved ones who passed away. As Julian's words flowed with his melody, my eyes welled. I turned to get a napkin to dab at them and saw that Robin's face was shiny with tears as she abandoned herself to the music. I pushed a few napkins in her direction.

Julian Lange appeared surprised and a little embarrassed by the crowd's enthusiastic response to his performance. His insightful lyrics struck such an empathetic chord in my psyche, I couldn't help but be drawn to him. And he was *hot*. I wanted nothing but to be in his arms, wrapped so tightly we became one animal, one mind. The depth of my yearning was shocking. It had been a long time. But then it hit me: *Oh wow! He reminds me of Peter.*

Stop it! I yelled at myself. *Just stop.* Any relationship, no matter how good, would only end in grief. There was nothing worth the pain that came with profound loss and turned into a dull, never-ending ache. Hadn't I already suffered all the loss I could stand? Hadn't I sworn never to expose myself again?

Oh god! I excused myself from our table and walked over to the table where Julian sat with two guys.

"Hi," I said to him, loudly. The jukebox was blaring.

"Hi," he replied with a gentle smile and blue eyes deep enough to swim in.

"I'm sure you hear this all the time, but I love your music. It really speaks to me." Julian's cheeks flushed pink and for a moment he looked ready to crawl under the table.

Then he gazed into my eyes and said, "Thank you." After a pause lengthy enough to teeter on awkwardness, the man sitting on Julian's right laughingly elbowed him in the ribs. Julian startled and gestured to the seat next to him, the only empty seat at the table. "Oh! Um, would you like to sit down?"

I glanced over at Robin and Lon. They were having a spirited discussion.

What am I doing?

"Yes, thanks, for just a minute. I'm Kerri Gordon," I said, shaking Julian's invitingly warm hand. Introductions were made 'round the table. The two sunny, wisecracking guys were Julian's friends. He introduced Jeffrey and Ben as members of a club band from Manhattan, one I had heard occasionally on WNEW-FM radio.

Ben, freckled and sporting a mound of bronze ringlets, faced me and said, "Julian here has written some of our best songs."

"Would you believe," added Jeffrey, a good-looking man with dreadlocks and high cheekbones, "tonight was Jule's very first time playing in public? Yeah, it's true! And he wrote every one of them songs." Jeffrey and Ben nodded approvingly in Julian's direction.

I looked at Julian with new admiration as his face pinked up again.

Ben flagged down the server and ordered a round for Julian and me. With a wink to Julian, his friends said they had to get back to the city for a late-night gig. They hugged Julian and me in turn, and Jeffrey gave me a kiss on the cheek. Laughing and romping like schoolboys, they went out into the night.

Julian leaned over and spoke in my ear. "I hope you're not offended, but are you here with an, um, adult? I mean, are you legal to drink?"

Oh shit! I'll have to perfect the makeup. I was well used to the question, and lately I'd started using a touch of makeup to appear the age I was supposed to be. Apparently, it didn't work too well. "It's no problem; I'm old enough."

Julian's eyebrows lifted and came together in a most charming way. "It's only . . . honestly, you look too young to be in a bar."

I gave him my best smile. "Really, it's fine. I'm carded a lot. I'm nearly thirty-two, but people tell me all the time I look a lot younger."

Julian slapped himself on the forehead. "Oh man! Sorry! You just . . . you look so young, and, well, um, I'm only twenty-nine."

"It's no problem, really. I'm used to it."

His eyes sparkled when he laughed.

From where I sat with Julian, I could see Robin grinning and giving me a thumbs-up, which I took to mean I should stay where I was. Julian and I began exploring each other with questions and stories. He described nights waiting tables to tide himself over while he developed his music business. I offered amusing anecdotes about my high school students, just to see Julian smile. He told me about growing up in Manhattan, and that his love of music had been fostered by the many concerts his parents had taken him to.

After I said I was especially moved by "Their Light Forever," Julian replied, "I believe we're surrounded by the love of those who've cherished us but passed on, and we can perceive that love by simply pausing to embrace it."

Something old and dark fell off my shoulders.

Before we took our leave, Julian asked for my phone number. Craving a normal life, I pushed back thoughts of the possible repercussions, wrote my number on a napkin, and handed it to him.

The next morning, Julian called, inviting me to a picnic lunch at his home on Lake Truesdale in South Salem. Could I make it that afternoon? As I ransacked my closet and drawers for the perfect outfit, I imagined Julian removing it. After nearly emptying my closet, I settled on a midriff-baring bell-bottoms set and threw it on just as the taxi blasted its horn.

The cabby couldn't find Julian's street and didn't have a map. Instead of radioing in to get directions, he kept driving around, searching. I became more and more annoyed at this display of macho, and livid when he ignored my requests to call dispatch for directions, turn down the music, or put out his cigarette.

Opening the window for fresh air had cooled my nervous sweat, but my hair blew around as if I were in a typhoon. After more than forty minutes driving around in circles, the driver at last radioed the dispatcher for directions, and I decided it was time I learned to drive. We arrived at Julian's in ten more minutes. I didn't give the driver a tip.

I tried to relax as I hurried down the driveway and, shivering, ran my fingers through my tangled hair. Julian's cedar-sided cottage above Lake Truesdale was set behind a split-rail fence nearly obscured by mounds of bleeding hearts, bluebells, and spiraea. The liberal sprinkling of pastel pinks and blues evoked one of Peter's Impressionist paintings. My finger shaking, I rang the bell.

When Julian opened the door, his smile and warmhearted greeting put me at ease, and his welcoming hug sent thrills pulsing through my body. I inhaled a hint of sandalwood.

I had never acquired a taste for modern decor yet liked the foyer's chic brass chandelier and the parlor's Danish furniture. Teak shell chairs with tan cushions sat opposite a matching sectional, all complemented with arched, brass reading lamps.

I was stopped in my tracks by a floor-to-ceiling mural of *Earthrise*, the photo taken from lunar orbit ten years earlier.

"A friend and I watched the *Apollo 8* broadcast on Christmas Eve," I said, gesturing toward the mural. "The picture is much more spectacular in color. If I remember correctly, one of the astronauts said, 'The vast loneliness is awe-inspiring and it makes you realize just what you have back on Earth.'"

"Yes, that was the command module's pilot, Lovell. He was missing his family at Christmas."

We contemplated the mural.

Then Julian asked sunnily, "Would you like something to drink?"

"Just water, please, no ice."

The back wall was entirely glass doors, beyond which a deck overlooked the lake. I could see Julian's grassy lawn with its flagstone path sloping gently down to the water, where a large weeping willow stood next to a dock and rowboat. A pair of swans crossed the lake's surface, the sun slanting off each ripple of their trailing wakes.

Julian handed me a tumbler, and I settled into a curved rosewood-and-leather lounge chair, its soft, buttery warmth wrapping around me. Putting his glass on a coaster on the teak coffee table, Julian took a seat on the sectional.

"I like your place," I said.

"Thanks. But the house isn't my doing; it belonged to my parents. I inherited it last year when they died. I'd been saving for a house of my own but hadn't made enough writing songs or waiting tables. My parents had just bought this house and lived here only a month before . . ." Julian hesitated and rubbed his eye. "They never had the chance to finish unpacking. Some things aren't my style, but I can't bring myself to change anything. I'm glad my folks had good taste."

"Yes, they did." Feeling Julian's pain, I said, "I'm so sorry about your parents."

"Thank you, Kerri. This year's been tough. As an only child, I was really close to them. When it happened, the cops called me at work and said my parents had been injured in an accident and were in serious condition. I practically flew to the hospital, but, once I got there, the doctors told me they'd been killed instantly. A truck ran them over in a crosswalk. I couldn't believe it and screamed that I wanted to see them." Julian worked his hands over his knuckles and palms as if trying to rub away greasy dirt. "I wish I could remember Mom and Dad the way they were before. Not that—that gruesome image."

"How awful," I said. My nails were digging into my elbows. I went to the sectional, sat down, and gave Julian a hug.

"I shouldn't have told you that," he said, head bowed.

"It's good you told me. That's what friends are for." *More than friends,* I hoped.

Julian pressed my hand. "What about you, Kerri? Tell me about your family."

I winced, not ready for that conversation. *Oh, what the heck.*

"I grew up in Philadelphia. When I was eleven, my parents, sister, and grandfather all became ill with food poisoning and died while we were on vacation in France. After that, I was raised by an aunt and a boarding school."

Julian paled. "Good god, Kerri! That's terrible! You were so young." Julian enveloped me in a consoling embrace.

I sniffled into his shoulder until I regained my composure, and then said, "It's okay. It was a long time ago, Julian."

We gazed at each other, eyes locked—the eyes, where two souls connect.

After long moments, Julian said, "Should we have our picnic?"

As we walked down the flagstones to the lake, I turned around and marveled that what I had thought was a cottage was in fact a three-story house built on a slope leading down to the lake. I admired the garden's emerging lilies, irises, and gladiolas. Thick-trunked red oaks edged the side yard to the right of the house. Because Julian's acre was on the lake's neck, it was quiet and private, though not so secluded we couldn't see the top floor of a maroon house peeking through lush trees on the opposite shore. We spread a blanket near the water's edge to have our lunch under the willow.

"Chicken and artichoke with Gruyère," Julian said, handing me a sandwich. Just then, a goose landing on the dock startled and scattered a nearby mallard and her half-dozen ducklings. We watched with amusement as the tiny fuzzballs paddled frantically to get back into formation behind their mother.

I took a bite of the sandwich and exclaimed as best I could with my full mouth, "This sandwich is delicious!"

"Mom's recipe." The corners of Julian's eyes crinkled with his smile.

Julian and I talked for hours that warm spring afternoon. Because his parents' death had caused him to face how short life could be, Julian had summoned the courage and drive to follow his dream of singing and playing in public the songs he composed. Julian said he'd enjoyed his first time performing for an audience and wanted to continue to do so, but he needed the steady income of writing songs for others.

Because Julian was too polite to pry, I found myself opening up more to him than I had with anyone besides Robin. I employed my skill at weaving together omissions and truth, so my conversation with Julian felt natural and full, although a sliver of guilt prickled my skin. As the afternoon waned, the lake shimmered and glowed with a new intensity—even the plainest rocks were now wondrous. Everything was more vibrant with Julian there.

Julian and I became inseparable friends that day and, before long, soul mates. Our ideas, philosophies, and interests were remarkably in tune. When we discussed politics, I thought it extraordinary for a twenty-nine-year-old to have such a mature perception of life, even wisdom. We had mutual concerns for the environment, the downtrodden, and the underserved. Neither of us could tolerate prejudice. Julian appreciated not just music but shared my love of the other arts as well. He and I had a surprising ability to finish each other's sentences, as if we'd known each other for decades.

One night about a week later, Julian drove me back home after a light dinner at the lake house. I unlocked the door to my condo and turned to him.

He whispered, "Good night, sweet Kerri," and bent to kiss me.

Julian's lips were soft and tasted of mint and wine. As his fingertips traced the lines of my cheekbones, I was certain sparks of electricity were visible between his fingers and my cheek. Our deep and lingering kiss sent the sparks flashing over my whole body. I had never wanted a man so much.

Still holding my face in his hands, Julian pushed my door open with his knee. We crossed the threshold as one and closed the door on the world.

When my world finally exploded into fractured lights of pleasure, I had no need for air, no need for light. Only Julian. Resting my head on Julian's chest as he gently stroked my hair, I luxuriated in his scent, musky and rich sandalwood in sunshine. I listened as his thudding heart returned to a calmer rhythm. It felt as if I'd been starving for years and had just dined on the most splendid meal. My world was complete. Serene.

I was nearly asleep, and still smiling, when Julian asked, "Kerri, where are the pictures of your family?"

My eyes flew open. "What?"

"Don't you have any family photos? Your walls are surprisingly bare."

I pulled away.

"Huh? What'd I . . .? Oh man, I'm so sorry, Kerri. I didn't—"

"It's nothing. I'm a little cold, that's all." I ran to the bathroom and wrapped myself in my robe.

<hr />

Ours was a whirlwind courtship, and Julian proposed two months after we met.

I panicked. How could I answer? I knew, I *knew* it was dangerous, but I already loved this man with an intensity that surprised me.

As Kerri, I was almost five years Julian's senior, but in truth, I was ancient. "Julian, doesn't it bother you to be marrying an older woman?"

Laughing at the notion, Julian replied, "In my eyes, darling Kerri, you are ageless."

Julian wouldn't have laughed had he known he'd unwittingly hit the bullseye. For so long, I had suffered a life apart, always a step removed from my friends, avoiding entanglements, and reinventing myself every fifteen years or so. I would have sold my soul to have a relationship in which I could love and be loved, fully and truthfully.

I was already happier and closer to Julian than to anyone since Peter, but for a while I felt disloyal to Peter. As I spent more time with Julian, I recognized that a person, instead of taking the place of another, could fill one's heart in different and important ways. Even so, because my agelessness remained a palisade to complete intimacy with Julian, I would always need to hold back part of myself.

Why couldn't I be upfront, just this once? Was our relationship strong enough to stand up to the truth? I couldn't answer the question but knew I would have to eventually. Just not today, lord forgive me. I forced myself to shake off my fears.

Wasting no time, Julian and I planned a July wedding at the lake house. He chose Ben as his best man. When I told Robin about Julian's proposal and asked her to be my matron of honor, she screamed and jumped up and down with unbridled glee.

On our wedding day, a glorious summer Sunday, I stepped out the rear basement door onto the patio and paused to wait for Jeffrey. A pair of swans sailed offshore, the brilliant white of their plumage playing hide-and-seek with the sun as clouds meandered by. Scents of phlox and summer sweet perfumed the warm breeze, and song sparrows trilled in celebration. Julian, sharply handsome in a beige linen suit, stood with Ben, Robin, and a Unitarian minister under a wildflower-trimmed gazebo near the dock. I wore an ivory moiré gown studded with pearls and had orange blossoms in my bouquet and twined in my updo. A sea of beaming faces near the gazebo turned my way.

I took Jeffrey's arm, and we stepped toward the gazebo. As another of Julian's friends began playing Grieg's "Morning Mood" on her classical guitar, something stopped me.

I'm only marrying Julian to make myself happy. What about his happiness? I am a liar and a selfish coward. This is terrifying. If he finds out the truth—if we're married, he will find out. How can I deal with this? Will he freak out and leave me? Will he hate me? What will I do when he dies? Oh my god, I can't do this!

My knees buckled, but Jeffrey's strong arm kept me upright. Julian stood at the gazebo like an angel bathed in sunlight.

I love him so much it hurts.

"Are you okay?" Jeffrey asked.

After a moment, I nodded. We proceeded toward the gazebo, Julian's love drawing me to him. Before I knew it, we were speaking our vows.

"Kerri, I promise to love you always, to listen to you, to help you shoulder any challenges. I promise to be your best friend. I will stand by you until I can stand no more. My life is yours."

At Julian's words, I could barely speak and fought to keep my tears at bay.

"My Julian, my everything, I promise to be by your side always. When times are hard, I will be there for you. I promise to help you reach your dreams. I will love you beyond time itself."

We shared a long kiss, husband and wife.

A massive, white tent in the side yard brimmed with nearly three hundred guests. In attendance were Julian's assorted relatives, friends, and fans, as well as Robin and Lon, some of my Du Bois Academy coworkers, students, and their parents. I felt my long-gone family's love surrounding me, just as Julian had said. I floated through the rest of our wedding day, dancing and smiling nonstop. Judging by the length and volume of the festivities, everyone had a great time dancing to music performed by Julian's friends and hoisting toast after toast to the bride and groom.

The menu we had chosen was a nod to Julian's German and Danish roots and included a traditional wedding soup and noodles and countless platters of smørrebrød, the Danish finger sandwiches with fancy smoked meats and fish on dark rye, each more delectable than the last. Julian and

I drank from a silver Hochzeitsbecher, an ingenious chalice shaped like a maiden holding a swiveling cup that allowed bride and groom to drink simultaneously without spilling a drop and symbolized our new, unified life. The wedding cake was a magnificent kransekake, a towering tree of almond and meringue rings stacked from large to small and adorned with loops of icing and slivers of candied orange. Instead of jointly cutting the cake as in American tradition, we lifted the top ring off the cake. Five more rings stuck to and lifted off with the first, while Julian's relatives hooted and cheered.

Julian whispered in my ear, "It means we'll have five children."

I drew back and looked at my grinning husband with wide eyes. *Oh god, what a mess! What have I done?*

We left on our wedding trip that evening, Julian calming me during my first airplane flight with the aid of a few mai tais. I stared out the window in wonder as we flew through an awe-inspiring sunset. Clouds in pinks and corals soon deepened to crimson and took on an iridescence and expanse I had never imagined. Then the sun withdrew behind us, and the spectacle darkened from electric purple to star-jeweled blackness.

Arriving at Bermuda's airport, Julian and I stepped into the balmy, comforting atmosphere that seduces people to lie on the pink sand beaches and stay. We had a fantasy vacation. Julian was an ideal travel companion, adventurous and willing to try anything. He rented motor scooters, and it was both hair-raising and exhilarating to ride them through Bermuda's green hills. Bermuda's cuisine was first-rate, especially the fish soup with fresh crusty bread and sherry pepper sauce, shark hash, and black rum cake. Best of all, some of the beaches were secluded enough to swim nude and make love enveloped in the fragrance of briny air and the sounds of surf and whistling tree frogs.

After a long day's work a few months after our wedding, I sautéed chicken piccata while Julian prepared the salad. We shared stories about our day.

I described ninth-grade biology class. "We were working on parasitic plants, and I was introducing haustoria, one of the mechanisms parasites use to get nutrients from their host plants. When I asked if anyone knew what a haustorium is, Lilah Sommer's hand shot up. She said, and I kid you not, 'My Mom says a haustorium is where hookers hang out.'"

Julian nearly choked.

"Exactly!" I said, as we burst into laughter.

"Kids say the funniest things," Julian said, still chuckling. He set down the chef's knife on the cutting board and came over to me, tenderly putting his hands on my waist and nuzzling the back of my neck. "*Our* kids will be amazing. Maybe we should start our family right now?"

I felt a chill. This was a dangerous subject. "So soon? Julian, we've just married. Heck, we've only known each other a short while. We should have some time for ourselves for a bit, don't you think?"

Still speaking to the back of my neck, Julian murmured, "Honey, I feel like I've known you forever. And to be honest, I worry about our age. I don't want your biological clock ticking away our chances for a family."

I flipped and prodded the pieces of chicken as I tried to slow my rapid breathing, afraid I'd hyperventilate. What could I say? *Ha-ha. Don't you worry about my clock, no indeed! It's the damn Duracell Drumming Bunny, it runs longer and longer still.* I had ached for a family for too many years. God, how I wanted to tell Julian *Yes!* I wanted to have that butterfly flutter of life in my belly, to feel the rush of electricity in my breasts when a rosebud mouth latched on, to hold a plump hand while walking down the street.

I had hope there was a chance my child might be ageless. If not—I would never, ever be able to survive the loss of another child. I couldn't risk that trauma on a hope.

I removed the skillet from the burner and turned off the stove. Dying inside, I turned to face Julian. "I'm sorry. We should have talked about this before. The truth is, I don't want to have children."

Julian's eyes widened in shock. "What the hell, Kerri? Are you kidding? You're damn straight we should have talked about this!"

I edged toward the sink, away from Julian's searing anger. "Julian, I'm so sorry. But I have my reasons."

He stood there, massaging his temples with his palms. Then, he pulled his fingers through his hair as if trying to comb away his pain.

"Before we married, we talked about so much . . . so many things. I thought nothing was hidden. I thought you loved me, Kerri."

"I do love you, Julian, more than anything. You have to understand."

"Understand what?" he asked, coldly.

I hesitated, preparing to speak the lie I had planned weeks ago. Julian's blue eyes were hard and icy. "Well?"

I reflexively brought a hand to my throat. "I was afraid, afraid to tell you, I didn't know how you'd take it. It would be a . . . having kids would be a risk, a big risk." I shuddered. "Hemophilia runs in my family."

How could I tell Julian the truth, that it would be unendurable to remain young while time dulled my children's eyes, curved their spines, and devoured their lives.

Julian glared at me, his lips in a tight, pale line. Then he muttered what sounded like a few swear words under his breath, grabbed his jacket and car keys, and stalked out of the kitchen.

"Where are you going?"

"I don't know," he spat. "I just know I can't deal with you right now."

"Please, can't we talk about it?"

"When I get back. If I get back."

I saw a vision of his car speeding, careening. "Please don't go! You're so angry."

"Nothing gets by you, does it, Kerri?" Out he went, slamming the door behind him.

I needed to speak to Robin, but I was so upset, I suddenly wasn't sure of her number. I opened my address book, but my tears wet the page and clouded the ink.

The next morning when Julian returned, he gave me nothing but icy looks and the cold shoulder.

Confronting me while I sat reading a book on the fourth evening of his silent treatment, Julian said, "Thinking about what you said and about what I should do got me nowhere. So, I talked to a shrink today. When you said you didn't want kids, I overreacted. I'm sorry. Since we have so much in common, I assumed you wanted kids. I understand why you don't want to chance having a precariously ill child, but I can't understand why you kept it from me. Kerri, I'm just asking you to be honest with me from now on."

I didn't want to lie again. "I'll try."

Julian's face reddened. "At least that's honest." He rubbed at the stubble under his chin, as if he'd found an unshaved area of beard. "What if we adopt? We could still have a family, a kid we could love as our own."

I picked at a corner of the book. Adopting was a big sacrifice for Julian. I had considered adoption when Peter and I remained childless, but now I couldn't because I knew the child would grow old and die before my eyes. I began to feel nauseated. "I'm not sure, Julian. It's not the same."

"Jesus, Kerri, why can't we just try this?"

He waited for my assent, but unable to answer, I stared at my book. Julian heaved a sigh and stomped downstairs. Soon the sounds of angry strumming blared from his music studio. I stood up and paced the room, my feet moving involuntarily in time to the beat. Not a day passed without Julian pressing me about adoption. He was ill-humored because I repeatedly demurred. After a week of this, no longer able to stand the distance between us, I allowed him to think I'd given in. Julian's elation made me weep.

A social worker came to our house to do an evaluation. When she phoned with a follow-up question, I told her adopting a child was my husband's idea, and I had gone along with it only under pressure. I said I could never raise another person's child. She sounded shocked, but agreed when I asked her to keep our conversation confidential.

Julian, thinking we had been rejected as adoptive parents, sought without success to learn why. Eventually, he stopped calling the agency and stopped bringing up the subject. But it seemed as if Julian's inner light had shadowed.

So, in addition to keeping my past hidden, guilt weighed heavy upon me. Being too cowardly to tell Julian the truth as I parried his questions and gave him partial answers or outright lies, I had deprived him of one of life's greatest joys. I had, without giving the slightest warning, let him marry into a nightmare.

My secret was an iron wedge between us that would grow larger as time went on. A lasting marriage required more than commitment, more even than friendship. It required the bonds of honesty and trust.

My brain churned. I had trouble concentrating on tasks at hand and sometimes forgot the mundane. I purchased five cans of noodle soup at the grocery store, although our pantry shelves were fully stocked with them. Occasionally, I forgot midsentence what I was saying in front of class. Once after work, I found my car battery dead. I had forgotten to turn off the lights when I arrived at school that morning.

I sorely missed the perfect love Julian and I should have had.

One warm night that September, Julian asked if I wanted to go for a moonlight row on the lake. He bailed rainwater from our aluminum rowboat while I finished creating a lesson plan for my ninth-grade biology class trip to Teatown Lake to study its ecology. Hearing Julian call, I put the work on top of unopened mail on the bookshelf above my desk and ran down the hill to the dock. After a kiss, Julian steadied the boat, and I climbed in.

Soft breezes kept autumn at bay and backlit clouds drifted across the sky. The moon shone full and bright white, casting an ethereal luster as we glided through the water.

This was it. It was time to take the leap. My heartbeats sprinted after one another and my muscles tensed so tight that my lungs strained for air.

"Julian . . ." My tongue felt swollen in my mouth. I told myself to calm down.

Julian pulled in the oars. "Kerri, what's up?"

"Julian, I have to tell you something I've never told anyone. And it's going to sound really weird." Those words out, my heartbeats slowed.

I unburdened myself as our boat bobbed on the lake's currents and we rode waves of emotion. Julian's expression changed from incredulity to rapt interest, to bewilderment and, ultimately, to stunned amazement. Finally, I had nothing more to tell. Julian slumped, head in hands.

Please, please, I silently begged.

After long seconds, Julian straightened. "Oh, Kerri," he said softly. His eyes in the moonlight were clearly lit with one sentiment. It was not disdain, but compassion. I blew out my breath in a long exhalation through rounded lips, feeling as if I had been holding it for centuries.

"Let's go in," I said. "I have something to show you."

Saying nothing more, Julian picked up the oars. As we rowed toward our dock, only the sound of oars slicing the glassy surface cut through the insects' ringing maraca chorus.

We walked wordlessly up to the house. Julian followed me into the bathroom and watched as I removed all my waterproof makeup with trembling hands. Beholding my youthful face, he grabbed onto the sink for support.

After collecting himself, Julian said with a wry smile, "I'll be damned. I knew I was marrying an older woman, but I didn't know how much older." Looking anxious, he said, "Or how much younger."

I reached out to Julian. We clasped each other in an embrace made pure by truth, and wept. I had at last gotten what must have been the strangest secret in history off my chest. I was free.

Drained, we lay down on the bed and held one another. Julian brought my hand to his lips. "Oh, Kerri. I . . . I can hardly find the words. This explains so much. You not wanting kids. No family photos. My god, what you've been through!"

"I want you to know, Julian, our love gave me the strength to finally tell you the truth."

I wondered how I would survive Julian's mortality. Then it occurred to me: surviving was what I did best.

He had more questions about my life, but my distracted mind at first couldn't take them in. I heard him ask, "Are you okay?"

I focused on Julian's eyes. "As okay as I'll ever be. What were you asking?"

"Do you think this has ever happened to anybody else?"

"I don't know. I've done a lot of research, but I still don't know. Have you heard of progeria?"

"Yeah, it's that disease where kids look really old." He paused, and then exclaimed, "Oh man! The opposite of what's happened to you!"

"Maybe. It's genetic, so maybe my, um, condition is caused by some sort of gene mutation. As far as I know, everyone in my family was normal."

"We can try to find out," Julian offered.

"I've thought about going to some of the scientists doing aging research, but I'm afraid of ending up a freak defined only by my mutation. Our life would be chaos."

"Kerri, I swear on our love, I'll never tell anyone your secret." He stroked my face and then asked, "Are you as healthy as a young woman? I mean, do you think you'll *ever* age, or . . . die?"

I twisted a long strand of his golden hair around my index finger.

"Julian, I haven't aged a day since reaching adulthood. I'm never sick, and my injuries heal almost immediately. So, as far as I know, barring a catastrophic accident that leaves me in pieces, or some other such horror, I'm immortal."

My blouse instantly soaked through with sweat. Uttering that word for the first time, I again saw myself alone at the end of the universe. Teetering on the edge of collapse, I keened, "Noooo!"

Julian clutched me tightly and rocked me, reassuring me that all would be well. My shaking subsided to shivers, and when I became still, Julian said, "Kerri, when we were on the boat, I was shocked and couldn't understand everything you said. Would you . . . would it be upsetting . . . could you tell me more about your . . . past? Your life?"

Julian listened raptly during the hours it took to recount my prior lives. He asked questions, gasped in surprise, laughed at the funny parts, cried with me over my losses and, above all, over the death of my child.

The moon was down and the day was breaking by the time I was through. My secret had been a rope knotted inside me for most of my life, and now it had come untied. In its place were both exhaustion and liberation.

Then the knife of guilt cut through. I said, "Julian, I lied to you. I should have told you the truth before locking you into this marriage."

Julian began to object, but I held up my hand. "Please, wait, let me finish. I am so, so sorry for what I've done to you. It's completely unfair. The truth is, I can't be a mother again because my child would die before me. You don't ever get over that kind of loss. Not ever. And now, I'm depriving you of the chance to experience the joy of being a parent. Julian, can you ever forgive me? I won't blame you if you want a divorce."

He breathed raggedly. "Kerri, life isn't supposed to be perfect. But I want you to know that mine is, being with you." He took my hand. "You did what your . . . extraordinary circumstance made you do. I understand, as much as I can. All I know is, our love is so strong that nothing will keep us apart. Not your age, not your past, nothing. We're here for each other, always. So, no, Kerri. I do not want a divorce. You are forgiven."

I smiled into Julian's eyes and said with all sincerity, "I am so lucky to have such an incredibly understanding husband."

Needing to be sure, I asked, "Julian, it won't be too hard living with someone who'll always be twenty, while you grow old?"

"I can't answer that; I just don't know. But I do know I will do, or be, anything for you. And, I agree about not having kids. Let's enjoy each day, Kerri, take it as it comes. Who knows, maybe I'll never reach old age, or maybe you'll die in a crazy accident. People would give anything to be in your place. I would have. But after learning your history, now I'm not so sure. You and I will do whatever it takes to make our marriage work. We'll figure it out."

Julian took my face in his hands and kissed me. "Everyone else tries to live to the fullest because, for us, life is so short. Your limitless life means limitless possibilities."

Yes! Limitless possibilities. I hadn't looked at it that way. Filled with a rush of optimism, I covered Julian's face with kisses.

"Thank you, my darling. You've given me a whole new lease on life. I feel like I could fly."

Julian grinned. "Please don't take off till I tell you how much I adore and admire you, Kerri Lange."

He studied me. "I wish I could have known your family, seen the ones who brought you into this world."

"Just a minute." Jumping off the bed, I went to the closet and dug out my hidden treasure lockbox of memorabilia and photographs, unopened for years, the sight of long-dead cherished ones too agonizing. Sometimes when their images came unbidden to my mind's eye like condolence cards strung along the stairway of my life, I was left staggering.

Yet that morning with Julian, I lovingly ran my fingers along each faded photo as if it were a bead on a rosary, before handing it to Julian and naming the faces.

For long minutes he studied the photos, speechless. Finally, he whispered, "So cool. I see you in them."

I pulled Trudy's locket from under my shirt and opened it. Cecile's curl shone. Julian, seeing my tears break free, cradled me in his arms.

"I guess you have a child after all, with me to manage."

Smiling, Julian said, "I hope you'll start using your real name again. Naissa. It's a beautiful name. You know what's ironic, right? *Naissa* means *reborn* in French."

"You remember you married a former French teacher, don't you?" We both giggled.

I did use Naissa again, but only between the two of us.

Some months later, Julian showed deep dedication to our marriage by having a vasectomy.

Julian found joy connecting with audiences through his music, sharing his feelings and giving pleasure and new understanding. He worked with an agent to sell more of his songs to other artists while still performing regularly. We were elated when he cut a record that received abundant airplay, and the royalties and numerous gigs made it possible for him to leave his waiter job. Even though we could have lived well off my substantial nest egg, Julian preferred to make his own way.

I continued to work at Du Bois Academy as a science teacher until it became too hard to pretend I was aging. I loved motivating the upcoming generation to care about the natural world and enlisting them as defenders of the Earth so the planet might be livable forever. The day I left the academy, using Julian's touring schedule as an excuse, I felt as if I were walking away from my salvation. I also had to minimize contact with friends so they wouldn't see through the makeup. This was most difficult with Robin, because having her in my life was a joy. We kept in touch by phone, but it wasn't the same.

Stepping away from my friend and from teaching was a steep price to pay for staying with Julian, but I couldn't refuse the chance to be with him long-term. I would do whatever was in my power to make our marriage work. Julian adapted well to my aberration, despite experiencing challenges. Once, I was making a dinner salad for us with produce from our garden, when I sliced my thumb, deeply.

Julian, who'd been getting silverware to set the table, yelled, "Holy crap, Naissa!"

He frantically grabbed a towel and wrapped it around my hand. "I *told* you not to use that knife—I still have to sharpen it. You've practically cut your thumb off!"

I unwrapped the white towel, and it was stained with a wide blob of crimson, the sight of which made Julian blanch. Then he gasped. The gash had stopped bleeding, and its edges were fusing.

"Ah! Thank god," Julian exhaled. His hands were shaking. He took the towel and tossed it into the trash can, and then did the same with the bowl of salad, which had been dressed with some of my blood. As Julian went back to the garden to gather more lettuce and tomatoes, I heard him humming a lilting, new melody.

Before long, my life of leisure didn't suit me. I deepened my environmental research and started writing letters under pseudonyms to editors of various newspapers and representatives, encouraging people to learn about the issues and support environmentally positive legislation. Piece by piece, legislation to protect the environment was adopted, but all battles were hard fought. The slow and difficult nature of change in the nation's culture and habits was at times discouraging.

I also expanded my creative range. When I was a girl, Father had taught me a little about jewelry making and design, and by this time my drawing skills had improved. Designing and creating jewelry seemed a good fit for a new challenge, so I hired a local, high-end jewelry fabricator to come to the house and teach me his art. The jeweler, Jonah Kleinicke, was the latest in a long line of German jewelers who owned a well-respected shop in nearby Peekskill.

I looked forward to my lessons with Jonah. Pouring myself into the work, I eventually became one of his suppliers.

With my hammering, and Julian's need for quiet while composing and recording, it was clear we needed separate spaces for our work. We designed and constructed two soundproof studios on the ground level, with plenty of space for Julian's collection of recording equipment and my tools and workbench.

<hr />

One midsummer day in 1984, I took the bus to White Plains to shop for lighting for my studio and a gift for Julian. His thirty-fifth birthday was coming up that weekend. The day had begun cool, but the high summer sun was aggravated by thick, swampy air. As I walked the crowded sidewalks, I scanned passersby as usual, hoping I wouldn't see a face from my recent lives.

I worried about people questioning my age and unearthing my secret. I was using heavier makeup to create the impression of facial lines and shadows, but I needed to do a better job of looking older. Julian, concerned about his limelight revealing my youthful face, stopped performing regularly to keep us out of the public eye and instead focused on his songwriting. I was still avoiding Robin and was becoming reluctant to go out with Julian and his friends. I cared for all of them very much, and especially loved going to Jeffrey and Ben's gigs because their music was so freeing and complex and, well, *fun*.

It was becoming harder to relax and enjoy myself. I stressed about the consequences of staying in one place years longer than I ever had. How would I create the appearance of a woman in her forties? Her fifties? Her eighties? Plastic surgery was out of the question because any alterations would likely revert and heal immediately.

While I was in Saks getting Julian's gift, I decided to stop at the makeup counter to see if someone could help my aging process appear more natural and convincing.

"Do you have anything to help me look more mature?" I asked the girl behind the counter.

Her brow furrowed. "Um, well, we have some Mary Quant from London. They've been around a long time, since, like, the sixties, I think."

I slowly exhaled my frustration and gave the girl's name tag a quick glance. What an odd spelling. "Tiffani, let's try this again. What if I want to look older, say in my forties?"

The face across the counter couldn't have been more than seventeen, even with the perfectly applied makeup: thin, penciled eyebrows, shimmery purple eyelids, rose-tinted cheeks, and frosted mauve lips. I was getting too old for this.

"You mean, like, for a costume party?" Tiffani asked, confused at my request.

I rolled my inner eyes at Tiffani. Who could understand wanting to disguise oneself, to hide the beauty of youth? I recalled the time I overheard Aunt Josephine and Uncle James talking about me and whether I was "marriageable."

"She's pretty enough," James had said, "but, alas, forgettable."

"Yes," agreed Josephine, "How does one successfully debut a girl who has no distinctive features?"

The memory of it still made me wince, but after all these years, I appreciated that an average face brought less scrutiny.

"Um, yes, a costume party."

"Well, okay . . . First maybe you can try a powdered foundation? And then use loose Airspun powder over that? To, you know, make wrinkles? Airspun even smells like old lady. And smudge a little sable below your eyes? And for sure stay away from mascara? If you want to look really old, you could, like, make some bumps with wax pencil. Do that before the foundation layer, you know?"

Like, really?

"Chanel makes this great matte color set, you could give it a try?" She pulled a box with a half-dozen rectangles in shades of ivory, beige, and purple and set it reverently on the counter in front of me. I choked when I saw the price but handed over the credit card anyway.

I couldn't get out of there fast enough.

Julian and I had been married fifteen years, and it amazed me that our love and closeness continued to grow. Not having children, we nurtured and devoted ourselves to each other. Apart from working and occasional socializing, our hours at the lake house were suffused with nature's bounty as we delighted in the changes the seasons brought.

On winter weekends, Julian and I cross-country skied on the unplowed road encircling the lake. Or, if the snow had been cleared, we snowshoed through the hushed woods where flurries and the calls of chickadees drifted on the frosty air. The most freeing and exciting experience was skate sailing: holding a small sail to glide on ice skates over the frozen lake. It felt like flying. Cuddling in front of the fireplace, Julian and I gazed out our picture window at a fairy tale snow kingdom with iced tree sculptures sparkling in the sunlight and fat snowflakes dancing on the wind.

By and by, warming rains washed away winter's cold whiteness and brought the land springing back to life with renewed colors and fragrances. Ducks, swans, and geese plied the lake with their downy families. Maples and oaks growing luxuriant with foliage and birdsong swayed over the yard, while young cottontails frolicked on the bright-green broadloom. The beauty of the spring flowers lifted our spirits.

Spring's green world gave way to hot summer days and cooling evening thundershowers, which provided an accompaniment to our lovemaking. Most summer weekends we swam and rowed on the lake, and summer evenings found us on romantic lake cruises. Julian and I watched the radiant bowl overhead go from backlit golden crimson and fuchsia to deep violet, then indigo, and finally onyx with sparkling stars, the moon-silvered clouds drifting by.

On blistering days, we went to Jones Beach. Bodysurfing in the ocean, Julian and I were part of the waves. Seagulls ambled around, heads bobbing up and down, searching for their dinner after most of the beachgoers had departed. Julian and I basked in the tranquility of the salt air.

Our organic garden in the backyard supplemented produce from the local co-op. To make a summer dinner, we just stepped outside and picked lettuce leaves and tomatoes, dug up a couple of carrots, and plucked raspberries from the berry patch. It was wonderful to have fresh, homegrown food. I even canned and froze the excess to augment our larder for the winter months.

Whirling maroon, marigold, and russet leaves heralded fall's arrival. If the weather cooperated, Julian and I made love on the deck in our double reclining chaise, underneath the stars and swooping bats. We picked apples at the local orchard and made applesauce on the stove, filling the house with the warm scent of cinnamon.

Instead of a bedside radio, the moaning winds, cawing crows, drumming rains, and breeze-rustled leaves serenaded us. I was also often serenaded with Julian's music. I marveled at the beautiful progression of his music over time and was proud of him for mentoring young, aspiring songwriters.

I spent hours content in my studio binding metal with stone to create unique and popular jewelry. The pieces I was most proud of were cameos I made of Suzanne and Robin. I modeled Suzanne's on her portrait I'd drawn in New Orleans, which smiled at me from my studio wall, next to my favorite sketch of Robin.

Our lives were fulfilled. Julian and I found joy in our work and surroundings. And in each other.

The year 2000 with its obliterating zeros was a flashing reminder that time would roll my world, my happiness—my Julian—forever into the past. From the first months of marriage, Julian and I had shared an awareness of impending loss most couples don't face until old age. Thus, every moment was precious and we lived life to the hilt.

At night as I waited for sleep to drift in, my mind focused on the shadowy vista of my enemy: time. Trembling, my bones chilled. Julian and I had only been together twenty-two years. It wasn't nearly enough. My love for him still grew every day. Surely, there would be many more years. I needed more.

I must tell research scientists my story. If they could find what I can't—a way to help Julian . . .

Impossible. I can't surrender myself to being a lab rat—it would kill me. And the inevitable notoriety would destroy Julian and his career.

Thoughts of the inescapable future made me retch.

The new millennium was an agent for introspection. I found myself sifting through a century and a half of memories. Too many old friends were gone. Others I had left behind, but I still corresponded with them as long as possible without giving myself away. Semler Family Law, my long-time attorneys, kept a post office box for forwarded mail from friends in my prior lives. I always opened those letters with a mixture of excitement and dread. Eighty-five-year-old Frank Miller was a regular writer, so I knew he and Bill Kuhn were still housemates in San Francisco. Two of my bygone friends had married and traveled the world by boat with their six children. By the time those friends grew old and died, they had grandchildren the world over.

When letters stopped, I wondered what became of their writers and whether they were still alive. After my painful experience at the library in Atlanta, I'd tried to stop caring about them disappearing into death. It didn't work, because when memories of them came back to haunt me, I felt their loss anew.

Eventually, the treasure trove of online information tempted my fingertips, and I surrendered to the urge. With public records and news archives as launching points, my searches meandered the Internet's labyrinth. I learned that Suzanne Durand died in 1986, having divorced her second husband since we'd last corresponded. I found a few of Cousin Claudia's descendants. Apparently, the Leighton family fell from society during the Depression and never recovered.

After a while, it became too distressing to see the demise of people I had known, so I decided again to try to find others with my condition. The Internet made it possible to reach far more people than I ever did with newspaper ads. I found online genealogy groups based around the world, and under fake IDs, posted that I was looking for distant relatives who might have family traits or individual histories of longevity and great health. There were more replies than I expected. Unfortunately, nearly all were spam: people looking for an inheritance, sex, or my credit card login. Some of the replies were viciously hateful. The whole exercise was another frustrating dead end.

———

Turning my head from side to side, I scrutinized the image in the mirror. Even the smallest flaw might have caused questions. And there, on the left side of my neck, was a ripple at the edge of the prosthetic transfer. I sighed, wet the brush, and smoothed the telltale edge. Next, I pulled out the palette of cream makeup and set to work.

Making myself look almost seventy took nearly an hour every time I wanted to leave the house, so I declined invitations more often than not. Even though I was well-practiced by this point, the prosthetics for an older woman were more substantial and the makeup more elaborate than what I needed a few years before. I used to put on my face in half an hour because the prosthetics were paper thin. Not anymore. Now, I even had to apply Pros-Aides to the tops of my hands.

I dabbed at the prosthetic skin on my face and neck with a stipple brush, applying a muted red mottling.

When I first met Julian, I'd been using touches of gray and brown waterproof grease pencils to appear older. A decade later, I was able to create authentic-looking crow's feet and laugh lines with wrinkle stipple and foundation makeup. Then, when I was supposed to be in my sixties, I began using prosthetic transfers, which were so thin and subtle, they were undetectable, even close up. I also found a way to use matte spirit gum to keep the prosthetics in place during hot and humid weather. Online videos were great for providing instruction in professional techniques.

After I sprayed a coat of sealant over my face and neck, I patted on another thin layer of powder. Then, I brushed on a hint of ivory mascara to lighten my otherwise dark lashes, and the effect was convincing. I dabbed on a touch of tooth color to slightly yellow my teeth.

"Naissa, are you coming?" Julian was getting impatient.

"Almost," I called out, and put on some pale lipstick before reaching for the thin, brunette wig with silver roots. It was a little crazy, I knew, trying to look like an older woman who was trying to look younger. One last inspection in the mirror and I was satisfied. I turned off the lights and ran upstairs to Julian tapping his fingers restlessly on the kitchen table. We were off to the polls, where I would vote for the first woman from a major political party to run for president.

<hr/>

Julian and I enjoyed as much of each other's company as we could manage. We attended shows in Manhattan and visited the city's many attractions. Sometimes we traveled to points of interest around the country and abroad. One of our favorite diversions was a game we called *Serendipity*. Going to parks and preserves at dawn, we rambled to see what we would find. We hiked the hills and used an inflatable boat to explore any lakes that turned up along our path.

A small piece of me died every time the end of our life together stole into my thoughts.

<hr/>

The antiseptic odor of disinfectant hit me as soon as I opened the door, but it couldn't mask the underlying stench of illness and grief. My flight impulse nearly won out. Robin, at the end of her life at only seventy-four years, had asked me to come and see her. Although Julian had offered to accompany me, I wanted to do this alone.

Robin and I had kept up our friendship over the years as she progressed through the usual milestones, all seemingly measured by her children: they entered school, excelled in school, graduated, repeat. Music recitals, athletic teams, plays, marriages, a grandchild on the way. Then stage four uterine cancer brought Robin down fast.

Robin's hospital room was flooded with the slanting afternoon sun. Mylar balloons vibrated in the golden glow among many bouquets of flowers. Robin was unrecognizable from the woman I'd seen only a few months ago. Her mottled skin hung slack over her bones, and she appeared to have aged fifteen years, as if someone had sucked all the life out of her with a straw and gnarled her tiny frame.

Robin must have heard my jagged gasp because her eyes opened and found mine. She smiled.

"Kerri, you're here," she whispered. "I'm so glad you've come."

My words stuck in a box I couldn't open. I nodded.

Robin gestured airily toward a putty-colored vinyl chair next to the bed. "Scooch over here. You look amazing. As always."

I sat down and reached for her hand. It was shockingly icy and felt like a small pile of sticks.

"Did you see the kids on your way in? Did you see my miracle grand-baby, Joy, my little Joy?" I shook my head. "Maybe they went for an early dinner," she said, turning her eyes to the door before fixing them on me again. Robin scrunched her sheet. "This is it for me, Kerri. I'm not going to make it through this."

I tried to object, but she quieted me with a small wave of her hand.

"Listen, hon, I got a favor to ask you."

"Anything," I said, and meant it.

After a moment of searching my face, Robin spoke again. "Why don't you tell me your secret? I swear I won't tell a soul." Her nut-brown eyes twinkled.

I tried to smile, and then shrugged. "You know me too well. Listen, I'm sorry you've had such a hard time this year."

Robin's laugh—a soft sputtering far removed from her grand belly laugh—was tinged with impatience.

"Of course, I do *not* know you too well, and that's the point, isn't it? You always give me agita by changing the subject. You've been my best friend for all these years, but I still hardly know a thing about you. Don't you think it's time to spill the beans? You gotta be real with me, for once. This is our last chance."

Robin had a point. She had always given freely of herself, even though our friendship had been one-sided. I had kept my secret from her by evading whenever she tried to get past my armor.

I knew more about Robin's life than I deserved. I didn't want to lie to my best friend again.

In a vase at the foot of the bed, a bouquet of orange zinnias with magenta centers exploded with color in the golden light of the late afternoon. An old feeling of tightness squeezed me, and I had to blink a few times to see the flower clearly. I glanced at the open door. Then, I got up and closed it, returned to my seat, and took Robin's weightless hand in both of mine.

"When you and I first met, I was nearly one hundred eighteen years old."

The corners of Robin's mouth upturned slightly. A perfect *Mona Lisa* smile.

After I told my story and showed Robin the family pictures in my locket, she managed a satisfied grin.

A short while later, Robin and I embraced goodbye. Then she clutched my arm and whispered urgently in my ear.

"You have to tell them, Kerri . . . *Naissa*. Tell someone. Scientists, so they can help you figure it out. You deserve that much. Salut, hon. I love you."

⁕⁕⁕

When I approached Robin's coffin at her wake, I gasped. The heavily made-up figure in the casket didn't look like my Robin. Nevertheless, I placed my fingers on her cold hand, leaned down, and whispered, "I love you, Robin. Goodbye, my dear friend. I miss you so much."

Tears blurring my vision, I was grateful Julian helped me back to my seat.

The next day at the funeral mass, I was too distraught to read the eulogy I'd written for my friend, so Julian did it for me. Afterward at the cemetery, I wasn't much better. The day was steamy, with a heavy haze in the distance. Perspiration ran down my spine and trickled from under my bra, and my makeup itched. Julian, in suit and tie, had wet strands of hair sticking to his reddened forehead. Hand in hand, we walked up a small hill to the gravesite.

Ahead of us, Lon and the children and their relatives moved haltingly up the hill. They pressed close together as if holding each other up, with Dawn and her infant daughter anchoring the small cluster. Robin's mother, staggering under the heat and grief, was supported on either side by Robin's father and brother.

By the time all the mourners arrived at the gravesite, the silver casket was laid on a green-skirted stand. The sun glinted so wildly off the shiny fittings, I reached into my bag for sunglasses.

After all were quiet, the long-robed priest began to drone, "We gather here to commend our sister, Robin Francesca Roselli Ames, to God our Father and commit her body to the earth."

I wondered how he could be in those robes in the same heat as the rest of us and still look cool as if it were a spring day. While the priest droned on, the hot air grew thicker and heavier, a leaden weight clogging my lungs and bearing down on my shoulders and eyelids. The scene around the casket wavered and disappeared.

I was back in Robin's hospital room, where the sun sparkled through the windows, illuminating the vase and zinnias bright as Day-Glo. And Robin, so slight and birdlike in her hospital bed, had pierced me with the steel of her nut-brown eyes.

You have to tell them, Kerri . . . You deserve that much.

Why did Robin have to go? Why did she have to suffer with cancer? At least she'd had three beautiful children, now grown tall and successful from her nurturing. At least she'd seen her grandchild before dying. But her time had been so short.

At the beginning of our friendship, I had silently judged Robin for watching too much TV, for not taking advantage of the new freedoms they called *women's lib*, for not packing up the kids and leaving Lon. Once, I'd needled her about her excessive TV watching, and she became exasperated.

"Kerri, it's like this. You know my marriage isn't exactly a fairy tale. Lon is never home, and he's oblivious when he *is* here. I get no help with chores at all. I'm treated like a scapegoat because problems are somehow all my fault. I've lost control of my children—you've heard how they give me lip. Everything is out of control. But escaping into my shows is something I can control. I can try to fill my emptiness with other lives."

She started to cry. "I'm so tired of yelling at my family. You just don't understand."

I hadn't realized how much of herself Robin had surrendered to her family. How awful to have been stuck in that marriage with a spouse whose only focus was himself. How alone Robin had been, staying with Lon for the sake of disrespectful children. I realized if I were ever a mother again, I would do whatever I could to make our relationships thrive.

I was sure Robin's cancer was a manifestation of stress, lack of respect, neglect, and the misery of unmet vows. Peering into the depths of Robin's sorrow and solitude, I wished I could have hugged her again and told her I understood. At least I'd had the chance to tell Robin the truth. Still, I was ashamed of how one-sided our friendship had been.

You have to tell them, Naissa . . . You deserve that much. You have to tell them.

Robin's voice echoed the phrase again and again in my mind until it gradually faded and the priest's recitation broke through.

"And may the blessing of almighty God, the Father, the Son, and the Holy Spirit remain with you forever."

Julian's arm was around my heaving shoulders.

Voices uttered, "Amen."

Robin's casket was already deep in its hole, flowers scattered over it like a child's game of pick-up sticks. Time reached into my chest and wrung my heart in its fist. Just to the side stood Dawn and her brothers, weeping and smiling as they encircled cooing Baby Joy.

Later, at the repast in Marcello's air-conditioned banquet room, I was unable to eat my food. Julian whispered comforting words as we sat at a back table. Robin's extended family was boisterous, and more than once I was startled to hear her wondrous laugh coming from different corners of the room.

I grasped Julian's hand and felt its heat and pulse of life. Backlit by wall sconces, Julian's Viking profile was as exquisitely featured as the day we met. However, I knew what more direct lighting would reveal: creases etched by time's hands.

Every passing minute was a step closer to another intolerable funeral, another hole in the ground. I fought to not think about it, but the dread stained my thoughts like spreading blood, and I had to grit my teeth to keep from screaming.

Adding to my gloom, I wondered if everyone we knew really thought I was in my late sixties. How much longer could my makeup fool people? Julian had long ago agreed we would assume other identities if it came to it, if my impersonation of an older woman became unworkable. But Julian's music career was still soaring. He had as much work as he could handle and an extensive waiting list. I couldn't let Julian dump the career that meant so much to him.

Robin wasn't entirely right: it wasn't what I deserved. It was what Julian deserved.

"Kerri?" I jerked my attention to Julian.

"Where were you? Didn't you hear me?"

"Sorry, Julian. What did you say?"

"Are you ready?" He looked theatrically toward the exit and held out his hand.

I took his hand. I was ready. I could delay no longer. I had to do something—for Julian.

⚜ ⚜ ⚜

One morning a week later, Julian and I sat on the deck with our coffee and scones. The overnight rain had cleared and broken the heat. Droplets suspended from every leaf and branch of the weeping willow sparkled in the early light. A mild breeze brought on a pattering as drops were loosened from their perches and fell on the vegetation below.

I blew on my steaming brew, the mug a world of warmth in my hands. "Julian," I began, "I think it's time we consider going public."

Julian set down his mug on the cedar table and turned to me. "What?"

"There's a place in Vienna, the Oberlin Institute for Medical Genetics. They're studying the genetics of aging. I think I should talk to them."

Julian blanched. "You can't be serious. I thought you didn't want to reveal yourself. What about . . . well, what they might do to you?"

"I've given this a lot of thought. The Oberlin Institute seems like a good match and their research is promising. If we went to Vienna and told them my story, they might be able to find an answer."

"But . . . but why now? It would change everything for us."

"There are advantages now. I've always needed to know *why*, and if there's anyone else like me. The science has advanced so much, the genetic basis can surely be found. Maybe now there are answers. Your career is strong, so there shouldn't be fallout."

Julian pulled at his sparse hair, causing it to stand up in little spikes. "But your privacy . . . you always said you didn't want to be a lab rat."

I leaned forward and took Julian's face in my hands. "My love. It's time. I must do this. For us."

A sunrise of hope slowly spread across his face.

"I'll call Semler and have them write a nondisclosure agreement. The firm's been really good to me over the years. They've done everything I've ever asked, everything I've needed—even under the radar. I have all confidence they'll write an ironclad NDA. We won't disclose anything unless the Oberlin Institute signs."

Julian's eyes strayed to the top of the willow, as if an answer perched on one of the arching branches. Finally, he sighed. "If you're sure it's what you want. You know I'll support you, no matter what."

It was not the first time I was thankful I had found such a perfect man.

⟡⟡⟡

There would be no appointment with the Oberlin Institute. On October 17, 2019, the day before my lawyers were to approach the institute, Julian died of a burst cerebral aneurism as he walked down the driveway with the day's mail. I saw him crumble mid-stride, letters and catalogs tumbling with him.

My best friend, my soul mate, was no more.

Oh, Julian! Why did my lungs still breathe? Julian's bright light had flared, ripped across the firmament, and was extinguished.

INTERLUDE

CONFIDENTIAL

MEMORANDUM

To: Dr. Alex Vasiliou, CEO

From: V.N. Singh, PhD, Researcher Emeritus

Re: Resignation

Background

The P_0 genome was isolated. Multiple carriers for use in transference methodologies were tested, with many failures. We identified a carrier, and small animal models have proven successful. Today, I was informed that a clone model is undergoing development and was directed to assume responsibility for the project.

I have repeatedly attempted to dissuade you and the rest of management from developing N^2GP therapy for use in the general human population. I have failed on that count. Furthermore, I object to the concept of a clone model and its development—especially without its capable subject—in the strongest possible terms.

Development of N^2GP technology poses substantial ethical and population issues. The risks for unintended consequences in human evolution are enormous to the point of folly. This use of N^2GP in the service of profit is, quite simply, unconscionable.

Resignation

For these reasons, and after thirty-one years of successful research collaboration, I hereby resign, effective immediately.

CONFIDENTIAL

CHAPTER SIX

2019

Naissa

⁘

WITHOUT JULIAN, I would never . . .
Stop!
I could not think. With a mighty effort, I emptied my mind and let nature's music fill it. How else to survive the graveside service, stay on my feet without collapsing, and not scream until my throat bled.

Rain fell in cold, steady beats. I closed my eyes and listened to raindrops springing off umbrellas, reverberating like the rapping of timbale drums.

"Dear God, grant that our brother, Julian Torsten Lange, may sleep here in peace until you awaken him to glory," intoned the minister in a voice on the edge of singing.

Like thousands of tiny fingers on a dayan, the small sister in a pair of Indian table drums, the rain plinked on the green tarp laid along the ground and over the mound of dirt. Far behind me, a torrent poured through a drainpipe with a deep, rhythmic bass, and drops clinked like struck cowbells on top of the pipe where it lay exposed. The pastor's singing stopped.

I opened my eyes.

The mound of flowers on the casket in front of me quietly accepted the rain's muted melody.

All around me, heads were bowed as attendants removed the huge spray of roses from the oaken casket and set it aside. A motor hummed and Julian was lowered into the ground, inch by tortured inch. When the motor at last clicked off, I pulled a white rose from the spray.

As if from a camera hovering above, I saw myself clutching the flower to my chest and falling into the muddy hole.

Coming back to myself, I beheld the rose still clutched in my hand. I willed my unyielding fingers to open and let the delicate bloom slide into the grave. One by one, other mourners dropped flowers onto my Julian in a muffled rhythm. Turning away, I took my leave of Julian and his only love, Naissa Nolan Lange, as the rain continued its lament on my empty soul.

All that remained were my mournful howls for the departed. *Julian. Robin. Frank. Suzanne. Marta. Cecile. Trudy. Grandfather. Father. Mother.*

I was alone, forever.

CHAPTER SEVEN

Rys

I WAS LIKE a wild animal, I know this now. I fought the doctor and aides tooth and nail. What did they expect, between the isolation and tests? You treat a child like an animal, don't be surprised if that's what the child becomes. Then somebody must have figured out that I was a human being because new people came into my life. Aunt and Uncle were scientists, but to me they were a different species from the doctor and aides. They talked to me, looked at me, and seemed to care about me. Eventually, they became a regular part of my life.

Uncle came to my rooms most days. He began by offering small gifts—treats and toys. About this time, more furniture showed up. There was a small table with two chairs, a new, more comfortable bed with a blue-and-white-striped comforter, a plush, golden chair, and wall-mounted lamp. They even screwed two large pictures into the walls. These fascinated me. One was a pristine, white-sand beach next to crystal-clear waters. Another was lush and green, with a family of brightly colored birds in the treetops. I couldn't imagine such places or creatures existed. And colors! They were breathtaking in my all-white room. I spent hours studying those pictures.

When I became less fearful of Uncle, he accompanied me to medical tests and examinations, helping to calm me down, promising treats and rewards if I behaved. I also started daily lessons in the school room. I hadn't even known the room was there because it was behind a previously locked door. The room had books on tidy shelves, a multiscreen on one wall, and a worktable with two chairs. Uncle used the multiscreen for my lessons. He taught me reading, writing, math, and later on, limited history and science.

Aunt arrived at dinnertime and was around overnight. She taught me table manners, helped me get ready for bed, and read stories. I liked the stories and saw myself in them, venturing in imaginary worlds. Some of the stories had fictional kids. I yearned to play and run with real friends, not just imaginary ones.

At night after I fell asleep, I don't know where Aunt stayed. In one of the offices, I guess. She showed up to comfort me whenever I had nightmares. Which was often. Sometimes she read me a story until I fell back to sleep. She was nice to me, but never loving.

As I grew a little older, some of the tests weren't medical. They subjected me to things I'd never seen before, like real animals, sounds, musical instruments, and pics and vids of unknown people. I remember the first time I heard music. It terrified me, but then I slowly uncovered my ears and felt its beauty. I assume they were testing my cognitive abilities. The animals—kittens and puppies, rats, small snakes, frogs, once even a small pig—were my favorites. Their eyes seemed to understand me. I petted them and talked with them, sometimes telling them stories. Other times, there were insects in clear boxes. I loved watching their movements, with their many articulated legs and antennae. I was heartbroken each time Uncle took the animals away at the end of a session. Afterward, Uncle asked me what I thought of the creatures. I never told him how sad I was when he took them away.

I remember the day aides brought what they called a multi-ex into my room. It was a multipurpose piece of exercise equipment and took up a whole corner of the room. I was supposed to use it daily to walk, run, and do strength exercises. At first I hated it, but then I began to enjoy running. I imagined myself on that beach in the picture, the sand between my toes, the sun on my face. I ran for hours. It was my escape.

There were cameras throughout my rooms, of course.

Most nights, a woman with a scarf on her head came in when they thought I was sleeping. She worked quietly dusting, cleaning, mopping, and emptying trash. She would glance at the cameras and then quickly smile at me, in a secret way that made me feel warm inside. Hers was the most beautiful smile with her straight, white teeth softly glowing in the room's dim light. But she was silent. She never said a word.

One night, the woman stopped by the top of my bed. She pointed to one of the cameras, held her finger to her lips in a *sh* sign, and then smiled and nodded at me. I nodded back. Then, she took a small bundle from her pocket and tucked it under the top corner of the mattress, by the wall. She did the *sh* sign once more, smiled, and went on with her cleaning.

I waited a few minutes, and then I rolled over toward the wall and, keeping my hand under the pillow, slowly reached under the mattress and pulled out the package. Sliding under the blanket, I quietly unwrapped it. Lying on a piece of white office paper was a small cube of dense, rich sweetness with green nuts. Now, I know it was pistachio halawa, but at the time, I had no idea. It was the most delicious thing I ever had. After I finished every crumb, I folded the paper up and tucked it back under the mattress. When I peeked out from beneath the covers, the door was quietly closing and the woman was gone.

When I woke in the morning, I felt for the paper, but it was no longer there. All through the day, I thought about the woman and her heavenly treat. It was the first true kindness I'd ever experienced.

I found myself living for the nights when the woman came through the door, softly humming as she worked while I pretended to sleep. I rushed through the days, concentrating on my lessons to finish them quickly. During medical tests, I distracted myself by wondering about the woman and why she was so different from the others. After I stopped fighting the aides, they seemed to be a bit nicer, and Uncle, too.

Every night the woman worked, or the next morning if I'd fallen asleep, there was an office-paper wrapped parcel with a goody of some sort: pretty cookies filled with fruit or nuts, a little cake, a handful of sweet popcorn with nuts. What a marvel popcorn was! I loved all her treats, but the nutty, fudgy cubes of halawa were my favorite. Burrowing under my covers, I savored my treats before folding the paper and slipping it back under the mattress.

When I had learned to read and write well enough, I snuck a pencil into bed. Before folding the paper to put it under the mattress, I wrote a question.

What is your name?

The next night's parcel contained a cookie filled with sweet, ground nuts, and an answer: *Khala.*

CHAPTER EIGHT

2019–2032

Naissa

⬥⬥⬥⬥⬥⬥

S TARTING IN LATE 2019, *a novel coronavirus caused a global pan-demic which, aside from the staggering death toll, changed the world in unforeseen ways. Followers of conservative leaders joined anti-vaccination movements, favoring individual rights over collective survivability. Social me-dia became a tool to harass and torment individuals, manipulate opinions, and influence beliefs about politics and global issues. Conservative govern-ments and isolationist nationalism multiplied around the world, compelling, for example, Great Britain's secession from the European Union and the US's withdrawal from multiple nuclear arms, climate, trade, and humanitarian agreements and treaties.*

For the first time in US history, a president faced prosecution for flouting national and state laws and attempting to overthrow the pillar of US democ-racy: the peaceful transition of power from one administration to another. A conservative Supreme Court reversed fifty-year precedent and abolished the con-stitutional right for individuals to control their pregnancies. As courts loosened gun laws and gun ownership soared, solo and mass shootings grew at exponen-tial levels. Polarization, government dysfunction, and extremism became tools for reactionary leaders to fundraise and threaten nearly 250 years of democracy. Civility hit new lows as gains in social equity, diversity, and the environment were attacked by conservative leaders and courts. Free speech norms were upended when books were banned from schools and libraries because they were deemed "corrupting" by right-wing States and groups.

At the dawn of the Fourth Industrial Revolution, ever faster, smaller, and more powerful computing using "smart" devices and the Internet of Things became required for many aspects of industry and daily life. Quantum computing took its first steps. Massive machine-to-machine computing systems enabled big data management, analytics, and forecasting for applications like marketing, finance, weather, and medicine. Artificial intelligence engines proliferated, offering great potential in areas such as research, automobile safety, and medical diagnosis and treatment. However, AI systems also threatened the authenticity of news, images, and videos, and the livelihoods of artists, writers, and educators. Materials science explored new structures and applications for metals, polymers, and ceramics, as well as developed new nano- and biomaterials.

The early twenty-first century also saw the sequencing of a complete human genome, as well as the advent of genetic manipulation via CRISPR gene-editing technology. Functional MRIs allowed researchers to peer into working brains. Robotic and laparoscopic methods resulted in faster healing and fewer invasive surgeries. Medical technologies of nanomedicine and 3D printing found applications in the generation of body parts.

Rising global population and environmental degradation reinvigorated the push for space exploration and colonization on Luna and Mars. Private corporations competed with national space programs to create efficient means for off-Earth technologies and settlements.

<hr />

Living in our home without Julian became unbearable. I auctioned our collectibles, sold the furniture and house, and donated the proceeds to the Juilliard School for scholarships in Julian's name. Julian would have been pleased to know he was still helping young musicians. By concentrating on the knowledge that Julian had made his individuality count with his music, I slowly stepped past mourning to whatever it was that made people keep going. I was changed. A vital part of myself—Julian—was missing. I called myself Dolores Stone and stopped using makeup to change my appearance. Traveling the globe, I wandered the continents' least populated corners and avoided interactions with others whenever possible. Fascination with places I hadn't seen before became glue with which I tried to fit myself back together.

My world tour came to an end in Amazonas, Brazil. I had hired a guide, Tiago, so I could tour the Madeira, the Amazon river's largest tributary, by peque-peque. The long, narrow riverboats, a primary means of transportation in the Amazon basin, were steered by pivoting an onboard engine to which was attached a six-foot propeller shaft extending beyond the boat's stern. The third morning of our trip upriver, a smoky haze settled over the water and brushed the top of the dense forest with wispy silver. By midday, the smoke was thick, yellow, and acrid. The sounds of heavy equipment echoed all around. Their crunching, roaring, and crashing grew deafening. Our boat rounded a bend and the world changed.

Tiago gasped and let out a breathy, "Ah, merda!" He took off his well-worn straw hat to wipe his brow, but his arm fell to his side, the hat dropping at his feet.

Past the steep riverbank on the east side of the river, for as far as we could see—which wasn't too far on account of the smoke—the forest had vanished. In its place was a rough and charred wasteland. It was as if the forest had ruptured and collapsed upon itself, morphing into hell. Pockets of fire glowed and smoldered. Huge shredders, backhoes, and dozers crawled at the edges of the fires, alien invaders angrily and methodically destroying every lifeform they encountered. Blackened stumps with shattered crowns were the scattered bones of life now gone.

I felt the carnage reach out and invade me as we slowly motored by. My face was wet and my knuckle bleeding from where I had bitten it. I tried to speak, but my throat had seized up. Finally, I croaked to Tiago, "Stop. *Stop. Now!*"

He regarded me with anxious, grieving eyes and turned to the western riverbank. Time stretched out and stilled as we moved around a bend and farther upriver. I didn't know if I sat there for minutes or hours. After the boat bumped into something, I turned and saw Tiago tying us up to a small dock. Crawling out of the boat on shaky hands and knees, I sank onto the dock's wide, weathered planks.

Hoarse wailing, as if from afar, reverberated in my skull. I realized it was coming from me. My anguish exploded as heaving sobs shuddered my whole frame. I couldn't stop the flood of grief.

Then there was a warm hand on my arm. I looked up to see a boy, maybe six or seven, with a worried expression on his delicate face. His ebony eyes were bright and concerned, and his black hair was shoulder-length and straight, with a neat part in the middle. Strands of seeds like garnets draped his neck

The boy grasped my hand with both of his and gently pulled. "Venha." He pulled again. "Venha comigo." From his small hands flowed the energy for me to stand.

I turned to Tiago, and he gestured up the riverbank with his chin. "You go with him, okay? I know these people."

I went with the boy to his family's hut. His mother gave me a blanket and a medicinal-tasting beverage and sat with me until I stopped shaking. After I calmed, the boy proudly introduced himself as Belam de Raon Mura, and his mother as Nalda Raon Pitangui Mura, his village's cacique, or chief.

Nalda showered me with kindness and allowed me to stay with her while I reoriented myself. When word came that borders were being shut down around the world because of a new and deadly respiratory virus, I found a rental a few miles downriver. Afterwards, I was a frequent visitor to Nalda's home.

The Mura tribe was a tight-knit, intrepid group. They revered their ancestors and their forest home and were blessed with abundant fish and game, as well as fruits, nuts, and edible plants. The adults devoted themselves to all the village's children. When the tribe's members weren't busy with the hard work of daily sustenance, their lives involved enjoying their natural environment and each other's company. Time seemed nonexistent as days ran into one another unmeasured in a limitless present. Their way of life suited me perfectly. I was grateful to be allowed to share that life, to be allowed time to heal.

I took a part-time job helping Tiago with his new business delivering items up and down the river. He and I became friends, and he showed me how to run a peque-peque through the river's sometimes tricky currents. Tiago also patiently tried to teach me rudimentary Pirahã, the Mura's spoken, hummed, and whistled language. As someone who learned languages with ease, I found my match in Pirahã.

The outside world, however, loomed over the Mura's peaceful lives and drew closer every day. A mostly paved road was being constructed to connect western Brazil to Manaus, the state capital of Amazonas and one of Brazil's largest cities; it brought with it an increasing stream of smoking diesel haulers and their twenty-first century goods. It was also an invitation to gold mining and criminal deforestation.

It was a rare day when the air didn't smell of smoke. The road brought diseases, too. During the COVID-19 pandemic, the Mura village remained isolated and fortunately unaffected, even while other tribes were nearly obliterated. Planes and helicopters whined overhead with increasing frequency. Electricity and plumbing replaced warm fires and cisterns. The people's battle to save their corner of the rainforest was no match for a thieving government, logging companies, developers, ranchers, and miners. As more acres of forest were destroyed, lakes and streams dried, and wild fish and game became scarce.

Nalda and I discussed the intrusion of "civilization" one morning while we were out gathering tucumã, the palm fruit used to make a favorite breakfast sandwich. We worried about the village's future because logging and farms were closing in on all sides.

"I worry most about the children," Nalda said. "What will be left for those who stay here? We are preserving our culture as best we can, but many of our youth will leave for opportunities on the outside. How will they survive in a city about which they know nothing? Most know little Portuguese, how to shop for groceries, or even what a number is."

Nalda set down her basket. "Lori, you told me you are a teacher, yes?"

I nodded. When Nalda used her nickname for Dolores, it made me feel a part of her family.

"Perhaps you could help. We teach our children the Mura way, every waking minute. But they need more, as insurance. Would you be interested in teaching the children to be ready for the future?"

"Of course! I would be honored. Whatever you need."

Nalda and I developed a curriculum, and a shelter was constructed for what became known as *City Class*. Several days a week, I taught the children language and skills they'd need if they ever found themselves living outside the forest.

Six years later, everything changed. Nalda received an official letter stating that the tribe's territory had been sold to a timber company, and the village was to be vacated in two months' time.

I told Nalda about my intention to go to Manaus and speak with the local head of FUNAI, Brazil's National Indian Foundation, to see if there were a way to halt the sale.

Nalda laughed bitterly. "Lori, please listen to me. The government *is* the problem. Ever since the president came back into power, the miners, loggers, and farmers—they all do whatever they want."

"But," I interrupted, "I know there are some in the National Congress who are friendly to the tribes."

Nalda paced back and forth in front of the fire. "You must not go to FU-NAI. I love that you are eager to join our effort, but this is not a game. Some have died—it happens all too often. The Waiapi cacique was brutally murdered by gold miners and his villagers terrorized. A few years ago, an entire uncontacted tribe was slaughtered by miners. The loggers are getting closer to us every day and they have guns. This fight is too dangerous, my friend."

"So, what do you propose? The loggers will be here next month."

"Perhaps they will."

"Of course they will! You have the letter."

Nalda sighed loudly and said, "We'll decide when the time comes. For now, tell me about City Class. How are the young ones progressing with their maths?"

Although I knew Nalda wouldn't approve, I needed to help. The next time I was in São João, I called Rodrigo de Ferro Jurema Alverez, FUNAI's regional director. To my surprise, the receptionist said he was free to talk. My research into Alverez's background had revealed an expertise in societies and civilizations, as well as degrees in botany and environmental sciences. I hoped our common interests might help my case.

"Senhorita Stone. How do you do?" Alverez's voice was deep and melodious.

"Thank you, Senhor Alverez, for taking my call."

"It is a pleasure, senhorita."

"I've learned that you and I share an interest in botany and environmental science."

As I'd hoped, Alverez warmed as we discussed our backgrounds.

"So, senhorita, what is it you wish to speak with me about?" he said, putting the small talk to an end.

I related the plight of my Mura friends, becoming more agitated as I went on. "I am pleading for the sale to stop. Otherwise, the tribe will be forced to relocate to an area far from their region and abandon the land they've known and loved for generations, and there are so few tribes left and they struggle so hard to maintain their lifestyles and with all the modern influences and troubles they keep losing ground, and soon there will be nowhere for them and—"

Oh good lord, Naissa! Of course he already knows this, so shut up and stop babbling! I shouted to myself, digging my thumbnail into the side of my hand.

Alverez was quiet for a moment. Then he sighed heavily.

"I understand too well the tribes' issues, Senhorita Stone. I wish with all my heart I could be of assistance. I say this to you in the strictest confidence. You may be aware that the head of FUNAI is a favorite of the president. His hate for the tribes is equaled only by his love for the masters of agribusiness and mining—and their money. Now, unregistered territories are sold to the highest bidders, as has been done with your friends' territory. As you must see, there is no one to whom we may appeal. There is nothing to be done. You must go no further with this."

I pressed him with the hope of learning more about the dynamics of the situation. But no matter how I tried, Alverez would say no more.

⚶⚶⚶

As the tribe's deadline to move grew closer, I was baffled to see no one making any preparations. It was unlike the Mura to be blasé in the face of difficulty. I asked Tiago about it one morning as we loaded a shipment of fruit and herbs bound for a settlement downriver.

"Ti, the government's deadline is nearly here. Why isn't anyone doing anything about moving?"

Tiago waved me off. "Everything is proceeding as expected. There is no concern. Here, please give this parcel to Yapohen before you go to São João."

He handed me a small package neatly wrapped in banana leaf, which I dutifully delivered to Yapohen in his hut before I took the loaded peque-peque downriver.

Two days later, City Class was in the middle of a lively discussion about bargaining versus bartering, when a shrieking came out of the woods. I told the children to stay put and ran to the central clearing. It was Yuaka,

Belam's best friend. Sobbing uncontrollably, he collapsed into the arms of his parents. Finally, he whispered a few words to his father. The man stiffened, and then took off in the direction Yuaka had come, whistling back over his shoulder for the top warriors to come with him. After an interminable time, they emerged from the forest with a limp body. There was a dark stain over the slender, bronze torso.

Belam.

A horrific scream rose from Nalda as she fell to her knees. Belam was dead, shot through the chest.

That night, a rock was hurled into the clearing. Around it was tied a note written in Portuguese and addressed to Nalda: "The bullet was meant for you. You should have stayed away from FUNAI."

I sank to my knees. Was this my fault? Was it because I talked to Alverez?

No, no, it couldn't be! There had to be another explanation, something Nalda and Tiago were keeping from me. Maybe FUNAI was funding the logging company? What *was* the tribe doing about it?

I finally dragged the answers to my questions out of Tiago. The tribe had been waging a guerilla war on the loggers encroaching the village, hoping the invaders would eventually abandon their work. My friends were responsible for the recent spate of burned equipment and logging camps about which I'd heard when I was in São João. But I still couldn't escape the possibility that Belam's death was my fault.

Drifting to sleep that night, I felt the cold presence of time beside my hammock.

I shook it off. *My friends have lived here forever. This is larger than the Mura. Without them to protect the rainforest, it will die. If the rainforest dies, the whole planet will die. I can't do nothing. I must help them!*

My grief ignited a hot flame of fury. *Damn those bastards! He was just a kid. I'd like to—I'll do whatever I can to help, even if it means using my freakishness.*

After Belam's murder, the tribe redoubled their efforts to defend themselves and their lands. I didn't let up until Nalda and Ti allowed me to join the fight. I'm sure they acquiesced just to stop my nagging. The night of my first raid, my hands shook as we painted ourselves with achiote and jenipapo tree ink. My job was to team with three teen boys carrying petrol. As we moved quietly through the forest, the leaders signaled with hand gestures and soft whistles. I tried my best to move as quietly as my comrades, but it seemed my pounding heart was loud enough to give us away.

Once our loads were poured over the targets at a logging camp and a match thrown, there was satisfaction in watching the fire take hold before we turned and ran back into the woods.

Back at the village, we quietly celebrated—and there were many jokes at my expense. Despite my awkwardness, the raid was a success. We destroyed two flatbed trucks and a log loader. Before our next raid, we stopped by the burned camp and used the ashes to mark our faces.

We went on raids nearly every day. My anger drove me with a restless fury. Our efforts made a dent in the loggers' equipment and camps, and several logging teams abandoned their jobs and left the rainforest. The remaining groups were heavily armed and, on the day of the deadline, they entered the village with the power of the government behind them and in their hands. The Mura were forced to pick up and move to state parklands twenty miles away.

I spent most of my time at the new Mura village, and only occasionally stayed at the settlement where I maintained a room. We continued the guerilla tactics, sometimes banding with other groups of Indigenous people for raiding parties. I learned how to handle the pistol I'd taken from a surrendering miner and was not afraid to use it—although we all did our best to avoid taking lives. It was understood the loggers and miners were in many cases the poorest of the poor, trying to make a living for themselves and their families. The tribe's bows, arrows, and borduna clubs mainly served as a warning to the invaders to go back to their own lands. We killed only to preserve our lives. Once, while we were spiking trees, I was shot through the forearm. The pain was excruciating but stopped almost immediately. When Ti later saw blood on my torn shirt sleeve, I waved it off, saying I was scratched by some thorns as we were running from the scene.

Ti leveled his dark eyes at me and glowered. When the moment became long enough to be uncomfortable, I said, "Really, it's nothing."

"Then show me. I know a bullet hole when I see one. It must be treated for infection." He reached out and grasped my wrist.

I looked around for an escape. Finding none, I had no choice. Slowly, I pushed up my sleeve to reveal my arm, stained with dried blood. Ti turned my arm this way and that, looking for the injury.

"What the hell?" He dropped my arm and said through tight lips, "Come with me."

Inside Ti's lean-to, he spoke in a quietly fierce voice. "What is going on here? You best tell me because this isn't the first time. You heal too fast. And you take too many risks. You don't care about being hurt. It may not matter to you, but your behavior is a grave risk for our people. So, explain. Or go home and never come back."

I cringed at his accusation of putting the others at risk, but I saw his point. I couldn't tell my secret, but I didn't want to lie to Ti.

"Please don't send me away. I *need* to be here, to help. If I don't, then . . . This fight matters to me—to the whole world's future. Please, you won't have to worry about me. It's okay. I don't have a death wish or anything, it's nothing like that."

"Then what is it, exactly?" Ti frowned and crossed his arms.

Shit. I was cornered. I let out a shaky breath.

"I—I've always been healthy. Injuries heal fast. I don't know why, it's just the way I am. And have been, for a—very long time."

"All injuries?"

I nodded.

"How long? In years."

I whispered, "A hundred and seventy-four."

Ti's eyes opened wide and he let out a low whistle. "I'm to believe you are some sort of superwoman?"

"Call it what you will. I am who I am, nothing more. I'm begging you, Tiago, please keep my secret. If it were to get out . . . I'd be locked away like a lab animal. *Please*, Ti. You can't even tell Nalda. I was so lonely, and the two of you gave me a place, a reason to keep going."

He looked out into the forest while considering my fate. It took all my will to practice the Mura patience I'd learned.

"All right, Dolores. You may stay, if—"

"You don't think I'm a freak?"

"No, of course not. I believe you are what you are. When you came to us, you were a broken bird. Now, I believe you were brought here for a purpose. I choose to believe that purpose is good."

"Oh, thank you, Ti! Thank you!"

Tiago brushed it aside. "If you stay, no more risks! You must follow the lead—and orders—of the other warriors without question. Agreed?"

The lightness of relief flooded me. "Agreed."

⊱─⊰─⊱─⊰

Outsiders concerned about the viability of the rainforest began to fund our group. We were outfitted with several drones and night-vision trap cameras for collecting evidence of logging and mining activity. In this way, tribal lawyers were able to report and stop a number of illegal operations.

The value of Amazon wood was so high—especially ipê, or Brazilian walnut—timber companies ran both legal and illegal operations to harvest the lumber. As soon as we took down one operation, another sprang up. Over time, the invaders became more and more violent. There were constant death threats, and friends were killed on raids or would simply disappear. The body count kept growing. Although each loss was grieved, the Mura dug in deeper. I became more adept with my weapon. I anonymously joined a social media campaign supporting the Indigenous people's struggle to preserve their lands and way of life. By then, satellite Internet allowed me to post my thoughts online, direct from the rainforest. My influencer pseudonym was *DefenderWithin*. One night after I'd been in Brazil almost nine years, we set out on a raid to burn a cache of cut ipê lumber one of the lookouts had found earlier in the day. The wood had been taken from several *mothers of the forest*, majestic trees in their prime age of seedbearing.

As we stood before the pile of wood with the smell of gasoline strong in the air, Nalda said, "Now we give these living pieces of ourselves back to the sacred ground. We can *never* let the brancos profit from our mothers and sisters. This war must end!"

Her face shone with tears as she lit the match and tossed it.

As we began our getaway, I heard the popping of shots. I ran hard with Nalda and Tiago, when suddenly Ti dropped back.

"My leg! I'm shot!" he cried.

Before we could turn and head back for him, Nalda shouted at me. "Go on, Lori, keep going. I'll bring him. *Go!*"

I ran ahead, but then heard Nalda cry out. I paused behind the interwoven trunks of an immense rubber tree and looked back. I froze.

There was fire where it shouldn't have been. I could see two silhouettes, one kneeling, one prone, both encircled by flames. It had been a trap!

Save them!

I must follow orders.

Go on, be the superhero.

I'm not a superhero.

But I love them.

I jumped out from behind the rubber tree and began to run toward Nalda and Tiago. Before I could take two steps, the flames built and filled the space around my two best friends, until all I could see was fire and smoke. Screams of agony pierced the air and clung to it as I breached the wall of flame. The pain was unimaginable, and I fought for every step forward. Suddenly, a burst of gunfire cut the screams into silence.

I was too late.

INTERLUDE

CONFIDENTIAL

MEMORANDUM

To: Mr. Donald R. Archer, CEO

From: Robert J. Henchon, VP Product Development

         Crystal Jacobs, VP Clinical Development

         Silas Traut, VP Finance

Re: N2GP Update and Recommendation for Production

Background

Our project team allowed six viable N^2 embryos to develop. At forty days gestation, all but the healthiest three were destroyed. Two of those died in the first trimester, while one made it to term and live birth. The subject has been thoroughly tested the last three years for both robustness and effectiveness of the N^2 genome. With the addition of day and night liaisons, the subject has shown marked improvement in prior aggressiveness, and is now generally cooperative with our personnel. Please see attached Report A.

In response to your request to evaluate product development feasibility and costs for the N^2 Genome Project, we assessed project data, distribution and demand models, and financial forecasts. Please see attached Report B.

Recommendations

Based on these analyses, and due to the tremendous success in isolating the P_0 phenomenon and transferring genetic material to normal cellular matrices and animal models, we are pleased to recommend a Phase 1 proposal be filed with the Global Health Administration (GHA). We should be able to proceed with production scale-up and Phase 2 and 3 clinical trials of N^2GP therapy within two years.

This further recommends educational testing be added to the overall testing regimen for the subject to fully evaluate cognition.

Henceforth, we propose the therapy be exclusively referred to by its new trade name, *reGenia*™.

These are exciting times for our company, and for the human race.

encl.

CONFIDENTIAL

CHAPTER NINE

2032–2071

Naissa

＊＊＊＊＊＊

W ITH EQUATORIAL REGIONS *becoming too hot for people to live
comfortably, migrations began to cooler climes northward and southward
toward the poles. Deforested areas of rainforest became more like African
savannahs than the lush jungles they had once been. Smog made outdoor exercise difficult and sometimes obscured things beyond a few feet of visibility. The
land became increasingly crowded, aggravated by rising sea levels and violent
storms.*

*The global number of known flora and fauna species continued to rapidly
decline. The daily news was a chorus of crowding, pollution, coastal flooding, ice
melt, drought, storms, famine, wildfires, and other disasters.*

*The late 2040s saw massive food riots in regions hardest hit by pover-
ty and the changing climate. Discontent with wealth inequality manifested in
protests and boycotts. Whole populations were stricken by epidemics, including the COVID-48 and DENV-49 pandemics, both of which echoed the awful
COVID-19 pandemic earlier in the century.*

*Medical advances, such as nonrejectable artificial organs, prevented many
life-threatening diseases and prolonged life. Cloning was beginning to successfully*

grow replacement organs, although whole human cloning was outlawed by most countries for ethical reasons. Worldwide, a woman's fertility continued into her late fifties, and average life expectancy grew to ninety-two for men and ninety-seven for women. The global population approached ten billion.

After Eastern Russia's entry into the European Union, and because all member countries in the European continent were now represented, the EU re-organized as New Europe. *A few years later, the countries of North and South America modeled New Europe and proposed a union of trade and government called* Canamericas.

There were protests against the union, culminating in the 2052 Day of Power, a multicountry march on both continents organized by a consortium of nationalist groups. The protests were so violent, their mission backfired and popular sentiment swung hard toward unification.

Technology continued its onward march in the Age of Iots. Iots were wireless smart devices formerly known as the Internet of Things, and came in stationary and mobile configurations, maneuvering on wheels, tracks, articulated legs, springs, and propellers. Iots performed menial jobs, such as minor repairs, maintenance, and cleaning. Mobile domestic service robots, DSRs, were found in most households. Municipalities used iots for maintaining and cleaning public spaces, and ultraspecialized iots performed medical diagnostics and minor procedures at microhospitals.

The first fusion engines came online, thanks to a breakthrough by a Rensselaer Polytechnic Institute team in 2042. Personal flying craft became commonplace for the wealthy. The world's aeronautics and space companies and agencies merged into the United Space Exploration Agency, or USEA, whose mission was to explore off-Earth habitation.

The first USEA missions, called Sol Horizon, took astronauts to Luna and Mars in solar system-capable spaceships. An experimental engine, the Roddenberry-Asaro, looked like a promising step toward near-lightspeed travel. The first attempt to establish a civilian colony off-Earth, China's lunar colony, Xìngyùn jiāyuán, came to a tragic end when a supply shuttle crashed into the residential habitat.

The village was devastated by the loss of Nalda and Tiago. Most of the people packed up and left, heading for settlements along the river or for villages farther afield. Some even moved away from the Amazon basin entirely.

As village cacique, Nalda was the one who had taken me in on that awful day I had fallen apart. The entire village had looked to Nalda for strength and guidance. She was the cornerstone in their battle to survive. Tiago was a sharpshooting archer and my brother in business and ecotage. He knew the names and histories of nearly everyone along a sixty-mile stretch of the Madeira and was beloved by all. Nalda, Tiago, and I had become the best of friends and comrades. I was numbed by guilt. All I had wanted was to help my friends, but I only made things worse.

I wished humanity would evolve to the point where everyone behaved like the Mura. If the rest of the world learned to respect, love, and protect the earth and one another the Indigenous way, perhaps they'd work together toward a promising future. If others could see through my eyes, they'd have no choice: unite to preserve our home—or let inaction lead to doom.

But how? Could I use my freakishness to push humanity to evolve? To work together? If I could turn my condition into our rescue . . .

Then it hit me, and a plan coalesced: to learn enough about the cause of my condition to develop a therapy for others. I would devote a piece of my infinite time so people could live long, healthy lives, and therefore have a vested interest in preserving our home for as long as possible. Plus, I'd find the nondying companionship for which I longed. Science had advanced enough to make this possible.

My heart sank. *Human overpopulation is part of the problem, as much as corporate greed. If people live indefinitely, population growth will kill the Earth and drive us to extinction.*

It was estimated the maximum sustainable human population on Earth was eight billion, which we'd already exceeded. Could thoughtful laws and universal access to better birth control limit population growth, as was now done in some countries? Or, what if ageless people were sterile? It would be a daunting choice: the cost of having a child would be mortality; the cost of infinite life—childlessness. There were moments when my solitude caught up to me, when I ached for a family. But the moments always passed. Aside from the tragically short life of my darling Cecile, I'd gone this far without adding to the population. It could be done.

After researching paths toward my goal of using my condition to help solve the big problems, I concluded that gaining expertise in biochemistry was the necessary first step. I'd always loved science and enjoyed teaching it, but I intended to do high-level research. For that, I needed stronger and updated skills. I needed to leave the rainforest and go back to school.

I couldn't return to the USA for school without documentation. My attorneys prepared a new Social Security card, passport, certificates of birth and death, and other necessary documents. I became eighteen-year-old Caroline Spencer, while eighty-year-old Kerri Gordon Lange "died." I had a funeral of sorts for Kerri before leaving the rainforest: I planted a few seeds from the giant waterlily, *Victoria amazonica*, in the loamy shallows of a clear, still pool in one of the tributaries. The strong and prickly wonders with their frying-pan leaves and exquisite flowers seemed a fitting tribute to my friends, and Kerri.

I applied to and was accepted by the University of Michigan's undergraduate biochemistry program. With deep sadness, I bade farewell to my remaining friends and returned to the United States.

<hr>

The biggest surprise after my time in Amazonas was the rapid change in technology. Classrooms were digital and school labs used virtual reality as tools for visualizing the molecular world.

Schoolwork was challenging but manageable, except for a required calculus course with concepts I had trouble grasping. I joined a study group and hired a tutor, but only muddled through. The course dented my GPA.

Although busy with my studies, I carried on my work as a covert activist and expanded my *DefenderWithin* campaign far beyond the Amazon basin.

Needing to be razor-focused on my goal, I couldn't risk social distractions. Foregoing friendships and relationships was an acceptable trade-off toward meeting my objective.

My determination and resulting grades were good enough to gain me admission to the next step in my plan, the graduate program in Molecular Biology and Genomics at Johns Hopkins in Baltimore, Maryland. Fortunately, most of my studies were fascinating, because otherwise I might not have survived the grueling program. I did, in the end, procure three stellar references from my professors in addition to a hard-earned master of science degree, setting me up for my next step.

Zurich's doctoral program in Genomics and Molecular Biology was known for its pioneering research and novel technologies. I spent three and a half years researching the molecular mechanisms of disease and aging, taking as much advantage of the institution's genius thinkers and resources as I could. Attending and presenting at conferences was a regular part of the curriculum—not to mention an excellent opportunity to create a network of contacts in the right places.

Everything led me to the goal I'd been working toward around the clock since I'd left Brazil ten years before: a postdoctoral position at the Oberlin Institute, the Viennese research facility I had planned to reveal myself to before Julian's death. I was going to Vienna—the City of Dreams.

<hr />

Vienna was almost as beautiful as it had been in the late nineteenth century, even with omnipresent air quality monitors and alarms. While the city's elegant character and buildings were as I remembered, the entire valley around the town center had become solidly urban all the way to the hills.

I rented a garden apartment in a chic neighborhood within walking distance of both shopping and the Oberlin Institute. The bright and airy apartment suited me perfectly. I planted a small herb, vegetable, and flower garden in the back, next to which I put a table and chair so I could enjoy my morning coffee among the growing things. Coffee was a luxury, but the Viennese were not to be denied their precious kleiner Schwarzer—the dark, espresso-like demitasse.

The researcher to whom I reported at the Oberlin Institute, Dr. Alex Vasiliou, was responsible for the institute's program on aging—my chosen path. I was disappointed to find, however, that my work was tedious. Rather than exploring new pathways as I'd envisioned, I was relegated, as a new hire, to running repeated experiments to confirm or reject hypotheses. The monotony was difficult to tolerate.

Even worse, my lab supervisor, Alain Dubuisson, had it in for me. He gave me assignments that should have gone to a lab tech—not a postdoc. Never referring to me by name or title, he refused to call me anything but *America*.

The trouble began on my fourth morning at the lab.

"America!" Dubuisson called in singsong. "You have not yet submitted the results report I asked for yesterday."

"I beg your pardon, Dr. Dubuisson, but I sent the report to you yesterday before end-of-business."

"But it is not here, come see. And you're on my list of approved contacts." He gestured toward the empty inbox on his display.

Incredulous, I knew I had sent the report. Biting my tongue, I fiddled with the dark tucumã ring Tiago had made for me. Carved and polished from the palm's seeds, tucumã rings were worn to show solidarity with the Indigenous cause and resistance to oppressors.

Dubuisson looked at me with mock sympathy. "Oh, dear, I need that report right away. You'll have to do it again."

I was regularly accused of failing to submit work, of errors, not cleaning my workstation, and other bogus complaints. As far as the higher-ups knew, I was a mediocre performer, or worse. It seemed that Alain did whatever he could to keep me from the research I was hired to do. Small, jittery, and pale, Dubuisson reminded me of a rat as he scurried about the lab. Over time, Dr. Vasiliou saw to it that I worked with her directly, assigning me projects which better used my skills. Although Dubuisson backed off a little, I couldn't shake the feeling that my failure was in his interest. The coworkers I confided in sympathized with my position, but there was little anyone could do.

Confounded by empty hours after work and on weekends, I worked harder on *DefenderWithin*. I also resumed sculpting, picking up where I'd left off in Florida over a century before. Sculpting turned out to be the perfect counterpoint to tedious days in Alain's lab with its inherent backbiting. Working with my hands stilled my mind and focused me on the act of transforming rough substances into objects with meaning. One of my most difficult pieces from that time was a pair of swallows in flight, dedicated to Nalda and Tiago.

My two-hundredth birthday came and went without celebration, but I did splurge and buy myself an actual book, a first edition of Darwin's *On the Origin of Species*. Its fragile pages were almost as old as I was.

<hr />

Dr. Dubuisson and I were in the café adjacent to the institute, discussing the lab's recent patent application for a novel delivery system for multi-CAS enzymes. My temper was growing.

I stirred and watched the swirl of cream blend itself into a steamy cup of kleiner Brauner. When the coffee was a uniform light brown, I set down the spoon on the plate next to the warm piece of apfelstrudel. The pastry was good, but not nearly as heavenly as what I remembered George's mother making. When I had returned to Vienna, I had looked into the Johnson family and found many descendants flourishing throughout the region, but none directly from George.

"What about the *Science* article?" I demanded. "You know the multivariate trellis was *my* work, yet I wasn't in the byline. And, you were supposed to include my name in the patent application. You told Vasiliou and Erics-dottir you would, but you never did!"

A sneer edged Alain's lips, transforming his narrow, pale face and large, fleshy nose into a gargoyle's countenance. "My mistake, America. Sorry."

Backstabbing sonofabitch! Without being published, I'd never get out from under Alain and never find the answers I craved. After all these years, my plan was twisting apart because of one asshole.

That night, I lay in bed wrestling with what to do. I couldn't resign and I couldn't continue the way things were. To make things worse, I'd been at the institute so long, I was starting to hear comments about my young looks. I needed to change direction. If only I could work on my genome!

That was it. I would tell them everything. And, I would insist on being part of the research team as a condition of my disclosure.

I laughed out loud. *Au revoir, Alain!*

After my attorney, Natalie Semler, approached the Oberlin Institute, it took a few months to get a signed nondisclosure agreement and a revised employ-ment contract. Her challenge was to entice the institute's deciders without providing too much information.

In the meantime, my challenge was to keep my mouth shut. My pat answer became, "Sorry, I can't talk about it on advice of my attorney."

Natalie worked her magic by saying we had something extraordinary to offer, potential Nobel Prize material. Oberlin Institute took the bait, and on a sultry Friday in late July, I sat in the OI boardroom with the institute's CEO, Dr. Dagna Ericsdottir, Natalie, and Dr. Vidyansh Navinder Singh. Dr. Singh, one of the youngest ever to graduate from Harvard Medical School, had soared to a brilliant career in molecular biology, becoming head of the OI's molecular genetics program by the age of twenty-seven. One of his labs was on the cutting edge of therapeutic cloning to develop replacement organs.

As I explained my quandary and showed proof of my age, Dr. Singh's brown eyes lit with barely contained delight. The man was well-nigh bouncing.

I could see the moment my story hit home with Dr. Ericsdottir. She paled and a faint sheen of sweat appeared on her upper lip. The woman was either terrified at the implications or having trouble counting the dollar signs—probably both.

"What a remarkable situation!" she gushed. "I wish you had told us sooner, Dr. Spencer—excuse me, Dr. *Nolan*—but now I understand your secrecy. While I need to touch base with our board of directors, I think it's safe to say we'd be delighted to partner with you to discover the source of your anomaly. If the board approves, we'll start work on it immediately, subject, of course, to running our own tests and reviewing your vital records."

At the conclusion of the meeting, Dr. Singh all but leaped over the table with ferocious energy to furiously shake my hand.

"Dr. Nolan, you cannot know how thrilled I am. Such an honor! We will find your answer, of that I have no doubt. As you well know, the science is very, very exciting at this point in time. I am humbled by your confidence in us. Thank you, thank you!"

"The pleasure is mine, Dr. Singh."

Dr. Ericsdottir said, "Thank you for trusting us with your secret, Dr. Nolan. We will guard it well."

<hr />

Natalie wasn't happy with the OI employment contract, on which the institute demanded agreement before working on my own project. Natalie's main objection dealt with ownership; all my work, inventions, biological samples, thoughts, and ideas were to be property of the Oberlin Institute. As long as I worked at OI, they would own me.

"I don't like the wording, it's too vague. But OI won't budge. You might consider stepping away from this and looking for someone else."

My heart sank. "I can't, Natalie. The thought of starting over—we're so close, I don't want to give up now. I *must* be on that project team."

"All right," Natalie sighed, "you're the client. But understand, this is against my better judgment."

I was elated. I would report directly to Dr. Singh, whose enthusiastic spirit was contagious. We needed to lay groundwork before actual work could begin: meetings to define project objectives, values, strategies, and candidates to interview. We also had to wait for our new lab space, which was to be housed in a massive underground expansion OI had been constructing for years. It took an agonizing six months to ready a secure wing for our labs and offices. Construction would continue around us on the rest of the expansion, but at least we would have a home.

Natalie and the OI counsel worked out the strategy for my transition from the Aging unit to Special Projects. I gave notice to Dr. Vasiliou, saying I took a project leader position in Singapore.

I moved to an apartment across the street from the back of the institute, adopted a different hairstyle and color, used EyeDye to color my eyes dark brown, and bought a nondescript wardrobe. In case of chance encounters with employees outside the Special Projects unit, I was given a new OI identity card as a twenty-four-year-old lab tech.

Our research project was top secret, so I entered and exited the building under cover of dark through a discreet, high-security entrance at the back of the building. Only a select few individuals, specially chosen after having undergone detailed background checks, were authorized to enter our lab. At first, construction noises were distracting, but over time the sounds faded into the humming of the ventilation system.

At first, my job was analyzing differences between my genome and the "normal" human one to isolate what part of the genome was responsible for my condition. This was a tedious process as I had to study one gene at a time, which took a number of years.

By the time we had a good idea of what differentiated my genome, security in my lab had grown tighter. Project members were given experimental wrist implants bought from a company named Shiwo. The Shiwo representative said the devices held a security and identity system keyed to our DNA, which would shut down if used or accessed by someone other than the authorized wearer. Shiwo wasn't completely foolproof, however, since the institute set mine up with a modified DNA sample to conceal my genome and true age. My implant alone must have cost OI a bundle.

While I was at the lab, I secretly prepared a cache of my blood cells. I slightly modified minor genes to make Shiwo identities apparently different from mine—just in case I needed new identities in the future.

We began testing normal cells and cloned organs to learn the safest and most effective way to insert my ageless genome into a living tissue at the cellular level. Monitoring each test's adverse events was a lengthy process, so our progress was aggravatingly slow.

Test after test failed, but we kept trying. I began to question the feasibility of my agelessness research.

Then, I found out what my employer was really up to.

⚜

Twelve years into my genome project, I talked the expansion construction manager into a quick tour of the nearly completed level below ours. As we walked down the hallway, a lab with an open door caught my attention. Inside, a piece of equipment was being installed.

I stopped by the doorway and gaped. The worker looked up, saw me, and slammed the door—but not before I got a good look at what she was installing. It was an amniponic incubator, like those used in therapeutic organ cloning. Only, it was much larger. Large enough to hold a fully developed human infant.

Stunned, I turned to the construction manager, who seemed about to panic.

"That's probably enough for today," she quickly said. "The rest is still hard hat only. Shall we head back to the elevator?"

Later, I couldn't stop thinking about what I'd seen: OI was working on human reproductive cloning—a banned science. That's why I'd received only mild pressure about the slowness of my progress; my project wasn't their biggest priority. No wonder, because human cloning—illegal or otherwise—would be immensely profitable. I was surprised I hadn't figured it out before.

It was one thing to use cloning for therapeutics, but reproductive cloning—there were so many issues. What a mess cloning would make of efforts to maintain sustainable population levels. Our world could be overrun. At least with my ageless project, population could be controlled by having the ageless genome be infertile, and the ageless would work their long lives to preserve the environment. With cloning—who knew? How could zero population growth measures possibly succeed? How could we save our world?

Not to mention the illegality of human cloning. And immorality! Reproductive cloning made mockery of what makes us human: our sense of autonomy and individuality. Who would want to grow up a shadow in the life of their identical parent? Or, what about clones reared as replacements for deceased children? They would never live up to the angelic ideal of their donor.

The institute was in it for the money, I had no doubt. It horrified me to think of human clones forced to live with the truth that their lives were purchased, like any other commodity. It was sickening.

I couldn't take one more paycheck from the devil, so I tendered my resignation, effective immediately, and demanded the institute halt further work on my ageless project. I walked out the front door and did not look back.

CHAPTER TEN

Rys

MY OTHERWISE STERILE world turned magical, thanks to Khala. It was exhilarating to share a secret life with her, to have knowledge unknown to everyone else. Each nibble of the goodies she shared with me exploded with the flavor of freedom. And the notes. As I got older, Khala told me more about places and things I could not see but believed I would, someday. Her notes were my salvation, my lifeline to a world outside my rooms.

From Uncle's lessons, I learned to solve story problems with math, to write about what I learned, and even make up stories. He taught me biology and chemistry and physics. I learned about what he called the ancient world, a place that used to be but was no more.

From Khala, I learned there were many places and people in the world, some beautiful, some ugly. She told me about people going to the moon and Mars, and about the invisible thing that controlled the sterilization iots in the med room, called *Immeda*. With Immeda, people talked to each other all over the world and in space, too. I could only use Immeda for the lights. Khala told me I was not the only child, that there were countless other children around the world. I lay awake at night trying to think how to get the sterilization iots to help me talk to the others. Khala said that many kids lived together with adults who loved them more than anything else. Even though I trusted what Khala had to say, I found that impossible to believe.

She taught me about different cultures, especially their foods. Cooking was a big part of her life. She said sitting down to a meal with others washed away differences and developed everlasting bonds. Once Uncle had a sandwich with me at lunchtime. I felt awkward at his grumpy silence. Perhaps he felt awkward, too, because he never stayed for lunch after that.

As I grew, my rooms changed around me. The school room's library books changed, and more challenging reading replaced the children's books. One day, aides installed what they called a window on my wall. It looked exactly like the monitor in the classroom, and when it came to life, I looked over a brick courtyard garden. There were trees and brightly colored flowers, a feeder with seed for chirping birds, and a cheerfully bubbling fountain. It was fun to watch the birds eat the seed, but magically, the feeder always stayed full. Over time, I noticed the view out the window began to slowly change into dry, rusty colors and rustling leaves. Then there were snows before the bright colors came around again. The whole cycle took a long time.

After an astronomy lesson one day, I realized I was experiencing seasons through my window.

I started asking Uncle questions he didn't seem to care for. When he was teaching me a math problem about the speed of two navicraft approaching each other, I asked him why I'd never seen such a vehicle. He said it was because navicraft existed only in the ancient world. Once I told him how much I wanted to go to the place in the pic on my wall, which he said was called Fiji. That's when he told me Earth was not like that anymore, that it had changed, and we needed to stay inside all the time to be safe. Later, I realized he was a smooth liar. I asked him where he lived, and he said in his rooms nearby. When studying a frog's reproductive organs, I asked where I came from. He ended the day's lesson right after I asked that one, saying he wasn't feeling too well.

Khala answered most of my questions, although she, too, never answered questions I asked about myself. I think she withheld answers to keep me from knowing the truth. She never disparaged Aunt and Uncle, or the doctors, and always treated me as though my life were normal, as if I were a normal kid. Best of all, Khala promised I would see the world outside someday. I loved her for that.

Still, it seemed something wasn't right, and I couldn't figure out what it was.

INTERLUDE

ETTING TO WORK is work itself. Once I am in the building, I go to Research Wing B's closet and get my cart, already filled with supplies for the night. I have space for my dinner pail on the cart's bottom rack. I push my cart into the conference room at the end of the wing. I look up at the camera and wave. Then, I wave my left wrist by the wall reader. A small monitor shows a picture of me as a young woman, and displays green letters: *Darwish, Zaina. Authorized.*

A hidden door slides open, and I enter the biocleaning airlock room. After I pass through the airlock and am decontaminated, I push my cart to the elevator and wave my wrist at another reader. My stomach jumps as the elevator rushes down. The door opens on Wing S2.

The air is different here, more sterile-smelling and dry. Stefan, one of the night guards, sits behind his desk in the hall's security area, reading. I stop at his desk and give him my lunch pail for inspection.

Stefan smiles and says, "Hi, Z. What's for dinner tonight?"

While he's opening the pail, I look at the images on the wall of monitors behind him. I am relieved to see the secret places are still off-camera.

"Tonight, I have sheikh al-mahshi—courgettes with chicken and yogurt. And ma'amoul with date and almond filling."

Three ma'amoul molds were the only things I carried with me when I left Syria during the West Asian War, during the siege of my city, Al-Hasakah. Each mold for making semolina cookies had a different design of a desert flower or star. The wooden molds belonged to my mother, and her mother before her, and so on. Two were burned by thieves on the journey through Türkiye.

"Looks and smells delicious, as usual." Stefan closes the pail and hands it back to me. "Have a good night, Z."

I nod to him and head down the hall to begin my work of cleaning the labs.

⁓⁓⁓⁓⁓⁓

On my dinner break, I wrap one of the ma'amoul in a piece of plain office paper I took from one of the labs, and the other in another piece of paper. Earlier, in one of my secret places unseen by cameras, I quickly wrote a message on the paper:

> *Hello, little Tayir. I hope your day was good. Today I saw a robin like the ones on your garden vid. This means spring will come soon. Be good tomorrow. I care for you. From, your Khala*

My heart aches for the girl. She is so small, so quiet, like a little birdie, a tayir. She is so like my own dear daughter, Allah Yerhamha. I called my daughter little Tayir before she faded away from hunger during the siege.

The first time the little one wrote back and told me her name, she asked for mine. It pained me that I could not tell her. When I started the job in Wing S, my boss said I would be deported and go to prison if I spoke to the girl or even looked at her. "Keep your head down, do your job, and you'll be fine," he said.

If the little one might tell my name by mistake, my life, such as it is, would end. Who then would hire me? It took so long for the girl to trust me, I could not harm her trust. So, I called her *Tayir* and told her my name is *Khala*. Auntie.

I go into her room to clean. She is awake but pretending to sleep. I dust the night table by her bed and quickly tuck the wrapped ma'amoul with the note under the corner of her mattress. I wish I had made pistachio halawa, her favorite. It is what I gave her the first night.

Later, after my Fajr prayers and before the end of my shift, I go back to her room with fresh towels. I take her note, read it, and shred it with the Wing S2's other waste papers before I leave at the end of my shift. On the way out, I give Stefan the other ma'amoul.

CHAPTER ELEVEN

2071–2087

Naissa

～～～～～～～

T HE WORLD HAD *much to contend with in the latter half of the twen-*
ty-first century. Governmental institutions continued evolving to favor large
corporations and the extremely wealthy, whose success, the populace was
deceitfully told, would result in success for everyone. The reality was a time of
worsening economic inequality, overpopulation, climate effects, depletion of food
sources, and poisoning of the environment. A generation of governmental dys-
function mired the globe in the status quo and prevented preparedness for and
solutions to global problems. Then, two calamities awakened the global mind to
the lethality of the problems and urgent need for drastic change.

On the morning of June 23, 2072, the Northern San Andreas Fault rup-
tured slightly north of San Francisco, causing an 8.1 magnitude quake. Its
intensifying energy propagated rapidly northward along the fault to the inter-
section of the San Andreas with the southern Cascadia subduction zone and
Gorda plate, near Mendocino, California. Offshore landslides by Mendocino
and Eureka triggered several tsunamis around the Pacific Coast. The San
Andreas rupture loaded just enough stress on the southern portion of the Casca-
dia Fault to trigger the first megathrust fault rupture on the deadly structure

since January of 1700. As the Cascadia rupture moved northward, it launched a deadly Pacific-wide tsunami.

Mount Shasta, where a fifth volcanic dome had been growing for almost two decades, exploded cataclysmically within an hour of the quake, sending 160 cubic kilometers of volcanic ejecta into the stratosphere. There, megatons of sulfurous gas emissions combined with water vapor to create reflective sulfuric acid aerosols, and for two years, this acidic veil in the atmosphere spread around the Earth and cooled global temperatures by 1.3 degrees Celsius. Insufficient sunlight and burning, acidic rain ruined crops throughout the northern hemisphere and into the southern, causing widespread famine and disease. The West Coast Disaster would become one of the largest in recorded history.

Five years later, no corner of the world escaped the devastating REOVID pandemic of 2077, in which most victims were under the age of ten. The trauma of losing nearly a generation of the youngest children was too much to bear.

Eastern Russian Deputy Prime Minister and Representative to the United Nations, Verunya Diakovna Kirova, proposed Consensus at the June '78 World Summit. She had lost her two young children to REOVID-77, and grief strengthened her message. With people misled into accepting a world of poverty and environmental disaster, Kirova maintained the salvation of the planet was in the majority's hands—not in the pockets of the few. "Our time is up— we are exterminating ourselves by inaction!" Kirova thundered. "Global issues demand a global approach. It is time for the people to decide. The people will set things right."

Kirova's plan was simple and radical: direct democracy on a global scale. Her model was based on Athenian democracy, updated to the twenty-first century: a virtual forum where proposals were debated and voted upon. Any person on the planet could submit proposals to local, regional, continental, and global councils, who would format proposals for voting and administer the global forum. Councils would use AIs to comb proposals without bias and weed out oddball detritus. Once initial proposals were formatted as proposed laws, they would be made available for debate and voting. Issues would be decided by simple majority and could be revisited, if necessary.

The Kirova plan was a hard sell, because the powerful never willingly ceded power. Yet, the first steps had been taken when Canamericas formed in 2053 to expedite trade and production throughout the Americas, and continental representatives were established to oversee the processes. Since most of the continents had begun to refer to themselves as countries—Canamericas, New Asia, New Europe, and New Africa—it wasn't a stretch to go further.

There were, of course, a number of despotic and autocratic regimes that initially refused to consider Consensus and tried to crush it. But the tide was too strong. In some places, widespread uprisings in favor of Consensus made it inevitable; a few presidents and premiers were assassinated. After China—the last holdout—experienced a widespread thousand-year flood event, it reluctantly permitted its citizens to vote on the proposal.

Since most people no longer trusted their governments to safeguard the common good, Consensus was approved by 94 percent of the world's voting population on the second day of December 2080. The follow-up vote two weeks later declared the new government to be the United Countries of Earth, *or UCE. The world became one nation.*

GlobeNet, free to everyone, integrated communications methods over short, long, and ultralong distances. Iots connected from everywhere to GlobeNet through its worldwide system of networks using wired, wireless, infrared, and optical communications. Lasers transmitted massive data streams almost instantaneously to and from Earth, satellites, colony projects, and spacecraft with pinpoint accuracy. Many of the older AIs, such as those used for controlling iots and databases, were merged under a universal AI, Immeda. Nearly unlimited information and tools were available anywhere just by asking.

In January of 2072, lumino physicist Bao Beldon observed waves of dark matter passing through Earth and space at velocities a thousand times light speed. Using a simple device to hold back dark matter waves at subluminal levels, the waves could be observed, have data loaded or unloaded, and then be set loose to proceed to remote receiver-transmitters. It was like putting one's hand perpendicularly into a stream of water to hold back the current, and then removing the dam to allow the stream to flow again. Beldon's wave tech enabled near-instantaneous communications between receiver-transmitters placed over vast distances. Seemingly overnight, GlobeNet became IntraSpaceNet, or ISN. It was possible to connect with someone across the solar system using real-time video messaging and converse as if the speakers were only a few miles apart. The relationship between humans and space was transformed. A short time later, Beldon waves were manipulated to create magnetic fields, enabling artificial gravity and a way to moderate acceleration and deceleration forces during space travel.

⁂

In the days after I left the Oberlin Institute, I needed to recenter myself. I found myself thinking of places I'd lived in times past, where life was safe and simple. Every generation must deal with new difficulties, but the extreme rapidity of change in this era and the magnitude of those changes had become overwhelming. I returned to my own hair and eye color, and had my lawyer create a "new" Shiwo identity for me: Naissa Nolan, age twenty.

Life always seemed simpler when traveling, so I decided to see parts of the world I'd never been. I journeyed through Eastern Europe, the Mediterranean, and Africa from Egypt to South Africa. From there, I lingered in New Zealand for a few months before moving on to Australia.

I had just arrived in Sydney and was relaxing at a harborside café not far from the skyport, sipping hibiscus tea with a drop of bush honey. A plate of fresh-from-the-oven biscuits sat on the table next to a cloth napkin and spoon, and a small vase held a colorful bouquet of cyclamen and paper daisies. That morning, I had heard reports of an earthquake and eruption, but it was so far across the world, I barely registered the news.

I would never forget where I was when the tsunami sirens blared. The tsunami sped across seventy-five hundred miles of the Pacific Ocean in just fifteen hours. Fortunately, there was ample warning for homes and businesses to quickly board up and for most everyone to reach higher ground. My hotel was well outside the evacuation zone, so I watched from my twentieth-floor balcony as the harbor emptied. A short while later, the sea rolled back in and rose in a roiling, muddy mass to inundate the lowlands. The noise was terrifying.

As the waters receded, damage was revealed. Whole sections of the city were wiped away, and mountainous logjams of debris were piled high with trees, vehicles, buildings, and everything else unlucky enough to be caught by the sea.

In the year following the disaster, the skies were tinged a dirty yellow and winter never fully turned to spring or summer. We in the southern hemisphere were the lucky ones to not suffer the worst effects, but costs for basic commodities jumped wildly, and hoarding was rampant.

I worked on cleanup, helping sort debris to be carted away, sweeping mud from streets, and flagging locations of bodies. It was a gruesome job, but I needed to be busy. Knowing the conditions could last for a few years, I was restless to go back North to help, but travel there was embargoed. Because most municipalities ran fusion reactors, the world was fortunate that power generation wasn't as compromised by the disaster as it might have been decades prior.

A year after the disaster, I returned to Canamericas, landing in Fernie, a town in the State of British Columbia, south of Calgary near Montana. There, I found a mountain cabin and volunteered with Replant, the state organization dedicated to reforestation of wasted areas. During the long winter, we sprouted native seeds under lights in a massive warehouse using a stacked aquaponics system, all powered by a small fusion generator. A closed-water system with tanks for indigenous fish species pumped nutrient-filled water to irrigate the seedlings and saplings. The seedlings would be ready for planting, and the fish for release, when the weather cleared and the sun shone again.

Every time I entered the growing center, I found joy in filling my lungs with moist, fir-scented air richly oxygenated by the growing things, and knowing my breath was also life-giving to the young seedlings. Brushing my fingertips over the velvety seedlings was better than any perfume.

~~~~~~~~~~

The snow crunched under my boots as Kit bounded ahead, leaping in arcs tall enough to fly over the snow and sending clouds of white powder high into the air. His luxuriant tail flashed through the powder storm in bursts of copper fire. Kit's joy infectious, I couldn't help but laugh. Last night's storm had dropped more than a foot of new snow, and the morning made it radiant against the sky's vivid blue. To the northeast, the Three Sisters Peak glowed blindingly. It was the first day of full sun in two years.

Before going to the barn, I stopped by the hopper—my personal driving and flying craft designed for short trips—to brush the snow off its solar rooftop. The sunny day would charge the batteries enough to fly a whole week without using the backup drive. I could have had Immeda, clear the snow using my pair of DSRs, but I liked doing chores because it helped fill my days.

Kit frolicked in the snowfall my hopper maintenance produced, snapping midair at the falling clumps in a dervish dance. He had adopted me the previous spring when he'd taken shelter from a late-season blizzard in a corner of my front porch. A fox pup whose eyes were just opening, he couldn't have been more than two weeks old. I left him undisturbed in hopes his mother would return for him. By the next morning, he was fading, and it was evident no parent would come to his rescue. I brought the tiny, shivering bundle of fur in by the fire and bottle-fed him for the next three weeks before gradually introducing pureed and then solid foods. I made Kit a bed in a dark nook in the barn to ready him for a return to the wild. I was thankful I had fully enclosed the chicken coop and yard because one of Kit's choice activities was running for hours around the chickens' enclosure, taunting the birds and looking for weaknesses in the fencing.

Kit bounced excitedly as I entered the chicken enclosure and latched the gate behind me, taking care not to give him access. After feeding the chickens, breaking the ice on their water, and collecting new eggs in a wicker basket, I left the run and securely fastened the gate. Then I tossed an egg toward Kit, my daily offering for depriving him of what would have been a favored prey. As usual, he caught the egg midair, and in an instant, there was nothing left but cleanly licked pieces of shell scattered in the trampled snow. I watched as Kit set off on his adventures for the day, bounding up the mountain to the woods in a spray of glistening powder. While I was glad Kit spent most of his life in the wild, I still enjoyed our morning ritual.

I unlocked the barn and fed and milked my two goats, squirting the steaming liquid into a clean, bioplastic bucket. The goats had given liberally, so I decided to make cheese and yogurt.

"Immeda, put lemons on the shopping list," I said. It still amazed me that Immeda was in the air everywhere. It was very *Star Trek*.

"I've put lemons on your shopping list," replied Immeda in its pleasant but disembodied male voice, a slight crispness to the accent as if he'd lived in Britain. I had customized Immeda's voice because I found the default cloying.

Today was a day off from work, so I was going into town to restock supplies. After showering and a breakfast of toast, blackberry jam from a coworker's larder, and hot milfoil and rosehip tea, I put the dishes in the dishcleaner, which whirred for half a minute and flashed a blue light before falling quiet. A mobile iot buzzed over and put the clean dishes back in the cupboard. "Immeda," I said, "prepare the hopper for a trip to Fernie."

"Preparing the hopper," the AI replied. "It will be ready in four minutes. Naissa, shall I preheat the compartment?"

"Sure."

In the time it took to gather my things and put on my coat and boots, Immeda had performed a preflight check on the hopper. As I settled into the front seat of the cozy compartment, Immeda said, "The battery is fully charged, for the first time in eight months. We can expect only four hours flying time at full throttle before a charge deficit, which means the battery has reached the end of its useful life. Therefore, I recommend replacing it with the new SuperVolt battery, which increases storage capacity by one hundred and twenty-three percent while reducing weight and size by eighteen percent, at a cost of thirty-seven credits. Should I add one Super-Volt battery to the shopping list?"

"Yes."

"I've added a SuperVolt battery to the shopping list. Our flight plan to Fernie, BC, North Main Street parking area has been filed. Winds are light from the west. Skies are clear and should remain so for the rest of the day. There is little traffic anticipated. We should reach the destination at 1046 hours."

"Affirmative," I said as I buckled into the harness. "Immeda, let's go."

With a low whirring, the hopper spun up the electric motor. The rotopeller positioned itself for takeoff and the hopper began rising.

"Would you care for some music this morning, Naissa?"

I thought for a moment. I was now headed eastward, climbing parallel to the south face of the Three Sisters toward the mountain pass leading to Fairy Creek Valley. "Yes, Immeda. Play songs from *Sensual* by Andover."

As the familiar guitar and piano prelude of "For Us" filled the air, it occurred to me the music was over eighty years old. I remembered the day Julian won the Andover contract and we'd celebrated with a dinner cruise on the Hudson. The summer evening was warm enough to keep the river breezes pleasant, and the city sparkled along the riverbanks as nighthawks soared overhead, feasting on flying insects. These days, my guilt over not using my genome soon enough to save Julian—and my friends—was compressed into a dull ache.

While I appreciated the solitude of my cabin, I sometimes pined for old friends, as I'd done the night before. Against my better judgment and with a generous glass of wine, I perused obituaries and genealogies for familiar names. I had kept in touch with Robin's children until after Julian's death, so I already knew Robin's eldest, Brian, had drowned a mere two years after Robin died, as he tried to save a child struggling in a riptide. It didn't take long to find the rest of her brood. Vinnie, Robin's nephew born with trisomy 21, had succumbed to complications from a heart abnormality in 2022. Lee, Robin's middle child, had lived a long, fulfilling life, dying just eleven years ago at the age of one hundred and two. Dawn was eighty-three when struck down by ovarian cancer. I shook as I searched for Joy, but I shouldn't have worried. Little Joy was now sixty-three, a USEA engineer serving as Senior Scientist on the EH2 space station. I toasted her and drained my glass.

Last night, I also decided to resubmit my article to more journals. When I wasn't working in town, I sculpted occasionally, continued my *Defender-Within* campaign, and I wrote. It started with my journal in Sydney, right after the disaster. I had so many thoughts on sustainability and survivability in natural and human disasters, I had to write them down. I used much of the material on *DefenderWithin*, but realized I wanted to reach a different audience. Trying to write a little every day, I researched and completed a scientific article on human and environmental survivability, which I submitted to a half dozen relevant publications. Several months had passed, and I'd received no replies. After I got back home, I would submit the article to other journals.

"Please prepare for landing," said Immeda.

After the hopper alighted in town and rolled into an empty parking space, its engines powered down and the rooftop collector panels entered full-charge mode. Iots flitted busily in and out of the town's shops as they swept, carried, scurried, and flew about their tasks.

Taking my parcels and collapsible shopping boxes from the rear hatch, I walked to the market for supplies. When I passed near the synthetic meat aisle, Immeda reminded me via my earpiece to get treats for Kit.

As I put Kit's treats in my boxes, my wrist implant added the items to my bill. Although I'd resented implantable technology at first, I appreciated the implant's convenience. The implantables market was booming because wrist capsules and similar devices had become a primary means for people to interface with Immeda. They securely contained our identity, financial, and medical data, as well as microphones for voice communication. Implantables were integrated with the Shiwo security system and were not hackable—as far as Shiwo knew.

When I finished shopping, I said, "Immeda, send me a PSR." Many municipalities provided PSRs, public service robots, for common use. They were parked at stations around town and could be used free of charge by anyone needing assistance.

I barely had time to double-check my list before a PSR was at my heels, awaiting instruction. "Take these to my hopper," I said, pointing to the boxes. I watched for a moment as the boxes were whisked out the door and toward the hopper. Its job completed, the PSR went back to its station, ready for the next job.

"Immeda, did you get the new battery?"

"Yes, Naissa. It's already installed and charged."

Back home, as the iots unloaded my supplies, a message dinged. It was from *Science*! I held my breath as I opened the recording.

"We are pleased to inform you . . ."

I was to be published.

Not long after my article was published, I was offered a fellowship at the University of Washington to help develop a sustainability curriculum and continue my research. All classes were remote because the University was still rebuilding after the disaster. While I would miss the college environment, I was happy to stay in my Fernie cabin with Kit to keep me company.

As the weather improved, I worked in my spare time to replant the trees I'd helped grow. It was backbreaking, messy work, but greatly satisfying to see a barren hillside come alive with young, green growth.

The following summer, Kit showed up after a two-week absence. Beside him was a young vixen with a luxurious coat, and evidently, she and I were being introduced.

"It's a pleasure to meet you, Kit's friend. Could I interest you in a treat?"

I grabbed two eggs from the coop, tossing one to Kit, who did his midair catch routine. I laid the other down and stepped back a half dozen paces.

Cautiously, the vixen came forward and furtively snatched the egg and scrambled off to enjoy her snack. She and Kit played around the barn for a while, while I had a mug of tea and enjoyed the show. An hour later, Kit scampered up to me and brushed his head on my leg. I reached down to scratch his ears, just as he liked. He and I looked into each other's eyes, and then he turned and scampered off with the vixen.

Sadly, I never saw Kit again. I like to believe he became involved in fatherly things and raised generations of his own beautiful kits.

In 2080, I was deep in research and teaching while the world prepared to vote on Consensus. It was a hot topic among my colleagues, but I had seen too many governments come and go. From my experience, it didn't really matter who was in charge, the problems were always the same. Consensus was a unique idea and I hoped I was wrong, but I wasn't holding my breath.

I focused my research on sustainability in extreme environments, like those due to climate change and natural disaster. In 2086, I was proud to have my book, *Creating Sustainable Habitats in Alien Environments*, published by the University of Washington Press.

Six months after publication, I was in Switzerland addressing an environmental conference. After my keynote, a rangy woman with silver hair introduced herself as Admiral Mary Keita from the United Space Exploration Agency, based in New York. I was puzzled as to her interest in my environmental work.

"USEA's Mars Settlement Project," she said, "is preparing for civilian colonization. We have need for expert leadership in establishing a safe, livable, and sustainable environment for Martian settlers." She looked at me intently. "Is this something in which you might be interested?"

I was dumbfounded. Mars? Of course! It made sense. What was a more alien environment than Mars?

Within the month, I was on my way back to New York.

CHAPTER TWELVE

Rys

RE YOU SURE you want to hear this? Okay, then. It happened like
this: Someone made a mistake, and everything changed.

It was a winter day, according to my window, with fresh snow on
the ground made brighter by the light of the sun. I had medical testing that
morning. A quarter hour into it, the doctor cursed under his breath and said
he forgot something, that he'd be right back. He rushed out the door and
the lock clicked back into place.

The doctor left his flexi on the exam tabletop.

I scooted it under my exam gown and wedged it into the leg of my underwear. I said aloud to the listeners that I was going to the bathroom and
went back to my room. There were no cameras in the bathroom anymore.
When I was around fourteen, the aides had removed them, saying they
weren't needed anymore.

The doctor's notes were open on the flexi. I didn't get past the first line:
RG Test 352.04: Neural response to introduced alkaloids in subject CloneN$_2$.

Clone? I'd learned about Dolly the sheep in science lessons. I puzzled
over what this had to do with testing. A chill ran through me.

I quickly went back to the medical room, hopped up on the exam table, and put the flexi back where it was, just as the doctor reentered the room. When he asked why I was shivering, I said the room was a little chilly.

Everything clicked into place. Why I was being kept. Why they wouldn't tell me anything about myself. Why all the people around me were doctors and scientists.

I was a clone.

My entire life, I'd been lied to. *Nothing* was as I had believed.

I was just someone's copy. But whose copy? Where was she? Would I ever meet her? I doubted it, since they wanted to keep me in my cage.

How could my . . . creator? original? I didn't even know what words to use to describe the relationship between us, to describe *her*. Whatever she was, she was sadistic for making me grow up in this horrible place. And Mean. Heartless. Pure evil.

I'm sorry to say all this, but it's what I believed at the time.

I was only sixteen, and everything I thought I knew was a lie. The injustice of it, the horror—it was unbearable. I fought to contain the hurt and hate that overwhelmed me, wanting nothing more than to scream and throw everything I could lay my hands on. But I had to act as if nothing was wrong because they were always watching. It was hell. I was in hell.

Why hadn't Khala told me anything? I had so many questions. I needed her to tell me the answers. Khala's notes had laid a foundation, made me aware of the world outside, so at least I'd suspected *something* was amiss. Maybe it wasn't an utter shock. That night, I asked in my note to Khala about who was responsible for my situation. I asked her *why* she hadn't told me. She wouldn't answer. She broke my heart.

I was nothing but a copy. I was nothing at all. I hated each and every one of the people responsible for creating me and feeding me nothing but lies for my entire life. I drowned in hate. The only thing to do was keep quiet and watch for an opportunity to escape. In the interminable two years that followed with no chance to escape, there were times I wished to forget I ever lived. Yes, of course, I know I'm not nothing. Please don't cry.

CHAPTER THIRTEEN

2087–2092

Naissa

◦━◦━◦━◦━◦━◦

F LEDGLING CONSENSUS, AFTER *a dozen years of learning from
bungles and triumphs, was settling into a well-running system of global government. Issues from local to global were addressed in online forums, and
proposals were written, debated, and voted upon.*

*The environmental crisis on Earth led to rapid developments both on Earth
and off. Global environmental preservation and restoration measures were en-
acted through Consensus and began yielding results in the form of cleaner air,
purer water, and a slowing of species extinctions. As the environment, nutrition,
and medicine improved, life expectancy began to rise after plummeting from the
West Coast Disaster. The global population rebounded to eleven billion, evi-
dencing a need for sustainable living and population controls. To manage the
growing population and as a bulwark against any further environmental crises,
massive resources were poured into development of synthetic and sustainable
food sources, fusion and other energy technologies, space travel, and off-Earth
habitats on Luna and Mars.*

*The time heralded the Fifth Industrial Revolution, an age of expansion be-
yond Earth also known as the* Extrerram *era (derived from* Extra Terram). *The*

USEA announced First and Second Colonies for civilians on Luna and Mars, respectively, in 2091. Sol Horizon missions explored potential colonies within the solar system, and by the early 2090s, the Sol Explorer project was initiated to expand our reach beyond the solar system.

⚬──⚬──⚬──⚬──⚬

Back in New York City, USEA housed me in a mod apartment in the elegant Bayside Towers waterfront complex, on the eighteenth floor of Building Thirteen, right next to the 219th Street seawall. I nearly fell over myself when I first saw the mod. There were five rooms, tastefully furnished with modern decor, interspersed with gorgeous, mid-twentieth-century antiques.

The view from the massive windows reached all the way to Long Island Sound. The balcony held a table and two chairs, perfect for enjoying sunrise and morning tea. Looking straight down, I could see Little Neck Bay and the seawall below. While it wasn't my Fernie haven, it was perfect.

I was assigned to the Habitat team of the Mars Settlement Project, which was responsible for settlers' habitat systems, HVAC, and recycling. I reported directly to Admiral Keita and liaised with the Safety teams.

Since I was joining the team already in progress, Milon Cody, whose specialty was dome systems, gave me a weeklong crash course in the project. Thinking of the Xìngyùn jiāyuán lunar disaster, the first question I asked Milon was about the habitat domes' durability.

"As you can guess," Milon answered, "domes must be strong enough to withstand small meteors, about two hundred of which strike the planet each year on account of the thinner atmosphere. It's similar to what orbiting vehicles experience. Small in this case means less than two centimeters. Larger ones are rare, so strike odds are low. Even so, more permanent structures connecting to the domes are being excavated subsurface and cliffside. These should offer full protection during larger strikes. Safety and Transportation teams are building alarm and evac systems, as well as evac procedures.

"The domes must also be radiation and dust proof—there's a ton of fine particulate dust on Mars. That's why we're using nano-textured Mazuderm to help solve these challenges."

"Mazuderm?"

"It's a lightweight, thin, alon- and graphene-based laminate skin for the domes, pliable, stronger than steel, and dust slips right off. The stuff's amazing. The graphene layers are conductive, so Mazuderm also serves as part of the solar collection system. They've started using a derivative of it on spaceship hulls."

His answers alleviated some of my worries about living on Mars. "Another concern I have is how people will deal when living permanently in such confined spaces. Aren't the domes a recipe for claustrophobia, especially if kids are involved?"

Milon shook his head. "There shouldn't be any of the cloister issues like they had with Lunar prototypes, when teams went stir-crazy. Second Colony domes are massive! We think the combination of above- and in-ground spaces should help prevent the problem. And with the ample power supply, crops and even trees can grow under the domes and sublevel, creating a more natural environment. Two-thirds of the living space is underground, and it's designed to be open and airy. Best of all, people can walk around without always bumping into each other the way we do on Earth. There are still a million details to work out, which is why we're thrilled to have you on our team."

I learned that, since the atmospheres of Luna and Mars didn't support life, having clean air and potable water was an ongoing issue. Water mining on Luna wasn't worth the expense, so it was far easier and cheaper to carry water from Earth by tanker and then recycle.

But on Mars, water was less expensive to excavate and purify in the quantities needed. Recycling and controlling temperature required gobs of power, but fusion reactors and orbital solar farms filled the need. Also, cryogenic methane fuel production supplemented other power needs. The challenge of learning Mars and creating a sustainable human habitat was one I embraced with my whole self. The days and months flew by. One day, I ran into Admiral Keita in the hallway.

"Well, Dr. Nolan, how are you finding USEA?" she said with a smile.

"Wonderful, thank you. The team is terrific and the groundwork they did is extraordinary. I'm thrilled to be part of it all. There's so much to be done, every day is fascinating."

The admiral's smile became broader. "I've heard quite a bit about your contributions so far. Question for you: What would you say to a position as Director of Environmental Sustainability in the first wave to Second Colony?"

"Wh—what?"

"If you want it, you're going to Mars."

<hr />

Before leaving the planet, I traveled by skyleaper—hypersonic commercial craft—to Italy and France for a brief holiday. My first stop was Rome, the lovely city with some of the planet's finest architecture, paintings, and statuary. I was especially taken with the two-thousand-year-old stadium, the Colosseum, a link to a less complex world. Drawn there in the late evening when there were fewer tourists, I had a feeling of belonging. Standing in the arena, the long-gone spectators' presence palpable, I was transported back to that time. The word *ancient* took on new meaning for me, since, after my more than two hundred years, two thousand years ago didn't seem so remote. I was in the company of a cohort—an entity that existed far longer than any other human on Earth.

Then the thought of leaving my ancient, scarred roots intruded, and I was cowed. Would I be able to extract those deep roots and plant them in an alien and inhospitable world? Would they grow? Could they even survive? It felt as if I were about to erase my entire existence, and it was terrifying. I looked around me at the ruins and heard the ancient, cheering ghosts who filled the seats, chanting for victory. Perhaps the Romans would have been terrified by the thought of life on Mars, which in their geocentric world was on the far side of the sun. More likely, they would have been excited to venture to the god of war's abode, to face new challenges, expand their empire, and create a new world of their own.

I drew in a deep breath and let the power and courage of the place fill me. With it came the knowledge that my roots were strong enough.

The next morning, I shuttled to Paris, where I stayed another week. It was the first time I'd been there in over two centuries. The mimosas, mums, and dahlias were in full blossom and the city overflowed with color. The sidewalk cafés and croissants were just as wonderful as they'd been long ago. I toured the museums and the Notre-Dame Cathedral—restored after a devastating fire at the beginning of the century—and browsed some of the city's quieter neighborhoods with their quaint shops, cafés, and gardens. While the city had changed considerably since I was a girl, much of it remained as stunning as it was then. Every now and then, I'd turn a corner and be taken back to my first visit to Paris, when my family was whole. The force of the memories knocked my breath away.

On my last day in Paris, I went to the necropolis at Père Lachaise to say goodbye to my family. On the way to the cemetery, I purchased dahlias from one of the street vendors. I gently laid bouquets of white, blush, and carmine dahlias, reserving one stem, at the feet of each goddess and stepped back to sit on the bench. I gazed in silence at the monument, my emotions overflowing. While years of grime and bird shit lay thick over many of the monuments, the elegant song of love to the family I adored somehow remained pristine. My family was forever in nature, in beauty. As I sat there, cooled by a gentle breeze, I was filled with love. *My family, my beautiful family, I miss you so much. I love you.*

And then, it was as if my family's love radiated back toward me through the arch, locking us together and magnifying the fierce and glowing power of our bond. In that moment, there was nothing else but my family, and there never would be. I basked in their embrace until night began to fall and I bade them adieu.

Following a different path to the exit, I came upon what I had intended to find, although I nearly missed him: Auguste Clésinger, who had died fourteen years after completing the Nolan family monument. He was set in a depression, with four steps leading down to his grave, his name barely legible on the plain, granite slab under which he lay. I lay a carmine dahlia upon his grave.

Rounding another corner, I stopped again. There she was. Milhomme's *La Douleur*. This time, with the spirit of my family close around me, I wished her my best.

On the flight home, my heart warmed as I learned a trust for the monument's maintenance had been established long ago by my dear Uncle William. I made a donation to the trust sufficient to tend the tomb for many, many years to come.

⚭⚭⚭

I followed the manual I wrote, required for all emigrants, including how and what to pack for moving to Mars. Daunted by the prospect of packing up my life to begin again on another world, I procrastinated. Once I finally plunged in, I found it liberating to weed out the detritus. I stuffed my life into USEA-issued modular, lightweight packing cubes and weighed each one carefully. Fortunately, cargo weight allotments were enough to bring the climate-safe case with my treasured sparkle box and its photos and mementos.

Two weeks before emigration, my cubes were sealed and transported to Wallops Island, where they were sent by maglev to Artemis station and loaded onto our ship. I had to endure two days of testing and inoculations at a UCE clinic. One of my vials of ageless blood from Oberlin Institute enabled me to pass scrutiny. I was issued a travel kit with a starter supply of antirad eyedrops, med patches, and radskins, the silky long underwear worn under clothing to protect against accidental gamma radiation exposure. What a waste of precious space.

When the day of departure finally arrived, I boarded a 6 a.m. USEA shuttle to the spaceport. Once at the spaceport, I met my fellow passengers—including half of my Habitat team—and nervously watched the bustling launch preparations through the waiting room's glass wall. Technicians performed their final checks on the *Enterprise IV*, our shuttle to Artemis station, where the USEA Spaceship *Alectrona* was docked and waiting.

An hour later, our group made its tremulous way to the *Enterprise* shuttle. With shuttles leaving every eight hours, it would take two days to ferry all the emigrants to Artemis.

The *Enterprise* was cramped and windowless, but large displays mounted on the walls showed images of the tarmac around us. I settled into the high-backed seat, and with shaky hands, buckled my restraining harness and adjusted the straps. Moments after the crew verified all were secured in our chairs, the whisper of the engines grew to ringing harmonics.

As we began to accelerate down the long track, a wave of panic rolled through me.

Maybe this isn't such a good idea. Wait! I can't leave!

Then I laughed. It was a little late, as we were on our way. The track's roughness smoothed as we turned upward, reminding me of a roller coaster. I relaxed a bit. This wasn't so bad. The blue sky on the displays grew more indigo as Earth fell away below and our gradual climb steepened. As I was pushed back more firmly into my well-padded chair, the cabin started shaking and the roar from outside the hull of the ship became deafening.

Tears slid down my cheeks. I had been on Earth nearly a quarter of a millennium. I'd visited and lived in many places the world over and had seen mind-boggling changes. I had delighted in the fragrant atmosphere after a rain, the hush of new snow, and the birds' spring melodies. Everyone I'd loved and lost was buried in Earth's sweet ground. Earth was my *home*. And I was leaving. Quickly, I rubbed my tears away. We rotated backward and were pressed more deeply into our seatbacks, as if by some giant hand.

I was thankful the prelaunch courses had prepared me for this voyage. Just as the weight on my chest became too heavy, there was a sudden release of pressure and I felt as if I were falling. The quiet was instant and absolute. My legs and arms rose of their own accord and my insides threatened to come up and out of my mouth. The hush of the cabin was broken by folks making use of their emesis bags. My hair floated around me like seaweed in undulating currents.

The displays switched to split views of Earth retreating and Luna growing larger, with superimposed speed and distance counters ticking rapidly upward.

"This is Captain Hiraku. Welcome to outer space! Please prepare for artificial gravity. AG will commence in five, four, three, two, one."

My hair fell back to my shoulders and my orientation returned to normal, even though we hadn't changed our angle. I was pushed gently back into my chair again as a humming grew louder. Fusion drives were accelerating us toward Luna.

On our approach to Artemis station, the displays presented magnificent views of the gigantic *Alectrona* nuzzling up to its berth like a massive, hunched creature. The *Enterprise* docked smoothly at the station, where we disembarked. We were shown to our quarters and to the commons where we would spend the next thirty-six hours until departure.

Everything was cramped and utilitarian, reminiscent of the Eurail sleeper cars I'd traveled in long ago. The walls of the commons area were filled with displays cycling through important reminders, as well as beautiful Earthen, Lunar, and Martian landscapes. My attention went to the few, small viewports along one wall, and I walked to the nearest one. Peering out, I shivered at seeing the real *Earthrise*.

⁂

When it was time to board the SS *Alectrona*, the first wave passengers, composed mostly of essential personnel and a few civilians charged with setting up government and social programs, buzzed with nervous excitement as we queued by the boarding gate and slowly made our way to the ship. Finally, I stepped through the thick hatch.

Instead of the technical gear depicted in old science fiction vids, we were looking at what appeared to be the interior of a luxurious ocean liner. In my work with the Mars Settlement Project, our mandate was the settlers' wellbeing, so we made every effort to maximize the familiar. The counterpoint to this was the view from the portholes: a star-pocked blackness rather than an undulating blue sea. Once everyone found their cabins and secured themselves into lounge chairs, the *Alectrona* began the two-month journey to Mars. I was relieved there was only gentle pressure and mild vibration when it accelerated. The Beldon AG automatically compensated for most of the acceleration and deceleration forces.

Soon, we were told to unbuckle and head for a mandatory orientation, where we learned about the ship's facilities, amenities, and rules. The *Alectrona* contained a full complement of amenities, including lounge, exercise room, and two mess halls. Afterward, passengers were free to explore.

The voyage was replete with seminars designed to help this first wave of civilian settlers acclimate to Second Colony. Passengers learned that the Martian atmosphere consisted of approximately 96 percent carbon dioxide, its gravity was about a third of Earth's, it was half Earth's size, its days—*sols*—were forty minutes longer, and its year was 687 days. The temperature varied widely from temperate to nearly 200 degrees below zero, depending on season and location. Mars had two tiny moons which could only be viewed from near or at the equator. The colony's primary industry was mining materials and precious metals for use by orbital autonomous manufacturing stations (AMSs), as well as export to Earth and First Colony. Settlers were told that anyone outside a dome without a self-contained envirosuit would quickly perish, and that no one under twenty-five was allowed on the surface without adult supervision. They were taught how to use EV suits and about compulsory, monthly EV drills. Even within the domes, EV suits had to be kept close by in the unlikely event of dome failure.

There was a seminar on healthcare for settlers. The town clinic was full-featured and included equipment and supplies—even bioprinters—for any emergency. Vaccines and medicines were being manufactured on one of the orbital AMSs.

By the end of the voyage, all were familiar with how Second Colony's Consensus government would take shape; the colony's near self-sufficiency for all essential goods; what facilities, opportunities, hardships, and responsibilities to expect; and the habitat's layout and operation.

I gave a seminar on the new dome habitat. The domes each enclosed about one square mile, into which my project team had introduced Earth-like biomes using select flora and fauna, including grasses, birds, and beneficial insects to sustain environmental balance. Using MOX3 systems, oxygen was extracted from CO_2 in the atmosphere, melted ice, and a network of underground lakes. Green walls throughout the domes provided not only supplemental oxygen, but also edibles and a welcome verdancy.

Hope Town, where this wave would settle, had industrially printed, ornamented structures, and had been assembled by iots over the last five years. Above-ground and sublevel structures used a composite made of Martian soil and rocks, bound with refuse from plants grown in the domes. I help familiarize the settlers with the tunnels connecting the domes, geothermal heat and cooling, solar and fusion generators, pneumatic delivery tubes, and waste and water transport. Everything was recycled. The group twittered with nervous excitement at the video introduction to Hope Town and had many excellent questions about our reuse and recycling processes.

It was exciting to see my team's hard work coming to fruition.

<hr />

After two months, the *Alectrona* went into orbit around Mars. I was anxious: would the settlers thrive in an alien environment? Would I? Could I live in a dome? The anxiety became almost unbearable by the time the Martian shuttles docked with our ship. It was a rough ride to the surface, with winds stronger than expected. Everyone applauded and cheered when we touched down on a landing pad next to our dome.

When the shuttle's hatches were unbolted, I needed to brace myself against the light flooding in. I strained to look outside but couldn't see beyond people pressing toward the hatch. Finally passing through the umbilical, I did my best to remain steady as I emerged in an open area inside a dome bright with full-spectrum light.

"Hello, everyone. I am Juana Chang, acting coordinator. I would like to welcome all of you—including the first settlers on Mars!—to Earth's Second Colony and your new home, Hope Town."

Her words were nearly drowned out by two borers emblazoned with "New Worlds Boring Co." rumbling past the dome.

"As you learned on the ship, you will be electing your permanent town coordinator shortly. When more of the domes are populated, colonists will vote on other government positions. What's that? Yes, yes, not to worry, your belongings are being unloaded and will soon be at your new homes via delivery tubes. Now please join me on the autowalk. You will arrive at the residential area in just two minutes. Please hold the rail tightly."

Eager to settle into my new home, I was relieved Chang's speech was brief. We followed her onto the autowalk, which descended below ground and sped through a lighted tunnel. Well-marked EV suit lockers were positioned at regular intervals along the walls next to message displays, while other areas were lined with glistening plants and grow lights.

Chan's amplified voice sounded through the tunnel. "At the break in the autowalk, please proceed to the autowalk on your *left*. To your left only, please."

Moments later the autowalk ended and the tunnel diverged into two. A sign over the right-hand tunnel read Hope Town Underground, and the sign over the left, Hope Town Surface. Be EV-Ready!

After the autowalk ascended, slowed, and stopped, and we were back in domelight, exclamations arose from the group as we set foot in our new town. While living spaces were situated mostly underground, each had a small room on the surface. These buildings were set in concentric rings around a park with gazebo and adventure playground. The first ring contained community structures, and the remaining rings, the houses. Although I was familiar with the town through mockups and vid feed, I admired the quaintly ornamented structures in front of me.

One of the things the Mars team devised was decorating the habitats with familiar, Earth-based designs to help settlers feel at home. It was an eclectic selection, with architecture styles from around the world, all details printed using native materials.

Through the clear walls of our dome, I could see the Kirova Dome with its nearly finished administrative district. The dome was named after Verunya Diakovna Kirova, who'd devised Consensus government.

My new home was Victorian in style, colored yellow and apricot with a tiny turret. Every household had a small yard, one young evergreen and some berry bushes—enough to support a small population of pollinators. Although similar in structure, each dwelling was unique.

Opening the door, I saw that a picture window looked out on the fenced yard, with its lawn and lone tree. Heaven. There was also a prominent EV-suit closet.

Downstairs, the house was spacious and bright with full-spectrum light. All the homes had most of their living space underground. My bottom two sublevels boasted a living room, bedroom, kitchen, bathroom, utility room, an entrance to the autowalk, and another EV closet. Instead of windows, large displays defaulted to a view and sounds of the above-ground neighborhood and were customizable to any scenes desired. I set one of the screens to rotating live views around Mars, including Valles Marineris, Hale Crater, and Mount Sharp. The kitchen was efficient and had a display above the sink. I'd wondered how I would adapt to living below the surface, but because the rooms were big and bright, it was easy to forget I was underground. I could always spend time on the top floor whenever I wanted.

After setting the house climate controls, I noticed my cubes had arrived at the utility room. I removed them from the delivery tube and began unpacking. I had just pulled my mugs from one of the cubes and was about to make tea when an announcement came over the intercom: dinner would be served in the communal cafeteria in one hour, with a town meeting and tour afterward.

This was the first of many congenial meals with neighbors. The food, organically grown or cultured, was relished by all. I particularly liked the mushroom and synthbeef lasagna. Following dinner, we were welcomed again by Juana Chang. After taking some questions and pointing out the emergency zones, Juana led us on a tour of the market, sports center, clinic, and community center.

I quickly settled into Second Colony life and busied myself with work. At home, I planted an edible garden in my tiny yard. It brought to mind the many gardens I had tended throughout my life. I began feeling more at ease in my new environment.

"Warning. Breach in Zone Six. Go to shelter stations *now*. Don EV suits now. Warning. This is not a drill. Zone Six lockdown in sixty seconds. Warning."

Immeda's emergency voice filled the dome with loud repetitions. Every display flashed red with warning messages and a prominent timer counting down the seconds until the sixth emergency evacuation zone would be sealed off from the rest of the dome. It was up to anyone unfortunate enough to be in Zone Six to reach shelter before the doors were sealed or meet their fate.

Each dome was divided into eighteen numerically labeled emergency zones that could be sealed off from the rest of the dome. If a dome suffered a meteorite breach or other failure, no matter where people were when the alarm rang, they were required to immediately move to the closest designated safety area—below-surface safe rooms, as well as the tunnels—and put on one of the emergency EV suits strategically placed at short intervals throughout the domes and underground spaces. Practice drills were run frequently, two of which we had already undergone.

I was in the tunnels on my way to work in Kirova Dome, midway between my house in evacuation Zone Fourteen and Zone Six, when the alarm sounded. When Immeda announced "This is *not* a drill," my skin turned cold and my heart banged against my chest like it wanted to get out. My bladder loosened a bit.

Somewhere down the tunnel, a woman's voice shouted, "Henry! It's the same as a drill! Stay calm! You know what to do."

With that reminder, I steered myself back from terror, and my mind ticked through the ERSEI steps we had learned and drilled:

1. Get to the nearest *EV suit*.
2. Put on its **Respirator**.
3. Move to the nearest **Shelter**.
4. Put on the rest of the *EV suit*.
5. Wait for Immeda's **Instructions**.

I took an EV suit from the wall and quickly put it on, respirator first. Then, all I could do was watch the wall display as it announced the sealing of Zone Six. After what seemed an age, messages displayed that everyone in Zone Six had safely sheltered prior to sealing, dome repairs were already well underway, and the "All clear" would sound in a matter of minutes. *Thank god.*

The colony would experience a couple of dome emergencies a year, but after my first, they fortunately weren't that distinguishable from the drills.

INTERLUDE

M Y HEART HAS been heavy since I left Al-Hasakah long ago, and now my old bones ache all the time. I should retire, but how can I ever leave the girl? Little Tayir is a bright light in my sad life. I must still care for her as if she were my own.

I wondered if something was wrong when she entered her teens, and the wastebaskets and lack of supplies told me she does not bleed. Then, everything was explained two years ago by a memo I found in the trash that said unholy things about the girl. Things I thought could not possibly be true, but now I know they are. My little birdie is a clone. They keep her here for their research. It is a sick violation of all that is holy. She is still like a child, innocent of the awful things around her. What believer would make an innocent child an apostate before she existed? I pray someday she is welcomed into paradise. Her innocence does not deserve hell.

My poor Tayir! She knows. She knows what she is.

I do not know how this happened. I strove to keep her innocent, but now my heart is in a million pieces.

She asks me who did this to her. She wants to know why I never told her the truth.

I cannot answer, and am filled with shame.

❦❦❦

When I go into my Tayir's room, I hear tears. She is turned to the wall, and her sobs fall, hard like almonds dropping from a tree. When I go to her bed to dust the table and give her a packet of halawa, I reach out to caress her forehead.

She jerks away and pulls the covers over her head.

My Tayir despises me. I am wretched. I would tear my hair and rend my face, but I must not let them see anything has changed, for her sake— and mine.

I cannot answer because I am afraid. My cowardice kept me from helping her long ago when she was still a young child. How many times have I wanted to take her away from this place? Have I not wanted to free her so we could be mother and daughter? I would cut out my own heart to keep her from harm.

❦❦❦

I must protect my dear Tayir. Even if it tears out my heart, even if it causes my death, I shall know she is safe. I will find my reward in paradise.

In the memo saying Tayir was a clone, a *parent* was mentioned, a person who is the girl's source, her real family. I try to recall the name.

At a public terminal, I look up the parent. She is easy to find.

I take the electrical tape from my bag and quickly put a small piece over the terminal's camera.

With shaking hands, I make the connection.

I am crying, face in hands. The lady was so angry. What have I done? My little Tayir—have I hurt her more? Will she ever be loved?

CHAPTER FOURTEEN

2092–2097

Naissa

G LOBAL SPECIALISTS PAVED *the way for civilian settlers, having worked with robotic resources since the formation of USEA to construct Extrerram colonies on Luna and Mars. Autonomous Manufacturing Stations began orbiting Luna and Mars, scaling up for nonstop mining, production, and manufacture of essential goods and materials. Power, water, and oxygen generators churned on the planets' surfaces and in orbit, and foods began to be grown and printed in agriculture domes.*

In 2094, scientists mapping Beldon wave networks detected an anomaly in the expected wave flow near one of Uranus's moons, Rhea. When the mapping probe approached the anomaly, its coordinates began fluctuating in microbursts between its position near Rhea and what appeared to be random coordinates. The scientists were befuddled. Eventually, it was assumed the probe was having some sort of instrument failure scientists couldn't correct. Then, one day around a month later, the readings settled and location data placed the probe squarely in Alpha Centauri. A portal across space had been discovered.

Further research showed that dark-matter filaments tied parts of space together. Vessels could ride along the filaments, which were called bridges *in homage to Einstein and Rosen. A second bridge was detected near Ceres, leading to Beta Eridani's neighborhood. Interstellar exploration and colonization became a reality far sooner than anyone anticipated.*

⌘⌘⌘⌘

Mars was beautiful. Its reddish desert landscapes were molded with sinuous channels and craters, and there were shifting dunes. The daytime sky was a pinkish-red or butterscotch expanse with occasional wispy pink, blue, and white clouds, and the sun appeared smaller and softer than it did on Earth. During the hottest days of spring and summer, hundreds of dust devils, their vertical plumes spinning up to six miles high, whirled over the plains. Every so often dry-ice snow fell over the South Pole and was said to sparkle like diamond dust, although I had yet to see it. Earth was a bright light in the Martian sky, and the thin atmosphere made it easy to spot orbiting construction and solar power stations.

Work kept me busy but gave me opportunities to explore some of the more fascinating areas of Second Colony. The Sustainability Center, where I had a spacious office, was in the Kirova administrative district, just a ten-minute autowalk from home. Meetings and paperwork tied up much of my time, but I often needed to visit habitats under construction as well as production and recycling facilities. Many of these were OOD (out of dome), which meant I became adept at putting on and wearing EV suits. I enjoyed the relative freedom and slight buoyancy of OOD, so OOD days were the best days at work. We traveled outside in specialized Skyleapers and high-speed rovers, or *bugs,* as we called them. The main problem for equipment on Mars was the gritty, talcum-fine dust, which, when stirred up, took hours to settle. And it clung to everything. Specialized iots were programmed to clear the dust from above-ground transportation, structures, and each other to prevent it from interfering with their functions.

Visiting the enormous agricultural domes was my favorite. Just twenty minutes south by underground maglev, the cluster of domes was impressive.

Supported by massive recirculation systems and drawing energy from the orbiting solar stations, the domes met all of Second Colony's nutritional needs. In addition to crops of soy, legumes, vegetables, fruit, and mushrooms grown traditionally, there were vertical gardens, farms for edible insects, extensive aquaponic systems for fish, and culture tanks for algae, fungi, and synthmeat. One dome was purposed just for 3D printing of food products from grown and cultured base ingredients. In the poultry dome, chickens clucked around and scratched busily in the grass and dirt.

Just beyond the ag domes were massive equatorial greenhouse domes in which grasslands and young forests grew. These domes were the basis of the atmospheric regeneration program and so were carefully protected. However, weekly tours were available to settlers so one could linger among the oxygen-rich green space. When time allowed, and for adventure and respite from the claustrophobia-inducing domes, I explored. I was invigorated after visiting the yawning chasm Valles Marineris. This massive rift on Mars's surface dwarfed Earth's Grand Canyon. It was nearly four miles deep and as long as continental America. The trip started aboard a Skyleaper so sightseers could better take in the valley's enormity. Once we set down on the canyon's edge, its size and the immense mesas and intricate geology were mind-boggling. Thrilling and frightening winds shrieking at the rim made me thankful for sturdy guardrails at the overlook.

I traveled to Tharsis Montes, a group of volcanoes on the other side of Mars. Olympus Mons, the mightiest volcano in the solar system, took my breath away. Soaring almost fourteen miles into the heavens, it was two and a half times the height of Earth's Mount Everest and had a footprint the size of France. My protracted life was only a molecule next to the wonder of Mars's immense, ancient beauty.

Mars was a world of extremes, from lofty to gritty. Worst were the wind and dust storms. The largest storms were infrequent but could last days, weeks, or months. These howling terrors had wind velocities up to sixty miles an hour and prevented all but essential OOD activity, so the need to venture outside became, by increments, overwhelming. The sun-dimming blights were the reason satellite solar technology had been developed. Mar-squakes were also a common occurrence. Most were minor and barely felt, but some were forceful enough to rattle dishes. Even knowing the tunnels were reinforced with the same strong conglomerate as the above-ground structures, my heart still jumped every time our world shook.

I resumed sculpting, renting a small studio in the commercial district. I designed in 3D on a flexi and, once I had a prototype I was satisfied with, I cut into chunks of Martian granite I'd selected from Tharsis quarry. The dark butterscotch rock with sparkling silicate was dense and hard like the finest Earth granite yet cut as smoothly as marble. As I worked on the stone, an iot hovering above my shoulder projected my design onto its surface so I could hew the lines I'd envisioned. Once I'd roughed out the sculpture, I stopped using the iot and worked from my heart as I listened to music, using the rhythm of the music in the strokes of my hammer.

I'd been on Mars five years when, after lunch one day, my assistant buzzed.

"Dr. Nolan, you have a call on line one. There's no vid and she won't give her name. She says it's an emergency, something about an Oberlin Institute?"

My blood chilled. The institute? What on earth could they want? And why no vid? This could not be good.

Heavily sighing, I said, "All right, put her through, please."

My flexi showed a connection, but a black feed.

"This is Dr. Nolan." There was a long silence. "Hello?"

A voice whispered, "You work at Oberlin?"

"Not now. I used to work there some time ago. What's this about?"

"It is—it is your daughter."

"My *what*? I have no children." This was obviously some prank.

The woman sniffled. Was she crying? *I should just hang up.*

"Yes. There is a child. A clone, poor little bird. They made you a clone. They keep her in a secret lab, underground."

This stretched credulity. Or did it? I wouldn't put it past . . .

"How do you know this? What's your name?" I demanded. Then, as emotion overwhelmed me, I yelled, "This is preposterous!"

"Please! I clean her room. I care for her, write notes, bring her treats, for many years now." The woman was sobbing.

This was simply cruel. "Who put you up to this?" I screeched as my anger reached the boiling point.

"Wait! Please listen! Her name . . . her name is Naryssa. Like yours. I saw your pic, you are the same. She needs you, she needs her mother. I beg you, please, *please* don't tell my boss it was me. That awful Dr. Dubuisson."

"T'mos!" I shouted to my assistant as I ran out of my office. "I have to go, cancel the rest of my day."

I dashed to the autowalk. I couldn't think. Overloaded with images and words, my brain was a jumble. Trying to clear my head, I closed my eyes and slowed my breathing. But my eyes popped open and my mind took off again. Back home, as the call replayed in my mind—the institute, secret labs, and the word *clone*—my heart quickened and blood pounded in my ears. My legs fell out from under me and I dropped, landing halfway on a kitchen chair. The pain in my thigh and tailbone brought me back, and I shifted fully onto the chair.

I had to find out more! Was there really a clone? Was this clone ageless, like me? She had to be. Yes, identical. Had my former colleagues made immortality a *fact*? Had they? Hadn't they? Without my permission!

Anger and doubt took hold as I grappled with the truth of it. Maybe it was all a hoax. I had to see for myself. Yes! I would go to Vienna. Would they allow me into the institute? I had to try. I had to know the truth. What should I pack? Where was my travel bag? I had to message Natalie right away—

I had to get a hold of myself. Trying to steady my shaking hands, I poured a glass of wine, drained it, then refilled the glass.

After more than two hundred years of being alone in my agelessness, in a state of constant loss, in terror of being alone forever, would I no longer be the only one?

If it were true . . .

I set down my glass. Laughing and crying, I sank to the floor.

The next morning, I took a flight back to Earth. Thanks to advances in fusion engine design, the journey took only three weeks—far easier than the two-month trip I endured on my way to Mars. My time was spent with work and strategizing with Natalie Semler about how to approach the situation with the Oberlin Institute. It was difficult to focus on work. My mind hadn't stopped spinning since I'd learned about the clone. Once my anger diffused to a manageable level, I had so many questions. What would the clone be like, aside from the obvious? No doubt she had a diametrically different childhood than I, so what was the impact of her being "born" at OI? Would her personality be like mine, or different?

The never-ending question was, what was she to me and I to her? She was my teenage clone, yes. But what sort of relationship would it be? What would that relationship even be called? I supposed she was my offspring, but what did that mean? Was I just a donor? Or was I a sister? An aunt, a parent? A mother? I didn't give birth to her, and yet, in a way I did. I couldn't reconcile the strangeness of it or my resentment at being forced into this position without my knowledge. A few days before our scheduled arrival on Earth, things suddenly resolved in my mind. Maybe it was the pull of Earth's gravity—the pull of home. Or perhaps my long-stifled desire for a family. But all of a sudden, a full-body knowledge filled me with yearning and certainty: I was my clone's mother, and she was my ageless child.

I activated my flexi and pinged Natalie.

Natalie Semler was extraordinary when she was on fire. She had the Oberlin Institute brass in her teeth and was shaking them hard. Natalie and I were in the OI board room, sitting opposite the CEO, Donald Archer, his Counsel, and VPs.

"Research in the name of science? Are you *kidding*? What you and your goonies have done to this poor child, *Mis*-ter Archer,"—Natalie made his name sound like razor blades—"is the same as those deviants who kidnap children and keep them prisoner for years in their basements, doing what they will, whenever they want, to their young hostages."

She roared, her voice trembling in anger. "This is a *human being* we're talking about, a *child*! A child raised as a lab rat in a locked, basement room, without her mother, without love or guidance. A child who's probably quite damaged by now. The DA will need to hire more prosecutors to deal with the *very* many criminal charges that will be filed against you. You will be shut down. You and everyone involved will live the rest of your days behind bars. Count on it!"

Archer had gone pale and glossy. As Natalie took a breath, he made as if to speak, but she held up her hand, silencing him.

"I am *not* done. I'm familiar with Dr. Nolan's contract and NDA. But creating a human life, making Dr. Nolan a *parent*—without her *permission*! How despicable can you people get? Frankly, in the face of this nightmare, I don't give one *damn* about your contracts. And neither will any judge, any-where. You'll all be bankrupt from the damages alone."

Archer looked to his counsel, who gave him an I-told-you-so look and shrugged. Then he looked to the other three members of his executive team. They all squirmed.

Finally, he sighed loudly and looked first at me and then back to Na-talie. "What do you want?" he said quietly.

Instantaneously, Natalie transformed from raging wolf to smiling fox. "Now, *that's* what I was waiting to hear. Before we talk about the financials, let's discuss where Naryssa goes from here. Because, despite your worthless contracts, there is only one answer."

INTERLUDE

SECURED CONFIDENTIAL

MEMORANDUM

To: Robert J. Henchon, VP Product Development

       Crystal Jacobs, VP Clinical Development

       Silas Traut, VP Finance

From: Mr. Donald R. Archer, CEO

Cc: Jaki Navarro, General Counsel

Re: reGenia* Approval

How the hell did this get out? I want the culprit(s) found, stat.

It is imperative our application obtains regulatory approval to market *immediately*. Expense is no object.

Make the reGenia* announcement immediately; we'll preempt them by letting the world know of our success. We must limit any liability.

I'll expect your call by EOB today.

/lts

CHAPTER FIFTEEN

Rys

T HE LOCK WHIRRED at an unusual hour of the morning. I rose from my desk when I saw Uncle coming through the door with a strange woman who was without a lab coat and smartly dressed. Behind her was an older woman, also well dressed. The first woman stalked past Uncle into the room—and froze.

For an instant, I thought I was looking in a mirror, but then everything stopped. My breath, my heart, my life, stopped. There was nothing but a loud ringing in my ears.

I was looking into my own eyes. My small nose. The dimple in my chin. My face, my shape. I was looking at a mirror—of myself.

The instant it hit me, my knees crumpled and I landed back in the desk chair.

Clone!

Simultaneously, the woman staggered. Uncle reached out to steady her, but she pushed him off.

After what seemed an eternity, Uncle cleared his throat and said, "Dr. Nolan, this is Naryssa. Your, um, daughter."

At that, we both—my source and I—turned our eyes on Uncle, startled. *Daughter?*

The woman started to cry quietly.

What did he call her, Nolan? *My name was Nolan, too!*

Uncle cleared his throat again and ran his finger inside his shirt collar, as if it were choking him. I wished it would.

After a long moment, the woman spoke to me. "I—I'm sorry. This is all so . . ." Her voice sounded strange.

Was that how *I* sounded? I didn't care for it. I didn't know what to say. My mouth was so dry, I don't think I could have said anything if I'd wanted to.

Finally, Uncle said, "Well. I know this is awkward. What if we—"

The woman straightened and cut him off, her eyes steely. "No. You be quiet."

She turned to me. "Naryssa, how would you like to get out of here?"

"But that's im—" began Uncle.

"I said, that's *enough*, Alain!" The woman's voice matched her steely eyes. She looked back at me, her eyes softening and holding mine, an eyebrow slightly cocked. "Well?"

I glanced at Uncle—Alain? The other woman was whispering something in his ear. The expression on his wrinkly face was as close to panic as I'd ever seen.

Was it true? I had a choice? I could leave this place? See the outside world, at last? My heart pounded furiously. This was my chance!

But. The moment I'd known I was someone's clone, I'd hated her with all my heart. And here she was, the object of my loathing and an utter stranger. Sure, she looked like me, but I had no idea who she really was. Or where she would take me.

Wherever she took me, I could have a better chance of escaping.

I looked around my room, the only place I'd ever known. The fountain gurgled and sparkled on the vid as a cardinal sat at the forever-full feeder. On the wall, the clear, blue water of Fiji still kissed the beach. The back corner of my bed, which had seen countless secrets passed, called to me.

No doubt sensing the cause of my hesitation, Uncle made a small noise. His eyes were on me, pleading.

"Let's go," I said to the woman.

As I walked past Uncle and out the door of my prison, it occurred to me: Khala's promise was coming true.

<hr/>

Outside the Oberlin Institute's front door was a complete, living, foreign world. All my senses were barraged by the painfully bright and noisy city life, but I absorbed the vibrancy the way a towel soaks up water. As I followed Dr. Nolan and her companion, introduced as a lawyer named Ms. Semler, to their navicraft (Navicraft! Uncle had lied about that, too), the energy in me grew and sparked until I felt overloaded, a bitter taste growing in my mouth.

In the quiet of the craft, Dr. Nolan said to Ms. Semler, "You were magnificent." They both smiled.

Then Dr. Nolan turned to study me as I gawked at the city streets.

"Are you okay?"

In truth, I wasn't sure.

I was shocked and angry and scared at the whole situation and thrilled to finally be outside. It was dizzying. But I nodded.

"Naryssa, I am so sorry I didn't learn about you until a few weeks ago. I had no clue you existed. I came as fast as I could."

She didn't know about me? Well, that was stupid. Since she gave her DNA, she had to know they were making me.

"I suppose we should say we're twin sisters, in case anyone asks."

I stared at her. I knew nothing about her, and I wondered what sort of doctor she was. If she, too, tortured kids.

"I don't know what to call you," I said.

She gave a start and glanced at Ms. Semler, who was piloting the navicraft.

"Naissa. My name is Naissa Nolan. But in private, you may call me something like *Mom*, if you want."

Ridiculous. She was not my mother. She wasn't even my donor, not really. A donor implies something given—she'd just stupidly let the doctors make me.

What life lay ahead with her? At least I'd had what I needed in my room. And I'd had Khala. What had I done? The bitterness I'd been tasting turned into nausea. I turned and squinted out the window at the infinite colors and people.

—————

It took less than twenty-four hours for Oberlin Institute to destroy my newly found freedom. Their press release announcing reGenia˚ therapy for agelessness ignited a paroxysm across humanity. For the first time ever, humans owned the Holy Grail. Not only did the institute trumpet their violation of my life and Naissa's genome, they named Naissa and me—the first successful human clone pair—as the "immortals" from whom the miracle of reGenia was made. Even worse, someone told the press the name of the hotel where we were staying.

"I'll bet it was Alain, that rat," hissed Naissa. She really didn't like Uncle.

"They're trying to preempt our case," worried Ms. Semler.

All the next day, reporters banged on the suite door and shouted at us. They swarmed on the street beneath our rooms and sent spy drones to loiter outside the windows. The hotel tried to keep our privacy, but the situation deteriorated. Finally, police grounded the drones and posted guards outside our door and the hotel. Our dinner was brought to our rooms, but someone snuck a recording device on the tray, which we didn't discover until dessert. After that, Ms. Semler said the recording was all over the news, which I wasn't allowed to see.

The uproar was terrifying and I couldn't stop shaking. I'd gone from one prison to another.

Naissa suggested we go to Mars as soon as possible. She said security was tighter there and we would have privacy. I didn't care what we did, as long as I escaped this madness.

Going to another planet was hard to imagine, after having been confined to two rooms my whole life. Despite how much I wanted to stay on Earth and see as much of it as I could, we took a ship to Mars early the next morning.

Aboard the ship, we traveled in a private suite and our meals were brought to us, so there were none of the problems as in Vienna. Every time I turned around, there was a new discovery. Immeda was a wonder; I'd never imagined just talking to the air and having it respond in so many ways. Naissa even gave me my own flexi.

———————

Naissa said Mars was a beautiful planet, that I would love it. She was wrong. In Vienna, for the first time in my life, I breathed fresh air and felt the breeze caress my face. Outside, the sun's warmth was golden and glowing. A thousand scents filled my head, and as many sounds sang in my ears. On Mars, we were cooped up in domes with an artificial habitat. The colors were subdued and rusty. Sure, there were plants and places to take long walks, but they were all indoors. In many ways, Mars wasn't so different from what I'd known most of my life.

After Naissa showed my room to me, she said, "There are towels, toiletries, and menstrual products in the bathroom, and food in the kitchen. Help yourself to whatever you need. If there's anything missing, just tell me, or you can order it directly from Immeda."

"Menstrual products?" I'd not heard the term before.

Naissa's sharp intake of breath told me I'd stepped into another of my ignorances. Great.

"For when you get your period?" she said cautiously. "You do get your period, don't you? Monthly bleeding?"

I shook my head in confusion. She was speaking a foreign language.

"How old are you?" Naissa asked.

"Almost eighteen."

"Oh my god. I'm going to kill those bastards." Naissa's face glowed red with anger as she hissed the words, but she quickly calmed herself.

"Okay, it's clear you and I have lots to learn about each other. Why don't you settle in and make yourself comfortable, and we can start at dinner. I'll have it ready in half an hour."

Every time Naissa walked away from me, I saw myself from behind. How weird. I couldn't imagine ever being comfortable again.

<hr />

I hated being alone when Naissa went to work. I explored the Hope Dome as much as I could, but I felt as out of place as a fountain in the Martian desert. People stared at me, whispering to each other. After a time, I was mostly ignored, although occasionally a reporter or someone recording would jump out in ambush. When that happened, Dome Security quickly appeared and escorted the offender away. Eventually, the harassment evolved from suffocating to just annoying. Most afternoons, a woman named Arrel came to the house for a couple of hours. Naissa had hired her as a tutor to help fill in what Uncle had omitted in my education. There was so much to learn, sometimes I thought I would never be on par with other people. Arrel was nice to me, but she was paid to be.

After a few months, I couldn't shake the feeling of being alone and penned in. I blamed Naissa. One morning Naissa asked if I was ready for the afternoon's lessons with Arrel. I yelled, "Back off, Naissa! You're never here, what do you care? I don't have to listen to you."

She stood frozen for a minute, and then closed her briefcase and quietly walked out the door.

I sat at the kitchen table, staring at the closed door. I wished I hadn't said what I did. I was so alone.

﹏﹏﹏

Once in a while, I escaped to the ag domes. After a life of plain white rooms, being with real growing things made me feel almost as if I were growing, too. I felt a peace I'd never felt before. The first time I spent the afternoon at the ag domes, however, the peace was short lived, because Naissa was waiting for me when I went home.

"Where were you?" she fumed. "I was worried sick!" She paced back and forth in front of the living room monitor. "You were supposed to be here doing your lessons. I was ready to call security."

"I was at the ag domes. I went out right after Arrel left. I tried to message you to let you know, but you didn't answer." The last bit was a lie. I thought I'd become proficient in lying while at the institute.

Her eyes narrowed. "You never messaged me! And you didn't answer my messages. I had no idea where you were. You could have been—" She paused to slow her breathing, and shook her head. "Oh my god, I don't believe this. Of course I messaged you."

"Relax, Naissa," I said. "I'm fine. I wish you'd stop patronizing me. You treat me like I'm a child, like you're my mother or something." I didn't need another Aunt or Uncle suffocating me.

She flinched at my words.

"But I *am* your mother."

This was too much. She was only an ignorant cell donor. "Mother? *Mother*? Hardly!"

I raced to my room and slammed the door.

﹏﹏﹏

Naissa tried to take me outside the dome. I had to wear an EV suit, which I hated as soon as I put it on. My mask kept fogging, and I felt like I couldn't breathe. Being outside the domes was even more confining than being in them. I breathed harder and faster, but the lack of air got harsher and harsher, until my vision started to blacken around the edges. Sobbing and gasping for air, I stumbled back to the airlock. By the time I was able to remove the helmet, I couldn't gulp air fast enough. Naissa tried to put her arms around me as I cried, but I only felt more claustrophobic by her embrace. I refused to go outside the domes after that.

Naissa sometimes asked me about the institute, but I wouldn't answer. I refused to relive what I knew was a mutant life, different from everyone else's: the life of a copy.

Besides, it wasn't any of her damn business.

One day, Naissa saw me drawing on my flexi.

"You draw? May I see?"

I gave her the flexi.

"This is beautiful!" she gasped. "Your style is powerful, yet sensitive. How long have you been drawing?"

"Since I can remember."

Naissa smiled at me. "You know, I draw, too—and sculpt. Would you like to see my studio? It's a quick trip by autowalk."

I liked Naissa's work, especially her sculptures. She made jewelry, too, and said her dad and grandfather had had a jewelry business. In the nineteenth century.

"Is it true what they say, we don't grow old and we heal quickly?" I asked. "I thought it was normal when I healed after all the tests, but the doctors seemed weirdly interested."

"Tests? What tests?" Naissa looked worried, but I didn't answer.

After a minute, she went on. "No, it's not normal. Everyone else is . . . mortal. They can become sick, or hurt, and eventually, they die. You weren't taught that?"

I remembered learning about old wars when Uncle taught history, and characters sometimes died in stories I read. "I guess so, but I didn't know *everyone* dies."

Naissa sighed. "Not everyone. You and I are the exceptions."

"Are there others?"

"Not as far as I know. At least, for now."

I was skeptical. "There were some really old comics in my library, about people called superheroes. They had special abilities and saved people from evil villains. You're saying there aren't any superheroes?"

She shook her head. "No, superheroes are only in stories and vids."

"Aren't you a superhero?"

She picked up a small statue of a pair of flying birds and turned it over in her hands, studying it. "No. I'm no superhero."

"Why not? You don't die and it doesn't matter if you get hurt."

She sighed and set down the statue. "I guess I'm not strong enough. I've almost always hidden my . . . superpower."

She paused, considering before going on. "I'm not a superhero, but I try to do good, to do the right thing. Problem is, I'm too human. I mess up."

Like you messed me up.

After that, Naissa and I would go to her studio when she had free time. She taught me how to sculpt. She let me use whatever tools and supplies I wanted. Mostly, I went to her studio to draw and try to sculpt while she was at work. I ordered watercolor supplies and started painting, too, mostly imaginary landscapes. I still longed every day for the Earth of my dreams.

⚜─⚜─⚜

"I can't tell you how glad I am to have you here with me," Naissa said while stirring the pot on the stove.

We were in the kitchen making Sunday dinner. I was prepping vegetables Naissa had picked up at the market. On weekends, she sometimes cooked and asked me to help. I'd never even been in a kitchen before coming to Mars, so I think I was more hindrance than help. Usually, she talked while we worked, and she told me about her life.

It was hard to believe she was that old. Some of what I learned in Uncle's class happened when she was young.

It was another era, another world.

"To be honest," she said, "it's been terribly difficult to always lose the people I've cared for. I've—I have waited lifetimes for family, for you. Now, we can..."

"What? Be friends forever?" I scoffed. "Sure." I don't think she saw me roll my eyes. I thought having someone for the ages didn't seem like such a bad idea. But it couldn't be her. Not the one who was responsible for my life's misery.

"You may not like it, Naryssa, but we're in this boat together, forever. I understand you've had a rough life so far and that it's difficult to adjust, but—"

"You understand nothing."

"Listen, I love you and I'm trying, don't you see that? Please let me in. You need to meet me half— *Wait!*" She pulled out a small knife from a drawer and held it out to me, handle first. "Instead of that large chef's knife to eye the potatoes, try this paring knife, and remember to hold your left hand as I showed you." She mimed her instruction, and I did as I was told.

"Anyway," Naissa continued, "being ageless can be awful *and* wonderful. It's important to have someone to celebrate good times with and commiserate with the bad. It will help both of us to share what we're going through, to be sounding boards for each other. Trust me, it will be wonderful to have company navigating our long lives. Someone dear to me once said that limitless life means limitless possibilities. In my experience, there's truth to it."

We were quiet for a while as I chopped and Naissa stirred.

"Naryssa," she said firmly, "I want you to know you can count on me, forever."

I handed Naissa the bowl of chopped potatoes and turned to wash my hands at the sink. I wanted to believe her, but I couldn't.

One morning I was flipping through the news on my flexi, when I heard the words "Oberlin Institute" and stopped scrolling. The story was about a Syrian woman who worked as a cleaner at the institute. Her name was Zaina Darwish, aged sixty-three. They said she had walked in front of a city transport vehicle and been killed.

Then they showed her image. It was Khala!

Realizing Khala was gone made me die a little inside. I couldn't imagine the world without her. Why would they blame her for being run over? In the vid of the accident, she seemed to be dazed, moving in slow motion, like something was wrong. Oh, why had I been so mean to Khala? Why, when she was the only one who ever cared about me? I cried the rest of the morning.

⌖⌖⌖

"Why do people call you doctor?"

Naissa looked up from her flexi. "I'm not a medical doctor. I have a doctorate degree in genomics and molecular biology, and those with PhDs are often addressed as doctor."

I was puzzled yet felt my anger rising. "Genomics? You study genes? You *are* like those people at Oberlin! I hate them!"

"I know you do. So do I," Naissa said. "In another life, I worked at the institute before you were, um, born. I wanted my genome to help people so they might have longer and better lives. I got the education and took the job so I could find out why I was different from everyone else. I learned quite a bit, but never fully unlocked the secret. Apparently, it took Oberlin another eighteen years to do so after I left. I know now, going to them was a mistake." She held my gaze.

I looked away. "Why are you a sustainability director now, if you're really a scientist?"

"The institute was only concerned with making huge profits. When I learned they had an illegal human cloning program, I left. They'd said they were researching medical cloning for replacing organs, nothing more. When I discovered the truth, I couldn't support their unethical research."

"Why didn't you report them?" If she had reported them, I never would have existed.

Naissa grimaced. "I wanted to. But there was a legal contract, and they threatened me if I were to violate it. So, I worked and fought for sustaining the environment, something I've done a good part of my life, especially after the West Coast Disaster. I want to help preserve our environments for future generations—and, in truth, also for myself. And now for you. My problem with the institute was—is—they own and control my genome. Based on their human cloning project, I didn't trust them to use my genome ethically, and I was right. Ms. Semler is pursuing a case against them now, and it looks like we'll get a nice settlement."

I had nothing to say to that, and Naissa returned to working on her flexi.

After a while I said, "I don't understand how you could work toward prolonging lives and then be concerned about sustaining the environment. With cloning and agelessness, wouldn't the population get out of control? How can you explain that?"

Naissa set down her flexi.

"I've always believed if people live longer or become ageless, they'll realize we *must* live sustainably to preserve our habitats for ourselves. I've been working with my wonderful attorney to write Consensus laws to create sustainability, as well as work toward zero growth—or ZPG—through universal access to better birth control and other incentives. We also must consider if people choose to be ageless, then should they be able to procreate? Maybe not."

She seemed too optimistic. I'd been learning a lot in my history lessons, and the common theme was people caring only about themselves. Naissa was wrong about people caring about where they lived. So stupid.

I answered, "But what about all the other planets? They're finding new ones all the time. People will just go there and mess them up."

"Colonization is only a partial solution, Naryssa. Life on planets in habitable zones is far superior to living in domes like this, but the exoplanets are rare. If immortal populations grow unchecked, we'll chew up every planet we come across. That's why I'm working so hard here on Mars to ensure humans live sustainably and with ZPG goals."

I agreed with domes being undesirable. Still, something was unsettling me.

"Why aren't you fighting cloning, too? Cloning's terrible for your ZPG goals. Why aren't you shutting down places like Oberlin Institute *now*? They deserve to be gone."

"I'm trying," Naissa said with a sigh. "The trouble is, change is hard. Setting up laws and using the courts takes time. A lot of time." She stood and walked to the monitor to watch the view, fiddling nervously with her hair. "I mentioned Natalie and I have been working on a case against the institute for a while. It's because—aside from what they did to me—to us—the ethics of human cloning are highly questionable. For years, no one attempted human cloning because of the huge risk of abnormalities and death.

"Clearly, that's been overcome." When she snorted, I cringed, but Naissa went on. "But I think human cloning throws everything we value as a moral society into the trash. On the scientific side, humans have evolved for millennia, thanks to natural selection. What happens when we screw with that prime directive, when we homogenize the gene pool with clones? Or when we take away their choices by making them sterile, as they did with you. If we lose our capacity to evolve, we'll never survive as a species."

The more Naissa talked, the more pain in my center grew and spread, until it felt as if the weight of the world were on my chest. They made me sterile? I don't know who she was talking to, but it sure wasn't me. Naissa went on and on, swept up in her strong feelings, while I became smaller and smaller. The worst part was that Naissa didn't believe in cloning. She didn't believe in *me*. Tears streamed down my face.

Finally, Naissa turned around, asking, "Naryssa, did you—?"

She blanched as she saw me.

"*Mother?*" I screeched. "What mother would make a copy of herself for a child?"

Naissa covered her mouth with her hand, but once started, I couldn't stop.

"Tell me, why was it so important for you to have me? It doesn't matter that you didn't know about me—in fact, that's part of the problem because it made me even more of a nonperson. You made me *nothing*. I can't even be a mother someday. And then, you abandoned me to those sadists? They tortured me! *Tortured* me! All they cared about was knowing why I healed, why I recovered from their sadistic shit. I was in prison my whole life, and now I'm in prison here. It's all your fault. You should have protected me. You're no mother!" I sobbed and then screamed, "*I hate you!*"

⁕⁖⁘⁖⁘⁖⁕

Around midnight, Naissa came quietly into my room. "Naryssa?" she whispered.

I pretended to sleep, and eventually she left the room, softly closing the door. I didn't want to be like Naissa. I didn't even want to be *with* her. Knowing we'd always be part of each other forever made me want to throw up.

When all was still in the house, I climbed out of bed, fully dressed. I neatly made the bed and retrieved my backpack from the closet. Earlier, I had filled the backpack with my essentials and a minicryo case with an ampule of Naissa's modified blood, which I'd snatched from her cryofreezer. It was her mistake to tell me about it. I'd also cashed out all the credits from the account Naissa had set up for me. Last, I'd written a note to be posted in the morning on the kitchen monitor where she would see it: *I can't do this anymore. I have freed myself to find my own life. Please don't look for me.*

As silently as possible, I left the house and took the autowalk to the transport hub. I had signed on as a USEA crewmember for a wage and free room and board, and there was a ship leaving for Luna in the morning.

Once aboard ship, I changed my appearance. While the media crush had died down on Mars, there was no telling what it would be like anywhere else. For my appearance, I installed programmable facial implants made of bodyforming nanobots. Because they weren't a part of me, I guessed my body would ignore them.

A technician led me through the process. "Here, drink this," she said, handing me a cup of milky liquid. "It's the nanobots."

I dutifully swallowed the syrupy, mint-flavored fluid filled with billions of the microscopic devices.

Once I handed back the empty cup, the tech said, "Now we tell them where they should go." She looked me in the eyes and said, "It will feel a little weird, but it doesn't hurt."

She held up a flexi in dual-view mode so I could see what she was looking at.

"Slide these markers over the image of your face to direct the nanobots. They'll cluster below your skin and change your facial contours. Like this."

She moved her finger on the flexi image to the left cheek and tapped. A strange, murky feeling went from my stomach, up my neck, and to my check, but it quickly subsided. I looked in the wall mirror. My left cheekbone was high and prominent. *Holy cow!*

"Nice, eh? Once the nanos are in the general area, you can fine-tune with these controls." She gestured to the menu bar on the flexi. "Just stay away from your eye sockets. And over here are pitch and timbre controls if you want to edit your voice." She ran her finger along an orange slider and my throat tingled. "Now, say something."

"Hello?"

I nearly jumped out of my skin at the sound of my deep bass. We both laughed. We spent the next half hour molding my face and voice until I was satisfied.

"At any time," the technician assured me, "you can tell Immeda or use the app on your flexi to make changes. When you want to go back to your original face, just tell the nanos to exit through your digestive tract."

The implants held. A few minutes later, I went to my appointment at the USEA office to retrieve my new identity card, for which I'd submitted Naissa's modified blood. From then on, I would be Rys Martin.

CHAPTER SIXTEEN

Rys

IT WAS CLOUDLESS and moonless the night we firebombed the worst of the cloning facilities, the one at the center of everything (I know you agree with that assessment). Yes, of course, we made sure the building was clear before we set it ablaze. Right after I'd shattered the front door with a large rock, we called building security to report several "suspicious characters" outside the front door. As soon as the three guards went outside, we detonated the charges. You should have seen it. Massive flames reached skyward, and boiling clouds of thick smoke covered the entire sky, eerily lit from below.

The fire brigade was quick to arrive. Even so, the place burned to the ground amid explosions of varying combustibles. No surprise, considering all the chemicals on site, right?

I can't begin to describe how happy this made me. I'm sure you can relate.

This action represented the culmination of two years of planning. My knowledge from time on the inside made all the difference to our success and insured no one was hurt. Because of the mission, I believed they would think twice before going forward, and those who thought they were mightier than evolution—mightier than God—might learn humility. We could save the world.

While I'm sure we set the stage for real change, I think we were naive to believe our small actions would have global consequences. I've since realized the way to make this change is through Consensus. Only when the majority agrees can we reach our goal. Yes, I believe it's possible. As you have, all along. But then, I saw everything differently.

After I left you, my mission on Earth was to stop human cloning by any means possible. *Any* means. I'm sure you understand why. A nascent anticloning movement was beginning to form, and it didn't take me long to find like-minded people. We moved around a lot, usually staying on the outskirts of cities with research and production facilities, and moving on after a successful mission.

Remember when we talked about superpowers? Those days, I felt like a superhero. I was fearless, always on the front lines. Nothing could stop me. It was a joyous feeling. For the first time, *I* controlled my life. I found who I was and my place in the world. I was proud, confident. And happy. A bit terrified, too. That much power can be scary.

But, as we marched through our missions, I began to acknowledge an unsettled feeling. As if a small being were nagging me, telling me I wasn't doing enough. The more I was in the world, the larger the picture I saw. I began to question the approach. I studied Consensus procedures, and realized there was more than one way to achieve real change.

I've decided to go to law school because I want to fight the cloning companies. They have complete freedom to do whatever they want, which will only lead to disaster. We need laws to control cloning and zero population growth, and I want to make those happen. Anyway, I'd taken the admissions tests and was waiting to hear from NYU when she messaged me.

O NE OF HUMANITY'S *greatest dreams was filled in the late twenty-first century: healthy, ageless, immortal life. The reGenia' genome was extracted and isolated from a living, human female born in 1850, and tested in her clone, who was born in 2080. Adults treated with the genome reverted to young-adult physiological age, were healthy, had injuries heal instantly, and apparently did not age or die. Researchers at the Oberlin Institute, which owned and developed the genome, escaped prosecution for violating human cloning prohibitions by arguing a "necessity defense," asserting that breaking the law was justified to advance the common good.*

Consensus programs for environmental sustainability and reclamation continued to reap benefits of a cleaner, more stable environment. The average global temperature remained steady at the post-WC Disaster level, thanks to multiple carbon abatement programs. Population issues remained a concern, however, and were aggravated by the advent of reGenia's agelessness.

First and Second Colonies on Luna and Mars developed and grew, although at a slower pace than planned. Given the economic and psychological costs of dome life and because viable planets were within reach, resources were

*diverted to more environmentally suitable planets for human habitation. In the
2030s, the former NASA's ARIEL mission had discovered the planet Sovak in
the Alpha Centauri system. Sovak orbited the sun Alpha Cen-B, in its habitable
zone, where conditions were favorable for the existence of water and atmosphere.
The first Alpha Cen probe sent through Rhea Bridge in 2095 confirmed Sovak's
Earthlike atmosphere and conditions.*

*On May 4, 2105, after deployment of several advance supply missions, a Sol
Explorer mission aboard the* Sally Ride *successfully landed humans on Sovak
for the purpose of establishing Third Colony. Other exploratory missions were
sent through Ceres bridge to Beta Eridani, where several promising planets had
been found.*

Naryssa left me to be free from the confines of domes. To be free from *me*.
She despised me and my role in her existence, of that I had no doubt.

I tried desperately to find her. She'd left on a flight to Luna, that much
I knew. But she disappeared after that; I could find no trace. When it occurred to me she might have changed her identity, I ran to my cryofreezer
to check my samples. Sure enough, one was missing. She could be anyone,
anywhere.

I was sick in bed for week before I could drag myself to standing. Even
though I'd only known Naryssa for a short while, losing her was like losing
a piece of myself. I understood why she hated me and held me responsible
for . . . everything. I would have felt the same way, in her shoes. But to realize
the depth of her hate and the lengths she went to disappear from me was
difficult to bear. It was pain unlike any I'd ever felt.

It had broken my heart when I realized she was ignorant of menstru-
ation, when I realized those soulless bastards had made her sterile. My
clone—my daughter—would never know any biological family other than
me. How could they have deprived her of that choice? I wanted to burn
down the whole thing and then curl up and die.

Ever since my time with Robin, I'd known how difficult it was to parent teens. And then I was dumped into the deep end of young angst. How much of our troubles were due to her simply being young? How much to the horrid environment in which she was raised? And so much because of my own stupidity. To be honest, it was easier without her daily arguments and attitudes—but thinking I'd never see her again terrified me.

As hard as it was to lose Naryssa, I hoped this move was good for her. She was so naive, so vulnerable. If she had truly changed her identity, as it seemed, maybe the vultures wouldn't find her, either. Worry became my constant companion.

Oberlin Institute paid—and would always pay—handsomely for their moral failures and lapse in discretion, Natalie made sure of it. But it was small compensation.

<hr/>

When cleaning Naryssa's workspace in the studio, I found a stack of her watercolors. They were intricate abstracts of watery shapes seeming to morph into more meaningful objects, while at the same time remaining vague and unnamable. Her work was excellent. I appreciated the blues and greens of the aqueous compositions, being weary of all the red dust. I hoped she would keep up her art.

Oh, Naryssa. My wish was that distance might someday bring us closer. Life used love and lust, as well as the craving for children, to ensure we passed on our genes. Sustaining life through procreation was the reason we were here. My child, however, was created in a sterile lab, and had proved hostile and frightened. My short attempt at motherhood snuffed out my inner peace. I intensely loved and as intensely resented Naryssa, who was both my core and my bitter pit. My child, the one I'd dreamed of for centuries, was nothing like my idealized concepts.

There were times I could do nothing more than sink to my knees and sob.

When Admiral Keita asked me if I wanted to be Habitat Administrator for the first human mission to Sovak, I was stunned. It would be a chance to build a sustainable, human environment from the ground up, something I dreamed of but thought I'd never see. Second Colony was doing well and becoming more self-sustaining all the time, so I wasn't needed there as much.

On Sovak, I would be much farther away from Naryssa, wherever she was, which I wasn't sure I could handle. But then, I realized she could easily find me, if she wanted. So, with nothing left for me on Mars, I decided to look to the stars for the self I had lost.

I was to accompany specialists from Earth, Luna, and Mars to establish Third Colony. How marvelous it would be to live outside domes, to be free, unencumbered by EV suits! Sovak was, as far as we could tell, a world of fantastically diverse plants and organisms. Vids and data sent from Sovak rovers showed rolling, bouncing creatures with intelligence evolved to that of Earth's canines. It would be an extraordinary adventure.

We would travel aboard the USEA Starship *Sally Ride*, a huge, Star Cruiser–class vessel. With Rhea Bridge and the *Sally Ride*'s fast Roddenberry-Asaro, or RA, engines, Sovak could be reached from Second Colony in just two years, even with extra time to minimize acceleration and deceleration forces. I packed my boxes and was ready to go in one hour.

My fellow crewmembers and I were given inoculations and physical exams preflight, even though I was known to be ageless. Blood was drawn, and our T cells were isolated and mixed into an antirad cocktail to be administered by medpatch once we arrived on Sovak. This was to repair our white blood cells and bolster immunity in the remote chance our bodies had absorbed solar or galactic cosmic radiation or endured other adverse effects during the voyage. We were given regimens of pills and eyedrops to prevent illnesses that might crop up during two years in space and taught to use specialized onboard exercise equipment to keep our bodies in shape.

Once in flight, I worked with the Habitat team on planning and policies. Most of the building materials and supplies needed would be dropped by the time we landed, including temporary housing pods. Once on the planet, we would construct our permanent residences and set up food production. For the first year, we'd work nonstop to ready the colony for the next wave of immigrants.

USEA had developed SimSense VR training materials about the planet, based on myriad data gathered by rovers and other iots. A session called *Explore Sovak* pulled many *oohs* and *aahs* from me. It was like being transported into one of Peter's Impressionist paintings: a lush tropical world in astonishingly soft and unusual shades, accented with gleaming primary colors. We were serenaded by the musical sounds of Sovakian wildlife as we enjoyed the balmy atmosphere scented with rich, floral fragrances.

The *Sally*'s average velocity was approximately 0.03 percent of light speed, so the trip from Second Colony to Third Colony took two years: a year and three months for the starship to travel to Rhea Bridge near Uranus, a month to travel along the bridge, and eight months more to reach Sovak. High-efficiency Roddenberry-Asaro engines with optimized fusion drives had reached ever-greater speeds. The highest speed recorded to date for a test flight was over 400,000 miles per hour, 0.06 percent of light speed.

I had serious doubts about my ability to withstand the interminable journey that lay ahead. After work one day, I made my way to an empty view lounge. Sitting in the room lit only by starlight, I remembered reading old stories about Earth's South Pole, in which station residents labored to control their mental and physical health during the six months of winter without sunlight. Four of those months were spent in complete darkness and the remaining two in twilight, so it was no surprise Antarctic residents frequently suffered depression. Although the USEA had made many adjustments to support *Sally Ride*'s passengers, such as full-spectrum lighting and the availability of countless activities, this journey through infinite space took a toll on one's mind.

I recalled science fiction stories where interstellar travelers used suspended animation for their long journeys. *Lucky them.* Cryosleep, in which people were frozen in stasis and then thawed, was being researched, and scientists were close to overcoming the problem of cellular damage due to crystallization. I wished we already had cryosleep, so prolonged space travel would no longer be such unbroken tedium.

Sighing deeply, I stretched, stood up, and went to my cabin for a nap.

I am still a mother.

I had come to recognize my failures as a mother. Even though Naryssa's behavior was understandable, where was the wisdom I should have gained from my many incarnations? With no better way to reach out to Naryssa, I wrote her a letter.

> *I know this is difficult for you, and I'm sorry. I apologize to you for everything, for my ignorance and carelessness that allowed your difficult childhood. After you came to Mars, I know I wasn't the best parent. I wasn't there for you when I should have been, and now I'm literally not there. Being a parent was much harder than I thought, and I really screwed things up. Teens don't come with instructions.*
>
> *I did the best I could. If I ever made you feel unloved, I'm profoundly sorry. Because the truth is, I love you more than anything in the universe. I have since I met you, and I always will.*
>
> *Please know how much I admire you, for your astounding courage and the wonderful young person you've become despite everything.*

I hope you're thriving, wherever you are, whatever you are doing. I hope one day you'll forgive me.

   I love you, Naissa (Mom)

I had nowhere to send the letter, so it remained in my files.

⧉⧉⧉

One morning about a month into our trip, I was about to change my radskin when my cabin door chimed. I told the door to open and beheld a statuesque woman with luminous, ebony skin. She was stunning.

"Good morning. I'm sorry to disturb you," she said in a rich voice. "I'm Valerie Mbiti. I've been assigned to be your assistant. Do you have some time to talk about the work?" She smiled widely.

"Nice to meet you, Valerie. Time is all we have on this ship." I laughed. The admiral told me I would have an assistant, but this was still a surprise. "Give me a minute, and we'll go for some tea."

Valerie waited outside because a single cabin scarcely had room for a bed, let alone another person. I stripped off my shimmery radskin, put it in the recycler, and hurriedly pulled on a fresh one.

Everyone on board was required to wear these suits at all times. Although the *Sally Ride* was encased in Mazuderm, similar to the dome covers on First and Second Colonies, extra layers of protection were required should the shielding fail.

For me, the radskin was likely unnecessary. *So stupid*, I thought, struggling as my left foot snagged in the radskin's leg. I was, however, not willing to be accosted and lectured to if caught without it.

Besides, once on, the underwear felt like a silky, second skin. At least it wasn't a corset.

A few minutes later at the always-open Stellar Café, Valerie and I sat at a table next to one of the viewports. We asked Immeda to bring us hot chai and biscuits.

As I blew on my steaming beverage, Valerie said, "I've been with Ship Services for years, so my transfer to the Habitat team was a bit of a shock. If it's not too much of an imposition, may I ask your help getting up to speed?"

"Of course." I took a sip of the spiced drink and felt the spreading warmth of its earthy flavors. I was surprisingly at ease with Valerie. "Whatever you need."

As Valerie and I talked, I found her fascinating. Her sense of humor was smart and ironic—something I had always appreciated—and her perceptiveness was keen. After I gave a crash course in the Habitat team's work, Valerie told me her story over our third cup of tea.

"I was born back in 2038, in Connecticut, and was raised in San Francisco. It was a beautiful town," she said wistfully. "Before."

"I fell for my only true love there, but a year later, I was flattened when she announced she was running off with a friend of ours who was like a brother to me. She broke my damn heart. I tried to forget her in an endless string of one-night stands which, of course, failed. Hollowed out, I decided a child would fill my emptiness. I married the first guy who asked. The marriage lasted long enough to produce two beautiful, amazing daughters. And then, my daughters died in a hopper accident, together with three of their high school friends."

My breath caught and I reached for Valerie's hand. Her pain reignited mine.

Valerie's eyes shone and she continued in a quavering voice. "I was . . . I was shattered. Not having the heart to even consider having more children, I had my tubes tied—which women did in those days for permanent birth control. I moved from job to job, affair to affair, all of them meaningless. By the time reGenia was announced, I was a bitter old woman on the verge of death from lung cancer, aching for oblivion. Then, I shocked myself by grabbing at the opportunity with both fists."

Valerie smiled and brushed a couple of braids from her face. "My do-over was like a birth in which I delivered *myself*. As I understand it, I owe you for that. Thank you."

I felt color rise to my cheeks as I smiled and nodded. It was the first time I knowingly met someone who had used reGenia treatment.

Valerie continued, "I've used what I'd learned from my failures to make a happier life. Looking for adventure, I signed up to work on USEA ships. And here we are."

Admiring Valerie's candor and grateful for her ageless companionship, I wanted to give her something in return. Pushing aside my usual fears, I told her everything about my life, including Naryssa. My temples throbbed by the time I was done, but I felt much lighter.

Valerie moved her chair next to mine and draped her arm around my shoulders. We sat like that for a long while, Valerie's tears dropping on my lap, my own tears leaving dark splotches on her orange pullover.

Then Valerie said in a soft voice, "You have suffered so very much, and I can imagine the depth of your pain. Since my daughters died, it's helped me to remember that love is forever, that the love my daughters and I shared is and will always be in my heart. Love endures all things. Love is infinite."

I felt a surge of gratitude. "Thank you, Valerie, for sharing your story with me, for listening to mine, and for your compassion and wisdom. I'll remember what you've said. From now on, I'll focus on the love I've known instead of on my heartache."

And then I laughed, with the first joy I'd felt in a long while. "And welcome to the Habitat team!"

We stood, embraced, and laughed through our tears.

⁂

At long last, we arrived at Rhea Bridge. We had been trained on bridge travel, but it was still nerve-racking to feel our ship bounce onto the span. Once we were skating across the bridge, there was nothing more than gentle vibration and an occasional jostling. Owing to the physics of bridge travel, all we could see through the viewports was infinite blackness and, rarely, flashing streaks. More than once, I experienced a wave of terror at the immensity of space and the fragility of our miniscule vessel with its gossamer skin.

The ride along Rhea Bridge took almost a month. To divert myself from the nothingness outside, I filled the journey to Sovak with listening to live music, exercising, reading, and attending lectures. Valerie often joined me when we weren't working. Sick of vids and VR, we began cooking our own meals, which became a favorite activity. The *Sally* had both hydroponic and mycelium tanks for fresh vegetables and protein-based food printing. While cooking sometimes intensified my longing for times gone by, I found satisfaction in using new techniques and combinations of ingredients. Who knew there were so many uses for soy paste?

⁖⁖⁖⁖⁖

Arriving on Sovak at the end of two mind-numbing years, I was overcome with relief. The lengthy trip in the confined environment of the starship had proved difficult for nearly everyone. Once the shuttle set down and the hatch opened, we took off running, whooping, and dancing in the dizzying embrace of sweet, fresh air. Because Sovak's gravity was slightly less than the *Sally*'s, more than one new Sovakian took a tumble in the velvety grasses.

We were overwhelmed and overjoyed by Sovak. Compared to the Sim-Sense VRs, the reality was staggering. Flower-painted meadows shimmered in a rainbow palate. The light-green sky was decorated with pastel clouds and Alpha Cen's two visible suns, one larger and brighter than the other. Their light cast a soft glow over the foothills, which rolled toward distant peaks blanketed by red and purple myanote trees. The air was scented with a delicate aroma reminiscent of orange blossom and honeysuckle.

We gathered refreshments of native fruits we'd learned about during our journey. The striped azleb, scarlet larimbos, and pearly kimanays were as delicious as they were beautiful. We drank large mugs of the palest pink water. After years of recycled, the fresh water was intoxicating.

Our settlement was to be on Crescent Green, overlooking the ruby-red ocean. There were shining trees with azure trunks and multicolored leaves, while others resembled palms with golden fronds; all had a startling depth and dazzle. The green held large flowerbeds with triangular and square-shaped blossoms in rich colors. The grasses were so vibrantly lush, they appeared to be in the very act of becoming grass. Tiny insects hummed eerie melodies and sparkled like darting jewels amid the bold, swelling fragrances.

This had to be the Garden of Eden.

Over the ensuing weeks, I selected a lot for my module with views of the ruby ocean and fantasy sunsets. I thought it likely I'd find solace in this paradise, despite my grief over Naryssa. I still kept the plush unicorn I'd given her by my pillow, but now it smelled of Sovak's flowery aura instead of Naryssa's sweet scent.

Days were twenty-six hours long, with daylight lasting between fourteen and eighteen hours, depending on the time of year. Nightfall was well worth the wait. When night deepened, nocturnal insects' soft music and bioluminescence enveloped the landscape, and the heady scent of night-blooming rystrika flowers filled the air. Forest-green heavens glittered with whorls of van Gogh stars and three jade moons.

Instead of birds, Sovak had flying mammalian life forms. Unlike Earth's bats, these violet-eyed obunds were diurnal, ubiquitous, and had iridescent golden fur. Aside from a few insect-eating species, Sovak's animals were herbivorous. The creatures were so tame and curious, they interacted with us like pets.

One morning as obunds swirled overhead, a small, egg-shaped animal—a melor—stood outside my door, its fuzzy purple fur glistening under the suns. As I tried to leave for work, it made happy-sounding clicks and rubbed against my ankles like a kitten. The next morning, I was too slow closing the door and it tumbled inside, making itself at home in the mod and in my heart.

Since self-reproducing melors were gynandromorphic, I chose to pretend it was male and called him Harry. Harry would sit on my lap while I worked at my desk and lightly click when I stroked his fur. He caught insects with his projectile tongue, and I supplemented his diet with mashed belza fruit. It was entertaining to watch little Harry somersault around the module. Somehow, he never rolled underfoot.

Daily work was long and hard that first year, but satisfying. We built out our modules into homes and constructed new modules for the next wave. All the iots were indispensable for clearing and construction. Once the essentials were established, I oversaw facilities for recycling and reuse, and managed the communal garden as part of my leadership of Habitat Administration. Agriculture iots cultivated essentials in broad fields below the hills. Our impact on the area was significant, but I was happy with the controls we put in place to minimize disruption to native flora and fauna.

By the time we welcomed the second wave, we had built a satisfying colony ready for them all—children included. It was thrilling to witness their first, joyous moments on Sovak. That evening, we threw a big dance party to celebrate.

Several years passed, and the creatures and their sounds, at first amazing, sadly became routine. I continued to enjoy my new home and the work I loved. After work, I usually sculpted or spent time on the Consensus Forum, browsing proposals and following the often-heated debates and deliberations.

Valerie was an excellent assistant who had perfected organization to an art form and learned to read my needs before I knew I had them. When our jobs allowed, we'd take long walks or continue our culinary adventures with Sovak's produce. I always looked forward to our time together. It was uncanny how we could pick up a conversation we'd left off weeks earlier.

As my time on Sovak grew, I had an inexplicable presentiment of the void closing in. It was nothing obvious, and, aside from missing Naryssa, I had no pressing issues or conflicts that might be the cause. My world was peaceful. Yet, something nibbled at my composure.

One morning before work, as I stood in front of the bathroom mirror brushing my hair, I found a couple of white strands. *Odd.*

⚜⚜⚜

I have been here . . .

I am thinking about how long I've lived on Sovak when, suddenly, I'm not sure. I have to look it up. It's been over ten years.

Something is very wrong. I was put on temporary leave from my job because I kept forgetting how to get to the Habitat Administration building. Even worse, I couldn't remember coworkers' names. There were days when I forgot I was even employed.

The other night, I found myself walking in the business district along an empty road lined with golden palms. Twilight receded and night sneaked out of the shadows to . . . to absorb me. Hissing winds picked up, bending the palms and sending a large azleb fruit crashing onto a nearby lamp, shattering it. When it began raining hard, I ran in the futile hope of getting home before complete saturation. Despite recognizing the area and racking my brain, I couldn't remember how to get home.

The power went out. Squinting and stumbling, I tried to make my way on the wet grass in near blackness. Then my silhouette, lit from behind, appeared in front of me. A navicraft was following me! I ran, sliding, bumping into things as a stitch in my side became a knife stabbing the breath from my lungs. My limbs, heavy and aching with fatigue, dragged more and more and more slowly. Then they slid out from under me. Before I could get to my feet, the navicraft hatch opened. A man reached down. A scream caught in my throat; the man and the female driver seemed somehow familiar, benign.

They helped me into the navicraft and wrapped a blanket around me.

⚜⚜⚜

There is no one. I am the last person left on Sovak. The loneliness is indescribable.

I wake up tossing, breathing rapidly, and find myself in Jahn and Wilfred Schultz's mod, the one next to mine. *Oh, I remember now.* It was Jahn,

Sovak's administrator, and her husband who rescued me from the storm. Humiliation joins with angst in the disordered labyrinths of my mind.

Unable to face my rescuers, I quietly put on my shoes and go home. I sip chorkroot coffee while rubbing Harry's fur and thinking about what to do. I've never needed a doctor in my whole life, but I can't muster the guts to consult a counselor or physician.

Taking Harry for an airing boosts my spirits. I watch him spin playfully among the flowers. He lunges for a blue-spotted wiplar, a creature like an Earth centipede, and just misses its trailing legs as it scoots down its tiny hole.

I giggle. "What's the matter, Harry? You too big to roll down its burrow?"

Harry looks at me and blinks.

Last night's storm has cleared, and the breezes from across the water are bracing and sweet. Long, wispy clouds of canary yellow stretch high across the greenish sky. My eyes drift to the suns' lustrous pencils shining through the golden palms, drawing the flowered lawns kaleidoscopic and sketching dancing shadow patterns over the streets. This reminds me of sparkling mornings on Earth when I'd go to the park with Robin and her kids.

I make my way home with Harry tumbling at my heels but pause at my door. An empty day with too much time to think lies in front of me. Without energy to sculpt or draw, I sigh and ask myself what I might do instead. As I step inside, a way to get my thoughts in order comes to me. *Why don't I do a memoir?* I have a lot to tell.

Before getting started, I message Jahn to thank her and Wilfred, and apologize for leaving without a word. Jahn pleads with me to see a doctor or counselor, but I refuse. Defeated, she asks for contact info of someone she can message in an emergency. I give her Valerie's info, not mentioning it's the only info I can give, as I have no one else in this solar system. Jahn hesitates before we disconnect.

In a resigned voice she says, "Naissa, I'm sorry to tell you this. Unless you get help, your leave will be permanent."

My insides chill. Furious, I try to remain composed. "Thanks a lot, Jahn. So supportive. I don't need therapy. I've gotten further than you'd ever imagine without it. *Life* is therapy."

I cut the link and fume around the flat.

Where is Valerie? I need her now.

───

Breakfast, plus another cup of chorkroot coffee, and I am relating my life story to Immeda. The work flows so easily, I'm unconscious of the passing hours. When my story is done, I eat a large dinner in the glow of my accomplishment. Afterward, wine glass in hand, I sit in my favorite chair in the sunroom, and tell Immeda to display my story.

I am flabbergasted, devastated. The life I effortlessly, confidently, outlined is not my own! It's a dreamlike hodgepodge of lives I've read about. I feel the same sense of loss as happens when I've roused from a vivid dream where I was a totally different person, someone whose life and relationships are annihilated upon waking.

Feeling unreal, I skim my journals to recollect myself, the logical thing to have done in the first place. My history seems alien, like it belongs to a stranger. Even worse, my current life is dimming as if it's a dream I'm no longer involved in, or a story someone once told me.

I know I need help, but the only move I can think of, messaging Valerie for advice, will have to wait because exhaustion forces me to lie down.

───

Awaking in darkness, I'm frightened. On my way to Mother and Father's room, I trip over something and have the wind knocked out of me. Trying to stand, I can't help whimpering. I carefully feel my way along the hall and knock on my parents' bedroom door. No one answers. I knock some more.

After waiting and waiting, I pound on the door. Then, I slowly open it. Dazzling light glares from the ceiling of a clothes closet. My parents, even their bedroom, have disappeared! Specks of rationality scatter, hot liquid rolls down my legs.

My cries and screams for Mother and Father sound grown-up. *Why?* Instead of their answer, a knocking comes from somewhere in this mind-boggling place. Turning toward the sound, I see an unfamiliar, brightly lit house. Thin, shrill laughter echoes inside my head.

A knocking coming from a large door grows more insistent.

Trembling, I ask, "Who is there?" in that strange voice.

A kind-sounding woman says, "Naissa, may I help?"

Who is she? I cautiously open the door. The stranger's eyes are alarmed and sympathetic.

"I want my parents, but I am in the wrong house," I whimper.

The woman looks at me a few moments before taking my hand. "Come with me, sweetie. Let's sit down and talk."

Joining her on a sofa, I catch sight of our feet. *Why are my feet as big as hers?* "My feet are too big!" I cry out.

Patting my arm, she says, "I have to leave the room for just a bit. I'll be right back."

I howl for my mother.

"Don't worry, help is coming," she says when she returns.

"But I want my mother," I moan between sobs, and howl for her again.

Soon, another nice lady comes in and sits down, and the first one says goodbye and leaves.

The new lady says, "I'm Dr. Mari Toma. Do you know your name?"

"Naissa Nolan," I blubber. "Where is my house? Where are my mother and father?"

She lifts her eyebrows. "Hello, Naissa. Can you tell me what year this is?"

What a stupid question. "It is 1856, of course."

"And can you tell me how old you are, Naissa?"

"I am six years old," I say through tears.

"I want to help you, honey. Let's try something. Why don't we have a look in the mirror?"

When we stand, the lady is my size! I don't understand. I'm a child and she's a grownup, so why is she my size? We go to a mirror. What I see makes me freeze. Instead of my reflection, there are two grownups standing side by side. One does my exact moves.

Shaking, panting, I push the lady away and scream, "I want to wake up now!" Remembering my protector, I shout, "George! I want George!"

Patting my shoulder, she says, "Everything will be fine, Naissa. Please sit down with me and we'll take some deep breaths together."

She removes a small bottle from her bag and opens it. "If you drink this, you'll be able to nap and then you'll feel better."

I study the bottle, and then her calm face.

She says, "It's all right, this will help."

After gulping the liquid, I lie down and she covers me with her overcoat.

An awareness of danger follows me through a withered, decaying forest. A bile-colored mist, a barely breathable haze stinking of sulfur threatens to . . . to dissolve me. I try to flee, but I am slow-motion running. My brain feels swollen in my skull and my feet in their shoes. My coat, smelling of wet wool and dread, is too heavy, but I divide my mind from my discomfort and struggle to move faster. Presently, my limbs and shriveled lungs are unable to sustain me, and my lips freeze in a silent scream. I decompose. *What is reality?* Dreams are reality, reality dreams.

⟨⟩⟨⟩⟨⟩

I wake to daylight. Still shaken by the nightmare, I remember I promised Trudy that I would help her sew a new dress for one of her dolls. I glance over at the clock, but it isn't there. Instead, I see numbers floating in the air! I must still be dreaming. Hoping to wake up, I quickly slide back under the blanket. When I dare to open my eyes and peek, everything is still different. What is this strange place? I pinch myself, but don't wake up. Heartbeats bounce off my eardrums.

Summoning my willpower, I get out of bed and walk to the window. There's a red ocean! Even the colors of the trees and sky are wrong. Sinking to the floor, I cover my eyes and tears slide from my palms to my elbows. Why don't I wake up? My terror yanks me to my feet and throws me back into bed and under the blanket. I pray Mother will soon wake me for lessons.

She doesn't.

Hunger wakes me. I quiver with fright because my hunger tells me I'm not asleep. Do I . . . do I look like me? I find a mirror, and staring back is the adult from last night's nightmare. Reason protests, sanity is indignant, but reason and sanity no longer prevail. My screams shoot out in loud, reverberating circles.

A familiar, dark-skinned lady comes running, wraps her arms around me and holds me until I've calmed somewhat. "Naissa, are you all right?"

"Why is my face so old?" I manage. "Why can't I wake up?"

"Please look at me. It's Valerie. Your friend. Do you remember me?"

Blowing on the coals of my being, her name breathes me into lucidity. Valerie has come to rescue me from the horror of an insane hell. My eyes overflow.

"Oh, Valerie! I'm so glad you're here. I don't know what's happening."

Valerie blots my tears with her sleeve. "It's okay, Naissa. If you're up to it, I can explain why you're having problems."

"Yes! Please, please tell me. What's wrong with me?"

We sit in the front room. I cannot stop shuddering. Valerie puts an arm around my shoulders.

"Naissa, do you remember the troubles you were having at work? Remembering things?" I nod, vaguely recalling, but I'm unsure where this is going.

"Well, apparently, there's something on Sovak that's affecting you."

"There is?"

"Yes. They think it's something in the environment, perhaps an unknown form of radiation. Whatever it is, it seems to be changing your genome."

My mind races. I flash on the white hairs. My confusion. The time I burned my wrist while using the laser cutter, a trivial wound that took a week to heal.

Something in the environment.

Valerie strokes my hand. "They're suggesting you leave Sovak because it's not safe for you here. Naissa, it's time to find you a new home."

A new home? Where? Earth? Another colony? I am too tired for this. No. I like it here. I'll take my life as it comes.

I look Valerie in the eyes. "I don't want to leave."

Drawing back, Valerie gasps, "What? Why not?"

"I just don't want to leave. This is my home now."

"But, being here is making you sick."

"Valerie, I've never been sick, not ever. I feel too tired to start over again somewhere else. I only had some bad dreams. I'm fine here. I'm not going anywhere."

"Fine?" Valerie responds, her voice rising to a frantic pitch. "*Fine*? You just spent the last thirty hours hallucinating, wandering around lost in a place you know, screaming for your mother! Begging for somebody named George. That's not fine."

Valerie pauses, a look of horror crossing her face. Her voice shakes as she continues. "I see what you want, Naissa. How could you? How could you be so damn selfish? You're my dearest friend. I love you. *Please!*"

My lips press tightly together. "Leave me be."

"At least . . . at least come with me to the health center. There's an infusion that might relieve your symptoms for a time."

"That *might* work? Shit. I don't want anyone meddling with me!"

"Please, there's nothing to worry about. You'll be in and out before you know it." Valerie's eyes plead.

My beloved friend. How can I let her down?

"All right. I'll think about it."

"And leaving here?"

"I'll think about that, too. Just give me a little time."

The relief flooding Valerie's face is worth the lie.

"Why don't we have some breakfast, okay?"

As we're eating, I realize something is missing. "Where's Harry?"

"He's next door with Jahn. We can go get him now if you want. Okay?"

That evening, I review the suggested procedure and tell Valerie I'll do it. The next day, after my blood is drawn and my DNA swabbed, I'm infused with a solution of my slightly modified DNA. I'm told everything went well. I hope for the best.

<hr/>

Valerie and I vacation together for nearly two weeks. Hiking the rainbow-colored woods and meadows, we come across whimsical wildlife. We visit a fiery canyon, swim under red waterfalls, and watch geysers spout pink steam. As Valerie and I experience these diversions and breathe Sovak's rich perfume, my angst dissipates.

Valerie and I continue the discussion we had the day we met about the endurance of love. Somehow, Valerie's deep understanding, the peace of our hikes, the loveliness of the landscape, and even our comfortable silences bring my history of love back to me as through a slowly clearing fog. I recognize the aching beauty of my long life's special relationships, one by one.

I tell Valerie about the people I've loved. I talk about Robin, about every detail I can remember of her life. As I talk, I regret never opening up to Robin as she had wanted and deserved.

When I talk about Naryssa, I crumble. "If I weren't so far away, I know I could help her."

Valerie holds me until I stop crying.

"Please don't worry. I know it's hard, love, but the important thing is, I'm sure she knows how much you love her. Remember, love transcends distance and time."

⟿⟿⟿

After my vacation with Valerie, I sit at my desk with the rosy sun warming my face. My ancient, paper journals are spread out like old friends, reminding me of times gone by. It's satisfying to read through them and pull out bits and pieces to weave together into a cohesive autobiography.

My azleb tea has grown cool. I look down at my flexi and tap Confirm. I have finalized a directive ensuring I will not be cloned again. Perhaps Naryssa will love me more if I can tell her about the directive.

CHAPTER EIGHTEEN

Rys

O UT OF THE blue, I was messaged by someone named Valerie. At first, I was thrown by her gorgeous face and didn't hear what she said.

"What?"

"I know Naissa; I'm a friend of hers."

My heart dropped out. And then I got angry.

"How did you get this contact?" I reached for the disconnect.

"No, wait! Naissa is sick."

"What?" I couldn't believe the nerve. "She can't get sick." I moved again to disconnect.

"Please, wait! It's Sovak. It's making her sick." There was worry on her face.

The colony in a different solar system? "Sovak? What does that have to do with Naissa?"

"Please, hear me out. I'm Naissa's assistant. She's my friend. We traveled to Sovak together over ten years ago. Lately, she's showing signs of . . . aging. A sort of dementia. They think something in Sovak's environment is affecting her genome."

This seemed like another hoax to me. Aside from Naissa's inability to get ill, I was having difficulty seeing Naissa in another solar system. There was, however, something about the woman that gave me pause. Her earnestness, maybe.

"Why is Naissa on Sovak?"

Over the next hour, Valerie explained what Naissa had been doing these last years, and how they became colleagues and friends. And how Naissa began deteriorating, while other people with reGenia treatment were unaffected.

"So please," Valerie begged, "come to Sovak as quickly as you can. Your mother needs you."

There was much to consider. In truth, I was ready for change. A trip to Sovak would be long; Valerie said six months each way with the latest ships. It was possible to do my coursework remotely, but not ideal. As much as I loved being on Earth, my ties to it were not strong. I could easily move my life, at least temporarily.

The real question was, what about Naissa? Valerie had called her my mother. I still bristled at the thought. I had distanced myself from my clone parent, to live my own life. And I was succeeding.

However, I kept hearing Naissa's words about having company to navigate our lives. I had friends, colleagues in my fight against cloning, but no real partners. I was, in fact, alone. Having been raised without family, and not aware I was without one, I was sufficient on my own. It was my normal. It took seeing real families to learn what I was missing and feel the pangs of loss. They say knowledge is power, but sometimes it's just hurtful.

Was a relationship with Naissa worth disrupting my life for over a year?

"If Sovak is making Naissa sick, why doesn't she leave?"

Valerie drooped as if a heavy weight landed on her shoulders. "She doesn't want to. She refuses."

What could that mean? She liked Sovak too much? Or was it exile? A death wish? I had no clue. I was a mirror of Naissa, my clone parent, and I had not one clue as to her state of mind. Pathetic.

"All right."

⸺⸺⸺

Over subsequent messaging during my voyage to Sovak, Valerie told me about the planet. I could see why Naissa didn't want to leave. It sounded wonderful. When I asked Valerie why she thought Naissa refused to leave, she shrugged and said, "That's for you and Naissa to discuss."

Valerie was devoted to Naissa, and I admired their fierce friendship. I loved that Valerie was straightforward, unafraid to answer questions. Over time, I came to believe she was honest. And that some of her friendship extended to me.

Not long before we landed in Sovak, Valerie asked me whether I viewed Naissa as my mother.

"She's my clone parent, that's true. But I think *mother* means something more than the biologic sense. It's someone who loves you from the day you're born. Who's always there for you."

Valerie's image studied me through the miles. "There may be a little more to it. Think about families who adopt. There is no relationship from the moment of birth, yet most adoptees view their adopted parents as their true parents—even when biological parents are on the scene. Or the loving relationships that can develop when an adult adoptee is reunited with their biological parent. Perhaps, then, the from-birth requirement is not necessarily accurate.

"From what she's told me, Naissa knows she made mistakes with you. It's easy to understand why she didn't emerge as a fully competent mother the day she learned of her grown daughter. But remember, once Naissa knew you existed, she fought vigorously for you. She *was* there for you. She tried. And she's never stopped hoping."

I thought about all the times Naissa had reached out to me, and all the times I'd rebuffed her. It was true. She'd tried. And I hadn't. In fact, I'd fought her all the way, because fighting those who had my fate in their hands was the only way I knew. And then I'd completely cut her off. My breakfast threatened to come up on a wave of remorse.

I took a sip from my water bottle and sighed. "I suppose she hasn't."

"Mom, I'm here. It's me, Rys—Naryssa."

She stood in the open door, a puzzled look on her face.

"Naryssa? Is it you? You look so . . . different."

I mentioned the bodyforming nanobots.

"Well, come in, please."

She'd been shocked to see me, but then her expression changed.

"Oh Naryssa, darling, I've missed you so much!"

I pulled her into my arms. We held each other for a long time, both of us crying softly.

"Why are you here?" Mom asked, drawing back and wiping tears from her cheeks. "I was afraid I'd never see you again."

I smiled sheepishly. "Valerie made sure I came." I laughed, "There's no point in arguing with her, as I'm sure you know. I came back to see you. And apologize for being so stupid. It's taken me this long to realize you were right."

"Right?"

I smiled. "Yes, that we need each other. You're family, the only family I'll ever have. We're family."

We hugged again, both sobbing with relief.

Mom had her good days and bad days. On the good days, we would sit on her sunny porch and swap stories. It was strangely freeing to tell her about myself. Her life story was incredible—I'd had no idea. We both laughed at our similarities and valued our differences.

My heart was full to bursting with the beauty of this new relationship with my mother. It was also breaking at the thought of losing her. How could she give up, after we'd only just found each other? I begged and begged her to leave Sovak with me. But she refused.

"This is where I've found the only true peace in my entire life. I'm tired, Naryssa. My life has been long, longer than it should have been." She reached out and held my hands. "And now you're here. You, daughter, are the greatest thing in my life. And I am the happiest I'll ever be."

M Y EYES OPEN on the day, morning light flooding my room. I see with newfound clarity. I've been driven my whole life by the fear of losing everyone I care about. My vulnerability caused me to selfishly hide my true self, to hold at a distance the people who've loved me, and not honor their love and friendship. I was challenged by the person I hoped to be. Oh, the damage I've caused.

My immortal family of two fell apart because I was wrapped up in my own troubles, because I didn't give Naryssa the love and attention she deserved. My dearest, tormented, and strong Naryssa. I should have listened more closely and loved you more for yourself. How alike we are, in more ways than I expected. If only I'd found you sooner. If only. At least we have done so, now. At least we have this short, glorious time together to share perfect love. It will live forever.

After beautiful months with my daughter, I feel it all slipping away. There is no more rebounding. Undone, broken like an overstretched Slinky toy, I sense my life winding down. I am emotionally ancient. I feel a creeping numbness, a ring of silence closing all around, annulling me.

It's harder and harder to hold on to the present, to reality. Sometimes I don't know where, or even who, I am. Is this a phantasmagoria? I've always liked that word. That's it, this is a phantasmagoric mise-en-scène.

⸙⸙⸙

Time and space shift. Inbound.

I am not alone, after all. My loved ones have brought themselves to the land of dreams. To be with them, I slip into dreams that are no longer shadows, but the substance of my life. Are you truly here? Did I invoke you with so much yearning and intensity that my memories of you put on flesh? Or are you antics of an addled brain? Maybe that.

I see a figure in bright light. It is Father! I run to his embrace, bury my face in his vest, and breathe in the spicy aroma of pipe smoke. Father strokes my hair. There's Cecile, holding out her arms to me. Oh, Cecile! I feel small hands in mine. And my dear Naryssa! My darlings. And here are Mother and Trudy. They kiss me. Peter is waving and Robin beckons. Dear Suzanne. Valerie embraces me. Julian! He's laughing and playing his music. I tell him how much I've missed him. What a delight to see Julian's smile again.

Am I asleep? Alive? Time stands still, as in the silence of a painting. Crouching. Ready to spring.

All at once, I remember the nightmare I had at five years old. It was about my actual, extraordinary life to come. When I was little, I believed real life was logical, sunny, and secure—unaware it can be quite the opposite. Too bad I didn't remember my life before I made my mistakes.

I am a bewildered 268-year-old. But I'm also Trudy's sister. An environmentalist, scientist, and sculptor endeavoring to shape legacies. A spirited young woman reveling in Peter's return from across the ocean. A friend, daughter, sister, a wife. A mother. A woman trying to fill the empty spaces left by death with new lives and new hopes. When I go to the places where these selves dwell in me, we share amazement at all that has happened to us.

We cry together and tell each other that, perhaps, I am still the child asleep in her bed, who'll awaken from this nightmare to an eternally joyful reality where I will be with all my loved ones forevermore.

⟡⟡⟡

Covered with quilts, I'm shivering with cold. I drift. Maybe . . . maybe if I focus hard enough . . . can I, like in my dreams, will myself back to childhood?

I will sleep, perchance to wake as the child I was. If not, I welcome oblivion. Both of these possibilities are . . . timeless.

Time doesn't win. *I* win.

Will there be silence, or endless joy?

EPILOGUE

Naryssa

~~~~~~~~~~~~~~~~

M Y SEAT BUMPS slightly and my cup rattles on the table next to me. Then, the ship steadies and soft starlight flows into the view lounge, washing away the darkness. I breathe a long sigh of relief. At last, we are off Rhea Bridge and back in Sol System. I don't like bridge travel. It's unsettling in a vague sort of way, as if every now and then one's heart is a half beat off. A flush of excitement swirls over me as I feel my proximity to Earth. I am homebound, and nearly there! Three months to go, but they will fly by.

My last days with Mom were the best and hardest in my life. I caused her great distress when we first met, but after we shared our life stories, we found peace together. Knowing her days were limited caused me boundless grief, but the love and beauty Mom showed in her passing helped soften it a bit. Mom filled the hole in my heart, and it will never be empty again.

And so, I turn and face forward. Before Mom passed, I used the implant app to instruct the nanobots to exit my face and vocal cords. That same, murky feeling as when the nanobots were first implanted oozed from my face to my gut. After a moment, Immeda said, "Nanobots disabled. They will exit via your digestive tract within eight hours. Although no discomfort is expected in the meantime, please let me know right away if you have any issues or concerns."

And that was that. When Mom saw me restored, she smiled and said, "Good." It was the last word she said to me.

⊱⊰⊱⊰⊱⊰

Since boarding the *Sally Ride* for the trip back to Earth, there have been only a few respectful requests for interviews. After several weeks, the interviews stopped. Occasionally people stared, trying to figure out how they knew me. Thankfully, that was it.

Leaving Valerie behind has been hard. Even though we message often, my life is emptier without her. Valerie is trying to get work on one of the ships destined for Earth. I hope she prevails. I miss her, too.

Returning home will be difficult. There are many mistakes to correct, many holes to patch with new mortar, but I'm determined to make it right, for Mom. I will move forward with her memory beside me, her heart inside me, her love guiding my steps. For the remaining time aboard the ship, I am considering how to rewrite my life. I could share my story so people might not repeat the mistakes that were made in my creation. We can solve our intrinsic problems the more people view our civilization and its troubles in a more enlightened way. Some of the first population policies have shown their weaknesses, and I plan to help with all that.

Cloning must end. In my mother's stead, I will fight that battle as a member of the United Countries and Colonies, and work within the system. Using what I've experienced and what I'm learning at law school, I'll craft new policies and laws for Consensus. I have many contacts now, thanks to my underground work. I believe the time is right for change. Even if it takes me lifetimes.

I see many beginnings, many paths forward from which to choose. There is much to look forward to. After all, as someone I loved once said, limitless life means limitless possibilities.

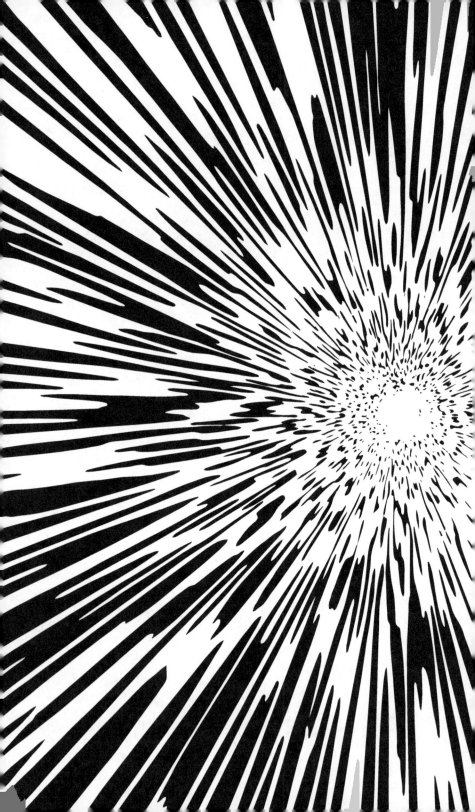

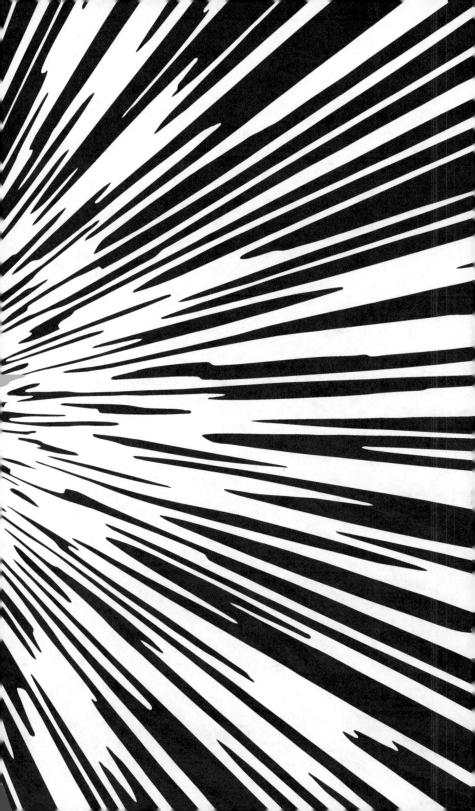

AUTHOR'S NOTE

T O MY EXTRAORDINARY editor, Erica B. Smith, words cannot express the depth of my gratitude for her invaluable contributions to this book. From the very beginning, she was more than just an editor; she was a collaborator, a trusted advisor, and a great friend.

Her guidance in helping to develop the story arc, craft compelling characters, and plan impactful scenes helped bring my vision to life in ways I never imagined. Her meticulous revisions and masterful editing honed the prose, and breathed new life into each sentence. Her keen eye and insightful suggestions were invaluable.

Her expertise went far beyond the text itself. She took the time to help with historical research, ensure authenticity, and envision the possibilities of future technology, all enriching the world of my story.

This book wouldn't be what it is today without her friendship, dedication, talent, and unwavering support. I am grateful for her to believe in me, pushing me to be my best, and celebrating every achievement along the way. I am deeply indebted to her and forever grateful for our collaboration.

SPECIAL NOTE

W HEN RENÉE CAME to me with her *Ageless* manuscript and asked what it would take for the novel to be published, I was naïve to an embarrassing degree. Most of my recent work had been business and scientific writing, editing dissertations, and graphic design. I hadn't worked on literary writing or fiction since it was one of my college majors—back in the stone age, as my sons would say.

Renée had always dreamed of being a writer, she told me, but had placed the dream on hold while her family was young. The manuscript she handed me represented decades of off-again, on-again effort. That she had persevered with her manuscript over all those years made a strong impression on me, and I wanted to help her get to the finish line.

After I gave Renée a report defining what was needed to make *Ageless* a publishable book, she looked me in the eye and said in her no-beating-around-the-bush manner, "I agree with everything you've said. I want you to help. How long will it take?"

Surprised, I drew a blank. A novel? I had no clue. It was a long moment while my brain raced, imagining the needed changes.

I answered with a feeble shrug, "A year?"

That year turned into a handful more, far beyond our original expectations. During those years, Renée and I debated vigorously, worked hard, laughed harder, and developed a loving friendship. When COVID-19 hit, I remotely accessed the manuscript on her computer while we talked over the phone. It wasn't as satisfying as working in person but we still managed to keep laughing and moving forward. Finally, *Ageless* was accepted for publication by CamCat Books.

It wasn't until Renée's last few months when we were beginning the editing process with CamCat that she revealed the illness from which, I later learned, she had suffered for several years. Even then, she minimized the disease. In those last days Renée was, as always, a fighter and remarkably upbeat. She remained full of spark and determined to finish *Ageless*. She spoke often of her greatest joy: the love of her family.

It broke my heart to say goodbye.

Renée leaves behind a loving friendship I will treasure the rest of my days. She leaves a strong family built on her love and example. With *Ageless*, she leaves us all a story whose protagonist reflects Renée's own perseverance and indomitable spirit.

On Renée's behalf and my own, profound thanks go to the entire CamCat Publishing team. They are exactly the sort of people you want in your corner in hard times. Sue Arroyo, CamCat CEO and Publisher, saw the potential in *Ageless* and gave it a chance. Helga Schier, Editorial Director, was generous with her guidance and compassion and pulled strings when they were most needed. Kayla Webb, Editor, provided brilliant ideas—as well as patience—throughout the editing process. *Ageless* is a stronger, more compelling book because of her. Maryann Appel, Art Director, designed a beautiful set of covers to choose from, and I'm grateful for her kindness and willingness to go above and beyond.

Ageless wouldn't be the book it is without its early readers. Olivia E. DeCaro and Sean E. Walsh twice read *Ageless* drafts, and I am indebted to their insightful and valuable suggestions and ideas. Karen Burka, Yeimy

Cifuentes, Edward Grippe, Susan Ann Hood, Robin Stephan, and Destiny Stephan all contributed significantly to making a better book.

Special thanks go to: Pat Pringle, former USGS geologist, geologic hazards specialist, professor emeritus, and family friend, for help imagining global geologic disasters and being the quintessential teacher in love with his subject; and longtime friend, Kathryn "KC" Clark, research scientist and former NASA Chief Scientist for both the International Space Station and Human Exploration & Development of Space Enterprise, for helping me decipher the biology of cloning.

Karen Burka, my dear friend and neighbor, introduced Renée and me, for which I am forever indebted. My thanks go to Laurie Spens for working hard to arrange a photo shoot for Renée, and to Susanne Ohland Winick, for advice on the beauty of Arizona.

I am grateful for Renée's family and their support during the evolution of this book. Dave, Cory, Troy, and Shaun Levine not only supported Renée but made sure I could finish the editing process and keep my last promise to Renée.

My heartfelt thanks go to my son, Sean, who was not only an early reader but provided a robust sounding board for all the random questions fired at him. I thank my lifelong friend, Elise Glenn, whose genius, humor, and steadfast support means the world to me. I am grateful to my family for being there for me through thick and thin, and to my late mother, Ramona DeLaney Smith, counselor extraordinaire. Finally, I thank the lucky stars for my husband, John F.X. Walsh, for his love, support, and picking up the slack when I needed it.

Erica B. Smith
Holmes, NY
3 February, 2024

ABOUT THE AUTHOR

❧❧❧

R ENÉE SCHAEFFER WAS fascinated by technology and where it may lead us, and when she was not writing, she was reading the latest speculative science fiction book. A lifelong New Yorker, she married her childhood sweetheart and raised three happy, successful children. An active social advocate, she believed in working to make life better for the less fortunate. Her favorite author's moment was the time she met famed science fiction writer Olivia Butler in a Greenwich Village bakery specializing in goods made by the homeless, and discussed with Ms. Butler the inspirations behind her books.

Ageless is Renée's debut novel. It was published posthumously.

If you enjoyed

Renée Schaeffer's

Ageless,

please consider leaving a review

to help our authors.

And check out

Meredith R. Lyons's

A Dagger of Lightning.

CHAPTER ONE

❦

*If you don't know where you're going, fine, just make sure you know
what you're looking for.* —Solange Delaney

"IM. IMOGEN! YOU'RE okay. You're alright, you're okay."

I awoke gasping, my ears throbbing as if my heart had established satellite locations. My eyes immediately locked onto a familiar shape, the feather swaying back and forth, dangling from the chain on our ceiling fan. *I'm safe. I'm in bed. With Keane. I'm okay.*

The orange glow of a street lamp filtered in through the open curtains. I reached up and lightly clasped Keane's forearm, his warm palm still gripping my shoulder, although he had stopped shaking me. I turned my head toward him, trying to take slower breaths. He'd angled himself just far enough away so that I wouldn't accidentally strike him. I must have been flailing.

"I'm awake. Sorry. Was I loud?" I never remembered these dreams when I woke. Only a sensation of falling and some vague knowledge that my grandfather had been there, either falling with me, or trying to keep me from falling, or . . . something . . .

"You didn't shout or anything this time, just thrashed around." Keane flopped back onto the pillows, sliding an arm beneath me and hauling me to his side. I let him, even though I was very warm and wanted air. The sheets beneath me were damp with sweat. I shoved the comforter down to my waist.

"Sorry I woke you. I've been trying to rest my ankle and didn't run yesterday." I always slept better if I were exhausted. I didn't process emotions the way most people did, and if I were unable to channel them physically, they liked to ambush me when I was unconscious.

"That's alright," Keane sighed, trailing his fingertips up and down my arm. Keane had been a good friend since college. Neither of us had ever married, in spite of cycling through many long-term relationships. At some point, after spending a mutual friend's wedding together as bridesmaid and groomsman for the umpteenth time, Keane had suggested that if we hadn't found anyone by forty, we should just wed each other. I'd drunkenly agreed. Now I was forty-five, Keane was nearly fifty, and six months ago he'd finally gotten my yes. I accepted a ring after insisting upon dating first, living together first, then living together for at least a year . . .until I'd run out of excuses. There were none. Keane was great. We got along great. Sex wasn't bad. Cohabitating was cheaper and made maintaining a home easier. And it was nice being on his insurance plan.

Settling, Imogen. You're settling is what you're doing. She'd been gone sixteen years and I could still *hear* my grandmother's exhale, could practically see her tossing a gauzy scarf over a small-boned shoulder as she gave me a *look* from beneath her lashes.

But what was wrong with that at my age? I'd come to the conclusion that 'true love' was a fantasy—although my grandparents had sure seemed to have it. Perhaps it wasn't in the cards for everyone. I'd looked around long enough. Fortunately, I'd never wanted kids, so I'd never felt that pressure.

"So, what are your plans for today?" Keane yawned, still lightly stroking my arm.

My stomach tightened. He had some kind of agenda. "Some more job applications, maybe—"

"You know, you don't have to get a job right away—"

"I *want* a job—"

"I know, Im, but you don't need one in the next twenty-four hours. Your dad's coming in next week, and . . ." He rolled toward me, pulling me even closer. "The guest room is still a mess."

My eyes dropped away from his. I turned my face skyward again and focused on the feather. "I know." The guest room would have been nice if it weren't for the large pile of cardboard boxes. All mine.

I *had* tried to whittle them down. But I didn't know what I'd need. I didn't know where I'd fit in this new place. Keane had received a dream job offer in New Orleans. He'd convinced me that this would be a great life for both of us. Wasn't I tired of the cold in Chicago? Wasn't I able to find friends wherever I went? Weren't we going to get married now? I had no good arguments, so I went with him. It made sense. We were engaged. Why not? I rolled my shoulders against the tightness threatening, trying to make a little more space between us. I didn't want to go through the boxes downstairs. Going through them meant getting rid of them, and I hated to let go of those little parts of myself.

I'd never found my calling. I liked to hop around. I was good at a lot of things, never great at any one thing. I never had a "tribe," but I was good at getting along. I'd find a job here too. Find things to like about it. I was good at adapting.

Grandma would have told me to keep searching. *You're different, Imogen, and that's okay. But you have a place. We all do. You'll know it when you find it. Just keep looking.* Well, she wasn't here. Besides, maybe this would be it.

"Okay," I said, taking a deep breath. "I'll go through the boxes today. Try to put some away."

"You could make a donation pile too," Keane said, pulling the covers back up around us. "What about all that martial arts stuff? You haven't fought in over a decade."

Something twisted at my center. "I liked fighting though," I said, quietly. I had loved sparring. It was another effective outlet for emotions packed down too tightly. And I'd been good at it. Although I was technically too old to fight competitively anymore, I could still train. "Maybe we could find a place here, we could do it together—"

Keane chuckled. "I'm still sore from soccer two days ago." He yawned again and pulled me even closer, eliminating any space I'd created by wrapping his arms around me. He pressed a kiss to my forehead, one hand rubbing my back. "You know, I was thinking when your dad's here next week, we could set a date for the wedding. Like, an actual date. Maybe something in the fall."

I felt myself go rigid in his arms. "Not the fall," I said. Keane's hand stilled on my back, but he didn't let me go. This was the only thing I had ever pushed back on consistently.

"Imogen—"

"My grandma disappeared in the fall. I don't like the fall."

"Imogen." Impatience simmered under his voice. "Everyone on Earth has lost a grandparent—"

"Lost, yes, had one disappear, no."

His chest inflated against my arms where I was still smashed against him. He exhaled slowly. "She was one-hundred-and-two, Im. You know she died. She probably left because your grandpa had just passed on and—"

"Her car was still there. All her stuff was still there. And she left me that message." The muscles between my shoulder blades tightened painfully.

Keane sighed. "She was quoting Stephen King—"

I knew exactly where this conversation was going and how I would feel afterward, but I couldn't help it, I took the bait. "No, she said, 'There might be other worlds to see,' not 'There are other worlds than these,' there's a diff—"

"So she misquoted—" Keane cut himself off when I started pushing out of his embrace. "Okay, baby." His voice lifted on the second word like he was asking a question. He held me slightly away, pushed my short hair back from my face, then tilted my chin up so I was forced to look at him. "I know you don't like to talk about this, so I'm not going to push it but . . . it's always something. First, you wanted to wait until I was sure about the job, then you wanted to wait until after the move, and now I just feel like you're making excuses."

"Just not the fall," I said. "Any other season—"

"How about this summer then?"

It was already June. Summer was technically days away.

"You want to get married in summer in New Orleans?" Honestly, this far south it felt like summer had been sitting on us for months already.

He didn't answer, just stared into my eyes, his fingers still at my chin, his arm at my waist, still holding me to him. Keane knew how to wear me down. If it was this important to him . . . what difference did it really make when it happened?

"Fine. Summer," I said, although a surge of distress slithered beneath my skin. "We can talk about it when dad's here."

"Really?" Keane grinned, the corners of his eyes crinkling. My heart softened. He really was a handsome guy. And he was good to me.

"Really," I said, smiling back.

He kissed me softly. "I love you, Imogen."

"I love you, too." The words came easy. We'd been saying them to each other as friends for decades. I forced another smile, the distress coalescing into eels tossing against my stomach. "I'm gonna head out for my run. The sun's gonna come up soon."

"Okay." He gave me a squeeze and released me. Keane knew what I was doing. And he was letting me. "Text me when you're close and I'll go out and get coffee for us." He snuggled back into the downy comforter.

"'Kay." I rolled out of bed and padded to the dresser in the soft brown light of near dawn. I snatched up some running shorts, a sports bra, and socks and slipped into the bathroom to get dressed. My sore Achilles still ached in spite of my rest day, but I ignored it. I couldn't get out of the house fast enough.

I stopped long enough to do a few heel drops on the front step to warm up my ankle before setting out, but that was it. The sky had lightened to pink by the time I hit the pavement. I loved the warm June mornings. Although I was leery of hurricane season, I couldn't complain about being warm all the time. No more treadmill-exclusive winters. I took off toward the levee. Running along the top at dawn was my new favorite way to greet the day.

I tried to shake off the tension from this morning's conversation as I ran. No one understood how hard I had taken my grandma's disappearance. We'd had a different bond. Even my father had said that he felt like an interloper sometimes when it was just the three of us together. I had a nagging feeling that Keane had used that attachment when he suggested the fall to push me into a summer wedding. I shoved that thought away. If he had, it was done now.

My mother had died when I was eight, which was about when I'd stopped emoting in the 'normal way.' I had to let it out physically. Running, fighting, acting. I wasn't a crier and I wasn't a talker. I think it was one of the things Keane liked about me. If something upset me, I waited until I felt safe to let it out, or I channeled it through my body.

Not for the first time, I wished my grandma was around so I could run this wedding thing by her. Ask her why I had these conflicting feelings about what was so obviously the right decision. I mean, I'd already followed the guy across the country.

Keep looking, Imogen, she would level her green eyes at me. *Keep exploring. No need to pin yourself down to this one. You've got time. I don't care what anyone says.*

Nevermind that she'd met my grandfather at eighteen and married him shortly after. Well, look where all that exploring had landed me. I had the most eclectic résumé on the planet and was now a forty-five-year-old fiancée.

"Get outta my head, Grandma. Keane's great and I'm doing this." I turned up my music, ignored my aching ankle, and picked up the pace. Running was one thing I'd always done, always loved, and always been good at. And Keane was obviously the right choice. Wasn't he?

I'd only logged about three miles when I had to stop to stretch my protesting Achilles and glanced up at the rising sun. Good clouds today. I pulled my phone out of its pouch to take a picture and noticed a text message. Odd for this early. Maybe Keane needed something. I clicked on the app and my heart lifted a bit when I saw it was Al from our soccer team.

I liked Al, although I was surprised to receive a text from him at dawn. Keane and I had joined a rec league this spring to meet people and Al was another charming newcomer. We'd gotten close with the team and I'd enjoyed harmlessly flirting with Al, even though I was probably technically old enough to be his mother. He gave back as good as he got, which was fun for me, and he and Keane got along like a house on fire. Didn't hurt that he was easy on the eyes and fun to talk to. The first time the three of us had hung out alone, we'd stayed up until midnight. My 5 a.m. run the next morning had been rough, but I hadn't regretted it.

Al: Hey! I know it's early, but since you're an early bird, I took a chance you might be up. You feel like meeting for some coffee? My treat.

My finger hovered over the screen and I started walking toward the next trailhead, almost absently. Keane was supposed to get coffee for us later. But Al had never asked me to coffee before. Maybe he needed to talk. And if I were being honest with myself, I wanted someone to talk to who wasn't Keane. Seeing Al was always fun. It would give my morning a lift. And I was feeling a little reckless.

Me: I am up! On a levee run actually. Which coffee shop are you going to? I'm less than a mile from the next trailhead and I could run there.

Al: What trailhead are you near? I'll come meet you. We can go together!

Directions given, I tucked my phone away and continued my run, my pace a bit faster—in spite of my Achilles—in anticipation of seeing my friend. *Calm down,* I told the tendon. *We'll have a shorter run than planned and a nice rest at coffee.*

When I approached the trailhead, Al was already waiting. He waved.

I waved back, slowing to a walk as I reached him. Strolling toward me. Wearing . . . a tunic and pants? Odd. His long blond hair was pulled neatly back and he was sporting the laid-back grin of a confident twenty-something without a care in the world. It was impossible not to smile back.

I pulled my earbuds out of my ears and tucked them into the pouch with my phone, shutting off the music. "Hey! Fancy meeting you here. Do you live or . . . work around here?" I gestured to his attire. Come to think of it, Al had never mentioned where he worked or what he even did.

"Not exactly." He smiled and reached for my left hand as if to shake, which I automatically extended. He cupped it in both of his.

I laughed. "Sorry if my hand is sweaty."

"It's not." His amber eyes glittered. The wind blew his earthy, sandalwood scent in my direction. I was positive that I smelled of nothing but sweat, but if he noticed, he didn't seem to mind. "I'm glad you were out. Thanks for meeting up."

"Sure, how can I help?" I pushed sweaty strands of my choppy, chin-length hair out of my face with my free hand and planted my foot on a rock, taking advantage of the pause to stretch again. He clocked the movement.

"Ankle?"

"Always." I smiled, pulling slightly on my hand. He gave it a squeeze and let go. His eyes dropped to my engagement ring as his fingers brushed over it. "Ankle, shoulder, uterus . . . getting old is no fun."

He moved closer. "Maybe I can help with that."

"With . . . my ankle?" I stepped away from the rock, fiddling with the zipper on my pouch, a warning bell pinging. Was this weird? It felt weird. I glanced around for Al's car and realized there wasn't one. Had he walked here?

"Among other things." His gaze flicked to my fidgeting hands then bounced up to my face. Something flashed behind his eyes. "How'd you like to know more about your grandmother?"

I froze. My stomach turned in on itself. "What are you talking about?" I tried to remember if I'd ever talked to Al about her, riffled through my memories of post-game bar visits.

Al cleared his throat, eyes on my nervous fingers, speaking quickly as if he could sense that I was ready to bolt. "I knew her. And I know you want to know where she went and where she came from. I can tell you everything about her."

I stilled, my heart hammering. How was it possible that Keane and I had just been talking about her and Al would show up minutes later claiming to know what happened to her? Grandma would have called it a sign.

"I can tell you about where that part of your family originated and what they were like," Al spoke again when I remained silent. "And you'll get to learn everything you want about Solange."

He knows her name.

He glanced up at the sky then back at me. He tilted his head. The corners of his mouth turned up. "All you have to do is come with me."

"Come with you where?" Electricity bounced through my chest. *How could he know my grandma?* "Al, this is—"

His eyes flicked toward the sky again, brow furrowing. I followed his gaze. *Is it supposed to storm or something?* I saw nothing.

I shifted my weight from foot to foot. My heart desperately wanted answers. My atrophied practical side scratched at my subconscious, telling me something was off, urging me to ask more questions. "Can we go tomorrow? How far is it?"

"I have to go now, Im. I promise you'll learn all about Solange, but it has to be your choice to come. If you really want to know." He swallowed again, his jaw bunching with tension. "Some of it is probably going to be hard to hear. Up to you." He held out his hand to me. An invitation.

I hesitated. These were questions I had asked myself for so long. And was it possible . . . could she still be alive somewhere? *There might be other worlds to see . . .* No. That was ridiculous. But . . . if I could get closure . . .

"I do want to know." Why was I even trying to pretend? "Okay, I'll go," I said. I could text Keane on the way. I reached for Al's hand. My fingers closed around his. "How far—"

He yanked me forward, pulling me hard against him. The earth fell away. The levee disappeared. We were plunged into blackness so thick it was almost tangible. I sucked in a sharp, panicked breath. There was no ground, no horizon, no sun, nothing but tumultuous current. I instinctively scrabbled to cling to Al, the only solid, visible thing around me as we shot through a void of black wind. He hugged me tightly, chuckling. "You're okay, Im. I gotcha." I could do nothing but hang on as the entire world vanished.

CHAPTER TWO

—~∞~~∞~—

It's how you handle the bad times, not what those bad times are,
that matters in the end. —Solange Delaney.

BEFORE I EVEN had time to consider a "what the hell," we landed hard.
My bad ankle received my full weight, and probably some of Al's. I couldn't
hold back a yelp as pain clanged through my leg up to the hip. *Oh God,*
please don't let my Achilles have ruptured. My leg buckled and Al hoisted me
into his arms.

"Cutting it close, Aloysius. We need to head out *now*," barked an au-
thoritative male voice. I tried to open eyes I had squeezed shut against the
pain, but the room was so bright I only managed rapid blinking. I was able
to discern at least five people in a cavernous space, with too-bright sunlight
streaming in through enormous floor-to-ceiling windows, but no other details. My heart lodged in my throat. *Where am I?*

"I know, sorry." Al was carrying me briskly away, sounding anything
but sorry. "She's hurt. If one of you can help, I want to turn her now, so she's
comfortable."

"Al, what the fuck?" I bit out through the pain. I was still hanging on to
him, my arms wrapped around his neck and shoulders. My entire body was
trembling, and I couldn't get enough air into my lungs. I managed to open

my eyes fully when we moved out of the bright room into a more reasonably lit hallway.

Al only squeezed me. "Bad part's almost over," he murmured and gave me a peck on the cheek. I smacked his shoulder, but there wasn't much behind it. My head was swimming.

The voice behind us said, "Llewellyn can help. I have enough people up here to get us going." Over Al's shoulder, I saw another gorgeous twenty-something striding from the bright room after us. As he got closer, I thought he looked like he could have been related to Al, only his long hair was dark red and he was taller, his muscles leaner. His face was edging to the irritated side of neutral.

"Thanks, Wells," Al tossed over his shoulder. "This is Imogen. Im, this is my brother. Imogen has a bad ankle. Among other things." He looked sideways at me, flashing his trademark rakish grin. "But she's still beautiful even when she's in pain."

"So not in the mood . . ." I puffed. I couldn't catch my breath. My ankle was throbbing. My heart raced. We passed by several identical doors, differentiated only by strange symbols above each one, along a seemingly endless corridor.

Al nudged one open, carried me into the small room, and gently set me down on some kind of narrow, padded table, the only furnishing. It reminded me of an exam table in a doctor's office.

I hissed as my foot made contact. "So, your name is Aloysius?" I gritted out, clenching my teeth, and trying to curb the now violent shaking taking over my body. Spots clustered in front of my eyes. I struggled to control my hyperventilating. "Well, *Aloysius*, I am about to lose my fucking shit. You said you'd explain some things . . ." I couldn't get my breath. *What kind of mess have you gotten yourself into now?*

"Leave it to Al to time everything poorly," Wells said as he entered the room and ambled around to the other side of the table, giving me a "what can you do?" smile, as if we were sharing a joke. He was the most beautiful person I had ever seen. His eyes were the color of a sunset. Just a shade lighter than his hair. But there was something . . . *other* about him that I couldn't categorize. I stared at him as he moved to stand next to me and gently took my hand. His friendly smile dropped. "Al, she's shaking all over. She's clammy. I think she might be going into shock."

"Could be. Let's do it now." Al sounded completely unconcerned. He grabbed my other hand, took my chin between a thumb and forefinger, and pulled my face away from Wells. "Look right into my eyes, Im. You'll feel so much better in a second."

My eyes locked onto his. "Now," he said. The skin where my hands made contact with theirs heated up to an intolerable temperature. Every nerve in my body lit up and exploded as if my blood were made of lightning. I couldn't scream as the air was forced from my lungs. Then I was gone.

⚜ ⚜ ⚜

I woke slowly, becoming conscious before I was able to move. I was lying on something soft. A bed? I heard the sounds of someone reading nearby. How was I able to *hear* a perfectly still person reading? I tried to move, but my limbs weren't ready to respond. I took a deeper breath and could smell . . . *everything*. The pages of the book, the spicy, musky, male scent of the person holding it, the soap he had bathed with . . .

I tried to move again. *Am I paralyzed?* Panic clawed its way from my chest to my throat. *Are my other senses heightened because I—* My foot twitched. Relief washed over me. I curled my fingers. Tried to move my head. It was so heavy. A tiny moan got stuck in my throat.

The person snapped his book shut. I heard him set it down and move closer to me. I desperately tried to open my eyes. Another whimper at the effort. My eyelids fluttered. I felt the bed sink next to my hip as he sat down beside me. *Where am I? WhereamIWhereAMI??* Gentle fingers brushed hair back from my face. I took another breath, tried again to open my eyes . . .

"That's it, Im. You can wake up. Everything's okay now." I recognized Al's voice. He continued gently stroking my face. I wanted him to stop. I wanted my goddamn body to respond to me so I could *throttle him*. He picked up my hand. "C'mon, Im. Almost there. Squeeze my hand, beautiful."

I tried to crush his hand. My fingers twitched. "That's it, good girl." *I am old enough to be your* mother, *pip-squeak,* I screamed internally. My eyelids fluttered. Fluttered. Blinked. Then opened. I would have yelped had my voice been awake.

Al was leaning over me, smiling as if Christmas had come early. He was still handsome, but . . . had somehow layered on that otherworldly beauty that I had been unable to put my finger on when I'd seen Wells. And not only that, I could see . . .

I could see individual threads in Al's tunic without trying. I could see grains of wood in the dresser on the other side of the room. There were flowing colors surrounding him. They were definitely attached to him, or emanating from him but . . . what were they? I blinked again, trying to clear my vision. *Did I hit my head?*

"There she is." Al cupped my cheek. "How's your ankle?"

My awareness instantly narrowed to my left ankle. I flexed and pointed my foot. No pain. No achiness. I rotated it 360 degrees. Nothing. Not even a click. "Seems okay . . ." I croaked. I cleared my throat. "Where—" Alarm squeezed my lungs, choking off my question. I struggled to push myself upright with stiff arms.

Al reached around my back, tucking his arm behind my shoulder, his palm supporting my neck, and helped me sit up. I wanted to shove him away but my arm buckled and I fell against him. I was wearing a short, gauzy, lilac dress. *Who the fuck changed my clothes?* Al's thumb idly stroked the side of my neck. I forced my elbows straight, locked my joints, and smacked him off. "Where am I? What did you do to me?"

The colors dancing around him brightened and sped up in response to the hardness in my voice, but soon resumed their slow swirling and cool palate. He smiled at me. It was the same charming smile Al had always wielded, but again . . . the 'otherness' . . . His blond hair was down around his face, amber eyes bright.

"Told you I could help. You won't hurt anymore. Your body won't start sputtering out. Take a look..." He indicated a full-length mirror, surrounded by a beautiful silver frame, affixed to the wall behind him.

I shook my head, my heart hammering. "How long have I been out? I need—"

He swung my legs over the side of the bed and helped me stand up. My limbs felt oddly foreign. As if every bone in my body had lengthened, although I didn't feel taller compared to Al. My reflection in the mirror was a punch in the chest. Al kept his hand on my low back, nudging me forward.

My short, dark, wavy hair was still there, but that face . . . that *girl*. I hadn't seen that face in the mirror in at least twenty-five years. My lungs spasmed. I staggered closer, my hands pressed into the wall on either side of the mirror as I stared at this, this . . . wrinkle-free, smooth face. My eyebrows pulled up in shock, but my forehead didn't crease. I squeezed my eyes shut. When I opened them, my twenty-year-old self was still staring back.

No.

No, I had left this girl behind. I was not her anymore. My breath quickened. I hadn't realized how much I had loved my forty-five-year-old reflection. Yes, of course, I had religiously applied retinol moisturizers and cleansers and had enjoyed it when people exclaimed that I couldn't be a day over thirty-whatever, but *what the fuck*. Had Al Botoxed me or something?

I put my hand to my face. The reflection mimicked me. I pushed my cheek up. The corner of my eye didn't so much as crinkle. My heartbeat accelerated. My cheeks flushed a delicate pink. It was me from twenty-five years ago, and yet . . .

I had been a gorgeous kid, no doubt, but not like this. The *otherness* had claimed me too. I was speechless. My eyes darted around my reflection. Willfully ignoring the colors I could now see swirling around me, too. Obviously I had some kind of concussion. Then I caught sight of my own eyes and stilled.

Those were not my eyes.

I leaned closer. My eyes had always been dark brown, just like my dad's. They were now a deep violet. "What did you do to my eyes?" I rasped.

Al rubbed my back. "Although yours were lovely, I did take some creative liberties there. That's the only spot." His calm smile in the reflection over my shoulder was maddening. It was as if he had designed me a dress to wear and had just altered a bit in a sudden burst of creativity.

I touched a finger to the corner of my eye and noticed my hands. Slim, long—my fingers had never been long. I took a shaky breath, pushed my hands into my hair, and in doing so revealed my ears.

Ears which now tapered to a delicate point. *Spock ears?*

I tugged on one. It stayed firmly attached. My chest tightened.

I pushed back from the mirror, taking in my entire reflection. My limbs had felt foreign because they *were* foreign. I had always had long, toned arms, but my legs had been shorter, runner's legs. Not anymore. My entire body was lanky, graceful in the stupid purple dress. I clutched at my now narrow midsection. Before I'd been more of a newspaper shape; my torso long and rather waistless. There was a slight relief at finding the muscle tone still present but . . .

I whirled on Al. Heart hammering. "What have you done to me?" My voice broke. I felt my lower lip quiver and smashed my mouth into a hard line.

His eyes softened with sympathy, and the colors surrounding him changed subtly. *Is that his aura? Can I see auras now? Do Vulcans see auras?* He gently grasped my upper arms. "You've been made sidhe," he said, smiling again, and pushed his curtain of blond hair back behind one arching ear.

"What?" I yelped.

"Like your grandmother was."

"I'm sorry, *what*?" My brain was exploding.

"Before Solange was human, she was a sidhe for centuries. And now so are you. You'll never get old, at least, not like humans do. You'll heal quickly. And you have time to do all of those things you've always wanted to do."

A choked guffaw clattered up my throat. This was insanity! Keane was going to flip out when I told him. My blood chilled.

"Keane . . ." I whispered. *How long has Al had me here?* My imagination played a short movie of Keane waking up with the sun filtering too brightly through the window of our bedroom. Checking the clock, seeing that it was far too late. Throwing back the covers, calling my name . . .

Al's swaggering smile flickered. "He never had your energy, your drive. Your adventurous spirit. He's fine. He'll be sad for a bit, but he'll be fine. You were wasted on Earth."

My stomach turned to stone. My spine stiffened. I slammed the heels of my palms into Al's shoulders and he staggered back. My proprioception was returning. This strange body was obeying me. "Take me back. Now."

"Calm down, you're just stunned, Im. You can't go back. Earth is a billion miles behind us and we won't be able to return for another century. Once you get used to everything, you'll be so much happier, I promise—"

My right cross arrowed to Al's nose carrying all of my fear and anger with it. Apparently this body had absorbed the training of the previous one. My weight shift was perfect and my aim was dead on.

He caught my fist. Barely.

I didn't hesitate and followed up with a left elbow to his temple. He blocked, but I was gaining momentum, fueled by terror and a newly surfacing grief. Al was defending effectively, but I was backing him up. Then he turned so quickly I didn't catch it between one blink and the next. He pinned me against a wall. I didn't have time to start jamming my fingers into pressure points before he said, "*STOP FIGHTING ME.*" His voice changed, ringing with a primal command that clanged through me. My body obeyed him. My limbs went pliant. I stopped fighting.

He blew out a breath, tension dropping out of his face. "There." He rubbed my arms. "I understand this is an adjustment but, Im, everything is going to be better for you now. I promise." He slid an arm around me, guiding me back toward the bed.

My mind screamed to pull back, to slap, to shove him away, but my body refused to fight him. *What the fuck is happening?* He guided me to a seat on the edge of the mattress, one arm hugging my waist. I couldn't make myself push him away. He brushed a stray lock of hair off my cheek and tucked it behind my ear.

"What did you just do to me?" My voice was shaking. Had he drugged me? I hadn't seen drugs. I didn't feel drugged . . . I forced myself to look into his eyes, my stomach flipping when I saw how close our faces were.

"Compulsion. Kroma. Humans don't have it. Or don't have control of theirs if they do." The corners of his mouth lifted. "You'll start to feel yours, too, don't worry, it just takes a while for your particular Kromas to manifest and for you to gain control of them when they do."

As if possessing alien powers was one of my top priorities right now. *He's insane. I've allowed myself to be kidnapped by a crazy person,* I thought. But I had been physically changed somehow. And he had taken away my ability to fight with a word. *He could do anything he wants to me.* His eyes dipped to my lips. My throat closed. He looked back up at me, brushing his thumb across my cheek.

"Since I'm the one who found you and turned you, I'm responsible for you. And you're new. I can make sure you don't hurt yourself or anyone else as your Kromas develop. We'll see what you end up with, but for right now, this is really safest. I can look out for you." His arm tightened around my waist. The hand at my cheek tilted my chin up. His thumb brushed across my lower lip and his gaze softened.

My body wouldn't pull back. I tried with all my might to shove him away but the most I was able to do was press my hands lightly to his chest. He hugged me closer, tilting his head. I whimpered when I realized where this could go.

His hand stilled on my cheek. He dragged smoldering eyes away from my lips to meet mine. I saw his aura shift when he felt me trembling. "Too much?"

I nodded. My heart pounding in my ears.

He nodded back. "Okay," he kissed my cheek, skimmed his knuckles along my jaw. "You've had a big day. I can wait. You probably have questions, we can just talk—"

"I want to go home," I whispered, my voice shaking. I dropped my eyes from his. They landed on my hands, still pressed against his chest. My ring was gone. "Where is my ring?" My voice steadied. Hardened. An image flashed across my mind's eye: the sun setting behind Keane when he'd worked up the nerve to propose and slid that ring on my finger, our friends beaming around us . . .

"You know that marrying Keane would have been a mistake," Al said, rubbing my arm, his aura spinning more quickly. As if he knew I was nearing an edge. "You let him talk you into it, but you knew it wasn't right. You're sidhe now. And you're free."

"You have a fucked up idea of what freedom is," I said, my voice breaking.

The colors swirling around Al paused for a blink and a flash of ochre shot through them. *Guilt?* A part of my brain still tried to make sense of things. But his aura resumed its usual dance after only a moment. Whatever his motives, Al didn't truly believe or understand that he was hurting me.

"I'm going to give you a good life, Imogen. A *long* life." He gave me a squeeze, one hand resting on my bare shoulder, his thumb tracing circles over my skin. "I want to make you happy. I want you to be able to do everything you want. Solange was so gifted. I know you will be too."

"I *was* happy," I choked. *Oh God, what is happening?* "I *was* doing what I wanted. *I am engaged to Keane.* He's going to be freaking out right now, Al, c'mon . . ."

His eyes dropped from mine and his focus seemed to go internal. I wondered if I'd struck a chord somewhere. I latched on. "You were friends with Keane too," I said, my words coming out quick and breathless. "He's going to be devastated, Al, you don't want to do that to him. We were just about to set a date—"

"Im, I'm going to need you to keep a secret for a while." His throat bobbed.

"Okay, what secret?" My heart picked up its pace. *Does he want me to say that I won't tell anyone he took me? Sure, I'll tell him whatever the hell he wants, get home and go straight to the goddamn police . . .*

"You can't tell anyone when we met." Caution darkened his amber eyes when they found mine again.

I nodded, encouraging him. *Sure, I never fucking knew you. Get me home, asshole.*

He cleared his throat. "You can't tell them about Keane. You can't say that you didn't know you were coming with me to Molnair."

I blinked. "What the hell is Molnair?"

"That's where we're going," he said. "That's my country on Perimov. *Your* country. Where Solange was from. That's home."

I was thrown. "I don't understand."

Al plucked one of my hands from his chest, kissed it, then kept hold of it, running his thumb over my knuckles. My shoulders tensed.

"We have eight months on Earth," he said. "We're supposed to find a potential partner with no less than six months to go or our search is terminated. It took me too long to find you, so I didn't have time to explain some things. But once I knew you, I couldn't leave you behind to fade away and die. So I . . . sped things up. I just need you to keep quiet about the fact that you were engaged, that you didn't know you were coming, and that we only met three months ago. Just for a while. Until we get home. And I promise I'll tell you all about Solange. You're so much like her, Imogen."

I was stunned, my brain whirling. There was only one useful thing I picked up from what he said. If he wanted me to keep quiet, that meant there were other people here who wouldn't approve of what he was doing. And maybe not far away. I couldn't fight, but I still had a voice.

I screamed.

Al clapped his hand over my mouth, but I didn't stop.

"Shhhh, Im, c'mon! Fuck." He pushed me down onto the bed, one hand still clamped over my mouth and stretched the other off to the side. A vial of silvery liquid flew into it. He pulled the cork out with his teeth, removed his hand from my mouth, and dumped the liquid in, covering my mouth and nose when he was done, forcing me to swallow. Once I had, he released me.

I coughed and gasped. Trying to catch my breath. Meanwhile, Al yanked back the covers and shoved me underneath them. "I'm sorry, Im. This is for the best. We'll get through this part."

My muscles went slack. My eyelids were impossibly heavy. "What . . ." I slurred.

Al knelt by the bed, tucking me in, brushing my hair back from my face. "Just an elixir for sleep, Im. You'll feel better in the morning. We'll get breakfast. We can talk." He kissed my forehead. "I care about you so much, Imogen. We're going to be great together."

You barely know me, I thought, but no words came out. I fought the elixir hard, but it had its hooks in me. I was still clinging to consciousness when I heard Al's door open.

"Did I hear screaming?" A male voice I'd heard before.

"Yeah, sorry, she had a nightmare," Al answered, still stroking my head. "I think she's a little disoriented. I gave her a sleeping elixir, she should be fine now."

"If you're able to take your shift, I can sit and watch her for a bit," the voice said. "With your close call leaving orbit—"

"Yeah, that would probably be a good idea." Al tucked the covers tighter around me and dropped another kiss on my forehead. "Thanks, Wells."

The claws I had dug into consciousness slipped and I went under.

⋙──⋘──⋙──⋘

When I opened my eyes, Al was sitting next to me. As if he had been waiting for me to wake up.

"*Imogen, keep the secret,*" he said in that ringing voice.

My heart crumbled.

I knew I was lost.

CHAPTER THREE

Do you think anything is what it's pretending to be? Hell, I'm not even who I'm pretending to be half the time! —Solange Aidair Delaney

AL BROUGHT ME down to the communal kitchen that morning for breakfast. He'd tried to get me to shower and change and I'd refused. I'd refused to do anything other than stare at the wall in his stupid, windowless room. My will had been taken from me. My life had been taken from me. What did it matter if I was clean? Some distant part of my brain still clocked the colors flowing around Al and tried to interpret them. Noticed that he was worried. At least that's what I thought those blue blacks in his normal sea green aura meant.

He hooked my arm around his and escorted me into the hallway. I didn't try to stop him. Perhaps I could get the lay of the land. Find a way to sneak out of here.

By now there was probably a missing persons alert at least statewide. If the soccer team had noticed Al missing also, the police had probably put two and two together.

The hallways were narrow, windowless, bare. Our unshod feet padded over a textured floor that felt like fiberglass. It reminded me of being on a boat. "What is this place?" I asked.

Al's aura flared. He reached over with his other hand and squeezed my limp fingers. They were the first words I'd spoken since he'd compelled me to keep the secret. "This is our spaceship, Im. The Promise. It's what we use to travel to Earth and back every hundred years. Only a few more days and we'll be home." He rubbed my hand then dropped his arm to his side. The colors around him flashed more vibrantly. He grinned at me. I didn't smile back. I turned my gaze back to my surroundings.

My heart sank. Were we really in space? This made getting out much more difficult. *Maybe he's lying . . .*

Al pulled me into the kitchen, which was set up like an over-large galley. I had expected some kind of cafeteria, but this was more like an open concept cooking area. It reminded me of one of those sushi restaurants with the kitchen placed so diners can watch the chefs preparing the pretty little sushi rolls. The three fae manning the stoves appeared to be cooking with . . . magic? I blinked hard and stared.

One would float a kettle of something over to another, who would point at the hearth and ignite a fire with a snap of his fingers. Another sliced a loaf of bread by shooting transparent green blades at it that materialized with a flick of his wrist. The loaf separated into neat pieces wherever the magic touched. The few people eating this early were sitting at one of two long tables, either having a conversation with their neighbor, reading, or just concentrating on their food. As if what the three chefs were doing was completely mundane. I couldn't help watching the magical cooking show. This was poking holes in a theory I'd been building that I was hypnotized somehow.

Then I felt Al tense and pulled my attention away. The redhead who helped Al turn me was strolling over to us. His brother.

"Hi Wells," Al said. I wondered if his voice only sounded strained to me.

Wells smiled pleasantly as he approached. He had a cup of some kind of liquid that smelled . . . like coffee and yet, not . . . "Good morning," he said to both of us, then cocked his head toward me, putting a hand in his pocket. "Was the rest of your night better?"

I want to go home. I don't know him. I didn't ask to come here. I tried to say. But the words caught in my throat. All I could do was stare into his sunset-colored eyes. My mouth wouldn't even open.

Al cleared his throat. "I think she's still a little groggy. We're just going to get something to go. I'll see you on the bridge later though." He tugged me along to the counter. "No meat except fish, right? Eggs are okay though?"

I swiveled my gaze behind us and found Wells still staring. His aura swirling with blue-blacks and orange-pinks. Concern and . . . curiosity?

Al put an arm around my shoulders and nudged my face forward with a thumb to my chin. "Look, Im," he pointed. "These are a little different than the muffins and croissants you're used to, but I think you'll like them. What looks good? I forget, do you like nuts?"

I stared blankly at the beautiful baked goods.

When I didn't speak, Al quickly ordered one of each item, two of the coffee-like drinks—which he called latkis—and hustled me back to the room.

I wouldn't eat.

"Im, you have to get something in your stomach. You were out for days after we turned you." Al was sitting crosslegged on the floor in front of me. I sat in the one chair in the room and stared at the floor, my warm latki next to me on the nightstand, his on the floor by his knee. He had flattened the sack he'd carried the pastries in and lined them up on top of it. He picked up a cinnamon-colored, flakey oval and held it out to me. "Look, I know you're upset with me, but I promise, eventually, you'll thank me and you'll be glad you're in Molnair. You're going to love it there."

I wouldn't look at him. "I want to go home," I said.

Al sighed and dropped his arm. He set down the pastry and buried his hands in his hair. "Im, we've been over this. There's no way to get you back. Not for another hundred years. Our magic has to have an anchor and we depend on the movement of the stars and planets en route to get us there and home." He looked up and took my limp hand in both of his. "Please eat something, baby. It's been days."

I dragged my eyes up to his. "I don't care." My whole life was gone. I might as well be dead already. Keane probably thought I was. Or he thought I'd run away. The ultimate wedding dodge. My stomach turned. I couldn't think of eating. I looked away and pulled my hand from his.

Al's face broke, then hardened. His aura fractured around him as he picked up a pastry and held it out to me. "Imogen. Either you eat it yourself, or I'll make you."

My stomach twisted. I held my breath. Which was worse? I imagined my body being compelled to eat . . . I snatched the food from his hand. "Fuck you," I hissed.

His aura cracked again. "You'll be better once we get home," he said. "You'll realize you belong there." I didn't know if he was trying to convince me or himself.

⌘∽☙∽❦∽☙∽❦∽☙∽⌘

Al tried again to get me to shower and change. Only after he threatened to compel me did I capitulate. He spread all the clothes he'd brought for me out on the bed. I had a choice between more feminine dresses or workout gear. I picked shorts and a tank top. Both of them were obviously not meant for casual wear. I could see his jaw clench, but he must have decided not to argue in favor of getting me in the shower.

I kept any tears quiet as the hot water beat against my skin. Vowing to find a way out. I had to at least try. There had to be an escape pod or something. I took my time showering, drying off and getting dressed.

I didn't want to go back into the bedroom. I stood in the tiny bathroom, fully dressed, my hair towel dried, and searched for an exit. Couldn't see an air vent. I checked the small cabinet. I checked the walls. I checked under the bathmat. No way to sneak out. I huddled in a corner on the floor and curled in on myself hugging my towel.

I flinched when Al opened the door several minutes later. His aura flared in surprise. The colors were brighter and easier to read since I'd eaten.

"C'mon, Im, get off the floor." He held a hand out to me.

Anger flooded through me. Frustration grated against my sternum. "Either take me home or leave me alone," I growled, but I did stand, disliking the feeling of him towering over me. "Better yet, just leave me alone and I'll find my own way home." Then, because I somehow knew it would get under his skin, I added, "I have a fiancé to get back to."

His eyes simmered as he dropped his hand. "You're behaving like a child," he said finally. "You didn't belong on Earth and you certainly didn't belong with Keane. You were more attracted to me than you ever were to him."

I threw the towel into his face as hard as I could. "I've been attracted to a lot of assholes, that doesn't mean they were good for me." I shimmied around him and stalked toward the door.

Between one blink and the next he was blocking my way. "Where do you think you're going?"

"Away from you." I tried to push past him.

He slammed his hand into the wall, blocking me with his arm. I glared up at him. He took a breath. "Imogen, let's talk for a minute—"

There was a knock at the door.

Al glanced at it, then back to me. "Stay there. Just a second." He kept an eye on me as he crossed to the door and opened it only enough to speak to the person on the other side.

"Yeah," I heard him say, "just let me get Imogen settled. Maybe ten . . . fifteen minutes?"

I didn't know what he meant by 'settle me.' I scanned the room, furious at being unable to fight him. The bed had drawers built into the base, no way to scurry beneath it. I could shut myself back in the bathroom. There was no lock, but maybe I could hold the door shut long enough to scream. I could—

Al closed the door and leaned back against it. "Imogen," he said, and his eyes lifted to mine. His aura had shifted. A strange crimson color was pushing through the sea greens and blues. "I have to take a shift, Im."

"I don't know what that means," I said, my voice hard. "You haven't ex-plained anything to me."

He blinked. "We all take turns powering the ship with our magic. I'm one of the more powerful people aboard. So is Wells, who you met. There are only a handful of people on board with our level of energy. They like at least one of us to be on duty when we're in difficult spots." He pushed off the door and took a step toward me. I backed up. "You've been pretty upset today and kind of volatile, so I'm going to suggest that you take a nap while I'm gone." He reached out his hand and another vial of that silvery liquid appeared within his grasp.

"No!" I jumped onto the bed to avoid him and launched myself back toward the bathroom. I got one hand on the doorframe before he had me around the waist, pinning my other arm to my side. I kicked and my heel connected with his shin.

I could fight.

Perhaps he can only compel one thing at a time. I redoubled my efforts, but he'd already brought me to the ground, using his weight to pin me down while he dosed me again.

"I'm sorry, Imogen," he panted as my body relaxed. "When you wake up, we'll talk about everything. I'll make time. I'll get Wells to take a double shift or something." He lifted himself off me and rolled me into his arms. "I promise you'll thank me someday."

"I'll always hate you," I breathed as my eyelids dropped shut.

<hr/>

When I awoke the room was dark. I was laying on my side and Al was curled around me, hugging me into the curve of his torso. I pushed out of his arms so hard I fell off the bed. He didn't stir. I noticed what looked like an empty bottle of wine on the nightstand. This was my lucky break.

My heart hammered against my ribcage. I didn't give myself a chance to second guess. I grabbed the empty bottle and managed to locate the rubber stopper. I brought both into the bathroom, rinsed the bottle and then filled it with water. Once stoppered, it was air tight. I wrapped it in a hand towel and nestled it in the sack of leftover pastries. Hopefully this would be enough to get me to Earth. Pending my ability to operate an escape pod.

Pending my successful location of an escape pod.

I slipped out of the room and shut the door behind me.

I scented the air in each direction with my sensitive new nose. Many people had gone to my right, fewer had passed to my left. I went right. If there were going to be escape pods, they would probably be in some central location. I jogged down the hallway, my heart lighter than it had been since I'd been taken. I was doing something. I was getting out. I increased my speed.

I turned the corner and ran smack into Wells.

And fell right on my ass. "I'm sorry," I mumbled. Before I could get my feet underneath me, Wells had grasped my arms and helped me up. "Thanks," I said, keeping my eyes down. I tried to disengage, but his hands stayed wrapped around my biceps.

"Imogen?"

I nodded. "Sorry for running into you," I said to the floor. I was sure that he had some kind of fae way of looking into my eyes and knowing that I was trying to run away.

Wells kept one hand wrapped around my arm, with the other he tilted my chin up until I was forced to meet his gaze. I was once again reminded of a sunset.

"Are you alright?" he asked.

"No," I said, and flinched. Had the magic worn off? I tried to follow up and say that I was kidnapped and wanted to go home. My jaw locked. I ground my teeth. *But there are some things I can say.* I tried to say Al had kidnapped me in every way I could think of. My mouth stayed firmly shut. I started shaking.

Wells scanned me from head to toe, still gripping my arm. He finally sighed and said, "Let's get you back to Al."

"No!" I twisted my arm out of his grasp and sprinted blindly down the hall. And crashed into Wells again. I stumbled but he caught me before I fell. *How did he move so quickly?* Had I starved myself so much that I was that slow? "I don't want to go back." I pulled against him and he released me, but stood blocking my way.

"Did something happen?" he asked.

"Yes," I said. A thrill shot up my spine. *Al took me from my life. I have a fiancé.* My mouth sealed shut again. I clenched my fists and blew out a breath.

"Alright, Imogen—" Wells took a step toward me, I took a step back. He stilled. I looked him over. He was taller than Al, leaner, with a longer reach. He was just as toned as his brother. And apparently very fast. I wasn't going to outrun him.

"Imogen, I need you to tell me what's wrong."

Such a reasonable request.

"I can't," I said, surprising myself. So I could tell him that I had restrictions. Interesting. I tried to remember all the terms of 'the secret'. There had to be some way . . .

"You can't, or you won't?" Wells asked, his russet eyes fixed on me.

"Can't," I said clearly. "I keep trying—" My mouth sealed itself shut as soon as I thought of telling him what Al had done.

"So there's something wrong that you cannot tell me?"

"Yes," I said, blowing out a breath.

"And Al compelled you to keep this quiet?"

"Yes," I said, my knees wobbled in relief.

"Imogen," Wells looked right at me, "did you want to leave Earth with Al?"

My lips clamped shut. I couldn't answer.

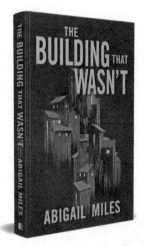
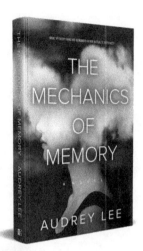
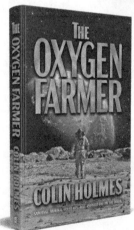

CamCat Books

VISIT US ONLINE FOR MORE BOOKS TO LIVE IN:
CAMCATBOOKS.COM

SIGN UP FOR CAMCAT'S FICTION NEWSLETTER FOR
COVER REVEALS, EBOOK DEALS, AND MORE EXCLUSIVE CONTENT.

CamCatBooks   @CamCatBooks   @CamCat_Books   @CamCatBooks